Chapter 1

While classic U2 played on the radio, Detective Dylan Black reviewed what he knew about the crime: white male, 58, lived alone, suspended in crucifixion position, gash in his side, wreath on his head, tortured. Like most U.S. cities, homicide was not uncommon in Normandy, Ohio, but ritualistic murder was a whole other game. This crime was unfamiliar territory for Black, who wasn't entirely certain he was ready for the challenge.

Looking out from the sanctuary of his Lexus, Black surveyed the melee: three news channels vied for a story, an ambulance and four police cars were parked like flotsam at the end of the circle. Several officers stood talking rather than working, likely caught up in the gruesome details of the crime. Black didn't see the chief medical examiner's SUV, and he wondered if she'd even been notified yet. By now, officers should have strung yellow crime tape and started combing the crowd. This was clearly an unusual case, and the last thing the Normandy Police Department needed were accusations of carelessness and incompetence. Black wished his partner was here; but last he'd heard, the station said she couldn't be reached. With a deep breath, he gathered his strength and stepped from the safety of the sedan into the balmy July air.

"Detective Black," one reporter yelled, and the swarm of media turned his way. He squinted into the glare of lights. "Can you tell us about the victim?"

"Is it true he was tortured?" another asked.

"Do you have a suspect?" a third called out.

With a dismissive wave, Black continued his insistent stride toward the dead man's apartment. Leaving reporters in his wake, he muttered, "No comment." Then he said to Officer Ari Davis, who looked like a Scandinavian model, "Handle them. Give them the basics and no more." Black patted the man's chiseled cheek. "They love that face of yours."

Black crossed the sidewalk and directed the show: He

ordered two officers to string crime tape, two officers to interview neighbors, and the rest to search the nearby park. Once everyone was on task, Black entered the apartment building. Inside the entryway, he was surprised to find his partner, Vivienne Sheffield, talking with another officer.

"About time you got here," she grumbled in jest.

"Was in the middle of washing my hair." He ran his fingers through his short, black hair. "Thought you couldn't be reached."

"Yeah, well they got me, and I beat you here. Listen, this murder sounds like a real mess: bloody, violent, staged, and rife with symbolism."

"Have you been in there?" Black asked.

She shook her head. "Was just about to enter. Ramsey was filling me in." Officer Ramsey looked a little green around the edges, like he'd just seen his first brain surgery. "You can go, Ramsey. I'll fill Detective Black in on the details."

"Okay," the officer responded, in an uncharacteristic quaver.

"Oh, and tell the techs to be ready to spend some time in there. And make sure the kid is okay."

Ramsey nodded and then turned to flee.

"'The kid'?" Black asked.

"Yeah. College student who found the vic. He's pretty shaken up."

"Where is he?"

"In Apartment C." She gestured toward the door. "Right across from the dead guy's."

Sheffield's blonde hair was styled in curls rather than harnessed into her customary ponytail, and she wore a full complement of makeup instead of her usual hint of eyeliner and lipstick. Vivienne Sheffield was an attractive woman, and tonight she looked a bit like a curvier Charlize Theron. Black animatedly looked his partner up and down, arched a brow and smiled.

"What?" Then she shook her head. "Don't say it." She ran her hands self-consciously down her fitted red dress. A self-confident woman in a world still dominated by testosterone, Sheffield suddenly wished her breasts weren't so prominent and her gown didn't accentuate her curves.

"At least you won't be able to tell if you get blood on your dress," he said. "You can go right back to your date."

She socked him playfully on the arm. "Shut up."

"I hope your date appreciates that dress. I'm jealous."

Sheffield knew the latter statement wasn't true, because Black had fumbled his opportunity. One night while working on a case, after long hours, some Szechuan chicken, a couple of drinks, and an unexpected touch of their hands, she had kissed her partner on the lips in the hope he would reciprocate. The kiss had felt wrong from the moment their lips touched. She apologized, he apologized, and then they talked it over briefly in clipped sentences. The discussion had ended with no closure, and the infamous kiss became their unspoken secret.

Dates were a rare commodity for Sheffield these days, but tonight's lucky man was a manager named Bill something, who worked for the electric company, drove a Porsche, and filled out a suit nicely. Regrettably, she wanted to be here with Black more than she wanted to be at the opera with Bill something.

"Let's go inside." She handed Black latex gloves and paper booties.

As her partner entered the residence, Sheffield stealthily eyed him from the back. Medium height, stocky, with black hair and blue eyes, Dylan Black filled out his Levi jeans in a way that made her pulse race.

Everything in the dead man's apartment had its place. Every line was sharp, crisp and even. *Maybe a little OCD*, Black thought. One wall of shelves was filled with books. Once he was close enough to read titles, whole categories were discernable: WWI, WWII, the Korean War, the Civil War. A vase of dying flowers served as the centerpiece on a heavy oak dining-room table. A bundle of mail was strewn across one end of the table like it had fallen from the sky. Magazines like *National Geographic* and *Newsweek* lay haphazardly amid white envelopes. The air was frigid, a stark contrast to the oppressive summer heat outside. No signs of struggle were apparent in the large, open living space. However, the master bedroom told a much more disturbing and macabre story. Moving in slow motion, the detectives stepped into the room, allowing the horror to hit them gradually. The only sound was their paper booties on the hardwood floor.

"Jesus!" Sheffield gasped.

"Literally," Black replied.

Lawrence Adams was suspended in crucifix position with one arm tied to each side of the bed's wooden canopy. His head hung forward, and a wreath adorned his white, thinning hair. The bed's gauze canopy had been removed and wrapped around the old man like a crude diaper. Bite marks covered his bruised and battered body, and a large gash in his side exposed tissue and bones. Staring at a bloody knife at the end of the bed, Sheffield bit her lower lip and wondered how long Adams had suffered before finally succumbing to his injuries.

"The perpetrator had control," she stated. "This wasn't an act of unrestrained rage. He toyed with him—maybe for hours."

"He pierced his side and suspended him like Jesus," Black said. "Is this supposed to look like a crucifixion?"

"There's no wooden cross."

"Maybe the psycho couldn't make a cross, so he opted for the closest alternative, suspending him from the wooden canopy."

"The killer must be a religious zealot." Sheffield leaned her head back and shook her curls away from her face.

Black groaned. "Damn, I hate when religion is involved."

"Isn't this guy a bit old for Jesus?"

"But an older man is easier to control than a young guy. It's probably more about the symbolism of the act than the physical similarities."

"Is that supposed to be a crown of thorns?" She pointed to the victim's head.

"Looks like shrubbery to me."

The detectives moved about the room with investigative intent—opening drawers, checking under the bed, and looking in closets. Black found a *King James Bible* in the top dresser drawer and wondered if Adams had been targeted because of his faith. On the nightstand lay a bloody tooth that didn't look human. Sheffield glanced at her partner and shook her head. Both surmised the killer had left the tooth as some kind of symbol, but neither had any idea what it meant. Next to the tooth was a Scrabble board with nonsense words written in game tiles: *yggdrasil, sleipnir, vegtam, mimir*, and *fenrir*. Black jotted the words on his notepad.

"Make sure they get a photo of this," he said, to no one in particular. "I'm not too up on my Bible trivia. Maybe they're anagrams. I bet our guy likes to play games."

"He has feathers in his back!"

"What?" Black looked up to see two large, ebony feathers protruding from the victim's shoulders. "Holy hell." Neither detective knew what to make of this. They moved closer and peered up at Adams's face.

"I think he's missing an eye," Sheffield proclaimed.

"Did Jesus lose an eye, or am I missing something here?"

Sheffield gently raised the dead man's eyelid, and bloody ooze dripped onto her latex glove.

"Let's bring the techs in." Black looked in the mirror and caught his own somber expression.

"Does he have a cat?" Sheffield asked, pointing. "Is that cat hair on the bed?"

The two detectives leaned over and almost bumped heads. Black poked the hairs with a gloved finger.

"Looks like pet hair," he observed.

"I'll tell the techs about this."

"Sheff?"

"Yeah, Dylan?"

"This one's gonna be ugly."

Chapter 2

The nondescript hallway outside Lawrence Adams's apartment was surprisingly quiet. Black unwrapped a stick of cinnamon gum and folded it into his mouth while he watched the hive of activity outside. *Are you standing in the crowd, enjoying the terror and pandemonium you've caused?* Black wondered. Seeing Officer Davis in the distance, Black once again was thankful for having someone else to handle the press.

The door to Apartment C unexpectedly opened, snapping him out of his daze. A paramedic emerged from the residence, and Black eyed her as if she might be the killer. The woman was almost as attractive as his partner. The stitching on her uniform read "Karen Stover." Given her line of work, Karen Stover had certainly seen more gore than he had—broken bones, severed digits, disfiguring burns. The truth is that Black couldn't do Karen Stover's job because blood made him queasy and suffering made him anxious. By the time he arrived at a crime scene, the torment was over, and the victim was lifeless; he was able to look upon the scene analytically and dispassionately. Still, gore grossed him out.

"Detective Black," the paramedic said. "He's pretty shook up, so I gave him a sedative and recommended he stay with someone tonight. The meds should kick in quickly."

Then Karen Stover did something that Black didn't expect: she touched his arm. He almost pulled away, then he wondered why that had been his natural reaction. A distracted "thanks" was all he could muster as she exited the building.

While his partner oversaw the crime-scene techs and forensic photographer, Black was supposed to interview the witness. Conducting interviews was one of his talents. He prided himself on getting people to remember things they didn't realize they had tucked away in their brains, cajoling killers into confessing, and reading subtle nuances that made him appear to be almost psychic. However, tonight he was feeling churlish and wished that his partner was conducting the interview so that he could avoid any effusive display of emotions or requisite tears. After one last glance outside, Black strode toward the plain white door marked "C" and knocked authoritatively. Officer Amadeo Perez answered.

"Where is he?" Black asked.

"He's pretty upset." Officer Perez spoke with a slight Hispanic accent. "He's in the restroom."

"Do you think he'll talk?"

"Yeah," Perez said. "He seems like a tough kid, but the drugs they gave him are kicking in fast."

"See if you can locate the victim's family."

Perez nodded and patted Black on the same arm that Karen Stover had touched minutes before. As the apartment door was closing, Black called to Perez, "What's this guy's name?"

"Trevor McDaniel," Perez responded, before disappearing from sight.

Black heard a door down the hall open and then saw a young man heading his way.

"Who are *you*?" the young man asked.

"I'm Detective Black. Officer Perez let me in. I need to ask you some questions."

Silence was the only response.

"I know it's tough, but it's best if we do this right away."

The college student looked about 24, only eight years younger than Black, and, around 5'9" and 175 pounds, he was almost as big as the detective. His bright green eyes were bloodshot from tears and glassy from the sedatives. With disheveled, dirty blond hair, indigo jeans, and a retro t-shirt, he looked like an advertisement for a mall store. Suddenly, the detective felt a pang of empathy for Trevor, and the emotion shocked him.

"It's important we question you while your memory's fresh," Black said.

"Okay," Trevor conceded. The two men chose their seats: one on the chaise, and the other on the couch.

"Tell me what happened," Black prodded.

Before he responded, Trevor closed his eyes and bowed his head as if envisioning the horrific scene.

"When I came home from school, I noticed that there were a couple days' worth of newspapers on Lawrence's doorstep, so I called his phone to see if he was okay, but he didn't answer."

"What time was that?"

"About 7:30. Usually, he tells me before he leaves, so I can take care of things while he's gone. I came into my apartment, put my backpack down, and got the key to his apartment."

"You have a key to Adams's apartment?"

The young man nodded.

"Where do you keep the key?"

"In the bowl on the counter." He slowly raised his arm to point. The sedatives made his movements sluggish.

"Have you ever noticed it missing or disturbed?"

"No."

"Does anyone else have access to your apartment?"

Trevor responded with a shake of his head.

"After you got the key, what did you do?"

"I let myself into his apartment. It was freezing in there, and I thought he'd accidentally turned the thermostat in the wrong direction before taking off. I called his name, but he didn't answer. So I turned off the air and grabbed his mail."

"Did you notice anything unusual or out of place?"

"No. Everything looked normal. There was an odd smell, but I figured he'd thrown something in the trash or down the disposal."

"When did you discover the body?"

"I checked around and didn't see anything wrong; then I opened the door to his bedroom." The young man paused and closed his bloodshot eyes. "He was just hanging there, and there was blood. At first, I thought he might have killed himself, but no one could tie themselves up like that. I panicked and ran into the living room to call 911."

"Did you disturb anything in his room?"

"No. The room stank, and I thought I was going to throw up."

"What did you do after you called 911?"

"I went back to his bedroom. I didn't want him to be alone." A tear slipped down the young man's cheek. "I know that sounds stupid, but he was like a father to me. I couldn't leave him alone, so I waited in his apartment for you to get here."

At first, Black was stunned by Trevor's statement; then he realized it was a collective *you* referring to the police and not a singular *you* referring to Black.

"I'm sorry for your loss." The words tumbled out instinctively.

"When I moved into Crest Ridge, I was afraid of how he'd react to me." The drugs were taking effect. Each blink lasted longer, and each word stretched further.

"Afraid?"

"Because he's older and ex-military, I thought he'd have a problem with my sexuality, but he didn't."

Now I see, Black thought. *Maybe he and the old man had some kinky, freakish relationship that turned sour.* Maybe this witness was actually the killer. After all, he did have a means with the key, and the motive could be any number of things. *Why me?* Black lamented. *Why couldn't Sheff have handled this one?*

"Your 'sexuality'?" Black tried to suppress his judgmental tone.

"I'm gay." Unabashed, Trevor made eye contact with Black as he said the words.

"And Mr. Adams?"

"He lost his wife about ten years ago to cancer."

"So he wasn't gay?"

Trevor was taken aback. "What? No. He was straight. My parents don't accept me, but Lawrence did. I'm a psych major, because I want to help other kids dealing with—"

Black's eyes narrowed.

"I'm sorry. I guess you don't need to know about my personal life."

"Does Mr. Adams have a pet?"

Trevor shook his head from side to side, and his movement resembled a drunk's.

If the hair on Adams's bed was left by the killer, how did it relate to Jesus or the crucifixion?

"Do you know of anyone that had a grudge against Mr. Adams?"

"No. Everyone loved him."

"Was he a religious man?"

"I know he was Catholic, but he didn't really practice."

Black flipped his notepad open and stared at the words he'd copied from the Scrabble board. His concentration was failing him.

Trevor fell back on the chaise and closed his eyes. "He was just hanging there."

"Like Jesus."

"Jesus?" Trevor's lips barely parted for the word.

"Can I call someone to stay with you?"

"Lawrence would have stayed." He opened his eyes briefly before closing them again. "He accepts me."

"We'll check in with you later to see if you remember anything else."

Black looked around as if expecting to find a smoking gun. Seeing nothing remarkable, he started for the door and then heard the young man mumble, "Not Jesus."

Chapter 3

The Normandy police station was unusually quiet as Sheffield and Black sat down at their desks—one organized and minimalistic, the other cluttered with files, pens, pictures, and sundry items. The first was photorealistic, the other a cubist painting.

Sheffield opened the folder she'd just received from the crime scene techs. "Guess where the animal hairs come from?"

"A dog?" Black tapped the side of his keypad to align it with the edge of his desk.

"Actually, a wolf."

"Where'd the killer get wolf hair?"

"If we can figure that out, we might have a chance of catching this son of a bitch."

"And the tooth? Is it from a wolf?"

Sheffield nodded. "Bingo. Give that man a booby prize. And the feathers are from a raven."

"A raven?" Black shook his head in disbelief. "So our killer has access to exotic animals."

"Maybe a zoo employee or a lab tech."

"Sheff, where the hell do we have a lab around here with wolves and ravens?"

"I'm thinking out loud," she retorted, standing up. "You know how my mind works."

"Are there even any wolves in Ohio? The nearest zoo is Cincinnati or Columbus."

"So we start with the zoos."

"Maybe Perez can help," Black said. A paperclip distracted his attention. His partner watched him take a mental jaunt somewhere far away, as was his habit. Whatever his process, Dylan Black was a good detective, and she wished that she could be inside his head as he shuffled facts to make deductions, connections, and leaps of faith. Neither one spoke as he traced the outline of the paperclip multiple times on a piece of notebook paper. It was tantamount to doodling for him.

"Anything else in the report?" he asked.

"The stuff on his head was mistletoe," she read.

"What's that have to do with Jesus? I could get it if it was frankincense or myrrh."

"Or gold. I did my homework and looked it up on the Internet. The wise men brought Jesus gold, frankincense, and myrrh." Sheffield arched her brows. A peripatetic thinker by nature, she took a respite and parked her derrière on the edge of her desk. "The bite marks all over his body are consistent with a large dog—"

"Or wolf."

"Most of the marks caused more bruising than tearing," Sheffield added. "There was no saliva, so they were not caused by a live animal. The killer has wolf hair, a tooth, and raven feathers lying around, and what—a *wolf jaw*?"

"How long did this bastard torment the old man?"

"No fingerprints," she continued. "The knife was from the vic's own kitchen. Either the perp wore gloves or wiped it clean."

"Any word from Dr. Petkov?" Black looked up from his newest tracing and caught his partner flipping her ponytail over her shoulder.

"Only to say she estimates the vic was killed sometime Wednesday evening. Hung there dead for two days. She said she'll try to get us something preliminary tomorrow. From the bruising and bleeding, she thinks Adams lived for a while."

"Anything else?"

"The Scrabble board was clean, too."

Black flipped open his notepad and looked at the strange words he'd copied from the Scrabble board. He typed the first into the Google search engine and received a surprising answer.

"I thought these might be code or anagrams, but the first one is a tree in Norse mythology." He typed in another. "The second is an eight-footed horse from Norse mythology."

"Norse? As in Viking?"

Black nodded.

"So, this killer is educated—may have a degree in history or religion. We've got to work on the animal thingies first. Then we can tackle this Norse stuff."

"And we've got to interview that McDaniel kid again."

Sheffield leaned toward her partner as if she was about to share a secret. "You considering him a suspect?"

"Maybe." Black looked out the window and thought of the student. "We've got to find out where he was Wednesday night."

"*My* money says you're barking up the wrong tree."

"He said something about it not being Jesus," Black replied. "What did that mean?"

Black shrugged. "I hate to say it, Sheff, but this one's over our heads. I was hoping the killer made a mistake."

"The doc's report might help." She sighed heavily. "You're right. We're out of our league."

~~~~~~

On their way back to Crest Ridge, Black thought about Trevor McDaniel—a psych major who wanted to help troubled youth. Many serial killers, like Ted Bundy, studied psychology. The wind whipped through the open windows of his vehicle as Black pushed to 55 in a 40 mph zone. Sheffield sat quietly next to him. While leaving the station, she'd ordered him to be nice to Trevor. The truth was that gay people made Black uncomfortable and self-conscious for reasons he'd never shared with anyone.

The Killers played on the radio as Black pulled into an open spot on the street. Scanning the milieu, he noted the resumption of peace in the apartment community. *This would be a nice place to live*, he thought, *if it hadn't been tarnished by the acts of a crazed killer*. The detective checked his gun, his notebook, his keys, and his cell phone as his partner exited the car and proceeded without him.

Entering the apartment building, Black decided a keyed entrance would be much safer, preventing just anyone from wandering inside and right up to a tenant's doors. Lawrence Adams's killer had probably done just that. An intercom system and video surveillance would be even better, but what could Black do about it?

"Detective Black," Trevor said when he opened the door.

"This is my partner, Vivienne Sheffield. You might remember her from last night."

Trevor waved the detectives inside. Sheffield entered ahead

of her partner and admired the décor of the apartment: powder blue walls, dark wooden furniture, and classical artwork. She started to comment on his style before realizing he'd recently been crying.

"We have a few more questions," Black said, flipping open his notepad. Trevor sat down on the chaise, and the detectives took the couch. Sheffield rubbed her hands over the textured damask material as though she were petting the sofa.

"Do you have any suspects?" Trevor asked. "I hope you catch this nut soon." Sheffield could sense her partner's suspicions pique.

"Do you remember anything you didn't mention last night?" Black asked, looking directly into the student's hazel eyes. He found them warm and kind—not the reptilian eyes of a psychopath.

"No, I'm sorry. I told you everything I knew."

"You said something as you were drifting off to sleep. You said, 'Not Jesus.'"

"Because you said Lawrence looked old for Jesus."

"He was hung with a gash in his side, wearing a crown of thorns. Sounds biblical to me."

"Oh." Trevor shifted in his seat.

Just as Black opened his mouth, his partner interjected, "What do you mean by 'Oh'?"

"Maybe you're right—about the Jesus thing."

"But you have another theory?" She realized she was still petting the couch and stopped instantly.

"I thought he was supposed to look like Odin."

"Who's that?" Black sounded irritable.

"Father of the Norse gods."

Sheffield looked over at Black, who didn't return her gaze. "As in Scandinavian?"

"Yes." Trevor looked from one detective to the other.

"Why do you think that?" Sheffield asked.

"Odin sacrificed himself on the World Tree with a gash in his side to acquire the knowledge of the runes. Just like Lawrence was hung up with a gash in his side."

"*Sacrificed* himself?" Black asked.

Trevor looked toward Sheffield, who seemed more sympathetic, before continuing.

"And he was one-eyed, just like Lawrence. Odin plucked out

his eye to drink from the Well of Knowledge."

"How do you know this?" she asked.

"I've always been fascinated by mythology—especially Norse." He pointed to a bookshelf cluttered with books.

"Did this Norse god—"

"Odin."

"Yeah…did he have pets?"

"An eight-footed horse called Sleipnir."

"Any ravens?"

"Yeah, two named Hugin and Munin. Their names mean 'thought' and 'memory,' and they flew out every day and then came back to tell Odin what was going on in the world."

"And a wolf?" Black asked.

Deep in contemplation, Trevor cast his glance on a replica mask of Agamemnon. "Not as a pet, but Odin was killed by a wolf, one of the children of Loki."

"Does this Norse god have some connection to mistletoe?" Black looked down as if consulting notes.

"His son Balder was killed by a sprig of mistletoe. Loki was jealous of Balder, so he tricked his blind brother into throwing mistletoe at him. It pierced his heart and killed him."

"I think I saw that once on *Hercules*," Sheffield commented, making Trevor chuckle but drawing a look of admonishment from her partner. "Well, I *did*," she said, defensive.

"The Vikings seemed to like killing their gods," Black said.

"Most of them died at the final confrontation between good and evil. It was called Ragnarok or Twilight of the Gods."

Sheffield was mesmerized by the college student's hazel eyes and soothing voice; he made a great storyteller. Black was not so enchanted.

"We found some words on a Scrabble board beside his bed."

Trevor nodded. "Lawrence was really good at Scrabble. Smart and lucky." The phrase hung in the air for a moment.

Black consulted his notepad. "You already mentioned the tree."

"Yggdrasil, the World Tree, where Odin hung himself."

"And the horse."

"Sleipnir, the offspring of Loki and a magical horse."

"Then there's Mimir?"

"He was a god who guarded the Well of Knowledge."

"Vegtam?"

"I think that's another name for Odin. Let me check." Trevor jumped up, selected a book from a shelf, and flipped to the glossary. A moment later, he answered. "Yep. Odin sometimes disguised himself and wandered among mortals to look for goodness and hospitality—just like Zeus—and he used the name Vegtam."

"The last word is…" Black held up his notepad. Trevor approached and read the word.

"Fenrir. He's the wolf who killed Odin at Ragnarok."

~~~~~~~~~

The tandoori chicken didn't stand a chance against the hungry detective; Sheffield finished the last bite while Black was still working on his chicken tikka masala. The Indian Kitchen restaurant was full when the homicide detectives had arrived for lunch, but now, half an hour later, the place was nearly empty. On the stark white walls hung pictures of India: the Taj Mahal, the Lotus Temple, a Bengal tiger, the elephant god, Ganesh. An Asian cover of a Britney Spears song played on the overhead speakers.

Sheffield mulled over the Adams murder as she flipped through a stack of printed articles. The first one, titled "Odin, Father of the Gods," had a picture of an elderly man wearing a cloak and a broad-brimmed hat and holding a cane. With a patch over one eye, the man looked more like an ancient vagabond than a deity. There were several other articles: "Norse Mythology: The Aesir," "All-Father Odin," "God of War and Wisdom," "Valkyries, Choosers of the Slain," and "Twilight of the Gods." A grainy print of the god riding an eight-footed steed captured her attention. The music stopped for a moment, the restaurant grew disturbingly quiet, and then the music resumed with a Cyndi Lauper cover replete with sitar. For a moment, in her mind, Vivienne Sheffield was standing once again in Adams's bedroom, wondering what monster had committed the heinous crime.

"So the kid thinks he was posed like this god Odin?" She held up a page.

"Yeah," Black replied, before popping a bite of naan bread in his mouth.

"Still think he's a suspect?" she asked.

"We still haven't confirmed he was in the library studying, like he said. It would be nice if he could name at least one person who saw him there Wednesday night when Adams was killed."

"What would be his motive?"

The bell on the door chimed as a young couple entered for a late lunch.

"Don't know," Black responded, "but he may be feeding us the mythology mumbo jumbo to mislead us. Maybe something happened between them, and he snapped."

"You just think that 'cause he's gay." She smiled at the couple as they walked by and then returned her attention to Black. "My sixth sense says that Myth Boy is not our killer; you *know* I trust my intuition, and my Spidey senses didn't even blip."

"I'm just saying I'm not ruling out any possibilities."

Sheffield took a sip of water and continued reading. "Any chance this could still be a Jesus thing?" she asked.

"The gash in his side, the crown, hung in crucifixion position. Maybe." Black waved for the waiter to bring him another Coke.

"Did we find Adams's fake eye?"

"Yeah, the techs found it under the dresser."

The waiter sat the drink in front of the detective and returned to folding napkins.

"Some of these articles Perez gave me about Odin show him with *two* eyes." She flipped through the pages. "What's up with that?"

In response, Black gave her a look of perturbation.

"It says here that Fenrir was the son of Loki and the giantess Angrboda." She looked up. "Her name means 'the Distress Bringer.' Well, *that* should have told him something."

"Doesn't it corrupt the myth to put the mistletoe in this Odin crime scene if it was used to kill the son and not the father?" Black asked, before sucking down half the Coke. Sheffield didn't answer. "And why would this psycho kill someone and make it look like the death of this god? Does he think the gods are out to get him?"

"This was the *father* of the gods. Maybe he's killing his father."

"Or showing how powerful he is—that he's…a god killer."

Chapter 4

The Normandy City Coroner's Lab sat on the corner of Second Street and Harriet Beecher Stowe Road. The crime-scene labs inhabited the west wing of the building, the office of the chief medical examiner occupied the east wing, and the Serology and DNA labs bridged the two. There were labs for ballistics and firearms, trace evidence, photography, fingerprints, documents, and computer crimes. From the outside, one might think the building was a bank or law firm, but the business inside was much more gruesome and grim.

Dr. Nikolina Petkov had been the chief medical examiner of Normandy for over three years. Originally from Bulgaria, she spoke with an accent that was easy to understand. Because English wasn't her first language, she occasionally used colloquialisms incorrectly or reversed words. To the average American, she sounded like Natasha from the *Rocky and Bullwinkle* cartoons—yet she was always very precise and articulate when she spoke about her cases. With high cheeks and a lean body, Petkov looked like an Eastern European mail-order bride, but her beauty belied her unsavory work with the dead. Because of her calm and quiet nature, people underestimated her fierceness. The post of chief medical examiner had been vacated after the previous CME was indicted for embezzling and misappropriation of funds. The standout in a dismal pool of family practitioners, Petkov had been the unanimous choice for the job, and she had uprooted her husband and two-year-old daughter and moved them from Topeka to Normandy. Within her first month as CME, she ferreted out the remaining muckrakers and hired new staff to replace them.

"Doc, how are you?" Sheffield asked upon entering the coroner's lab.

"Fine," she answered. "Is hot today, and my car's air conditioning is out, but no complaints."

"How is your daughter?"

"Petia is good." She drew the last word out as if there were extra o's. "When will you get family so I can ask *you* such questions?" She pointed to both of them in turn.

"Believe me, I'm trying," Sheffield responded.

"I know nice man in lab. He is from Ukraine, is very handsome. Only problem is he is quiet—and you are *not*." Black laughed out loud, and his partner nudged him roughly. "Vivienne, you know I mean nothing bad. I introduce you. He is maybe your type."

"Doc, I don't know if I have a type anymore."

"And you?" Petkov turned to Black.

"I prefer to be a loner."

"Is no good for you, Dylan. Will make you grumpy." His partner nodded in assent.

"Come to my office." Petkov scooped her arm in a big arc. She led them past her secretary, RayAnne, and into her office, where a large map of Bulgaria dominated one wall. Her desk, bookshelves, and filing cabinet were light colors, making the office warm and inviting. After directing them to the couch, Petkov rifled through folders on her desk to locate the Adams file.

"Mr. Adams's death was caused by blood loss that weakened his heart," the CME said.

"Based on bleeding, he was still alive when two bird feathers were inserted subcutaneously. He was gagged; there is residue from tape that was wrapped around his face."

"That's why none of the neighbors heard anything," Sheffield stated.

Petkov walked over to a skeleton suspended by the bookshelf.

"The wound at his side was made by killer standing on right and stabbing with kitchen knife." She imitated the motion on the skeleton. "This wound was not deep enough to puncture organs; killer did not do this to kill."

Sheffield turned to Black. "The killer used Adams's own knife against him, just like Odin used his own spear to pierce his side."

"Do you know if the attacker was a man or a woman?" Black asked.

"Anything is possible." Petkov removed her green jacket,

exposing a cream-colored silk blouse. "I have no evidence to verify sex of killer."

"Fair enough," Black responded.

"The bite marks are strange. I am most disturbed by these. They are consistent with the protruding canines of wolf. Dogs don't have such protruding canines. No saliva, so I am certain these bites were made from skeleton of *Canis lupus* jaws."

"So how were they made?" Sheffield asked.

"I think your killer clamped the upper and lower jaws of skeleton and squeezed with great force, imitating bites from the animal. In several places, the canines and incisors punctured the epidermis. There was more bruising than lacerations, though." The CME looked at the detectives with her piercing green eyes and enunciated her next words distinctly. "This was torture."

"The killer was being the wolf who ate Odin," Black said.

"And the tooth from the nightstand?" Sheffield stood to relieve her restlessness.

"Belonged to wolf, but not the mandible used on victim. The tooth is lower carnassial of adult wolf and appears to be many years old."

"The murder scene was very controlled. This guy meant to torment the victim and act out some sick fantasy."

"Yes, murder of Norse god Odin," Petkov said with a Bulgarian flair. "You told me this on phone."

"We're pretty certain about it." Black felt the need to stand to be on eye level with the women.

"Was Mr. Adams drugged?" Sheffield asked.

"No. Toxicology showed no drugs in system."

"Is there anything else?" Black asked.

Petkov looked down at the autopsy photos and shuffled a few of them around.

"This killer tore out Mr. Adams's glass eye savagely with hands and caused bleeding in socket."

Black winced.

~~~~~~

Julie Nereid sat in the front pew of St. Mary's Sacred Blood

Church on Webster Street. Though the body of her father rested in a casket twenty feet away, her face was expressionless. At her side, a young boy in a black suit fidgeted in his seat. His Power Ranger action figure kept him distracted, but he really didn't like to sit still for so long. Moreover, he didn't know why he and his mom had boarded a plane and traveled so far from their home in California. Until today, the boy had never been to Ohio or inside a church.

As the only surviving family member of Lawrence Adams, Julie was front and center at the ceremony, but father and daughter had barely spoken since her mother's death ten years before. Anne Adams had chosen to forgo radiation and chemotherapy to treat the cancer that had spread throughout her body, and Julie had directed her anger toward her father. Now Julie was a mother herself and needed to say farewell to the man she had pushed away so long ago. There were no tears, no visible emotions, no sense of loss. It was as if he had died ten years earlier, and she was being called back a decade later to say good-bye. At her side, six-year-old Ryan finally grew tired, unfolded his body on the pew, rested his head in his mother's lap, and went to sleep. The priest offered comforting words, quoted scripture, and called for prayer. Staring blankly at the casket, she heard nothing he said. For a single moment, while stroking her son's hair, she regretted her actions, pushing her father away. She was sorry that Ryan had never met his grandfather, because she saw so much of her dad in him.

From the back row, Black watched the proceedings. Noting the daughter's lack of grief, he wondered about her relationship with her father. Although family members are often prime suspects, Julie was not. If she'd hired a hit man, the assassin would have exterminated Adams judiciously without all the mythology symbolism.

A few war buddies, church acquaintances, book-club members, and neighbors had come to say their good-byes. Adams was well-liked, but his cadre of friends was small. Black knew that the killer would get a thrill out of coming to the funeral, but he couldn't find a boogeyman in their midst.

Two lone figures, an elderly woman and a twenty-something man, sat in the same pew about four feet apart, and Black felt sorry for both people. Grieving was difficult; alone it was worse. Black had met the woman before the service and knew that she was a friend from the library where Adams had spent hour upon hour reading books. If he were a betting man, he'd wager that the librarian had fancied Adams more than the old man had known. The second lone figure was Trevor McDaniel. Though Black couldn't see his eyes, he knew they were rimmed in red. It was clear Adams was an important figure in the young man's life.

The cell phone in Black's pocket began vibrating. Seeing his partner's number, he rushed outside to answer it.

"It's me," she said on the other end.

"Yeah?"

"Are you at the funeral?"

"Yeah."

"Don't suppose you've seen our killer, the Wolf?" Black could hear the traffic in the background and Sheffield swearing at another driver.

"No. Almost everyone here is old enough for social security."

"Damn."

A man in a robe nodded sympathetically to him as he walked past.

"I'm outside now. I'll look around to see if anyone is watching the church."

"Is Myth Boy there?"

"Yeah. He's pretty upset."

"I'm glad we confirmed he was at the library so you can stop suspecting him."

"Just because his card was used doesn't mean he was the one there."

"Trust me, wrong tree, Dylan. Anyway, what now?"

"I don't know, but I'm taking off."

Black pressed the end button on his cell phone and then glanced back at the church. He wondered if the Christian God and the Norse Odin were old pals.

~~~~~~~

An inconspicuous man in a church robe watched the detective breeze by speaking into his cell phone. Before the ceremony, the man had greeted people at the door, ushered them to seats, and offered condolences. During the ceremony, he gathered the guest book and extra programs and packed them up for the deceased man's daughter. He was ecstatic to know that Lawrence Adams had been a father; even better, he had apparently been a *bad* father. Adams's daughter had abandoned him years ago and hadn't shed a tear yet. The man in the robe surveyed the crowd with his black eyes. He imagined Adams berating his precious little girl—just as his own father had berated him. He imagined Adams controlling his daughter's life and brandishing his education as if it made him superior to her. He imagined Adams making Julie feel as if she were a failure and deserved punishment from the gods. For his crimes against his children, father had suffered. He had paid for what he'd done, and retribution was so satisfying.

The man stripped off the robe, hung it on the rack, and exited the church in time to see the detective pull away in his shiny black car.

Chapter 5

Situated southwest of downtown Toledo and north of the Maumee
River, the Toledo Zoo was divided by Highway 25, otherwise known
as Anthony Wayne Trail. At the entrance, a bald eagle kept a
watchful eye on visitors as they filed into the zoo. A blue '94 Jetta
heading west on Broadway pulled into a parking spot, and the
woman behind the wheel fixed her name badge before getting out of
the car. Wearing khaki shorts and shirt, the woman entered the zoo
through the staff entrance. By all accounts, she was plain and
forgettable. Her wiry, brunette hair was pulled haphazardly into a
ponytail with wild, stray tendrils waving in the wind. Once, for a
ninth-grade dance, she had worn makeup; but her family had
laughed at her and said she looked like a clown, so Millicent Deaver
never wore makeup again. Unfortunately, genetics had not gifted her
with sparkling eyes, chestnut hair, or flawless skin. Her teeth seemed
too large for her small head, and her nose had an unsightly crook in
it. Generally, no one paid much attention to the mousy zoo
employee. Eventually, Millicent had learned to turn her attention
from cruel, rejecting humans to predictable, nonjudgmental animals.
The zoo became a sanctuary for her, and there wasn't a job she
refused to perform, from nursing baby camels to cleaning up bison
feces to helping a snake shed its skin. Though her income was paltry,
the satisfaction made up for it; the animals accepted Millicent in a
way that humans never had.

    Then, one day, everything changed when Millicent met a
mysterious man with sultry black eyes and a bald head. When he
approached her and struck up a conversation, she couldn't believe
her luck. He was so handsome, he made her feel something she'd
never felt. Thinking it was a cruel trick, Millicent was suspicious
when the stranger asked her on a date. The next day, they went to the
Toledo Museum of Art and took a cruise down the canal. The man
with the broad shoulders and baritone voice made her feel beautiful,
and he seemed fascinated by her work at the zoo. Before the date

was over, Millicent had already begun to think of him as her boyfriend.

The next day, her coworkers, who usually paid little attention to her, noticed that she had more spring in her step and a smile on her face. They razzed her about having a special someone, but they joked behind her back that he must look like Quasimodo, and as quickly as they developed an interest in who this mysterious guy might be, they forgot about him.

After the third date, her new boyfriend became her lover. Millicent had only had sex with one other man, a drunken frat boy who had simply rammed it in her, bounced up and down a few times, rolled over, and fallen asleep. The next morning, the hungover man had looked at her and said, "Oh, fuck, don't tell me I poked an ugly chick."

But sex with her new lover was entirely different. In fact, it was un-fucking-believable. Millie, as her new boyfriend called her, was falling in love. The only problem was that he lived three hours away, in southwestern Ohio. Every time he left to return home, she sobbed uncontrollably. Desperate to be close to him, she considered applying for a job at the Cincinnati Zoo, but when she mentioned her plans, the bald man with black eyes became enraged, so Millie did what she did best: she apologized and shut up.

Their recent weekend together had been splendid, albeit too short in Millicent's opinion. He had breezed in on Saturday and treated her to a picnic. Before leaving, he requested she gather some odd items from the zoo. One time, he'd asked for a collection of penguin feathers and returned two weeks later with a homemade card that had an image of a panda made from the black and white penguin feathers. So the next time he asked for animal items, she gladly complied and then awaited her reward, but it never came. At first, a question rose in her throat—*what could he possibly do with these things?*—but it tasted like trouble, so she swallowed it. When Millicent gave him a plastic bag full of wolf hair, she asked for no explanation.

~~~~~~~

"The Columbus Zoo has Mexican wolves," Officer Perez

reported while tapping a pencil on the desk. "The Cincinnati Zoo, too. The Mexican, also called 'lobo'"—he pronounced *lobo* with distinct Hispanic flair—"is the smallest of the five subspecies of gray wolves, which aren't necessarily gray."

Sheffield paced by her desk while Black, consumed by a paperclip, hunched over his.

"And the hair was from a Mexican wolf?" she asked.

"A juvenile with tawny fur. The people I spoke with at both zoos said that hundreds of people keep wolves or wolf-dog hybrids as pets in the United States alone; then they proceeded to tell me why that was inappropriate, as if I was asking how to buy a wolf pup on the black market." Black spread the crime scene photos across his desk, while his partner glanced at the pile of Internet articles strewn across hers. "The animal hairs from the victim's room were not cut. They had most likely been shed." Perez reclined in his chair, spread his legs before him, and folded his arms behind his head. Both detectives noted how large his biceps appeared in that pose. "There's almost no possibility they could have been collected in the wild, because this is an extremely rare wolf, probably extinct except for captive ones."

"Can we match these hairs to the hairs of a specific animal?" Black asked, while looking at the photo of the wolf hair from Adams's bedroom.

"I suppose, but DNA tests would be expensive. We'd have to start by collecting samples from every wolf we could find—but how many people have access to exhibits or other places where these hairs may have been shed?"

"We should interview anyone who works directly with the Mexican wolves," Black said.

"I'll get on it, since I've already made first contact." Perez spun his chair around and scrawled a note on paper.

"Don't alert them to the hair left at the murder scene," Black instructed.

Sheffield looked like she was pondering a philosophical conundrum as she plopped her butt on her desk and put her feet in her chair.

"And the raven feathers?" Officer Perez spun his chair and rolled closer to their desks.

"Ravens and crows are both from the same family," Black

responded. "Did you know that a group of crows is called a 'murder'?" Perez and Sheffield both looked to see if he was joking. "It's true. People believed that a flock of crows would kill a member crow for bad behavior; also, they frequented battlefields to feed upon human carcasses, so a group is called a murder of crows. Anyway, ravens are *not* crows. They are bigger and have a different beak. The ornithologist I called told me that ravens can be three feet tall and form monogamous pairs for life. Our feathers are definitely raven, not crow. They could be from the wild, but they're relatively clean. Very few spores or trace materials on the feathers, so the source is likely a captive animal."

Sheffield stood and brushed the front of her gray slacks. "As fascinating as this zoology lesson has been, I wish we had a lead." She thought it was her turn, so she picked up a folder from her desk but stopped when Black started again.

"Let me tell you what I found out about mistletoe. Apparently, mistletoe is a parasitic plant, feeding off its host, so it's also known as 'the vampire plant.'" Sheffield gave him a "get out of here" glance. "You'll love this," Black continued. "It was associated with many ancient cultures, including the Vikings and the Celtic druids. According to what I found, our current habit of hanging mistletoe at Christmas and kissing underneath it relates back to these ancient cultures. The Greeks did it; the Celts, too. The early Germans and the Norse all had some powerful beliefs about the plant."

"Isn't it poisonous?" Perez asked.

"It is in very high doses. According to the lab, the mistletoe around the victim's head was from a holiday decoration. After it was dried, it was made into a wreath and then sold to the public. So far, no lead on where it came from, and, unfortunately, it's likely a dead-end."

Now it was Sheffield's turn. Preempting the bad news, she tossed the folder dejectedly on her desk.

"I've read every interview conducted at the scene of the crime and gone through the profile of every neighbor who lives in Crest Ridge. No one there has a violent record. A few residents have misdemeanors, but nothing serious. We really didn't expect that our killer lived in the same apartment complex, but I'd hoped someone in the crowd didn't belong. The only guy who no one recognized turned out to be a brother of a resident, visiting from Kansas. Ironclad alibi: was at the movies with his niece seeing a tween flick. Brave uncle."

Perez chuckled and then announced, "Well, I'm off to do some digging."

The detectives watched the officer walk away. Short and stocky, Perez was built like a badger. Sometimes, Sheffield called him *el oso*, "the bear."

"No prints, no clue where the animal stuff came from," Black sighed. "We got zip."

~~~~~~~~

After a test in Sociology and a shift at the museum, Trevor was feeling listless and asocial. Dinner consisted of a frozen Mediterranean pizza and root beer. Before the murder, he rarely worried about closing his curtains in the evening, but now he found a need to shut out the world. Not surprisingly, his parents offered him no solace and simply grumbled about "the cruel world we live in."

A hot shower dulled the physical ache. He missed his friend and neighbor and was haunted by images of his lifeless body suspended like a side of beef. He turned on the Discovery channel with the volume low. Then he started his Art History homework— using six terms to describe Lord Frederic Leighton's painting *Flaming June*. The warm colors, gossamer gown, and seductive repose of the painting had always captivated and enthralled him. Every time he stared at her, he imagined a life for this woman named June. The terms he chose for his essay were foreshortening, asymmetry, chiaroscuro, contrapposto, composition, and organic shapes. A half-hour later, he hit "print," stapled the paper to a postcard of *Flaming June*, and stuffed the assignment into his folder.

Given his job at the art museum, he should have been ashamed of his sophomoric paper on one of the world's greatest masterpieces, but it was a matter of self-preservation—so much homework and so many distractions (like finding his friend murdered). Besides, something else had been interfering with his concentration: much to his chagrin, he couldn't stop thinking about Detective Black. It had been two weeks since he last talked with the homicide detective, but not a day went by that he didn't wish to know what the detective was doing. Trevor found himself wondering what Black's private life was like, why he had become a detective, and whether he had a girlfriend or wife. On three separate occasions, he had entered Black's phone number just to erase it before hitting "send" on his cell.

After shoving his textbooks and folders into his backpack, Trevor turned off the TV, and perused the mythology books on his shelves. Choosing a book about Greek myths, he sat down to read again about Apollo and Hyacinthus. Once he'd finished, he laid the book aside, thought about Detective Black, and fell asleep.

~~~~~~~

Black lay in bed purging his brain of all of the evil he encountered on his job. Gone were the thoughts of the eight-year-old boy killed by a friend showing off his father's gun. Gone were the images of a homeless woman beaten to death in the alley behind a movie theater. Gone were the scenes of Adams's body hanging in crucifixion position from the canopy of his bed.

But one thing from the past two weeks wouldn't go away. In his head, conversations replayed as if on a movie screen. Black saw the calligraphy letter "C" on the white door, the large framed print of a half-naked woman, the replica gold mask, and the chaise covered in silky blue and beige fabric. Mostly what he remembered, though, were those green eyes.

Chapter 6

Four months after Lawrence Adams was found suspended from his bed with a gash in his side, feathers piercing his back, mistletoe adorning his head, and bite marks covering his body, the investigation had faltered. There were still no suspects and no leads. The closest they could get to the killer was through the wolf hair left at the scene of the crime, which had almost certainly been gathered from a captive individual, since Mexican wolves were believed to be extinct in the wild. However, there were dozens of zoos that housed Mexican wolves in the United States and thousands of humans who had access to a little wolf fur.

Though the case was far from being closed, it occupied less and less of the NPD's time. The homicide detectives moved on to other crimes—a white man who killed his black neighbor for playing his hip-hop music too loud, a sixty-year-old man who stabbed his wife because he thought she was trying to bombard him with radiation from the microwave, and an unsolved death of a strangled jogger—but they kept going back to the Wolf case in hopes something would surface. The news stations had forgotten the bizarre murder, and the residents of the Crest Ridge community had put it behind them. Two people, though, had most certainly not forgotten about Adams's murder.

The young psych student who had thought of Adams as a father was still plagued by nightmares. More often than not, he slept with a light on in his bedroom. A Hispanic family had moved into Apartment D, and their five-year-old son would run to the park and back, laughing and squealing with delight. They seemed completely unaware of the heinous crime that had taken place in their new home. For the student, one semester had ended, and a new one began, and one course kept him mesmerized. Twice a week, Trevor headed to the University of Normandy to listen to Dr. Straymore's lectures on Criminal Psychopathology. During every class, Trevor thought about the Wolf and how he fit the theories the professor presented.

Someone *else* remembered Lawrence Adams's death and replayed it every night in his head. The visions were so real, the sensations so visceral, that it was as if he were back in the victim's bedroom, pressing the wolf's jaws into the old man's skin. Why did fear have such a distinctive smell? It was the single most satisfying night of his life. He needed that intense exhilaration again—the urge was overpowering. Occasionally, a forgotten detail about the murder—like the ping of the glass eye when it had hit the mirror or the way his prey had struggled when he had dug the raven feathers under the skin—would resurface in his brain and induce a state of morbid euphoria. Only four months after the murder of All-Father, the need to kill was too strong to ignore. He ached to live out another fantasy, and he had so many.

Now it was mother's turn to die.

~~~~~~~

While the tub filled with warm water, Sheffield opened a can of cat food and scooped it into the dish. Louis and Lestat came running. The lavender aroma rose from the warm water as she discarded her skirt and blouse, bra and panties. The flame of a lemon scented candle danced a wild flamenco. She felt the warm water soak into her muscles as tension seeped from her pores. With her eyes closed and her head back, images of Dylan Black filled her mind. She slowly, intentionally moved her hand between her legs. A slight rub with her palm, a lick of her lips, a flicker of her finger, a soft moan. Dylan Black had the perfect amount of hair on his chest, and in her fantasy, it tickled her breasts erotically. While her left hand cupped her breast, her right hand explored her delicate areas. Sheffield imagined their kiss again, but this time his tongue entered her mouth and met hers. Nothing turned her on more than a passionate kiss. If a man could give pleasing kisses on the lips, then he could certainly give even better kisses in other places. Her clitoris was swollen, and she rubbed it feverishly as she thought about stroking Black's penis. Once he slipped his cock inside her, his thrusts would build to an orgiastic crescendo. Next, her tender lover would lick his way from her nipples down her torso. The fantasy always finished with his tongue lapping at the sensitive areas between her legs. Her body quivered, her face grew flushed, and she slid her finger between her labia and rubbed intently. Soft moans escaped her lips as her insides flooded and convulsed in pleasure.

No one was there to hear her soft cries as ecstasy surged through her body.

And no one was there to hear her sobs as she lay in bed trying to forget about Dylan Black.

Chapter 7

The base of the lamp was fashioned after the bust of Nefertiti, and fit perfectly next to the replica funerary mask of Tutankhamen. Kneeling Tuthmosis sconces, obelisks covered in hieroglyphs, a scarab jewelry box, and kitschy globe pyramids adorned the adjacent shelves. The blue fabric on the display counter was covered with rows of five-pointed white stars. It was a profusion of ancient Egypt. Imitation red carnelian, blue lapis lazuli, and green jade made the Egyptian area sparkle and gleam. Trevor loved working at the gift shop in the Normandy Art Museum. Sometimes when he handled a piece, he would pretend it was an authentic artifact. He loved unfurling the papyrus scroll of the Egyptian Book of the Dead—the name a misnomer—that provided the deceased with spells, incantations, and directions to successfully navigate to the afterworld. Holding the facsimile before him, Trevor felt like a priest of Ptah during the reign of Ramses the Great.

The museum paid him little more than minimum wage, so on the weekends he waited tables at the steakhouse by his apartment. After high school, he had delayed college for four years while deciding a direction in life. During that time, he worked as many as three jobs concurrently and stashed away money for when the college bug bit. At the age of 22, he finally matriculated to the University of Normandy. Sometimes, he considered giving up the museum job for one that paid more, but he loved it too much.

To finish the Egyptian display in the gift shop, he searched for a book to place beside the Nefertiti lamp. After much deliberation, he found the perfect one: *Curse of the Pharaohs: My Adventures with Mummies* by Zahi Hawass. It had an amazing cover, a limestone bust of a pharaoh with the *nemes* cloth around his head and the *uraeus* cobra on his brow. As the glowing limestone eyes peered at him from the cover of the book, Trevor thought of his murdered friend who had once met Dr. Hawass.

After his shift at the museum, Trevor headed to the gym to

kick start his endorphins and fend off the blues. After his last triceps exercise, he headed toward the elliptical machines and noticed an attractive blonde woman about to step onto one next to him. By the time she had lodged her water bottle into the holder and entered her settings, he realized who she was.

"Excuse me," he said tentatively, "but aren't you Detective Black's partner?"

"That'd be me. Vivienne." When she recognized him, her eyes widened. "Hey, you're Myth Boy! The one who found—" she altered her phrasing—"you helped us piece together the whole Norse god thing."

"That's me. Trevor."

"You a member, or doing the free trial like me?"

"A member. I try to get here three days a week." Then, unable to control himself, he blurted out, "Are there any leads in the investigation?"

She shook her head and increased the resistance on her elliptical machine. The detective wore powder blue sweatpants and a white t-shirt. Her blonde mane was pulled up into a high ponytail.

There was a moment of silence while he mounted the machine beside her, and then he asked, "How is Detective Black?"

"Fine." *Uh-oh, Myth Boy's crushing on Dylan*, she thought.

"I know I rambled a lot when we talked. He probably thinks I'm crazy."

"Trust me, he didn't think that." As she continued her elliptical steps, she flipped open an old *Vanity Fair* and propped it on her machine. "He may act rough and gruff sometimes, but he's really a softie. Don't tell him I said that."

Trevor chuckled. "So, does *he* work out here, too?"

"No. I see enough of him already, so I don't want to work out at the same gym."

"Actually, you look like you're in great shape," Trevor replied. "And I'm *not* coming on to you."

"Oh, I know," Sheffield acknowledged, with a hint of a smile.

Trevor realized that Black must have told her that he was gay. To prove his ruggedness, he stepped quicker.

"Thanks for the compliment, though," she said between huffs. "If I was about five years younger *and* you were straight, I'd be flirting like a schoolgirl."

"That's the nicest thing anyone has said to me today," Trevor laughed.

"We should drag Dylan in here sometime and make him do a set of squats right in front of us. Trust me, he could balance a truck on those shoulders."

"I bet he could."

"He comes from good farm stock. Dylan is going to have that hard body way after my body starts to fall apart. I hate him for it."

"Me too," Trevor said. He laughed, and Sheffield smiled wickedly. They continued to step without saying a word, and both knew they could never hate Dylan Black.

~~~~~~~~

In early November, Renee Davis was relieved to finally be back in Ohio after four days at a conference in Tulsa. She mindlessly watched the empty conveyor belt travel along its serpentine path. Eventually, bags flowed out of the gaping metal mouth, and, for the first time in her life, her bag was the very first one to emerge from the depths. When she reached for it, a young man swooped in and pulled her burgundy Samson bag off the conveyor for her.

"This must be yours," he said flirtatiously.

"Yes, thank you," she answered.

"Is this home for you?" the stranger asked.

"Yeah," she responded, while trying to raise the bar on her luggage. The guy was cute, but Renee already had a man.

"Take care," he said, flashing a grin.

"You too." *Sorry, baby, but this sista ain't buying what you're selling.* Damon was all the man she needed, and he should be waiting for her in the pick-up lane in front of the airport. Unable to resist, she hit the button on her cell phone to dial him.

"Hello," he answered.

"It's me," she cooed. "I had to hear your voice. I can't wait to see you, baby."

"I missed you, sweetie."

"I got you something in Tucson," she said. Actually, it was a dreamcatcher she had bought from Native Americans, and she'd purchased a second one for her roommate, Kelly.

"Where are you now?"

"Look to your right, baby," she told him, as she exited the airport terminal near his car. Damon leapt from the vehicle and picked her up in an ebullient embrace. After kisses and tight hugs, they threw her luggage into the trunk and headed toward her place on Arcadia Drive. On the ride from the airport, Renee and Damon planned a quiet night alone: drop off her luggage, say hi to her roommate, and then head to Damon's apartment for some of that "sexual healing" that Marvin Gaye sung about.

When they entered the house, a foul odor assaulted their senses. The heat was off, and the house was frosty—something was definitely not right. Renee and Damon tentatively entered the premises as if they were walking into a minefield. Her roommate's car was in the garage, but the place seemed abandoned. Renee wondered if the heater had gone out. The light on the answering machine blinked, but she passed by without stopping to listen to the messages. If Kelly had needed her, she should have called. Renee began to worry about her roommate. She called out to her, but there was no answer. Nothing in the living room was out of place, but everything seemed wrong.

With Damon at her side, Renee knocked softly on Kelly's bedroom door. No response.

Finally, she turned the handle and pushed the door open. The room was dark, and the rancid air made her stomach turn. Then Renee clicked on the overhead light, and before she could even scream, she fainted.

Chapter 8

Red strobe lights passed over the neighborhood like ominous rays from a lighthouse. A young African American couple sat in the back of an open ambulance while Officer Perez questioned them. Reporters had not yet arrived when the two homicide detectives pulled up in Sheffield's Lincoln.

The house on Arcadia Drive was a hive of activity. The yellow siding looked wan and uninviting in the artificial light. Tucked in their homes, afraid of what horror had invaded their community, neighbors peered out their windows. Officers searched for signs of forced entry, footprints, and trace evidence. When Sheffield and Black entered the frigid premises, Officer Davis directed them to the homeowner's bedroom.

The prostate body on the bed had been defiled in the most disturbing ways. It was the worst that either detective had seen.

"Oh, my God," one detective uttered.

"What the f—" the other whispered simultaneously.

Momentarily silenced by the butchery, the detectives stood by the bed, trying to process the horrific scene. Not only had Kelly Robison's head been severed from her body, but a huge harpoon protruded from her abdomen, as if she'd been shot by an oversized arrow. Blood had saturated the sheets in a halo around her head and dried a deep burgundy. Her pale white lips were stitched shut, and her black hair was plaited with gold cord. Strips of white cotton fabric were wrapped meticulously around each finger and up her arms, as well as around her toes and legs, and crude stitching closed an incision running from her sternum to just above the harpoon's point of entry. It was as if she was Frankenstein's monster and the Mummy rolled into one. An oddly folded red cloth extended from her right hand, and a metallic dildo rested in her left. On top of her bare breast lay a lone black feather.

Sheffield ventured closer to Kelly Robison's corpse.

"Looks like she may have been sexually assaulted."

"What makes you say that?" Black averted his eyes from the carnage. He took in the room: lavender walls, maple furniture, a large sun mirror hanging over the bed, a purple comforter with yellow flowers, a glazed bowl filled with potpourri, and a large ficus tree.

"The exposed breasts and the dildo in her hand make me think this was a sex crime."

"The doc will check for signs of rape."

Sheffield couldn't help but think that, in life, Kelly Robison had been an attractive woman.

On the nightstand, next to the alarm clock, lay a severed hand not belonging to the victim. Sheffield spotted an odd, brown lump on the bed.

"Is that a scorpion?"

Black instinctively took a step back before he even spotted the object. Though it appeared to be dead, it still looked menacing.

"There's another. And *another*." Sheffield's voice raised an octave. "How many *are* there?"

Black only shivered in response.

On the dresser, lined up like guardians, were four white jars stained with ribbons of blood and topped with lids in the forms of heads. One was a human head with vacuous eyes and a flat smile, another was a monkey head with a protruding snout, the third was a dog head with pointy ears, and the last was a bird head with a beaked nose. They seemed anachronistic and occult and gave both detectives a sick feeling.

"What the hell?" Black said.

"Those are disturbing." His partner curled her nose in disgust.

With a gloved hand, he carefully lifted the bird lid and saw human viscera. His stomach rolled, and he dropped the lid. Aware of her partner's aversion to gore, Sheffield looked inside the other three. All were filled with bloody organs. Black turned his attention toward the jewelry box.

"It certainly wasn't a robbery. There's enough gold in here to make a brick for Fort Knox."

"Does this look like a repeat of our Odin killer?"

"Could be, but that eye and that thing are Egyptian, not Norse." To the left of the sun mirror, an Egyptian eye was painted in black on the lavender wall. On the opposite side was a cartouche.

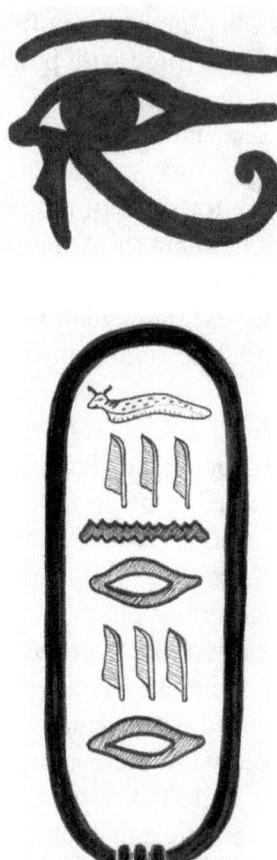

Sheffield pointed to the drawings. "It's controlled, it's symbolic, it's hands-on. He must be jumping from Norse to Egyptian mythology."

"So who's she supposed to be, and why is she beheaded?" Black chewed on his bottom lip. "And what's with stitching her mouth shut? To silence her?"

"I don't know," Sheffield admitted.

"I think we need some help here. I'll have someone contact the university to see if they have a history prof who can answer some questions for us."

"What about Myth Boy?" she asked, shrugging her

shoulders.

Black had already considered the possibility. Something struck him as he gazed at the crude artwork on the wall.

"Hey, Sheff—this cartouche is somebody's name."

"Whose?"

"Take a guess."

She studied the image.

"There are six letters, and the fourth and sixth are the same," Black explained.

"Fenrir. The son of a bitch *has* struck again. Looks like we have ourselves a serial killer."

~~~~~~~~

The detectives parked in the visitor lot at the University of Normandy and walked a short distance to Bainbridge Hall. Students wandered along the labyrinth of sidewalks on their way to class.

"Did you actually talk to this Classical Humanities prof?" Black asked as they approached the building.

"Nope, the secretary. Hope he knows we're bringing pictures."

As the two entered Bainbridge Hall, Sheffield reflected on a brief but gratifying affair she'd had with a French exchange student during her junior year of college. Best sex of her life, and the memory brought an immutable smile to her face. They descended the stairs and located room 096. Bold letters on the door read "History and Classical Humanities Department." After brief introductions, the secretary led them to an office.

"Dr. Radford, I'm Vivienne Sheffield, and this is Dylan Black. We appreciate you taking the time to see us."

Radford stood but did not extend his hand. "I must admit that I was intrigued when Beatrice said two homicide detectives wanted to know if anyone here could answer questions about ancient mythology. Curiosity got the better of me."

Books, papers, and folders were piled all over the office, including atop his desk; many threatened to spill over should a gust of wind or a gentle tap strike them. Everything looked old—the scarred oak desk, the dented, gray file cabinet, the metal chair with vinyl padding, the sagging bookshelves, and the dilapidated credenza. Even some of the papers sticking out of the stacks were yellowed with age. Books were heaped precipitously on nearly every surface in the room. The only modern amenity was the flat computer monitor on his desk.

Sheffield was surprised at how young Radford appeared—no older than 40. With curly, black, unkempt hair that was sorely in need of a trim, he looked like a mad scientist. His deep-set, dark eyes exacerbated her uneasiness. The burgundy button-down shirt appeared as if he'd slept in it, and a grease stain above the pocket resembled a Rorschach inkblot. Sheffield saw no sign of a tie, but a tan corduroy sport coat hung on the back of his chair. *I'd be afraid,* Sheffield thought, *if I walked into a class and saw this guy was the teacher.*

"Please have a seat," the professor said. "The chairs aren't very comfortable. It helps keep the students from staying too long during office hours." The detectives sat in the cracked, red plastic chairs across from the classicist.

"Dr. Radford, we've had two homicides that seem to be highly symbolic," Black stated.

"We believe both victims are meant to resemble ancient gods."

"So you'll be visiting the Psychology Department after this. They're across campus so you'll have a bit of a hike. They get a new twenty-million-dollar building, while *we* get stuck in this bomb shelter left over from World War II."

"No, sir," Sheffield responded dryly. "We have access to our own psych experts."

Black continued. "We have some pictures of the crime scenes, but we must warn you that they're very disturbing. The killer tortured the victims."

"Which two?" the professor asked.

"I'm sorry?" Black asked, befuddled.

"Which two gods were the victims supposed to represent?" *No subtlety from Dr. Sensitivity,* Sheffield thought.

"The first was a Norse god named Odin," Black answered. "From what we've learned, he was the main god in Scandinavian mythology. The second one we haven't figured out. That's why we're here."

"I'm not an expert on Norse mythology. My area is strictly Greco-Roman history."

"We understand that, professor, but we've called every college in Normandy and no one is," Black said.

"At the second murder, there were Egyptian markings on the wall," Sheffield explained.

"I'm not versed in Egyptian mythology either. In fact, it's complicated, because it evolved over three thousand years."

"See, that's more than I knew." She thought, *Stroke the ego if that's what it takes.*

"We understand that Odin died at a battle between the forces of good and evil," Black stated. "The idea of gods dying is a new one to me. I can't imagine the Christian god dying."

"Yet his son did. That's similar to Norse mythology. In ancient societies, the gods were more powerful versions of people. They were flawed; they had personalities; and yes, in some ancient religions, they died."

Black tried a second time. "Did an Egyptian goddess die?"

"The god Osiris died when his brother Seth killed him. I don't know of any goddesses in the Egyptian pantheon that died, but again, this isn't my area."

"Dr. Radford," Sheffield interjected, "we understand that. The department secretary said that you'd know more than anyone else."

"She's right." Radford leaned forward. "You said you have pictures."

"Yes," Black held up a folder. "The woman was beheaded, and her mouth was sewn shut; and there was a man's severed hand found in the room."

"That doesn't sound familiar. Is that in the pictures?" Both detectives ignored the question.

Black added, "Drawn on the wall above the bed was that eye that you see everywhere in Egyptian pictures."

"The Eye of Horus," the professor stated.

"And there was a cartouche."

Sheffield picked up where Black left off. "There were scorpions on the bed. The victim had been pierced with a large fishing harpoon, like one used in deep-sea fishing. In her hands, she held a bloody sheet and an artificial phallus."

"A dildo! I'm sorry, but even with all that, I'm not sure who it is."

"There was a feather on her chest."

"Sounds like Ma'at, the goddess of truth."

The two detectives paused, and there was a moment of silence. A phone rang in the outer office, and they could hear the secretary's voice.

"Let me see the pictures," the Classics professor demanded before softening his tone. "I'll see if I can put together more pieces for you."

"Again, I'll warn you that the photos are very disturbing and graphic," Black cautioned.

Staring at the detective with a look of boredom, the professor simply extended his hand, and Black relinquished the file. As Radford rapidly flipped through the gruesome pictures, the detectives looked around the office. Various degrees hung in frames on the wall: a bachelor's from Brown, a master's from Columbia, and a PhD from Johns Hopkins. Finally, Radford looked up.

"I'm sorry. I don't recognize the symbolism. She could be any Egyptian goddess—if she *is* even supposed to be a goddess."

"Any guesses?" Black asked. Then he held up a picture of Kelly Robison's right hand holding the bloody sheet.

"In her hand, she holds an ankh, the symbol of life in Egyptian religion. Many deities held the ankh in Egyptian art. And I don't remember any scorpion goddesses."

"Thanks for your time, professor." Black and Sheffield stood.

"If the killer picks a Greco-Roman myth, by all means come back to see me. I'd love to see what he does with that."

~~~~~~

"Well, that was a waste of time," Sheffield said, as they walked briskly to the parking lot.

"Can't say we didn't try." Black pulled his collar to block the wintry air.

"He knew less than Myth Boy about this stuff."

"He seems humorless and creepy," Black commented.

"And what was with the crack about 'if there's Greco-Roman murder'? Sounds like he's hoping for one."

"Maybe he's feeling left out."

Once inside the car, Sheffield pushed the speaker button on her cell and dialed. "We need to see what the lab came up with."

After two rings, Perez answered cheerily. "So how was your meeting with the professor?"

"Ugh!" was Sheffield's reply.

"What did the doc say?" Black asked.

"Dead since Friday," Perez answered. "Looks like she was tortured for hours. He tied her down till he was done, sewed her mouth shut while she was still alive, and killed her with the spear or harpoon or whatever it is. By the time he took off her head and opened her up, she was dead. Some of her organs were removed and placed in those animal jars, and salt pellets were stuffed inside her before she was stitched up. When she's got more, she'll call."

"Thanks, buddy. We'll see you at the station." Black waited for his partner to turn off the phone and then added, "Maybe it's time to talk to psych and get a profile of this guy."

"And I think we need to talk to Myth Boy," she added. "I forgot to tell you, I saw him at the gym last week."

Black tried to react nonchalantly. "I thought your gym was all women."

"Yeah, women and gay men, because we get along so well," she quipped. "Not that one, dumbass. I have a trial membership at another gym close to where he lives, so I went there to check it out." She pulled out of campus. "It was nice. Anyway, we talked about you."

"Shut up." He was taken aback.

"We did." She gunned the engine to make a yellow light and smiled at him. "He asked if you worked out. I told him that underneath that button-down shirt was a flabby, grotesque body."

"Speaking of, let's stop and get lunch. I'm starved."

"It's late. It's almost dinner time."

"Yeah, and I haven't eaten, so let's stop somewhere."

"Okay, let's do Mexican."

"Fine."

The two were quiet as Sheffield navigated the one-way

streets and headed toward Taco Palace.

"I still think we should talk to Trevor," she said.

"I think you're right," Black finally responded.

Chapter 9

The bitch is dead. Head severed from her body. Lips sewn shut. Organs removed, but not the right ones. Her freakish arachnids couldn't protect her. Now she will learn that she should've loved and protected me. Now she resides with father in hell.

The harpy had to die. She stood by and did nothing when father attacked me. When he berated me, belittled me, she said nothing. After his tirades, I sought her comfort, but she blamed me for bringing out his wrath. What a cold, heartless monster. Maybe she's the one who named me Fenrir. She allowed his abuse. For that, I loathed her more than him. She was an empty shell, devoid of love. When I left a toy in the dining room, mother tattled to father in order to provoke his fury. At night, mother came to me. Did she bring me food to stave my hunger or water to slake my thirst? No. She came to tell me that the gods were watching, and that they punish little boys who don't obey their parents.

Sometimes, mother, little boys grow up to be gods themselves. Then they pass judgment on you for your sins. Good-bye, mother. May your soul wander eternity forever.

Chapter 10

Thanksgiving was less than two weeks away, and Trevor expected to spend it alone, rather than watching it pass in slow motion at his parents' house. In the kitchen, his controlling, overweight mother would watch QVC while constantly "taste testing" everything that wasn't still raw; and in the family room, his alcoholic father would watch football, drink beer, and cuss at the TV. Both would ignore their only child until they were ready to launch into a harangue about his "sinful lifestyle choice." As he poured syrup on his waffles, he tried to think of an excuse to get out of going to their house for Thanksgiving. And Christmas. And every other holiday.

The phone rang, startling him. The number on the caller ID looked familiar, but he wasn't sure why. Before answering, he turned the volume down on the TV, reducing Pink's belting vocals to an inarticulate growl.

"Hello?"

"This is Dylan Black," the baritone voice said. "I spoke with you a couple of times in July."

"Detective Black, I remember you," Trevor replied, a bit too excitedly. "Have you caught Lawrence's killer?"

"Actually, there's been a second murder. We're pretty sure it's the same perp."

"Fenrir?"

"I was hoping to ask you some questions. We're a little confused by some of the mythological symbols."

"Is it the same M.O.?" He surprised himself using cop talk.

"Not exactly."

Trevor could hear the tension in the detective's voice. He plopped down on the lounger and stared at the couch where Black had sat twice before.

"It's not Odin?"

"No. What do you know about Egyptian mythology?"

"I know *some*. Mostly the major gods and goddesses."

"Could we talk today?"

"I have class this morning and then work until 6:00."

"That's fine. Would 6:30 be okay? At the bistro on Tannenburg? I'll buy dinner."

"I'll be there."

After hanging up, both men clutched their respective phones and thought about the impending meeting.

~~~~~~

After six hours on the phone, Sheffield's back was aching, and her desk was more cluttered than usual. She had identified the maker of the canopic jars, the ones that held Kelly Robison's viscera, and located a dozen stores, mostly online, that sold them. Several retailers had provided the names of everyone who had purchased the stone replica jars within the last year. Of course, the list only included those who had paid by credit card; the ones who had paid by cash were untraceable. The salesperson at the gift shop in the Luxor Hotel in Las Vegas said he'd sold a set to a customer who had paid in cash about two weeks prior. Sheffield's interested piqued until he describe the customer: an elderly man from St. Louis confined to a wheelchair. She thanked him for the information nonetheless.

Intended for a much different audience, the fishing harpoon was a whole other story. Used to spear sharks, swordfish, and giant bluefin tuna, it was sold mostly by fishing stores along the coasts; however, two stores in Ohio actually carried the model the killer had pierced through Kelly Robison's body. The five-foot shank was made of steel alloy, and the dart that screwed onto the tip was made of bronze. The tool was a menacing weapon against large marine prey and had the same devastating effect when run through a human. Officer Perez retrieved customer lists from online vendors and the two stores in Ohio that sold the harpoon. By quickly cross-referencing the lists, the homicide team determined that no one appeared to have bought both the canopic jars and the harpoon. In fact, almost no city in Ohio was duplicated on the lists. Tracing the jars and harpoon quickly grew fallow.

"Damn it," Sheffield exclaimed as she held up several

printouts and paced by her desk. "The killer could be anyone on this list. I ran all of the names of those living in Ohio, Indiana, and Kentucky through criminal records and got no violent offenders." Angrily, she tossed the papers down.

Perez was sitting at Black's desk. "I'm still waiting on receipts from two companies," he said.

"Just run what you've got. See if it kicks out any names. I'm going to check ViCAP for other murders made to look like assassinations of gods."

"Doesn't it sound sacrilegious?" Perez raised a brow. "Killing a god?"

"This guy is a megalomaniacal freak who thinks he *is* a god," she averred. "When I catch him, I think I'll shoot him, just to make sure he doesn't get off on a technicality."

"I'd be careful saying that out loud."

Sheffield placed her hands on her hips, and Perez could see her Beretta in her shoulder holster. She grimaced and then groaned.

"You're right," he finally said. "I'd shoot him, too, if I were you."

~~~~~~

When Trevor arrived at 6:30, the restaurant was hopping with hungry customers, mostly twenty- and thirty-something professionals who frequented the bistro to dine on specialty bagels, croissant sandwiches, and unusual soups. The black and red modern décor attracted an artsy crowd, and monochromatic prints adorned the walls. Below the "order here" sign, a dozen customers waited impatiently. When Trevor entered the restaurant, Black stood up from a booth in the corner and motioned him over. The detective had been writing notes, and the table was cluttered with files, forms, notebook paper, a cell phone, and a cup of coffee.

"Have a seat," Black said.

Trevor laid his coat and book on the seat and slid into the booth. He couldn't help but notice that the man across from him wore a black sweater that accentuated his athletic physique.

"Here's a menu." Black held one aloft. "Let me know what

you want."

"I've been here before. I'll have a chicken-salad croissant, potato soup, and hot chocolate."

"Be right back."

Trevor watched him walk away and then looked at the papers on the table in front of him. He considered perusing them but then thought better of it. He didn't want to get arrested for interfering with a police investigation or tampering with evidence or something like that. But if *Black* was doing the arresting…

He liked that the detective was confident, just a bit cocky. Black walked and talked with authority and that was *très sexy*. From the booth, Trevor stared at Black and wondered where he hid his gun. A few minutes later, an employee behind the counter slid a tray toward the detective, and Trevor averted his eyes.

When Black returned to the table, he said, "Let me clear this stuff and let's eat." He stacked the items into one big pile and pushed them against the wall.

"So, who was the victim?" Trevor asked. Black picked up his roast beef sandwich and looked at Trevor without saying a word. "Does he live in my neighborhood?"

"Actually this was a *she*, and she lived south of town. Looks like an Egyptian theme."

"This killer has eclectic interests."

"Mm-hmm."

"Since you ask me what I knew about Egyptian myths, I brought this." He held up a book titled *Who's Who in Egyptian Mythology*.

Black gave a half nod, and Trevor couldn't decide if it was dismissive or encouraging. He hated that his feelings for the detective made him paranoid. He sipped his cocoa and felt the whipped cream tickle his lip. He was nervous and rushed to fill the silence.

"Actually, I love ancient Egypt, but the mythology is a lot more complicated than Greek or Norse. Since the hegemonic power in Egypt shifted from city to city, there were multiple stories of things like cosmology."

"That's the creation of the world?" Black asked before taking a bite of his pickle spear. Trevor nodded.

"And you're certain she's meant to be a goddess and not a

pharaoh like Cleopatra?"

Though he was seeking information, the detective wasn't prepared for the young man's ramblings.

"Let's eat."

"Oh. Okay." Feeling chastised, Trevor crumbled crackers into his soup and diverted his gaze toward a photo of a lone Joshua tree.

"Is your food good?" Black asked.

"Yeah." After swallowing a bite of soup, he blurted out, "I'm sorry I talk so much."

"You're fine."

By now, the bistro had filled to the brim. Customers wandered in circles, looking for an empty seat, and Black seemed oblivious.

"Got big plans for Thanksgiving?" the detective asked, reaching for his soup.

"I guess I'll spend it with my family." Trevor speared a tomato wedge.

"You don't sound too enthused."

"We aren't close. What about you?"

"I'll spend it with my folks. They live a few hours north of here, on the farm where I grew up."

"Can I come, too?" Trevor asked with a chuckle.

Black took a bite of his sandwich and looked at Trevor like he was waiting for the punch line.

"Just joking."

"Yeah." Black looked away.

As the two finished their meals, they made idle conversation. Why had Black wanted to be a detective? How were Trevor's classes going? Once they'd polished off the food, the detective cleaned up the mess. As he returned the tray, his phone rang.

"It's me," his partner announced. "You talk to Myth Boy yet?"

"We just finished eating. Thought it was best not to talk about death and dismemberment while we were stuffing our mouths."

"Always thinking on your feet; that's my partner. Listen, I've got some of the lab results. Interesting stuff. Get over here when you're done with the interview."

"If you're at the station, how about I bring him there, and you can hear what he has to say, too?" Black looked at Trevor, who was pretending not to be listening.

"Fine. I'll meet you in the conference room."

After hanging up, Black nodded toward the door. "Do you mind?"

"Should I follow in my car?" Trevor asked.

"I'll drive and bring you back when we're finished."

Trevor was excited that he'd get to ride in the Dylan-mobile.

~~~~~~~

The conference room was dismal and uninspired; with walls the color of mud and carpet the color of clay, the room had little hope of being warm and inviting. The large, laminated table in the middle of the room seated eight. Abstract, blurred photos of people in motion served as art. Trevor thought the space desperately needed an HGTV makeover. Sheffield adjusted the light by flipping one switch off, making the room look less like an overexposed picture. She filled a plastic cup with water and offered it to Trevor.

"What have you told him?" she asked Black.

"Nothing, except that it's Egyptian and a female vic."

Sheffield leaned against the table and crossed one leg in front of the other. Her purple blouse and black slacks made her look chic. As Sheffield flipped her blonde ponytail over her shoulder, she winked at Trevor, who wondered if the two detectives were sleeping together. Black laid out the details.

"The woman was in her early thirties, attractive, black hair, brown eyes. She was beheaded and harpooned. We're fairly certain it was our guy because of this." He tossed a photo of the cartouche from the wall in Kelly Robison's bedroom. "According to what we found on the web, it translates to 'Fenrir.' And he drew this." Black slid another photo in front of the student.

"The Eye of Horus," Trevor uttered. "It was torn out by the god Seth. It's a symbol of healing and renewal."

Sheffield said, "I knew we brought you here for a reason."

"The victim's arms and legs were wrapped in strips of fabric," Black continued.

"As if she was partially mummified," Sheffield added.

"These four jars, called 'canopic jars,' were on the dresser." Another photo.

"The four sons of Horus," Trevor said. The detectives gave no response. "Each jar held a specific organ and was protected by a different goddess."

"Her abdomen had been cut open and some of her organs removed and placed inside," Black continued.

Sheffield jumped in. "Like her liver and her heart."

"That can't be right." The words leapt from Trevor's mouth. The detectives exchanged inquisitive glances.

"Why not?" Sheffield asked, standing.

"The Egyptians believed that the heart was the source of thought and emotion. During mummification, some of the organs were removed and placed in canopic jars for protection, but the heart had to remain with the body for it to function in the afterlife."

"Maybe our killer doesn't know as much as he thinks," Sheffield smirked.

"Or maybe he did it intentionally," Black proposed. "Do you know why her mouth would be stitched shut?"

"To keep her from making it in the afterlife," Trevor said, affirming Black's lead.

"Huh?" Sheffield shot him an inquisitive glance.

"The embalming process was to help the person live in the afterlife. After mummification, there was a ceremony called 'the Opening of the Mouth.' The bandages around the mummy's mouth were cut open so that the deceased could recite spells and incantations to reach the Afterworld."

"I thought you didn't know much of this Egyptian stuff," Sheffield said. Trevor blushed.

"And bad people went to hell?" Black asked.

"If a person was bad, their soul was eaten by the Swallowing Monster. It was like a combination of a crocodile, a hippo, and a lion." He flipped open the book and showed them a picture of the beast Amam. "Here he's called 'the devourer.'"

"Lovely," Sheffield responded.

"By removing the heart and sewing the mouth shut, he was

effectively denying this woman the right to an afterlife."

"Do you have any idea who she represents?" Black asked.

"Isis. That's my guess."

"Why?"

"Because she was beheaded."

Sheffield began to pace. "So Isis was killed?"

"Not killed, but she was beheaded by her son Horus, because she interfered in his battle with Seth. Isis controlled magic, so she was able to recover."

"There was a severed hand in the room." Black leaned back in his chair.

"Isis once cut off Horus' hand."

"What? She cut off her son's hand?" Sheffield stopped in mid-step.

Trevor paused and smiled. "Because it held the semen of Seth."

"This is what I love about mythology," Sheffield said, rolling her eyes.

"After Osiris was killed, Seth and Horus fought for the right to the throne. One day, Seth tried to molest Horus to defame him, but Horus caught the semen in his hand. Isis cut off the hand to keep it from polluting his body; then she restored his hand with magic."

"So the Wolf left the hand as proof of the mother's *interference*," Black posited aloud.

"Maybe this Seth thing is the reason he placed the dildo in her hand," Sheffield postulated.

"Nope." Trevor cast a look of contrition.

"After Seth killed Osiris, he cut up his body and scattered the pieces. Isis found all of Osiris' body except his penis—it was swallowed by a fish and gave the Nile valley its fertility—so she had to make a fake one before she could copulate with him."

"Okay." Sheffield flipped her ponytail behind her. "And was Isis harpooned?"

"Not that I know of. Let me check." Trevor flipped feverishly and scanned pages quickly.

"Ooh. It says here that during their great battle, Seth and Horus transformed themselves into hippos and submerged themselves in the river. Isis was worried Seth would kill her son, so she threw a harpoon—but pierced Horus instead of Seth."

"Oops," Sheffield uttered.

Black tapped a pencil on the table. "Was Isis associated with animals?" he asked.

"All Egyptian gods were associated with animals, but Isis was usually portrayed in human form, often suckling the infant Horus—like Mary with Jesus."

"Was she a bird goddess?"

"Not really."

"What about scorpions?" Black asked.

"There was a scorpion goddess, but not Isis. Let me see what I can find." As Trevor flipped to the S's, Sheffield smiled at Black. "Here it is. Scorpions accompanied Isis to protect her."

"Seven of them," Sheffield muttered. "We found them on the bed surrounding the deceased."

"How'd he get scorpions?"

"That's what we'd like to know," Black grumbled. "And there was a feather on her body."

"Her son, Horus, was the falcon god."

"So it will turn out to be a falcon feather," Sheffield said. "This whole thing is a big 'fuck you' to his mother." She looked at Trevor. "Sorry, I have a potty mouth."

Black pulled out two photos; each showed the bloody cloth in the victim's hand.

"We spoke with a professor at your school. He told us that the thing in her right hand is an ankh."

"I don't think it is."

The detectives both met his gaze. The room was eerily silent.

"See how the sides of this one are folded down? This is the *tyet*." Trevor sketched two images on the pad of paper.

"The one on the left is the ankh. The other is the tyet, which is a symbol of Isis. I don't know what it represents."

"So this sheet is a symbol of Isis," Sheffield said. "Figures." She filled Trevor's cup with water as Black jotted notes: Check paint used for eye and hiero. Motive for killing gods—represent real people in killer's life? Follow up with Radford—gauge his reaction to Isis. How did killer learn myths?

Suddenly, the door to the conference room opened, and the receptionist, Jan, waved a piece of paper at the two detectives.

"There's news," she told them.

"Is it about the Robison case?" Sheffield asked.

"Someone claiming to be the killer mailed a letter to the newspaper."

"The *Normandy Times*?"

"Yes."

Sheffield reached for the letter as Black moved to her side. Trevor flipped through his books to find out more about the tyet while the detectives read the letter.

Dear Ms. Rhodes,

By now you probably know that I have taken two lives. Both were punished for their crimes. The first was father. He thought that his wisdom made him better than all of us, that he could lord over us as if we didn't matter, but he was wrong. I, Fenrir the Wolf, made him suffer for his wrongs. I devoured him whole. Now All-Father Odin is dead.

The second was mother. She was complicit in father's crimes. In fact, she constantly threatened to turn me over to his wrath. Isis suckled her son Horus just to meddle incessantly in his life later. Now she is in Hel with father. I, Fenrir the Wolf, have recused mother of her maternal duties.

Warn the world: Fenrir is here to punish the wrongdoers for their sins. Even the gods bow at my feet. Even the gods die at my hands. Tremble at my name, fear my wrath.

Yours truly,
Fenrir the Wolf

P.S. A Slut Erred.

Chapter 11

A light snow had begun to fall in the city of Normandy as Officer Amadeo Perez merrily navigated the streets toward the bistro where Trevor's car remained. It was the first snow of the year, and there would be no significant accumulation, but the officer was elated anyway.

"Man, I love the snow!" Perez gushed. "You?"

"I like it for about a month," Trevor responded. "Then I'm ready for it to be over."

"I grew up in New Mexico," Perez replied, "and never saw snow till I came to Ohio."

"I've lived here all my life, and sometimes I want to hibernate my way through winter."

Perez adroitly swerved to miss a stray dog in the street. "So how'd you learn all this mythology stuff?"

"Some kids read about dinosaurs. I read about mythology."

"That's cool."

"It makes me a geek."

Perez chuckled. "No, it doesn't. Geeks talk about theories and formulae, and they're socially inept. That's not you."

Trevor looked at the officer and appreciated his sexy Latin features—smooth, olive skin, full lips, wavy black hair, and dark, soulful eyes. And he smelled so damn good! Then he noted the wedding ring on his hand. Perez twisted his wedding band with his thumb, and Trevor looked away, admonishing himself for his lust.

"You used the Latin plural of 'formula,'" Trevor said, to break the silence.

"Huh?" Perez stopped for a red light.

"You used the correct Latin plural of 'formula.' Most people don't use Latin endings like phenomena or datum."

"Yeah, two years of Latin in Catholic school did it to me."

"It's impressive, Officer Perez."

"Call me Amadeo. Did you think I was a buffoon?"

"No, not at all," Trevor insisted. "I didn't mean to imply—"

Perez laughed and slapped his passenger's leg. "I'm just giving you a hard time."

"*Si*, Amadeo." Trevor flashed a wry smile.

"I like you."

Trevor tried not to read into the words. Instead, he watched the snow fall delicately.

"And I know Dylan and Viv appreciate your help. They're like family to me."

"I think I ramble too much when I talk to them."

"Dylan make you nervous?" Perez didn't wait for an answer. "He acts all cool and macho, but he's got a heart of gold. When my dad died, Dylan was really there for me. It's just the kind of guy he is."

It wasn't Black's tough-guy attitude that made Trevor uptight.

"So, you got a boyfriend?" Perez asked, without warning.

Caught off guard, Trevor was silent for a moment, uncertain where the conversation was going. His heart beat quickly, and his throat felt like it was closing. Though he wasn't looking for a fling with a married man, he had to admit that he'd jump at the opportunity to sleep with Officer Perez, even if it meant being secret lovers.

"My wife's brother is gay," Perez clarified. "I could hook you up if you wanted."

After the wave of disappointment dissipated, Trevor was impressed that a straight man was trying to set him up on a date with another man. He thought, *My opinion of Officer Perez just ramped up a gazillion points.*

"Actually, I'm not seeing anyone," Trevor answered.

"He lives in Chicago."

"That's six hours away!"

"I know, but he comes here to visit sometimes, and I thought the next time he came to town, you two could get together to see if you click."

"Thanks for the offer, but I'm not *that* desperate—yet."

"He's a good-looking guy. I think you'd like him."

"I appreciate the offer."

"If you change your mind, just get in touch with me at the

station."

The snow had already stopped when they pulled into the crowded parking lot. Trevor pointed to his vehicle, and the two men said their good-byes. *Damn, I need to get laid*, Trevor thought. He shivered, but whether from the cold or his unsatisfied libido, he wasn't certain.

~~~~~~~

Even at nine o'clock at night, the offices of the *Normandy Times* were buzzing. Agatha Rhodes was much younger than her name might lead one to believe. Her shoulder-length brown hair was parted right of center, fluffed, moussed, and shellacked into a helmet. About 70 pounds overweight, the reporter was dynamic, bold, sassy, and gregarious. She liked to tell people that with a name like Agatha (though most people called her "Aggie") she was destined to be an investigative reporter, a job she took very seriously. Usually imperturbable, Aggie Rhodes was visibly distressed when the homicide detectives stepped off the elevator.

"Ms. Rhodes, I'm Detective Sheffield, and this is Detective Black," Sheffield said, as she extended her hand.

"Please call me Aggie. So this isn't fake?"

"We don't think so," Black responded.

"How many people touched the letter?" Sheffield inquired.

"Me and my assistant and my boss."

"We will need to get the fingerprints for all three of you."

"You already have mine," she offered casually, as she bit a fingernail. The two weighed her admission and said nothing. "I had some threatening letters a few years back, and the police took my prints then," she explained. "I'll tell Eddie and Mort that you need their prints. The letter's in my office over there." She pointed.

The trio navigated around workstations and past employees and soon peered at the innocuous-looking paper that lay in the center of Aggie's desk. It had no distinct features, such as tears, colors, or embossing. It appeared to be inexpensive printer paper with black inkjet print. With a gloved hand, Black held it up to the light. The white envelope had an adhesive strip and a peel-and-stick stamp, so there was no likelihood of saliva with DNA. The address was printed directly on the envelope with "c/o Agatha Rhodes."

"When did you discover this?" Sheffield asked.

"It came today in the afternoon mail." Staring at the letter as if it was virulent, the reporter picked nervously at a button on her mauve suit jacket. "My assistant, Eddie, opened it and thought it was a joke, but the tone was so disturbing. It didn't seem like a crackpot. He seemed to have inside information."

"Did your assistant show this to anyone else before he brought it to you?" Black asked.

"Eddie is a *she*, and she didn't show it to anyone else."

"So you were the second person to see it; is that right?" Black slipped the letter into a plastic bag.

"Yes. Then I showed it to Mort, our editor in chief. After that, I called the precinct and faxed it over to your assistant." Sheffield spotted several awards on the reporter's credenza. "I'm working on an article about the killer and this letter. I want to add a comment from you about the investigation."

"Can you hold off one day to print the article?" Black requested.

"I really want the story in tomorrow's paper. He may have sent letters to other reporters, and I don't want the *Times* to lose the story."

"Give us until noon tomorrow, and we'll get back to you with a statement," Black offered.

"And you'll comment on the record?"

"If you hold off, then yes."

"So this is all true, what he said in the letter?"

"Unfortunately, it is." Sheffield watched her partner pick up the plastic evidence bag with the letter and envelope in it.

"So, a serial killer has now opened up shop in our little corner of Ohio." Her voice grew tremulous. "Do you think my family is in danger?"

"We have no reason to think that, Aggie," Sheffield said, "but it's best to be cautious."

"You can bet your *ass* I'll be 'cautious' until this psycho is behind bars!"

~~~~~~

The next day the temperatures climbed back up into the

sixties, and all evidence of the snow from the night before vanished. The vicissitudes of Ohio weather seemed like a joke Mother Nature played for amusement. Dylan Black was driving to the station when his cell phone rang.

"I'm sorry to bother you, Detective Black," the voice on the other end stated, "but I wanted to let you know what I found out."

"What you found out?" Black repeated, confused.

"About the Egyptian stuff I said I'd look into. Is this a good time for you?"

"Sure, Trevor; tell me what you've got."

"The tyet was called 'the Blood of Isis,' 'the Girdle of Isis,' or 'the Knot of Isis.' It probably represents the uterus and was usually made of red carnelian, red jasper, or red faience."

"So he killed Isis and then placed a symbol of her own power in her hand?"

"He even knew to use a red sheet."

Black edged his Lexus into traffic. "The sheet was originally white," he said. "It was red from the victim's blood."

"Oh." Trevor sounded repulsed.

"Anything else?"

"I found that Seth transformed himself into a scorpion to sting Horus, but the god Thoth came and healed him. Don't know if that matters, but we talked about scorpions."

"So scorpions protected Isis and harmed her son. This guy has got to love this mythology stuff."

"Yeah."

"That it?"

Trevor closed his Egyptology book. "I know it doesn't help."

Black realized he'd sounded brusque. "In case you're wondering, I'm not always a jerk."

Trevor laughed. "I never thought you were."

"Liar."

"Seriously. You just seem...*direct*."

"*That's* what they're calling it these days."

"One last thing," Trevor added. "The Opening of the Mouth ceremony was done on statues and mummies. It wasn't a literal cutting of the bandages, like I thought. It was symbolic to awaken the senses."

"Looks like he carried out his own ritual."

As Trevor packed his book bag, one of his textbooks caught his eye. "I'm taking a Criminal Psych class this term, and I keep thinking about Fenrir. What makes him tick, what kind of childhood he had."

Black pulled into his parking spot at the station. "If you figure that out, give me a call."

~~~~~~~~~

Officer Perez contacted the Columbus Zoo again and found out that there are more than 1,200 identified species of scorpions all over the world, that they are related to spiders, and that under ultraviolet light, they glow.

The seven scorpions found in Kelly Robison's room were from the western United States. They had residue on their exoskeletons from an ammonia bath, most likely to kill and preserve them. Two were giant, hairy scorpions; and five were the more common striped-tailed scorpion, otherwise known as the 'devil scorpion.' They could have been bought on the roadside or captured in the desert. A quick Internet search led to several sites selling live scorpions—some lethal—as pets.

The feather led to a conversation with a falconer, who gave Perez a plethora of falcon facts: the family Falconidae contains over 60 species; the peregrine falcon is the most widespread species and the fastest-known animal; falconry has been around since the Middle Ages; and there are dozens of raptor centers in the United States alone. The lab determined that the feather found resting on Kelly Robison's bare breast belonged to an adult peregrine falcon. Trace elements, like dirt and pollen, indicated the bird had lived in eastern Canada. Eventually, Perez informed Black and Sheffield of what he'd learned about the feather and scorpions before returning to the harpoon receipts to try and track down the killer.

~~~~~~~~~

The fingerprints of the severed hand left on the nightstand in Kelly Robison's bedroom matched fingerprints for Joseph Sanders, a construction worker in Louisville, Kentucky, who had been arrested when he was 19 for breaking a man's jaw in a bar fight. Eight months prior to Robison's murder, Joseph Sanders slipped on a wet roof and fell three stories. The impact broke several ribs, both legs, and a vertebra in his neck. When a coworker turned him over, the jagged vertebra sliced into the spinal cord, effectively ending Joseph Sander's young life at 23.

His mother, Valeen, lived alone in Normandy and associated with no one. She survived month-to-month at the poverty level. With no family and no money, she held no services for her dead son. The day after his body returned to Ohio, it was cremated. The ashes were disposed of by the state, and Valeen Sanders returned to her sad, solitary existence to grieve for her only child, whom she had unfortunately outlived.

When Black questioned him, the funeral director broke out in hives while insisting that nothing like this had ever happened to a body in his care. Black was unable to ease his anxiety or get any useful information from him. The police report from the break-in supported the veracity of the director's story. To be on the safe side, Black ran a check on all employees of the funeral home. Black and Sheffield called Dr. Petkov's office before they pulled away, and she requested they come immediately to the coroner's lab.

Chapter 12

Whether wearing an Anne Klein suit or hospital scrubs, Dr. Nikolina Petkov exuded power and self-assurance without impugning her femininity. Even when traversing a crime scene, she moved with grace and poise. Though she worked with the dead, she was generally cheery and good-natured—but today, her mood was somber. The detectives followed her into her office. Sheffield sat on the red suede sofa, while Black and the CME enjoyed the comfort of the two sleek, black leather guest chairs. An abstract sculpture of a bird in flight adorned the stone coffee table.

"Doc, what can you tell us?" Black asked.

"Ms. Robison was killed on Friday around 10:00 p.m."

Black consulted his notepad. "She was at work until 5:30 that day. After work, she had drinks and dinner with a coworker. Told her she was going home to relax and watch a movie."

"Johnny Depp," Sheffield added. She and the victim apparently shared a love for the sexy actor. Based on Petkov's smile, she, too, shared a love for Depp.

"A neighbor said she arrived home around 6:45, so the murder had to take place sometime after that," he confirmed from his notes.

Petkov flipped through a file without reading it. "The killer bound Ms. Robison's hands and feet with strips of cotton sheets. He stuffed her mouth with a ball of the same fabric."

"He used the victim's own sheets from the linen closet," Black commented.

"To sew her lips together, he used a curved needle, like quilter's needle, threaded with nylon fishing line," the CME explained.

"So our guy likes Jo-Ann Fabrics?" Sheffield quipped. "Quilter's needles, nylon thread, and gold cord."

"Ms. Robison was alive when he stitched her lips," Petkov continued. "There was extensive bruising and bleeding, a sign that she fought back. As you can imagine, it would have been very painful." The CME shook her head and pursed her lips in disgust.

"After he did that, I bet she lay there suffering while he painted the eye on the wall and his name in hieroglyphs," Black theorized. "Then he stood by the bed, ripping the sheets into strips. It would have been psychological torture."

"Ms. Robison's blood-alcohol level was very low. No other drugs were found in her system. She may have gone into shock long before he plunged that spear through her thoracoabdominal cavity." Petkov pointed her finger at her own stomach to demonstrate. "The tip slid between sacrum and L5 vertebra, killing her instantly. After she was dead, he cut from sternum to pelvis with scalpel and removed organs—heart, liver, stomach, and part of left lung." She crossed her leg, revealing a shapely calf.

Black referred to his notepad. "He was supposed to remove the lower intestines."

"They were not removed." Petkov laid the file on the stone coffee table.

"Our guy was deviating from the normal mummification process on purpose," Black averred.

"He filled thoracic cavity with rock salt and stitched her up with same needle used on her lips." Her Bulgarian accent made the last word sound like "leeps."

"The Egyptians used salt to embalm bodies," Black said.

"Yes, natron salt." Petkov unbuttoned her jacket and then leaned forward as if she intended to whisper the next lines. "Her head was removed with a hacksaw, same one used to remove the hand found on side table."

Sheffield tugged on her ponytail. "The killer must have brought the hacksaw to the crime scene and taken it home with him, because we didn't find it. From fingerprints, we determined that the hand belonged to a construction worker named Joseph Sanders— who died eight months ago."

"The hand was originally preserved in formaldehyde. I discovered something strange: dried semen on the hand. We've done a DNA test, but no matches." Petkov leaned back in her chair as if there were no more secrets to share.

"Didn't Trevor say Isis cut off her son's hand because it held the semen of the other god?" Sheffield asked Black.

Windows stretched the entire wall behind Petkov's desk, allowing the rising sun to flood the room with natural light. The polished-stone table glinted in the sun's rays, and the skeleton cast an ominous shadow on the wall.

"So, before our killer left Kelly Robison's house, he spent a great deal of time setting up the scene," Black said. "He braided her hair, he partially mummified her, he placed scorpions around her and a falcon feather on her breast, and he put a phallus in one hand and a bloody sheet tied into some ancient symbol in the other."

"Was she sexually assaulted?" Sheffield asked.

"No." Petkov drank a swig of water, reached for the file, and began flipping through the pages. An auburn curl fell forward, and she instinctively tucked it behind her ear, looked up, and said, "If I find more, I will call you."

"Thanks for your help, Doc," Sheffield said.

"This is very disturbed killer," replied Petkov. "Please stop him before I have another body like this in my lab."

~~~~~~~~

Fenrir the Wolf had already planned his next attack. He was having so much fun that he couldn't stop now. Why *should* he stop? He was *better* than the gods. In his head, he replayed the executions of father and mother, and it gave him chills. The satisfaction tasted like honey on his lips; actually, it was more like ambrosia, the food of the gods. Now, Fenrir was hungry again. Each murder took planning, but he'd been preparing for years. Dozens of items had been procured in a variety of ways over the past ten years. Some from far away, like the scorpions and the falcon feather. Some at the same time, like the harpoon from the last murder and the fishing net he would use next. The dumb detectives would never trace these last items to a boat called *Glory Bound* in Key West; they couldn't track the wolf tooth to a stuffed wolf from a cabin in Montana that he burned to the ground; they would never be able to trace the paint from a children's art set he bought with cash from a discount store; they would never link the canopic jars to an elderly woman in Lima, Ohio, who visited her sister in Florida, during which time he ordered the jars on her credit card; they would never know he caught the scorpions himself in the Arizona desert; and they would never figure out that the falcon feather came from a raptor center outside of Kingston, Ontario. He was above the law, better than the Normandy Police Department, better than the forensic psychologist, better than the bumbling detectives. He was better than his domineering father and his pernicious mother.

Once again, his deeds were on the front page of the paper. Now, he was a celebrity. Now, the masses realized that he was an unstoppable force, ready to take down whomever he chose. The people of Normandy would grow more fearful. The game had begun. He loved the headline "Two Dead at Hands of Serial Killer, the Wolf." At first, he was angry at Aggie for not reproducing his letter word for word, but she had written a chilling article about the "violent murders" and the "serial killer among us." At least his name was there—Fenrir the Wolf. But the postscript was missing. The bitch, Aggie Rhodes, was like everyone else; she was too dumb to see a clue right in front of her fat face. Relishing each word, he read the article a second time and then a third time. The terror and panic were palpable, and it gave him a rush. With care, he clipped the entire article and pressed it into his scrapbook. There were other articles about the murders, but this one was his favorite, because it identified him by his chosen *nom de guerre*.

Neither the dumb reporter nor the incompetent detectives had figured out the clue he'd given them in the postscript; they stunk at the game. They were no good at anything except failure. Even if they *did* decipher his message, they couldn't stop him. He was the God Killer. He was Fenrir the Wolf. He committed the Myth Murders. Soon, his next crime would throw the citizens into a new panic.

Chapter 13

Returning from Thanksgiving in Middleboro, Dylan Black chose a different exit off the highway than he normally took.

After dinner, his parents had asked about his work. When talking about the God Killer case, Black found himself sharing more than he expected about Trevor, including the fact that the young man was spending Thanksgiving alone. When Margaret Black heard that, she chastised her son for not bringing him to their place; then she insisted he take the "poor child" a box of goodies. Margaret and Andy Black were just those kind of people—loving, caring, nurturing—even to strangers. They'd welcome anyone into their home. The detective knew he was lucky to have grown up in that environment.

Black turned the Lexus onto Sycamore Lane and parked illegally in front of the apartment. Trevor could not have been more surprised when he opened the door and found the detective standing there in indigo jeans and a blue sweater that matched his eyes.

"Detective Black."

"I have a treat for you."

Trevor wondered if he was dreaming. Was the detective going to profess his love and ravage him on the sofa? Black lifted a box in the air.

"Momma Black insisted I bring you a decent Thanksgiving dinner."

Trevor waved the detective in. "You really didn't have to do that."

Christina Aguilera's voice emanated from the Bose speakers. The faint scent of cinnamon and pumpkin lingered in the air. Black flashed a smile as he sat the box on the counter and began to scoop out the goodies.

"Actually, I did. You don't know my mother."

Speechless, Trevor felt an intense desire to touch Black. Instead, he retreated to turn off the CD player.

"Are you hungry?" Black asked.

Standing with his hands in his back pocket, Trevor shook his head. He wore black chinos and a white-and-purple-striped button-down shirt.

"Well then, you can put it in the fridge and eat it tomorrow."

Happy to distract himself from his libido, Trevor obeyed, piling the plastic containers in the refrigerator. "This was so nice. Tell your parents I said thank you."

Black turned and walked into the living room, where books were strewn in an imperfect arc around the chaise. "Doing some light reading?"

"Just some homework. I have a test in Criminal Psych next week and a paper due in Anthropology."

Black saw the textbooks, but next to them were other books: *The Encyclopedia of Norse Mythology; The Children of Odin: The Book of Northern Myths*; *Greek and Roman Myths; Gods of the Egyptians; The Vikings and their Religion.* He wondered if the Wolf owned these same books; and for a second, he wondered again if Trevor could be the Wolf.

"Do you mind if I sit?" he asked.

"No. Please do."

Black plopped heavily onto the couch and looked around the room, studying the various pieces of art. Then he said, "I don't want to spoil your holiday, but I wondered if you'd tell me what you make of the letter from the Wolf."

Trevor returned to the living room with a plate of pumpkin bread and a glass of milk. "Here. I made it myself." The detective scooted forward on the couch and took the plate as Trevor moved to the chaise. After swallowing a bite, Trevor responded. "About the letter: it was exactly what I'd expect from a psychopath. 'I'm the Great Oz—blah, blah.'"

"Yeah, but the last line didn't make sense: 'A slut erred.'" Black took a bite and mumbled, "This is good."

"It's like he's toying with the police." Trevor downed a gulp of milk.

"Could it have anything to do with Isis or some other mythology?"

"There were lots of goddesses that were...*promiscuous*— Aphrodite, Ishtar, Freya. I don't know what he meant by 'a slut erred,' unless he's pissed at some woman who spurned him. Maybe he's referring to Isis, but she wasn't really promiscuous by any stretch of the imagination."

Black polished off the last bite of his pumpkin bread, sat the plate on the table, and then downed the entire glass of milk. "And he misspelled hell. I'm surprised his spellchecker didn't catch that."

"It's not misspelled if you're talking about Fenrir's sister. The Christian purgatory is usually spelled with two l's, but the Norse goddess is usually spelled with only one."

The detective sat back and folded his arms in front of him. "I should have known it wasn't a mistake."

The student leaned forward as if he was tumbling to the ground and grabbed a book from the floor. "Here's a picture."

The goddess was a woman whose left side was a rotted corpse while the right side was a living female. Underneath the disturbing image was written "Hel, Goddess of Withering Things."

"She's a beauty." Black curled his lip in a sneer.

"The Wolf has taken out two biggies: the father of the Norse gods and the mother of the Egyptian gods."

"Mother and father. What's next?" Black stared at the ceiling and chewed on his lip.

While the question hung in the air, Trevor finished off his milk. "There's one thing I don't understand," he finally said.

"What's that?"

"If he wanted to target a bad mother, why would he go for Isis? He should have gone for Hera. She's the one who threw her own son from Mount Olympus."

Black rubbed his chin, giving him a quizzical look. "Maybe our killer doesn't know about Greek mythology."

Trevor shrugged. "Maybe. But I would think if he knows about Isis severing the hand of her son Horus and Odin sacrificing himself on the World Tree, then he's got to know about Hera." Black watched Trevor wiggle his naked toes.

"Why did Hera throw her son out?"

"She was jealous of Zeus' affairs, so she parthogenetically conceived a child, Hephaestus."

"Partho—*what*?"

Trevor chuckled.

"She conceived a child without a mate. Some animals can do

it, like earthworms or something. The child was so monstrous she
threw him out of heaven."

"Interesting. I think I'm beginning to get into this mythology
stuff."

Trevor narrowed his eyes in mock disbelief. "Are you being
facetious, Detective Black?"

"No." Black raised a hand. "Really, it's interesting."

While a wintry wind raced outside, the only sound inside was
the tick of the wall clock that read 9:46. Trevor looked down at the
book on Egyptian mythology.

"I just don't understand why he chose Isis; she was
practically Mary."

"But did Hera's son behead *her*?"

"No." Then the revelation hit him: the Isis myth provided
more violent images for Fenrir to recreate. Black raised his brows as
if to say "see?" Hera was mostly known for her revenge, but
relatively little happened to her: she was stuck to a magical throne
made by her rejected son, Hephaestus; and when the infant Heracles
sucked too hard on her nipple, she pulled away, and her breast milk
formed the Milky Way. The beheading of Isis was much more
graphic than any of that.

Trevor's cell phone unexpectedly rang, startling them both
from their private thoughts. Jumping up, he retrieved the phone.
Recognizing the number, he flipped it open with a pit of dread in his
stomach.

"Hi, mom."

Silence.

"I know, but I couldn't come today."

Silence.

"Now's not a good time. I'm with a friend."

Worried that Black would take umbrage to being referred to
as his friend, Trevor glanced apologetically at the detective, who
rose from the couch.

"No, mom, it's not like that. Mom—"

Black moved closer and could hear the woman on the other
end of the line in mid-harangue. He caught the occasional word—
"abomination," "sin," and "evil."

Trevor's head was bowed, and the phone was pressed tightly
to his ear as if he were listening to a secret code. Black moved

within inches of Trevor.

    Black spoke loudly on purpose. "Is there a problem, Trevor?" The diatribe on the other end of the phone ended abruptly.

    "No, it's my mom." Trevor felt overpowered by the detective's proximity and embarrassed by the situation. He wished to disappear.

    "Calling to wish you a happy Thanksgiving?" Black asked.

    "I guess," Trevor muttered feebly.

    "Tell her *I* said 'Happy Thanksgiving.'" He stared directly into Trevor's eyes.

    "Mom, we're getting ready to eat dessert, so I've got to go." There was a pause. "Bye."

    "I thought we already had dessert," Black joked.

    Trevor sighed heavily. "Sorry about that."

    "No problem."

    "Can I ask you something? Do you have any gay friends?"

    "The way Sheff talks about how hot Dr. Petkov is, you'd *think* she was a lesbian. But no, I don't have any gay friends."

    "When I was 16, my parents found a picture of Keanu Reeves in my notebook, and they freaked out. They told me that I was going to hell."

    "Not everyone should be a parent." Black placed a hand on Trevor's shoulder.

    "When they freaked out about the picture, I knew I was gay. I blurted it out: 'I'm gay.' They told me to leave, so I left and slept in a park. When I went back home, they told me that I could stay if I promised to work on becoming straight."

    "Is that even possible?"

    Trevor shrugged. "Not for me. I was afraid to be on my own, so I shut my mouth and pretended."

    "Forget about your parents."

    "You know Officer Perez offered to hook me up with his brother-in-law?"

    "Really? Amadeo was trying to play matchmaker?" The detective was surprised, but then again, Perez was one of the good guys who didn't have an ounce of bigotry in his body. "And what did you say to him?"

    "The guy lives in Chicago, so I said 'pass.'"

    "I don't know, Trevor. Maybe you should take him up on it.

Perez's wife is gorgeous. They got that whole Latin thing going. *Muy caliente.*"

Trevor laughed out loud, and it felt good.

~~~~~~~

Vivienne Sheffield actually spent Thanksgiving morning at the station, reviewing progress on the Myth Murders. Looking at her watch, she realized that it was time to go home, shower, and dress for her Thanksgiving meal. Viktor Edwards, a financial manager at a local firm, was cooking dinner for her at his house. She scooped up a jumble of papers from her desk, clipped them together, and placed them in her desk drawer. For a moment, she looked at the desk across from hers and thought of Black. An aching sensation washed through her like a traveling tsunami. Once it passed, she turned away and headed home.

Chapter 14

Jennifer Phillips Black didn't go back to her maiden name after divorcing Dylan Black. It was simply a matter of convenience; all those forms, all the paperwork, all the bother. She just didn't have time. After a whirlwind romance that lasted six months, Dylan Black, the handsome detective-in-training, asked for her hand in marriage, but after only a year, things changed. Dylan spent more and more time at work, and when he was home, he seemed distant. Their sex life became nonexistent. Suspecting he was having an affair, she started calling at random times and dropping by the precinct unannounced. After months of quiet despair, Jennifer began to drink. A sip in the morning, a few when she arrived home, a half a bottle before going to bed. Within a couple months, Jennifer Black had become a secret alcoholic.

Rather than detox in Normandy, she went to Nevada to dry out. During her recovery, she looked back on her life and realized how her childhood had contributed to her addiction: parents who were always at each other's throats, boyfriends who cared only that they were dating a hot cheerleader. No one valued Jennifer's dreams or feelings—until Dylan Black, that is. And when their relationship soured, Jennifer reverted to old habits and blamed herself. During her twelve steps to sobriety, her husband didn't abandon her. He called every day, sent flowers once a week, and visited her twice in Nevada. After gaining control over her addiction, she did the unthinkable: she forgave her husband for ruining their marriage. Jennifer knew that she'd always love Dylan, and maybe that's why she kept his name. Five years after the divorce, they still stayed in touch.

Reading about the serial killer in Normandy sent chills through her. Though it was early, she picked up the phone and dialed her ex-husband.

"Dylan, it's me. What're you doing?"

"Getting ready for work."

"Do you have a minute?" She took a sip of hot tea.

"One or two."

She heard him turn off the faucet and realized he was either shaving or brushing his teeth. A couple days of stubble on Dylan was a good thing.

"Is anything wrong, Jenny?"

"No. I wanted to see how you're doing. How're your mom and dad?"

"They're great."

"And the little ones?" She was referring to his parents' dogs.

"Good. Hold on."

She imagined he was wiping shaving cream from his face and took the opportunity to apply lipstick.

"I'm back."

"I read about the killer in the paper, and I'm a little freaked out." She zipped her suede skirt and stepped into her pumps.

"This one's bizarre. We can't seem to catch any breaks."

Jennifer sighed.

"I'm worried about you, Dylan. This isn't some street thug. This is a real psycho. Promise you'll be careful." Despite their troubled past, their relationship had evolved into something special. In some ways, they were better now than when they were married.

"I'll be fine. Don't worry. You know I can handle myself."

"I can't help it," she confessed. "This whole thing gives me goose bumps. I'm going to worry until this guy is caught."

"What do you want me to say? Should I sing you a song?"

She blotted her lipstick before responding. "I always loved your version of 'Sister Golden Hair.'"

"I remember." She heard him snap his shoulder holster.

"Are you dating anyone, Dylan?"

"No. I'm stuck with Sheff all the time."

"Ah, poor baby. How *is* Viv?"

"She's been working a lot of hours. I've been spending too much time with Petkov and this college student named Trevor who knows a hell of a lot about this mythology stuff." He didn't know why he'd just mentioned Trevor to his ex-wife, but it was done.

"Just take care of yourself," she insisted, as she dabbed Bulgari cologne on her neck. "Give me a call every once in a while to let me know you're okay." She made a kissing sound into the phone. After she hung up, Jennifer tried to imagine the college student. Trevor—nice name. Though she had yet to share her suspicions with anyone other than her therapist, for years Jennifer Black had suspected that her ex-husband might actually be gay.

~~~~~~

Given the dearth of progress in the Myth Murders, Black and Sheffield decided the time had come to call in Dr. Edgar Canter, a forensic psychologist who worked with the FBI and several precincts in Ohio. An expert on compulsive killers, Dr. Canter had interviewed hundreds of murderers, including several serial killers, among them Edmund Kemper who had dispassionately described in great detail murdering his mother and stuffing her vocal chords down a garbage disposal. Black and Sheffield sent the psychologist information about both murders and a copy of his letter.

Holding several thick files, Sheffield walked into the conference room and quietly selected a seat across from Canter, who was jotting notes in his own secret code. The psychiatrist was a round man with a nearly bald pate and doe eyes. Though he was very overweight, he always dressed impeccably and never seemed to sweat. He also made direct eye contact when speaking. Some believed Canter's nonjudgmental mien and soft, methodical speech could calm a bear. It had effectively cajoled dozens of killers into opening up about the most violent aspects of their crimes.

"How are you today, Detective Sheffield?" the roly-poly man asked.

"Good. Please call me Viv. Black should be here in a minute." She flipped her blonde mane over her shoulder and unbuttoned her jacket. The door to the conference room opened. Black rushed to greet the forensic psychologist.

"Dr. Canter, sorry to keep you waiting. Thanks for meeting with us."

"Please call me Edgar."

Black selected a seat at the end of the table. "Okay. Edgar it is. I'm Dylan."

"I'm afraid that you have yourself a full-fledged, organized, predatory killer here." Canter waved his hand over the documents on the table in front of him. Gruesome crime-scene photos peeked out like glimpses in a sadist's family-photo album. "A psychopathic personality disorder, if you will. Let me tell you my first impressions: Your killer is male; otherwise, she would have chosen a female *nom de guerre*—after all, there are plenty of female monsters in mythology. He's probably white, since all of his victims have been white, maybe in his 30's, plain looking, ordinary. My guess is that he's in a relationship with a woman, but she isn't part of his violent fantasies, so she's safe. He probably holds a mundane job that requires little education, and he performs poorly—bad attendance, shoddy work."

The two detectives were extremely attentive as the large man eloquently profiled the Wolf. The psychiatrist pulled out the copy of Fenrir's letter and read it silently before continuing.

"As you know, he takes great pride in duping the police. He's teasing you, challenging you. For example, he tried to make the first murder look like the crucifixion of Jesus, though he knew you'd eventually figure out it wasn't. Like all psychopaths, he has a grandiose self-image and thinks he's better than everyone else— including you." He nodded to each detective in turn. "He can treat people as objects, with no remorse. Your guy is at least normal intelligence, but likely gifted. Obviously, he knows a great deal about ancient mythologies, and that may be your hook in catching him."

Black was jotting notes.

"Do you have any ideas how?" Sheffield asked.

Canter shook his head. "His childhood was almost definitely troubled. My guess is his mom was domineering and overbearing, but maybe it was his dad. His parents held him to some unreasonable standards that he couldn't achieve. Most definitely he was exposed to this mythology stuff through his parents or primary caregiver. He grew up with this. Maybe it was held against him, used as psychological torture. Clearly, he thinks he is like a god. He sees nothing wrong with doling out punishment or exacting revenge like any god might. He's acting out a fantasy. These killings are well thought out, preplanned, and full of symbolism. Have you checked for prior killings?"

"I ran it through ViCAP using several key words." Sheffield ran her fingernail over a crack in the table. "I found no matches."

"Hmmm. Good that you checked nationwide, because serial killers are notoriously mobile. Maybe he didn't use the symbolism with such a heavy hand before. It's obvious his fantasy is to kill off individuals who represent someone who's hurt him." Canter paused, arched a brow, and looked at a macabre photo from Kelly Robison's bedroom.

"The Greeks and Romans anthropomorphized their gods— philandering husband, prodigal child, jealous wife. They're like archetypes really. It's odd to me that your guy is not just killing his human foes, but rather a godlike version of them. It's as if he's saying he's so powerful, he can even kill the gods.

Black said, "One of the people who knows this mythology stuff says Isis was a relatively good mother."

"Maybe he's following an undiscerned pattern here: Norse, then Egyptian; wolf, then falcon; father, then mother. Or maybe he's chosen these gods because of physical characteristics. Maybe his father was one-eyed; maybe his mother had long, black hair. Could be he's simply flaunting his knowledge of these myths to display his intellect."

"He had to *love* a myth about a wolf eating a god." Sheffield tapped a finger on the table to drive home her point.

"The wolf is a powerful predator, the perfect animal totem for our killer," Canter explained. "Imagine growing up on these myths, especially if they were used to threaten you or control you." Black folded his arms as his partner pushed her chair back from the table. "Compulsive killers are extremely talented at choosing victims, but they're also opportunistic. He could see his victim in the grocery store, in traffic, in the park. It may be that he chose Lawrence Adams from a crowd because he was missing an eye."

"We thought the same thing," Black confessed.

"Your guy has rehearsed these murders so many times in his head—and spent an enormous amount of time collecting props, I might add—and he needs to externalize his fantasies. Now, it's self-sustaining. Four months after his first killing, he did it again. As you know, the murders usually escalate over time as the serial killer begins to degrade.

"My suspicions are that this killer is hidden among us very well. He looks relatively normal and behaves in an acceptable manner, although he may be a little odd, slightly off. Most likely he comes across as a bit of a loner, with very few people close to him. He loves publicity, because it feeds his grandiose ego. I don't envy your task."

"Any good news?" Sheffield clicked her heels in a *rat-a-tat* on the floor.

"Yes. Eventually, he'll get too cocky and make a mistake."

"What do you make of this postscript?" Black pointed to the letter.

Canter picked it up with his sausage fingers and responded, "Odd."

"Do you think we could trap him somehow?" Black asked. "Bait him into selecting a particular victim?"

"No," the psychologist answered. "He doesn't have one type he's pursuing. He's not picking up brunettes at dive bars or gay-male hustlers in parks. I see no pattern at this point. Next it might be a teacher who belittled him, a brother who picked on him, a girlfriend who cheated on him."

Sheffield paced behind her chair. Black continued. "You mentioned finding a pattern to the murders. Norse, then Egyptian; father, then mother. Can you think of any patterns that might help us anticipate his next move?"

"Detective Black, I wish I could. He's likely going to switch mythologies once more—maybe Celtic or Babylonian or Mesoamerican this time. He's already planning it, collecting items, rehearsing it. Even if we knew he was going after his uncle as Zeus, we still would have no clue how to track him down. I can almost guarantee he'll write the press again. Have you attended the funerals of his victims?"

Both Sheffield and Black nodded.

"We didn't see anyone out of the ordinary," Black said.

Edgar Canter folded his arms over his big belly. "This killer likes the hands-on approach that involves torture over a length of time, and it may get him into trouble. A roommate may come home early, a neighbor may spot a suspicious vehicle. If so, you might get lucky."

"There was no forced entry either time," Black shared.

"Which makes me think he presents himself in a nonthreatening way, maybe under some guise like 'repairman.'"

"So far, the killing has been restricted to the bedrooms."

"He most likely has issues with bedrooms. Maybe he was confined to one."

"So he's one sick bastard?" Sheffield made eye contact with the psychiatrist.

"That's not how I would describe him in court, but yes. Your perpetrator is an antisocial personality disorder. Or, as you put it, 'one sick bastard.'"

Chapter 15

Dr. Straymore wrote three phrases on the blackboard at the front of the room while 30 college students watched. "Today we're going to talk about the Kelleher Typology of female serial killers: the Angel of Death, the Black Widow, and the Revenge Killer." His gray seersucker suit and deep, resonant voice gave him an air of authority and expertise. This man was made for academia, and yet he only taught one class a year. His fulltime job was counseling violent criminals and teenagers with rage issues, but every fall semester he taught one evening course in Criminal Psychopathology at the University of Normandy.

"How many of you can name a female serial killer?" the professor asked. Several hands went up.

"Besides Aileen Wuornos." All hands fell. "So I take it many of you saw the movie *Monster*." Chuckles arose.

As Dr. Straymore continued his lecture, the students leaned forward and settled in for the ride. The class had learned the characteristics of killers according to Anne Rule, a popular author of true crime as well as world-renowned expert on criminal behavior. They had discussed paranoid annihilation, contemptuous delight, narcissistic rage, the grandiose self, Macdonald's triad of sociopathy, and predatory versus affective aggression. The class had been reminded of the differences between mass murderers and serial killers and had discussed the theory of an impaired limbic system and the reptilian concept, which contends that serial killers are cold and unfeeling, lacking warmth and empathy, just like reptiles.

After his Criminal Psych class, Trevor often thought of his friend Lawrence and grew melancholy. And he thought of Fenrir the Wolf. Who was he? How much did he resemble the characteristics of Anne Rule? Did he have reptilian eyes? What had his childhood been like? How did he know about the gods? Did people around him think he was normal? Where did he live? Which god would he choose to kill next?

~~~~~~~~~

Friday and Saturday nights, at Sexcapade Lounge in downtown Columbus, women stripped in the front of the bar on the large main stage lined in pink neon, while men stripped toward the back, on the smaller stage lined with blue neon. One could stand anywhere in the strip joint and see everyone else.

The Herculean stripper known as "Tank" was 6'2" and 245 pounds and built like his name implied. From the time he'd lost his virginity to his sister's babysitter at the age of 14, he knew his looks gave him power. By the age of 16, Tank, who was then known as Brad or "Bender," was having sex regularly: high-school girlfriends, his boss's wife, the twin sisters next door, the quarterback on the football team, his sister's best friend. His good grades in Spanish had nothing to do with how well he spoke it; the bonus at his landscaping job wasn't due to how well he pruned trees. Tank used his body to his advantage.

Much like Tank, Star, whose real name was Felicity Roth, had learned that her looks could make men open their wallets. For the pleasure of watching her strip, they would lose their religion, forsake their families, and shell out their savings. Like Tank, her attributes were all god-given. When she was on stage, her breasts high in the air, her long, blonde hair whipping behind her like a mane, Star was the star of the club. The stares, the tips, the betrothals of love, and the adoring fans made her feel successful, needed, and loved.

Only a handful of fellow dancers knew that Tank and Star lived together in a loft in downtown Normandy. They were proverbial birds of a feather who understood each other. More than once, they'd fucked the same person. Sometimes, a two-way turned into a three-way at the request of an adventurous date. Sometimes, lovers left behind tokens of appreciation—namely, *cash*.

When a plain-looking man with a limp approached Star and Tank in the parking lot of Sexcapade, neither felt threatened. The disabled man spoke nervously.

"Excuse me. Can I ask you a question?"

"What is it, baby?" Star had a habit of using terms of

endearment with friends and customers.

"I just wanted to tell you how much I enjoyed watching you."

"That's sweet," she purred.

Tank clicked the button to unlock their Mazda while Star attended to her fan.

"Are you a couple?" With a bum leg, wild hair, an unkempt beard, and broken glasses, the man appeared to have had a tough life.

"Hey, buddy, I'm Tank." The behemoth spoke, and the lame man actually recoiled in fear. "Star and I are friends."

"Oh." It was the sound of disappointment. "I thought you were a couple." Ashamed, the man looked down at his worn work boots. "I have a problem—a *sexual* problem."

"Sorry to hear that, dude." Tank put an arm protectively around Star's shoulder.

"I have trouble getting hard and coming." He cast a wary glance at Star. "But you excite me."

"Thank you, baby. So what're you getting at?"

"I might be able to orgasm if I watched you two…" The man trailed off nervously.

The dancers exchanges glances, and Tank asked, "You want to watch me and Star fuck?"

The stranger became flustered; he turned to walk away and then turned back. Next, he reached in his pocket and pulled out a roll of cash.

"I've never done this before, but I hoped…" His voice trembled.

"What do you have in mind, baby?" Star guessed there was a thousand dollars in his hand.

"I'd just sit across the room and jack off while you two…" He seemed ashamed to say the word. "If I watch…"

Star and Tank looked at each other and shrugged.

"Okay, buddy." Tank reached out and took the money. "Looks like we're going to do a show for you, and you're going to fuckin' love it."

~~~~~~~

One day, while working out his biceps, Trevor noticed a dark-haired hunk across the gym perched on the sit-up bench, looking his way. Trevor smiled and nodded casually, and the hottie in the tight tank top did the same. Trevor headed to the cardio equipment and stood, deciding between a treadmill and a bike.

"You have great form on your bicep curls." It was Mr. Hot Body. He was stunning—good physique, angular face, movie star smile.

Trevor fought to appear calm. *Please don't let my voice crack.* "Thanks. So, you do a lot of abs?"

"Yeah. Got to work the six pack."

"I'm bad about skipping abs." Was the cutie flirting?

"Well, you look like you're in good shape," the dark-haired hunk said.

"Thanks. You, too."

"I'm Marc."

"I'm Trevor."

"Have you ever been to the Dark Room?" It was a popular gay bar in Normandy. *Score*, Trevor thought.

The two continued to flirt like teenagers and made plans to go on a date Thursday night. Trevor's last date had been months ago, with a guy who couldn't stop talking about himself. Now he was ready to get back on the horse, so to speak. When Thursday night rolled around, the dark-haired stud arrived with a single red rose in a halo of baby's breath, a portent of a romantic evening to come. Greeting Trevor with a hug, Marc exuded charm, charisma, and sex appeal, and Trevor knew he was in trouble. The meal was Italian. The conversation was uneven, but Trevor learned that Marc was one year younger than him and worked at a fitness store. The movie was a historical action film with millions of dollars' worth of special effects and a hot male lead who spent much of the movie without a shirt. Though he hated to admit it, Trevor was horny and lonely. Big trouble.

When they arrived back at Crest Ridge, the two exchanged pleasantries and then grew silent. Trevor made his move.

"Would you like to come inside?" Trevor waited for the verdict.

"Sure."

Trevor couldn't stop smiling as he got out of the car. "We

can make banana splits."

"I'll split one with you," Marc said. "I've got to watch the carbs."

"It just *one* banana split."

"Seriously, I've got to monitor what I eat pretty closely, or I get a little pudgy around the middle." He raised his shirt and slapped his abs to drive home his point.

Please let him be more than a musclehead, Trevor thought, as they entered his apartment. "You can live a little tonight. It's our first date."

"So there might be another?" Marc asked. Trevor turned to smile at Marc, then raised his eyebrows playfully, and Marc responded with an "Oh, yeah!"

Marc looked around and whistled. "I love your place."

"Thanks. Did you say your parents live in Seattle?"

"Uh-huh."

"What's the gay scene like there?"

"About like *here*. It's okay. I'm not really into parades and gay bowling."

Trevor gathered the ingredients. "That's not really my cup of tea, either. I look forward to the day when we can walk down the street hand-in-hand or kiss in public, and it's a non-issue."

"I don't care about that. I'm not really into PDAs. No one needs to know I'm gay."

Trevor sliced a banana into two bowls and scooped ice cream on top. "But don't you think gay kids need to see gay adults to feel normal?"

Marc shrugged. "You and I survived, and I certainly didn't see many homos when I was growing up." Trevor focused on the whipped cream and toppings and added a cherry to both bowls. "So are you out to your family and your coworkers?" Marc asked. Trevor handed one bowl to his guest and kept the second for himself.

"Yeah. It's not the first thing I tell people, but it takes too much energy to live a lie."

"I don't agree. Let 'em think you're straight, and save yourself the grief."

Trevor shrugged. Time to abandon the topic. Being playful, he scooped up a spoonful of ice cream and fed Marc. He wiped the chocolate off Marc's lips with his thumb, and then Marc sucked

Trevor's thumb into his mouth. Both libidos revved into high gear. After the ice cream, he and Marc were going to have sex—and it was going to be damn good.

~~~~~~~

The Normandy homicide detectives were gathered at their desks, reviewing crime-lab reports and discussing their progress—or lack thereof—in what was being referred to variously as "God Killings," "Myth Murders," and "the Normandy Slasher case." The trail to the canopic jars and harpoon was ice cold. How had the killer procured these items without leaving a trace? Had he bought them with cash? Purchased them outside of Ohio? Stolen them? Similarly, the animal items had led them down several dead ends.

"With all the items the killer brought to the crime scenes, you'd think something would lead us to his door," Sheffield said. "Instead, they've led us on wild-goose chases."

"So what do we have?" Black was a list person, and he reviewed. "At Adams's, he left wolf hair, the tooth, mistletoe and raven feathers. We've checked them all out."

Perez jumped in. "At Robison's, he left the canopic jars, the harpoon, scorpions, a falcon feather, elastic cord, and paint."

"Don't forget the hand of Joseph Sanders," Sheffield reminded him.

"Seems like he's taking a lot of chances." Perez sat down and spun his chair to face the detectives.

Black played with a paperclip. "He feels confident."

"But why?" Sheffield was agitated. "How can he be so certain?"

"Some of the items he used were in the house already." Black rattled off the list. "The Scrabble board and knife at Adams's. The needle, thread, rock salt, and dildo at Robison's. Finding these items must seem fortuitous to the Wolf." Black looked at the papers in front of him. "The paint analysis shows that he used nontoxic children's paint. It comes in a kit with a bib."

"I wonder if he painted the Eye of Horus and the cartouche while she watched in horror." Sheffield stared out the window as she imagined the scene.

Black mindlessly opened and closed his stapler repeatedly. "The bastard is really getting off on leaving these things at the crime scenes."

"If I were a gambler, I'd wager he's stealing them," Perez said.

"He's planned these attacks for a long time, so he could have gotten some of these things *years* ago, far away from here." Sheffield fished a Payday candy bar from her desk and opened it eagerly.

"Okay, so let's say he gathered the wolf hair, the raven feathers, the falcon feather, and the scorpions in the wild." Black leaned toward his friend Perez as if he were asking him a personal question. "Where the fuck does he *go* for all these?"

"Yellowstone." It was a joke, but no one laughed. "That type of wolf is extinct in the wild, so it had to be a captive animal."

Sheffield stared at the remains of the candy bar. "What is he, Dr. Doolittle?"

"We've had no luck looking at employees of zoos and animal-shelters," Perez said.

"What are we missing?" Black asked. "Can we track *any* of these things to our killer?"

Then a familiar voice called to them.

"Black, Sheffield, in my office!" It was the chief of police, Titus McNally.

~~~~~~~

Aggie Rhodes looked at the letter in disbelief. When she wrote her first article about Fenrir—quoting directly from his correspondence—she knew that she'd forged an uncomfortable alliance with the devil. As precautions, Aggie had begun carrying Mace and driving her two kids to and from school every day.

Now she had been touched by evil again. The letter in her hand reeked of malevolence.

Dear Ms. Rhodes,

Thank you for the flattering article about me. You really

are a stupid bitch. Not as dumb as the inept police,
especially the Keystone Kops Vivienne Sheffield and
Dylan Black, but you still have no clue just how powerful
I am. Soon you will see once again that I am superior,
even to the gods.

It is time for you to write about me again. I miss the
attention. You'll inflame fear and panic with your effusive
descriptions. Remind the public of my name: Fenrir the
Wolf, killer of the gods. Apparently, you missed the clue
in my last letter. I'm disappointed in you, Aggie.

I look forward to your new article. I'm certain you'll do
me justice. Remember, I'm better than you, and I can't be
stopped.

Yours truly,
Fenrir the Wolf

P.S. As Much Is By Doubt

Certain it was from the killer, she felt ill when she read the
contents. While waiting on the homicide detectives, she studied the
letter. What the hell was with the stupid postscript again?
On the side of her desk was the crossword puzzle that she
hadn't completed from the day's paper. That was it! The mixed-up
conglomeration of words in the postscript had to be a word game, an
encrypted message. The killer was leaving clues to see if she could
decipher them. She feverishly set about solving the riddle. First,
Aggie rewrote the five words, one underneath another, on a piece of
paper. Hoping to make a word from them, she studied the first letter
of each word, but it made no sense: AMIBD. Could it be an
anagram? The only thing she could make of it was "I'm bad".
Deciding that she needed another approach, she scrawled all of the
letters from the postscript, leaving no spaces. Now it was just one
long string of 15 letters: ASMUCHISBYDOUBT. Allowing her
"puzzle mind" to take over, she searched for new possibilities. Soon,
she had several words jotted down: boy, basis, hum, him, dutch,
butch.
It was the last word that brought it all into focus. From

"butch," she instantly leapt to "bitch," and Aggie knew that the message was an insult directed at her. After another minute of unscrambling, Aggie Rhodes had the hidden message from Fenrir the Wolf written before her.

"As Much Is By Doubt" was an anagram for "You dumbass bitch."

Chapter 16

Titus McNally, the Normandy chief of police, was an irascible, brusque man, and the officers of the NPD both feared and respected him. At 59 years of age, he was still a powerful man, though his love of sandwiches and cookies had given him an undeniable Santa belly. His skin was the color of roasted coffee beans, and his short hair was salt-and-pepper. Over the years, he'd grown so myopic that he needed glasses, which he usually refused to wear, just to read a police report. Though Normandy was a predominantly white city, with as many Latinos as blacks, McNally never gave a thought to being a minority when he took the job as Chief of Police.

Black and Sheffield generally liked McNally and thought he did a damn good job. Still, when he shouted, "In my office!" their eyes met in a look of dread. There was no denying that the chief was displeased with the Myth Murders case.

"So what's the status with this serial killer?" he asked, standing by the window watching a bird on the ledge.

Sheffield spoke first. "Well, we've been investigating the items left at the scenes."

Black stuffed his hands in his pants and added, "Since some of these items are so unusual, we thought we'd be able to narrow down where he got them. We started by tracking receipts and calling zoos about the animal items."

"Still no luck?" the chief boomed.

"No, sir. We looked into all Ohioans who purchased the jars and the harpoon in the past year," Sheffield responded.

The cardinal returned to the window ledge, and the chief seemed momentarily distracted by it. "Did you consider expanding your search to the tri-state area?" McNally asked.

"We haven't yet, but we're planning that next," Black said.

"It seems this guy is very careful," Sheffield added.

"Why're these sons of bitches always so smart?" His gaze returned to the detectives. "Whatta you need?"

Black beat Sheffield to the response. "Officer Perez has been helping us. We'd like to keep him, if that's okay."

"Fine. Tell him that he's now officially part of your team. We'll call it a task force. The goddamn media always wants a task force. Expand your search to include Indiana and Kentucky. Go back two years."

The detectives nodded in unison. Stoic, Black continued to stand with hands in his pockets, but Sheffield shifted her weight like a child who wanted to run and play.

"What's with the hand he left behind?" The chief plopped down hard into his chair. "It belonged to a dead man?"

"Yes," Black answered. "A construction worker who died on the job. The night before the cremation, the funeral home experienced a break-in."

"And no one noticed the guy was missing a hand before they cremated him?"

"Apparently not."

"Holy hell! People can't even respect the dead. We've dealt with some goddamn freaks, but this one's *got* to be the worst." The chief bit into a Nutter Butter cookie and scowled. Then he growled like a bear.

Black continued, as if prodded to fill the silence.

"This guy plans these killings well in advance and procures these items in a manner that's hard to trace. He may even steal them. There's debris on one of the feathers that indicates it's from Canada."

"Canada! Christ almighty!" Though he was a pious man, the chief liked profanity with religious reference—except around his wife, Dolores.

Sheffield muttered, "Seems our guy travels a lot."

"So Indiana and Kentucky may not be a big enough radius." The chief polished off another Nutter Butter in one bite.

"The wolf hair from the first case was from a Mexican-wolf pup," Black said. "They're extremely rare. As far as we can tell, all of the Mexican wolves in Ohio are in zoos or sanctuaries, so we've interviewed everyone we could find that had contact with these animals."

"Perez has been in touch with zoo officials," Sheffield shared. "He's had his zoology lessons."

The chief grunted. "And you talked with psych about this?"

"Yes, sir," Black answered. "Last week. Dr. Canter gave us some ideas about our killer's motives. He thinks our guy was exposed to this mythology stuff as a kid. Strict home, smart but an oddball."

"Like *that* narrows it down." The chief furrowed his brow as if debating whether to eat another cookie. "Do you have any suspects?"

"No, sir," Sheffield answered quietly.

"And he's writing this reporter?" The chief looked at the newspaper before him. "That's just what we need."

"Aggie Rhodes at the *Normandy Times*," Sheffield stated. "She just got a second letter."

"The killer left no DNA or fingerprints on them," Black said.

"These psycho killers always love publicity, don't they?" McNally squinted as if he was reading his computer screen. "And you've spoken with a professor at the university about the mythology?"

"Yes, sir," Sheffield answered. "Quite frankly, he wasn't very helpful. He's an expert on Greek and Roman mythology. The killings were based on Norse and Egyptian myths."

"The student who found the first victim has helped some with the mythology," Black added.

Sheffield snorted, as if to say "more than some!" "His name is Trevor McDaniel," she said, "but I call him Myth Boy. He knows these myths pretty well."

"Sounds like a suspect to me," the chief said gruffly. "I hope you eliminated him as one."

"Alibis that checked out during both murders," Black responded.

"Well, keep him reeled in tightly. What does Petkov say?"

Hesitant to deliver the bad news, Sheffield paused before answering, "So far, nothing to lead us to the Wolf."

"What's your next move, besides expanding your search?"

"We're going back through the items left behind to see if we can come up with something new. Especially the animal stuff."

"Okay, okay," McNally said, with a wave of his hand. "Just keep working on this, and let me know when you find something. I got people who don't know shit from Shinola chomping on my ass about this one." He picked up the empty cookie wrapper and studied it longingly.

~~~~~~~

Trevor was unaccustomed to having a warm body next to him, but he knew he could get used to it. The sex had been hot, but there was one problem: Marc wouldn't kiss; he turned his head every time Trevor moved in for a smooch. After sex, Marc drifted off to sleep, but Trevor stayed awake. The soft cadence of Marc's heartbeat was soothing. Trevor's arm fell asleep, and his neck was bent awkwardly, but he didn't care. Even in the moonlight, he could make out the curves of Marc's chest, the definition in his abdomen, and the cleft in his chin. Though it had only been the second date, Trevor wondered if this might be a relationship in the works.

As Trevor shifted his shoulder to wake his numbing arm, Marc stirred and opened his eyes. He smiled at Trevor, and Trevor's heart melted. Then he rubbed the back of his hand over Trevor's cheek. It was sublime.

Marc sat up and announced, "Well, I'd better go."

"Why? Can't you stay for breakfast?"

"I don't want my roommate to ask a lot of questions."

"Don't you ever stay out all night?"

"Sometimes, but I should get going." Marc reached for his clothes. Trevor watched him slip on his t-shirt, jeans, and sandals.

"I had a great time last night," Trevor said.

"Me, too. We should do this again soon."

"Yeah. *Definitely.*" Trevor leaned over to kiss Marc on the lips and only got his cheek. So the date ended with Trevor watching the gorgeous man run off into the night, as if he was a secret agent called in for a mission.

~~~~~~~

The second letter from Fenrir was like the previous one: same paper, same font, and same dire, self-aggrandizing message. It was postmarked from a zip code in Springfield, about 20 miles away. Black and Sheffield stood over Aggie's desk, reading the letter a second time.

"See the postscript?" Aggie moved toward them until she was pressed against Black.

"Seems like a message." Sheffield leaned closer as if she'd glean some additional knowledge.

"Like the last one," Black added.

The reporter gesticulated excitedly, as if she'd had too much caffeine. "It is. This message is meant for me. It's an anagram. Look!" Aggie held up a piece of paper with a jumble of letters, many with lines through them, and a hodgepodge of words, some real and some made-up. Below the words was a circled sentence: "you dumbass bitch."

"What is this?" Sheffield asked.

"Just what you think—an anagram. And the last postscript was the same."

The two detectives watched Aggie reach for another pad of paper. The odd phrase from Fenrir's last letter was written at the top in all capital letters with no spaces: ASLUTERRED. Hash marks again canceled out letters. The page abounded with words: dread, lust, star, red, tree, sad, salt, reed, read, slate, rustle, adult. Again, at the bottom, enclosed in a circle, was Aggie Rhodes's solution: "adulterers."

"Son of a bitch," Black muttered.

~~~~~~~~

"Trevor, I'm wondering if you could answer a question for us." Black was on his phone at his desk, watching his partner fight over a Chinese menu with Officer Perez.

"Sure."

"Oh, no—another murder?" Trevor pictured Lawrence, bruised and bloody in crucifixion position.

"No. The killer sent another letter to the newspaper. Seems the postscripts are a message."

"A message?" Trevor could hear Sheffield ordering sweet-and-sour pork.

"It's an anagram: adulterers. Are there any gods who fit the bill?"

"Too many to name. The gods didn't tend to be faithful. Almost all of the Greco-Roman gods had affairs. Especially Zeus."

"From what you know about our killer, any guesses about what he's planning?"

"Dylan, I don't know." Trevor immediately chastised himself for using the detective's first name. "First, he went for father, then mother, so maybe this is an unfaithful girlfriend."

"That's kinda what we're thinking. Could you make a list for us?"

"A list of adulterers?" Trevor asked, as he bit into a dark chocolate bar.

"Is that too much to ask?"

"No, I'd be glad to. I've got class and then work, but I'll see what I can put together."

"I'll buy you lunch."

"You don't have to do that, but it would be nice to see you again."

There was a prolonged pause before Black responded.

"Yeah, same here. Call me once you've got something."

Chapter 17

"Where would you like us to do it? Here on the couch?" Tank asked. Star was dancing around like Salome asking for the head of John the Baptist. As she swayed gracefully, the scent of gardenia candles wafted toward the lame man.

"I prefer the bedroom," the man with the limp answered furtively. Star and Tank traded glances, as if carrying on a psychic conversation. He wore tight jeans and black tank top, and she had on a pink skirt and white corset top.

"My room's right up there." She pointed to the loft above. When Tank picked up Star, she wrapped her legs around his waist. He carried her as if she weighed nothing at all.

"Are you going to be okay coming up the stairs, honey?" she asked the stranger.

"Yes, I'll be fine."

Over Tank's shoulder, Star watched the crippled man pull his left leg behind him. *I thought his right leg was the injured one*, she said to herself.

Once inside the bedroom, Tank turned and ran his hands over Star's ass. "Tell us what you want to see."

Star leaned backward, letting her shirt ride up and her hair dance seductively behind her. "Yeah, baby, tell us what you want."

"Well, you can undress each other." The man sat in the vanity chair and leaned forward. Covered in flannel and khaki, he looked like a mountain man, and the layers of clothing hid his burgeoning erection.

"Sure, baby," Star purred. "I *love* Tank's muscular body."

The blonde flipped her hair forward over Tank's head and shoulders. Using his body like a pole, she unwrapped one leg and rubbed a knee against his crotch before sliding down to the ground. Tank offered no protests as she unfastened his belt and jeans, removed his tank top and licked his torso. Tank almost delicately unbuttoned her camisole, pushed it off her body, and unfastened her bra, exposing her plump, round breasts.

From the side of the room, the man trembled nervously.

"You okay, honey?" she asked.

"Yeah. I think this is going to be just what I needed."

"You like my breasts?"

He gave an adamant nod. "Can he suck them?"

"Sure, baby." She knelt on the edge of the bed and beckoned Tank with a wave of her fingers. Then she gently guided his face toward her bosom. He teased each nipple with his tongue before sucking it into his mouth like a hungry newborn. Smelling her citrus perfume, hearing her soft moans of pleasure, seeing her engorged nipples quiver, the lame man was enraptured.

"You gonna get it out, baby?" Star looked at him as she ran her hand down Tank's back and into his jeans and squeezed his ass. "This is all for you, sweetie."

The man squeezed his crotch. "Not yet."

"You want more?" Tank asked, continuing to suck on Star's tits. Star undressed Tank slowly, deliberately, as if unwrapping a special gift. It took some effort to push his jeans over his beefy ass and past his massive thighs. Once his clothes were off, she turned Tank around so that his erection protruded toward the man paying for the show; that way, he could see what was about to invade her body. She reached around and stroked Tank's cock while sliding off her skirt. Then she stepped from behind Tank and playfully slipped off her thong.

"Can you be on top?" the man asked coyly.

"Sure. Tank won't mind that."

"Hell, no," the big man responded.

"If you want to talk dirty, I like that, too."

"Sure, baby. You want me to tell Tank how much I like his big cock inside my wet pussy?"

Tank followed her lead. "I'm going to fuck you good, baby, and make you come."

The lame man slid forward in his seat. "That's hot."

Star pushed her roommate roughly back onto the bed. "I'm gonna climb aboard and *ride* that big dick." And she did. The two moaned as her body undulated. Tank cupped her breast and pinched her nipples as they continued their sexual talk.

"You like what you see, baby?" she asked the lame man, as

she flipped her mane over her shoulder.

"Yeah, but I have a favor to ask." He pulled out another wad of money. It looked like another thousand dollars. "Would you handcuff him to the bed? I like when a woman takes control. It turns me on."

Star stopped her movements and looked down at Tank.

"Fuck yeah, baby!" he said to her. "Handcuff me to the bed and take advantage of me."

The man moved tentatively toward the bed to hand Star a set of handcuffs. He held up the key and laid it on the vanity beside him. Star fastened a cuff around her roommate's right wrist and then reached through the slats in the headboard to fasten the left one. Next, she slapped him lightly and playfully across the cheek before kissing him hard. Both chuckled at the game. They knew this was better than any porno the lame man could rent. Her hips moved more quickly. Tank arched his back and moaned loudly as he tugged at the cuffs. Star was in complete control.

"I love your big dick inside me, honey. Don't come yet. I'm gonna ride you till my pussy explodes. I'm going to come, baby. I'm going to come while I ride you."

"Yeah, baby, do it!" Tank gasped.

While cupping his balls in her hand, Star bounced vigorously on Tank's shaft. Arching her back and pushing her breasts into the air, she was lost in ecstasy and thought only of her G-spot and the building pressure. Neither stripper paid attention to the lame man who'd hired them to fuck. Neither noticed the stranger reach into his pocket and take out a weapon.

Star moaned loudly and her skin flushed bright red in spots. All she could mutter was, "I'm coming." She continued to shudder for several more seconds as Tank growled,

"I can't h-hold it any longer! I'm c-coming!"

Both strippers were spent as Star fell on the bed beside Tank. Before either could say anything, the lame man reached out and zapped Tank with a stun gun. The large man convulsed on the bed as his lover jumped to her feet. Before she could scream, the man charged at her and struck her hard across the face with his fist. He held her tightly and stuffed her underwear, which he had surreptitiously picked up from the floor, into her mouth and threw her roughly onto the bed. The frightened woman flailed violently to get free, but the man struck her again hard, almost knocking her unconscious. As Tank mumbled incoherently, the stranger stuffed a thong into his mouth and then zapped him a second time. Then lame man stood there, eyeing his prey.

"Hello, my lovers. I'm Fenrir the Wolf."

~~~~~~~~

Trevor reclined on the chaise with a pile of books on the floor beside him. Rather than working on homework, he was instead creating a list of mythological adulterers for Black. At first, Trevor thought that it would be an easy task, but it proved to be more challenging than he expected, because it was tough to decide which gods were actually considered *married*. Couples like Isis and Osiris were definitely committed. Hera and Zeus were the most famous couple of Greek mythology, but most of the other gods were not committed to one consort. Apollo, for example, had many lovers, both male and female, but no wife; so, by strict definition of the word, he couldn't really be an adulterer.

The list soon grew to include nearly every Greek god, with the exception of the virgin goddesses Artemis and Athena. Hera apparently never had an affair either, so she was off the list. Trevor decided to add Helen, though she wasn't a goddess, because she was the daughter of Zeus and had an affair that launched a war. Similarly, he added the demigod Heracles, who once slept with 50 sisters in one night.

After exhausting the Greek myths, he considered other religions. The Egyptians were big on fidelity, and very few of their myths involved extramarital affairs. He could find only one: Nephthys, who was barren when she lay with her husband/brother Seth, disguised herself as their sister Isis, and seduced their brother Osiris to bear Anubis, the god of embalming.

Next, Trevor moved to the Norse pantheon. Most of those gods were known to have spouses. Certainly, Odin and Frigg were husband and wife. Thor, Loki, and Frey all had wives. Freya, the fertility goddess, was known to have multiple lovers. If Fenrir felt an affinity for Norse mythology, his "slut" may be Freya—but could she be considered an adulterer? Trevor wondered what props the

Wolf would use for the murder of Freya.

The last name he jotted on his tablet was Ishtar, the goddess of love in Mesopotamian mythology. The *Epic of Gilgamesh* provided a list of Ishtar's dalliances. According to the rants of King Gilgamesh, Ishtar's lovers suffered a variety of fates, from being turned into a wolf to death.

Suddenly the phone rang, distracting Trevor from his list.

"Trevor, it's Marc. How're you?"

"Great," Trevor answered. "I've been thinking about you."

"Yeah. Me, too. I had a great time."

Trevor smiled. "Maybe next time you won't have to leave the minute you wake up."

"So you're up for another date?"

"Sure," Trevor answered excitedly. The two made plans for a third date. After hanging up, Trevor closed his eyes to dream of Marc's hot body, and the phone unexpectedly rang again. This time, it was Black.

"Is this a bad time?" the detective asked.

"No."

"I'm parked outside. Would you mind if I came in?"

Trevor bolted upright as if Black had said, "The call is coming from inside the house." He gathered himself quickly. "Of course not."

As soon as he hung up, he jumped to his feet and looked around to see if everything was neat and presentable.

"Sorry to just drop by," Black apologized as he entered the apartment. Trevor hadn't realized it was snowing again. The temperatures were ridiculously low, typical of February in Ohio. Black kicked off his boots to avoid leaving wet footprints.

"No problem. Can I get you anything?" Trevor's anxiety was causing him to breathe irregularly. It didn't help that the detective looked so damn good dressed in all black and a skullcap.

Black moved toward the couch, saying, "No, I'm fine. I know I haven't given you much time, but I wondered if you had any ideas yet."

"I was just working on the list." Trevor held up paper as proof. He stacked the books from the floor into a pile and plopped down. "If the Wolf really likes the Norse theme, then he might choose the fertility goddess Freya. She was known to do things like sleep with elves in exchange for a necklace, but she wasn't really married, so I don't know if she'd be considered an adulterer."

"What does she look like? Any distinguishing characteristics, like one eye?"

"She was the most beautiful Norse goddess. Since she was leader of Odin's Valkyries and chose part of the dead to dwell in her hall, Freya was sometimes portrayed as wearing battle gear—a shield, helmet, and corselet—and holding a spear." Trevor pointed to an open book on the occasional table. Black studied it inquisitively. "Since she was Scandinavian, we can surmise she had long, blonde hair. The necklace was important because she believed it made her more beautiful. Also, she had a coat of falcon feathers that allowed her to fly."

"Great. Falcon feathers again." The detective laid the book down and removed his coat, but not the skullcap.

"'Freya' means 'lady,' and she rode in a carriage drawn by eight cats."

"Cats?"

"Yeah. Many of the Norse gods had carriages led by animals. Her twin brother, Frey, had a chariot drawn by a golden boar."

"The killer brought seven scorpions to the last victim's house. Guess he could bring eight cats to the next one."

"Ooh." Trevor twisted his face in disgust.

"Tell me about it." Black opened his notepad and made some scribbles.

"Of course, there were other gods and goddesses who cheated." He handed over the piece of paper.

"Quite a list. So you're leaning toward the Norse goddess?"

The mythology buff self-consciously ran his hands through his dirty blond hair. "Freya? I don't know."

"So we should look for a victim with long, blonde hair."

"In a carriage drawn by cats," Trevor deadpanned.

"Maybe he would choose a woman who works at a pet store or animal shelter. That would give her a connection with cats. If we could find a woman with blonde hair and a fancy necklace who works with cats, we may be able to catch our guy."

Trevor gave him a skeptical glance before asking, "And what if it *isn't* Freya he's after?"

"We've got to go out on a limb here, because this guy isn't

going to stop."

Black felt like they were onto something, so he called Sheffield to share the Freya theory. Clearly, Sheffield, too, was skeptical, but when Black hung up his cell, he was smiling.

"What does she think?" Trevor asked.

Black shrugged. "I owe you a lobster dinner."

"No, you don't." Suddenly, Trevor felt a *vibe*, something he couldn't explain. It was sending an electric charge to his brain. "You'd better be careful, Detective, or I might get used to your company."

Black gave him a wry smile.

Nervous, Trevor decided to make a joke.

"Then I'd start stalking you, and you'd have to arrest me. Trust me, it could get ugly."

Black chuckled and said, "I'm not worried."

"Unless I can make things work with Officer Perez's brother-in-law." The detective arched a brow. "Or things work out with this guy I'm seeing."

"So you met somebody?" Black closed his notepad.

"Third date on Tuesday."

"Congratulations." Black stuffed the notepad, along with the list of mythological names, in his pocket. "Thanks for the list."

"You know that most of the days of the week are named after Norse gods," Trevor began rambling, trying to keep Black from leaving. "Tuesday is named after Tyr, the god of war. Wednesday is named after Odin, whom the Germanic tribes called 'Wodin.' Thursday is 'Thor's day.' Friday is 'Frigg's day.'"

"Did you say that Wednesday is named after Odin?"

"Yeah." Then it clicked. "Lawrence was killed on a Wednesday and posed like Odin."

"Exactly. Maybe it's a coincidence, but with *our* guy, I don't think anything is by accident."

Trevor sat forward excitedly. "And Isis is the Egyptian Frigg. He killed the second victim on a Friday, which is named after Frigg."

"No days named after Freya?"

"In some places it says that Friday is named after Freya and not Frigg."

"So we may have until Friday to find our victim?"

Black walked toward the door, and Trevor followed. The ache he felt was unlike anything he'd experienced before. It was uncharacteristic of Trevor to fall for a straight guy, but that was exactly what was happening. He spoke without forethought.

"Dylan, I need to say something to you."

The detective pulled on his coat. "Sure. What is it?"

"This is tough for me to say, and I feel badly."

Black slipped on his boots, stood, and looked Trevor in the eyes. The two men were face-to-face and inches apart.

"It's just that…you're a nice guy, and I…" Trevor was unable to successfully articulate the words. But even without the words being spoken, both men understood exactly what was being communicated.

"It's okay," Black reassured him.

"I'm sorry about this, but I thought you should know." The young man looked into the detective's blue eyes. Black patted Trevor's shoulder, and Trevor pushed his hands into his pockets. "Maybe I shouldn't have said anything."

"You really *didn't* say anything," Black responded.

"But you know what I'm trying to say?"

"Trevor, you're a nice guy. What you feel doesn't bother me. It's not the first time."

Intrigued by Black's admission, Trevor's green eyes narrowed. The air inside was still, and there were no sounds. A winter wind whipped furiously outside the window. Trevor was certain that Black could hear his heart beating. Both men were confused; neither knew how to end this well. Trevor smiled feebly and rocked back on his feet.

"Sorry," the young man muttered.

"Ah, fuck it," Black said, and he grabbed Trevor by the shoulders.

With a final shake of his head, Black kissed Trevor on the lips. At first, the kiss was awkward, but it soon grew passionate and tender. It was the best kiss of Trevor's young life, and there was no telling which man was more shocked by it.

Chapter 18

After the kiss, Black held Trevor by the shoulders as if the young man might lunge at him. Panicked, the detective uttered a groan of regret and shook his head.

"I don't know why I did that," he confessed. "I have to go." Without even zipping his coat, Black fled into the night.

Trying to figure out what had just happened, Trevor stood frozen in place, staring at the door. Suddenly, he squealed, "Yes!"

Black felt his Lexus fishtail as he left the scene of the indiscretion. His heart continued to race; his mind wouldn't let him forget; even in the cold, he felt his palms sweating. For the first time in a long time, Dylan Black felt like punching something. Of course, he reminded himself, it wasn't like there hadn't been other men. Most of his gay encounters had been brief affairs involving no discussion before or after. In most instances, Black had blamed alcohol for his lowered inhibitions, and yet not one of these liaisons had occurred when he was actually inebriated.

His first tryst was with a fellow football player his senior year of high school; the second was his sophomore year at Ohio University with his roommate's friend. His last affair with man didn't take place until the first year of his marriage to Jennifer. It started when a glass of ice water tumbled into his lap while he sat studying for the detective exam in a café. A hapless customer had bumped into a waitress, thereby causing the unfortunate accident. As the man apologized profusely, Black detected a speech impediment and realized he was deaf. Dark haired and light eyed, the man had an infectious smile and warm personality. His name was Colin.

The next time they met at the restaurant, Black invited him to sit at his table. Colin read lips extremely well, and Black learned to look directly at Colin while speaking. The two continued to meet at the café and quickly became friends. Colin divulged that he was gay, to which Black responded, "I have other gay friends." It was an innocuous lie.

Three weeks later, Colin needed help moving a couch, and Black volunteered his services. The hide-a-bed sofa weighed more than the two men bargained for, and it took all their might to carry it to the basement. Colin attempted to stuff money in Black's shirt pocket to pay him for his help, but Black refused. The two men engaged in what looked like an absurd dance. Once Colin's arms were wrapped around Black, the men froze in an awkward embrace. Colin jumped back and began to cry as his emotions overtook him. He uttered the hardest words of his life: "Dylan, we can't be friends anymore." Rather than leave, Black kissed Colin on the lips. The two men went to bed together, and Black made love to another man for the first time without the ruse of alcohol. Resting in Colin's arms, he imagined coming home to that every night.

For a month, they shared blissful moments and tender embraces. Then one day, on his way home from the café, Colin failed to hear the approach of an oncoming car, and the young driver, showing off for his buddies, failed to see Colin. The deaf man was dead when Black arrived at the hospital. He envisioned walking into the jail, drawing his SIG, and shooting the driver in the heart, destroying it like his own heart had been destroyed. Ultimately, he regained his senses; then Dylan Black grieved in secret. He couldn't tell his wife, his partner, or his parents. At Colin's funeral, Black said good-bye to his lover after everyone else was gone.

Six years later, Black had met Trevor, who was funny, bright, kind, and attractive. Black had been inexorably drawn to him the first time they'd met, after Adams's body had been discovered, but did his best to ignore the emotions. Trevor was vulnerable and fragile, and Black wanted to take him in his arms, protect him, and hide him from the evil of the world. Instead, remembering Colin, the detective suppressed his feelings. But those green eyes and full lips, that disheveled blond hair, and that athletic body sparked Black's repressed desires. Now Trevor had confessed his feelings, and Black had reciprocated with a kiss.

That night he slept fitfully--with nightmares that his secret was out.

~~~~~~~~

Between wails, TaShanda Payne screamed, "My mother's dead! Who killed my mother?"

Inside the loft, the body of LuWanda Payne rested on the cold linoleum floor next to the folded morning paper. Like an owl's, her head was turned at a precarious angle, casting her dead gaze toward her right shoulder. The killer had wrenched her neck with such violence that it had snapped. There were no signs of forced entry, and the body had been dead for approximately five hours when it was discovered by her daughter. Black and Sheffield looked down at the gray-haired woman in a floral print nightgown. Nothing in the loft seemed out of place; if not for the dead body in the foyer, the scene would be an ideal picture of hearth and home.

"We can't interview the daughter while she's like that," Sheffield said, as she wandered into LuWanda Payne's bedroom. Through the window, the downtown vista and the suspension bridge over the Independence River were visible.

"The second ambulance should be here soon to take the body to the morgue." Black opened drawers and closets.

"Not a robbery. There are things of value here in plain sight." She held up a diamond tennis bracelet as proof.

"He didn't even take the rings on her fingers," Black said.

"Maybe the perp was interrupted and fled before he got anything."

"No report of suspicious activity. Let's talk to the neighbors."

It was time for the techs to do their work, so the detectives exited the residence.

"You get that one, and I'll get this one." Black pointed to one apartment and nodded toward the other. Faust, the lone Normandy canine officer, sniffed intently around the dead woman's front door. Black watched for a minute with fascination. "He got something?"

"Looks like it." Officer Thomas, an ex-Marine who looked like he could survive alone in the woods with the German shepherd, responded. Faust followed his nose down the walk to the curb and then back toward Black. Without even a casual sniff his way, the dog passed by the homicide detective and headed toward the neighbor's door.

"That's where I was headed." Black stated. "Anyone home?" Officer Thomas shrugged as an agitated Faust growled and scratched at the door. "I'm going to knock," Black said.

Officer Thomas called Faust. The dog sat back on its haunches without taking his eyes from the door. No one answered, so Black rapped again louder. No one answered the second time. The third attempt was forceful enough to wake anyone on the premises. Faust hunkered down and growled. Black tried the door; it was unlocked.

Stepping inside, Black immediately called out, "Police! Is anyone home?"

Then recognition set in, and his bowels turned to ice. The loft was freezing cold, as if the heat had been off for days; there was the faint scent from a candle or air freshener, but the air was too cold for him to discern the fragrance. His skin bristled like he was in an electric storm. Drawing his gun from his shoulder holster, Black called out again. He checked the downstairs: nothing out of the ordinary. Heading upstairs, he braced himself. There was one bedroom on the left and a bathroom door just to the right. His back to the wall, Black eased up the stairs, and with each step, he kept his eyes trained on the open loft bedroom. Once he reached the top, he holstered his gun and called his partner on his cell phone.

"Looks like our guy just doubled his body count."

Chapter 19

Again, I have proven my dominance. This time, I ended two lives. They didn't think I'd find out about their little affair, but they were dead wrong. That lying, promiscuous bitch; that stupid toad of a man she chose to fuck. They both had to pay for thinking they could cheat with impunity.

The gods are not supposed to bleed red, but I like that it ran red when I cut them. What fools to believe that I was lame and ugly! I am Fenrir the Wolf; I am strong and beautiful, more powerful than the gods themselves who now die at my whim. While they bled, I wrote down the names of their bastard children, then the names of her lovers, then the names of his lovers. With each name, I punished them. Wrath is mine, not theirs.

I relished the fear in their eyes and their cries of pain. I liked the feel of their twitching bodies beneath me as I held them down and choked them, cut them, maimed them. I made her watch as I pummeled him, and I made him watch as I sliced her. Given the gurgling in his lungs, he lasted longer than I expected.

And that damn neighbor saw me enter the house, so she had to die, too. It was an inglorious but necessary kill.

Chapter 20

The bruised and bloodied bodies were covered in a large fishing net that looked like a giant, decaying spider web. Naked and supine on the bed, they appeared to be two lovers fallen asleep. A quick glance around the room confirmed that Fenrir had not used as many props, nor was this murder as bloody as the last. At least their heads were still intact with their bodies. On the vanity, six pewter figurines cast metal stares—only slightly less disturbing than the severed hand in Kelly Robison's bedroom.

"Who're they supposed to be?" Sheffield pulled on latex gloves.

"I don't know," her partner replied.

On the vanity mirror, written in red lipstick, were six Greek letters:

"Yep, it's Fenrir." Sheffield approached the bed.

"No drawings, like the Eye at the last scene."

"Maybe he was rushed."

"Or it wasn't part of this myth." Black looked over the railing and down into the living room below.

Lifting the net delicately to see their faces, Sheffield felt pity for the dead couple.

"Based on the letters," —she pointed—" I guess they're Greek gods. Our adulterers. Call Myth Boy. He'll have an answer."

Black walked to the bed and looked down at the victims' faces. "There was an s."

"What?" Sheffield asked.

"It was *plural* in the note. We missed that. The anagram was 'adulterers'—plural. He told us he was going to murder a couple."

"At least he didn't behead them."

"Looks like he cut off junior." He pointed to the man's genital region. Sheffield threw back the net and saw the full extent of the damage. The sadism was worse than she'd thought.

Black remembered the lifeless body of LuWanda Payne with her twisted neck. "I bet the neighbor got a gander at him. This can't be a coincidence, her murder in the apartment next to these two."

Sheffield walked to the ledge and directed an officer below to check for calls from LuWanda Payne's residence to either 911 or the police station the previous night. Black looked at the six painted pewter figurines. The largest was sitting on a throne and held a lightning bolt in one hand, another rode a horse and carried a trident, the third wore a cap and held a scepter while a three-headed dog sat at his feet, the fourth carried a staff with two snakes wrapped around it, the fifth carried both a lyre and bow and arrow, and the last held a bunch of grapes in one hand and a staff topped with a pine cone in the other hand. Black knew these were gods, though he could confidently identify none of them.

"Found the guy's member," Black announced. "On the vanity in the Mason jar. And there's a gavel next to it."

"Why the hell would he cut off his penis?"

"Part of a myth, I suppose."

Sheffield studied the bodies closely. "My god, he's bruised all over, and she looks like she's been cut with a dull, serrated knife. From the bruises on their wrists, it looks like they were bound while he tortured them. There're burn marks on his side."

Black leaned in close to see what his partner was referring to. "I've seen those marks. He used a stun gun. That explains how he subdued this big guy."

"Maybe he drugged them, too."

Both detectives jumped as an officer spoke from the stairwell. "No call to either 911 or the station from LuWanda Payne's house."

"Jesus!" Sheffield exclaimed. "Don't sneak up on me when I'm leaning over a dead body."

"Sorry, ma'am." The officer began his retreat.

"And don't call me ma'am," she insisted. "Oh, and thanks."

Black couldn't help but smirk.

"So Ms. Payne probably saw our guy, and he silenced her before she could talk. But how'd he get inside her house without any signs of forced entry?"

"Good question. And for that matter, how'd he get in *here*? Is he posing as a traveling missionary? Because so far everyone's let him in without a struggle."

"Maybe LuWanda knew him. Maybe these two knew him," Sheffield said. She opened the closet doors and flipped through the abundance of clothes. *Damn, she had good taste.*

"But there hasn't been any forced entry at any of the homes. He's a manipulator who knows how to work people."

Sheffield looked at the once-beautiful woman. "God, look at her cheek."

Black commented, "Looks like he bludgeoned them with his fists. *His* wounds look completely different from hers."

"Let's get the techs in here. Is that hair?" Sheffield pointed to a place on the bed between the fallen pair.

"I think that's wolf hair."

"He's leaving his mark again."

Sheffield couldn't tear herself away from the horrific scene. She kept wondering what this woman's life had been like—and what her death had been like.

"She was pretty. Think he raped her? Maybe made the boyfriend watch."

"It's possible. I'm sure the doc will check. She should be here soon." Black paused and glanced down the hallway to the other bedroom. "I don't think he's the boyfriend." When they entered the second bedroom, it was clear that it belonged to a man: sparsely decorated, men's cologne, men's clothing.

Sheffield looked at Black, confused. "So they weren't a couple?"

"Not really adulterers then. Unless they were cheating on their partners with each other."

"So why'd Fenrir pick them?"

Black took out his phone. "Maybe we'll know once we get some background on them."

Officer Ramsey came to the door but avoided looking at the

bodies. "We got an ID. The female's name is Felicity Roth. The male's name is Brad Bender. They both work as adult entertainers at a club in Columbus called Sexcapade."

"Strippers?" Sheffield said, incredulous.

"Maybe that's your answer." Black raised his eyebrow. "Thanks, Ramsey." He scanned the numbers in his cell for a particular one and dialed. As soon as there was an answer, Black said, "Trevor, we've had another murder."

No beating around the bush, Sheffield thought.

Black couldn't give Trevor time to bring up the kiss, so he quickly continued. "It's a couple, and they're naked in bed. He's been beaten pretty badly, and his penis has been lopped off. She's been cut repeatedly. They're under some kind of net." Pause. "Uh-huh. Yeah, there are Greek letters on the mirror." Pause. "You're sure?" Pause. "Yeah, me too. We will."

Sheffield followed the entire conversation up until the end. She knew Myth Boy had not let her down. Obviously, he'd be able to identify the scene from Black's description.

"He says they're probably Aphrodite and Ares—goddess of love, god of war."

"Damn, he's quick. You'll owe him a blowjob after this."

He shot her a perturbed look. "You're not funny."

"I think I am." She flashed a big smile and put her hands on her hips.

"The severed penis makes no sense, but the net clinched it for him."

"Well, he hasn't led us astray so far." Sheffield opened the drawer and found half-naked pictures of the dead man. "His costume was a military uniform." Sheffield held up a camo thong as proof. "How much closer could he get to killing the god of war?"

~~~~~~~~

Sitting at his new desk near Sheffield's and Black's, Officer Perez looked at the computer screen and then back at the photograph from the murder scene. He jotted down notes: *phi, epsilon, nu, rho, iota, rho.* "Surprise," he said sarcastically. "It says 'Fenrir' in Greek. The killer likes to leave his mark like a wolf peeing on a tree."

Sheffield wandered over to look at his notes.

"He knows his name in Greek," Perez said.

"He would," she responded, unimpressed.

Black arrived with a large file containing crime scene photos. They laid them out on his desk and studied the handiwork of the Wolf: the carnage and the symbols. Painted pewter figurines, Mason jar with the victim's penis, fishing net, raw and inflamed wrists and ankles, gavel, jagged cuts on Felicity Roth's body, burn marks from the stun gun, bruises on Brad Bender's body, lipstick signature in Greek letters on the vanity mirror. Suddenly, they came to an unfamiliar painting of a woman, followed by one of a man. A series of photos followed, showing unusual names written on a wall.

"I didn't know about these," Perez commented.

"Neither did we," Black uttered.

"Did they get mixed up with your crime scene photos?" Perez asked.

"Are those paintings of Ares and Aphrodite?" Black asked. "Where are they painted?"

Suddenly, Sheffield recognized the wall. "I'll be damned. It's the sliding partition wall in her bedroom. It was open when we got there, and we didn't close it."

"The killer painted their pictures and wrote all these names on the wall during the murders?" Perez asked, to no in particular.

Black lined up a dozen pictures of the retractable wall. One showed a crude drawing of a naked woman, with the same features as Felicity Roth, standing on a clamshell. They all recalled the ubiquitous painting by Sandro Botticelli, the *Birth of Venus*. In the second painting, a man who looked like a warrior wore a crested helmet and held a spear and a shield. Though they were amateurish and unfinished, their inspiration was evident. The remaining photos of the wall showed four series of Greek names. One cluster read, "Enemies: Hephaestus, Helios, Diomedes, Athena, Poseidon, Heracles." The next cluster read, "Your Bastards: Phobus, Deimos, Harmonia, Eros, Anteros." The next photo was "Her Lovers" and "His Lovers," with several names each. The black letters stood out dramatically against the beige laminate of the retractable wall. They appeared to be lists proving the infidelity, philandering, and cruelty of Aphrodite and Ares—justification for their punishment.

"We need to go back and look at this," Black said.

Sheffield began to pace behind the other two. "I agree. Why the hell would he take time to write all of those names and paint those pictures?"

"These are the sins of Ares and Aphrodite? Isn't this the reason they were punished? These names prove they're adulterers. They had lovers; they had children together."

"So they weren't married?" Perez asked.

Black tapped the photo of Venus on the half shell. "No. She was married to another god but cheated on him with Ares."

Sheffield folded a piece of gum into her mouth. "So she *is* an adulterer in the true sense of the word. And our victim, Ms. Roth—was she married?"

Perez sat in his chair and slid over to his desk. "According to her file, she was never married. Clean as a whistle. No arrests, no history of drugs, no prostitution."

"Same true for the guy?" Sheffield asked.

"Yeah," Perez responded. "The owner and manager of the bar—a Mr. Harry Whitehead—says they were model employees."

"Looks like we should talk to Dr. Radford," Black said. "He wanted us to come see him if we had a Greek-based murder. Maybe he can impress us this time."

"I doubt it." Sheffield rolled her eyes and tapped the heel of her boot on the floor like she was trying to chip off a piece of tile. "And we've got to talk to Trevor." Her partner gave a dismissive wave, and Sheffield wondered, *What the hell's his problem?*

Black grabbed his coat. "Let's go back to the loft first to check out Fenrir's artwork in person. Then, we'll hit the campus to talk to Dr. History."

Chapter 21

The sidewalks of the University of Normandy were cleared of the latest onslaught of snow and ice. Except for the overflowing parking lots, the school looked deserted on the outside. Sheffield was glad she had worn her wool slacks, cashmere sweater, and heaviest leather coat. She looked like a sexy spy—Emma Peel or La Femme Nikita. The staccato click of her heels on the pavement reverberated in the cold courtyard and announced the detectives' arrival.

"You know," Sheffield said through her scarf, "I really don't like this guy much."

Her partner picked up pace. "Yeah, I'm with you on that, but let's see what he's got to say."

"And let's make sure he has an alibi for Sunday night."

The detectives entered Bainbridge Hall and descended the stairs to the History and Classics Department. It had been three months since their last visit, shortly after Kelly Robison's dismembered, mummified, and harpooned body had been discovered. The secretary greeted them warmly by name and led them to Dr. Radford's office.

"Detectives." The professor quickly closed a window on his computer and flashed an exaggerated smile. "Did your killer finally choose a Roman god?"

Trying to hide her displeasure, Sheffield lowered her head and picked lint from the front of her sweater. *Let Black do the talking*, she thought, *because this guy pushes my buttons.*

Black responded, "Actually, yes. It was a young couple left under a net."

"Ah, that's how Vulcan trapped his wife, Venus, and his brother Mars when they were having sex." The professor drummed his finger on his cluttered desk.

"So we hear." Sheffield couldn't deign to look at the sanctimonious buffoon.

"Those are Hephaestus, Aphrodite and Mars in Greek?"

Black asked while consulting his notepad. With a look of incredulity, Radford nodded. "Can you tell us the story, Professor?" Black asked.

"Not much to it really. Classic example of revenge on a cheating spouse. Venus was married to the blacksmith god, Vulcan, but had an ongoing affair with Mars. The sun god, Helios, spotted them and reported it to Vulcan, who forged an indestructible net to ensnare them."

"They weren't killed?" Black asked.

"The other gods were called in to laugh at the captured lovers, but the Olympian gods didn't die. Sorry to disappoint you, Detective Black." *He really does sound like a haughty prick,* Sheffield thought.

"Was the god Ares…err, I mean Mars, married?"

"No, but he had several lovers and many progeny. Most of his offspring were monsters."

"Vulcan didn't harm Ares?" Black asked.

"He pierced his foot with his own sword. One that he'd forged just for Mars, no less."

As his partner stared coldly at the professor, Black flipped a page in his notepad and wondered how much to divulge to the man.

"We found the victim's penis in a jar. What do you make of that?"

The professor actually smiled—quickly, but perceptibly—and Sheffield felt a need to stand and distance herself from the man.

"There's nothing in the myths about Mars being castrated, although his great-grandfather Uranus was."

"The severed genitalia, the jar—they have no meaning?" Sheffield asked.

"Not really. Even when his great-grandfather, Uranus, was castrated, there was no jar. The genitals were cast into the sea. This had nothing to do with Mars and predated his birth."

"The painting of Venus by Botticelli—" Sheffield began, but Radford cut her off.

"According to Hesiod, Venus was born from the foam of the sea when the genitals of Uranus were thrown into it. Other sources, like Homer, claim she was a child of Zeus and Dione. It's the way of mythology, I'm afraid—differing versions."

"And Mars?" Black asked.

"He was a confirmed son of Jupiter and Juno. On that, all

sources agree."

Black felt his partner pacing behind him and could imagine her pinched expression.

"There was also a gavel at the scene. We believe the killer might have left it."

"Was either a god of justice?" Sheffield interjected.

Radford laughed sardonically, as if she mispronounced "Uranus" as "your anus." "Hardly. The statues of the blind woman holding the scales is the goddess Themis, whose name means 'justice.' According to the Greeks, Ares was a violent, warmongering god who acted like a spoiled child. Athena represented just war, but Ares represented bloodlust. The Greeks essentially feared Ares; however, the Romans loved and revered him. Of course, they called him Mars, and they claimed direct descent through his sons Romulus and Remus. Although, he did rape their mother when he impregnated her."

Sheffield's stopped in mid-step and eyed him suspiciously.

"And Venus?" Black asked.

"Everyone loved her. The Romans claimed descent from her through the Trojan hero Aeneas. It's all in Virgil's *Aeneid*. You have *heard* of it, I presume." Now he was being blatantly condescending.

"Thanks for your time, professor." Sheffield said, as she turned for a hasty retreat.

"Love and War in bed together." Radford tapped his fingers, as if emphasizing a point. "But her husband was a monster, so you can't blame Venus for adultery."

~~~~~~~~

Jennifer Phillips Black saw the news about the latest murders in Normandy and worried that her ex-husband was up against an extremely dangerous monster. There were few details about the victims or the manner of their deaths, but the TV station ran many reactions from concerned citizens who questioned whether the police were doing enough to stop this madman. Jennifer was shocked to hear that there were three victims; the killer was ramping up his kill quotient. The quote from her ex-husband was, "We're working on several leads. We ask the public to be vigilant but not to panic."

When asked directly whether they had any suspects, he declined to comment.

Jennifer had to admit that she was worried about Dylan's safety. What if Fenrir the Wolf came after him? Every time she talked with him, he expressed his frustration with the case. She also worried that Dylan was one of those lonely people who buried his pain in his work. Jennifer knew that several years before, her husband had gone to the funeral of a hard-of-hearing man whom he'd never mentioned. She knew because she'd followed him. After he had left the church, she'd slipped in and gazed at the picture of the sweet-looking man with dark hair and blue eyes. She ran her fingers over the name on the program: Colin. Without ever discussing it with anyone, most of all her husband, she knew that they'd been lovers. Jennifer Black immediately left the church, headed home, and drank herself into a stupor.

Now she wondered about this college student, Trevor. For a moment, she debated telling Black what she knew; then she thought about taking the easy route and sending an e-mail. Ultimately, she decided to do nothing at all. She'd let it go once more, but only for a little while longer. One day soon, she'd tell her ex-husband that she knew he was gay.

~~~~~~~

"Well *that's* subtle," Sheffield said, referring to the neon sign above the strip club's entrance. In a series of three light changes, the neon woman went from clothed to bare-breasted to naked, including a red heart between her legs.

"They don't open for another half an hour," her partner stated, "but the owner said most of the dancers would be here now."

Sheffield parked her Lincoln next to the building. When they stepped out, the arctic blast assailed their exposed skin, and they all but ran to the entrance. Black aggressively yanked open the large metal door, and they dived inside. Three security men looked their way, and one behemoth positioned himself like a human barrier underneath the arch leading into the club. Black pushed his badge into the man's face, and the massive bouncer flashed a smile and blithely stepped aside. When the massive man nodded toward Black and made a kissing gesture, Sheffield laughed out loud. Black turned around, but his partner simply shook her head dismissively.

"Come on," the bouncer said to Sheffield. "I'll take you to his office." He put his hand on Sheffield's shoulder. She would have paid money to see him put his hand on Black's shoulder instead.

White lights washed out the neon bulbs and exposed every nuance of the nightclub. Sheffield thought, *Not so sexy all lit up*. The stage floor glistened, the dance poles sparkled, music thumped, and she fell in step with the beat. Passing through the club, Sheffield wondered what it looked like during business hours, with half-naked women on stage and horny men carousing.

"Detectives, please come inside." A heavyset, balding man, Harry Whitehead spoke in a warm, smooth voice an octave higher than expected. He looked like Boss Hog but sounded like Truman Capote. Not believing the décor of Harry's office—mahogany wood, Tiffany lamps, and art nouveau vases—Sheffield almost whistled aloud. It looked like something in a swanky hotel in Vegas, rather than at a strip joint in Columbus.

"Mr. Whitehead, we need to know if you have seen anyone suspicious recently, maybe someone paying too much attention to Ms. Roth or Mr. Bender."

"Ma'am, there are a lot of 'suspicious characters' that come in here. I'm afraid it's the nature of the business." The manager/owner waved toward matching leather club chairs. When Sheffield slid into one, she felt like she was sitting on a throne.

"Did either"—Black struggled to find the right word—"*performer* complain about anyone harassing them?"

Harry Whitehead selected a spot directly in the middle of the love seat across from the detectives.

"Detective Black, Tank and Star were very popular. If you could have seen them on stage, you'd realize why."

Sheffield flipped her ponytail over her shoulder and then caressed the leather arm of the chair. "No problem customers who got a little handsy?"

"Most of our customers are harmless. They're just lonely men and women who need a little diversion. And if anyone gets too 'handsy,' the bouncers take care of them immediately. You saw my bouncer Sean. Gentle giant, really, but he's fiercely protective of the dancers."

"Any new customers in the past few weeks who stand out?" Black persisted.

"We have regulars, but every night, we get newbies." Whitehead fixed the sleeve on his burgundy dress shirt. "I'm back here most of the time while the club is open, so I don't see much on the floor."

"Maybe the dancers saw something," Black said.

"I've told them you were coming. They're a little shaken up." He had a hint of an accent, almost southern. Thinking of Whitehead as an oxymoron, Sheffield wondered how such a well-mannered, unassuming man came to own a strip club.

"We'll try to make this quick, Mr. Whitehead."

The owner proceeded toward the doorway, but stopped to face the detectives. "I must warn you that the women may hit on you."

"Can you handle that, Black?" Sheffield slapped his arm.

The soft-spoken man looked at her. "You, too, Detective Sheffield."

"Oh."

Black shot her a wry glance.

Barely missing a beat, she added, "Good. My ego could use a boost."

"I apologize in advance if they're inappropriate. You have to understand the psychology of adult entertainers. Many have troubled pasts, and they all like to be the center of attention. Really, they just want to be loved. They simply seek it out in nontraditional ways."

When the detectives entered the dressing room, the women continued donning costumes and applying makeup. *The show must go on*, Black thought. After Whitehead made quick introductions, the detectives asked if anyone, like a spurned customer, had had a beef with Tank and Star.

"I don't think anyone was giving them problems," a stripper said while applying body glitter. "And we were pretty close. We even dated for a while."

The detectives didn't know which stripper she was referring to.

Another jumped in. "Is this psycho coming for one of us next?"

"No, no." Before any chance of a meltdown, Sheffield waved

her hand to silence them. "He wouldn't take a chance coming back here. You're all safe."

"There've been two strange men recently," a dancer in a zebra-print dress offered. The strippers described the men: the first, African-American, scrawny, poorly dressed, with bushy hair and body odor; the second, middle-aged, white, with a mild case of Tourette's. Neither seemed to fit the bill. Fenrir was endearing and sly. He wouldn't be walking around smelling badly or blurting out obscenities. Still, they'd look into it.

Blacked ended by saying, "Mr. Whitehead has our number if you think of anything."

Miss Body Glitter stopped applying makeup. "Aren't you going to stay? I'm on first, and you'll like the show."

"Thanks for the invitation," Black stammered.

"What about you, cutie?" She stared at Sheffield like an addict eyeing blow. "My stage name is Jasmine, but my real name is Amber."

"I would love to, but I've got to catch a killer, Amber. Some other time."

"I'll hold you to it," Amber purred. Then she walked over to Sheffield and handed her two purple hair sticks with bronze suns. "You got beautiful hair. These'll look good in it."

"Uh, thanks."

Harry Whitehead met the detectives at the door. "Did you get anything from them?"

Sheffield looked down at the hair sticks in her hand. "Maybe."

He handed them a list. "I've highlighted the names and numbers of the employees who aren't here."

"None of the male dancers are here tonight?" Sheffield asked.

The owner shook his head. "The women strip six nights a week. The guys, only on Fridays and Saturdays."

"We'd like to send a sketch artist to get a drawing of some of your patrons."

"Why don't you search the surveillance tapes? I'm sure they're on there."

"You have tapes?" Sheffield's excitement was evident.

"Yes. I guess I forgot to mention that. It's a very high-tech

system. The camera is embedded in the arch when you first enter."
Harry led them through the arch and pointed up. "See? The eye of
the camera is small. It's in the face on the sun."

"Son of a bitch," Black muttered. Sheffield made eye contact
with the smiley bouncer.

"How far back do you have tapes?"

"Four weeks."

"Can we get the ones for Fridays and Saturdays?"

"Sure. I'll get them now."

As Harry Whitehead walked away, Black turned to Sheffield
and said, "It's a sun. Radford said the sun god saw Ares and
Aphrodite together. Maybe the sun also caught a Wolf in human
clothing."

~~~~~~~

They viewed the tapes in reverse chronological order,
starting with the Saturday before the murders. They searched for the
two "strange" customers, even though they were unlikely killers, but
the detectives didn't stop there. Anyone who was alone, between the
ages of 20 and 40, and physically fit was deemed a possible suspect.
They passed over anyone they believed was too old or physically
incapable of carrying out the crimes. They passed over the blind guy
(and wondered how he enjoyed the show). They skipped by the
bachelor parties and the college boys who arrived in groups—their
killer was an unsocial wolf, not one hiding among a pack. They
passed by the guy with a bad limp, the guy in a wheelchair, and the
guy missing an arm. They skipped over all the women, because Dr.
Canter had indicated a female killer would have chosen a female
monster's name rather than Fenrir the Wolf.

Their eyes grew bleary as they watched hour after hour of
man after man filing through the arch. Officer Daniels, a young,
quiet, tech-savvy cop who served as the NPD media specialist, froze
the surveillance tape on anyone pegged a "potential" and captured a
grainy image. Before long, they had over a hundred prints. There
was no way to know if Fenrir was in these photos, but they believed
that he was. Now the trick was to narrow the possibilities and catch
their killer, a task that was nothing, if not daunting. While Officer

Daniels continued the search, the homicide team phoned the remaining Sexcapade employees, including the male strippers—one of whom ironically wore a cop uniform in his act.

~~~~~~~~

Black, Sheffield, and Trevor were once again united in the police station's conference room. This time, they were joined by a fourth party: Officer Perez. Files decorated the table in an irregular pattern. One was open to a photo of the dead couple, Fenrir's latest "god killing." Sheffield briefed Trevor on the scene and summed up Radford's information.

"Still think this is Ares and Aphrodite?" Black looked into the hallway and not at Trevor.

"Yes," Trevor responded.

Sheffield studied the two curiously. Whether it was a woman's intuition or a cop's sixth sense, she detected a new dynamic between the men. *Oh hell*, she thought, *Black must have offended the student, maybe by uttering a homophobic slur*. She nodded toward the photo.

"Trevor, these are our adulterers?"

"Yes." Trevor focused on her. "And he killed them on the 'Sun's Day,' probably as a reference to the sun god Helios, who caught them having their affair." He glanced at Perez, who was leaning back in his chair with his arms folded behind his head.

Black kicked his heel against the counter for no apparent reason. "So, he's keeping with his theme, killing on the day of the week that best fits with the myth."

"The woman has unusual gashes all over her body," Sheffield said. "They're like nothing I've ever seen. Any ideas why he did it?"

"No," Trevor said, "but I remember Aphrodite was injured in the *Iliad*. During the Trojan War, a Greek soldier pierced Ares in the side. Aphrodite rushed in to save her wounded lover and was pierced in the hand. I don't know why Fenrir would cut this woman all over."

Perez sat forward. "She was stabbed in the hand, and he was stabbed in the side."

"But why all these other gashes?" Sheffield asked.

"He needed to ramp up the violence, go beyond the myths," Black posited. He edged closer to the table but stopped midway. While Trevor and Black were certain that no one else sensed the tension between them, both Sheffield and Perez picked up on it and followed Black's unusual movement with their eyes.

Sheffield turned back to Trevor. "And the man was bruised severely, as if he'd been beaten with a bowling ball."

Trevor looked down at the photo and grimaced. "I did a report on Ares in my mythology class last year. He and Athena didn't get along too well. Once, she threw a stone and knocked him down. And I know Heracles and Ares fought on a couple occasions."

"So maybe he used a stone and beat him." Black walked over to the water dispenser for a drink. "Fenrir appears to be taking on the role of their enemies. All of them."

"And they had children?" Sheffield asked.

"Ares and Aphrodite? Lots of them, but only three together: Panic, Fear, and Harmony."

The three cops looked inquisitively at each other.

"Their children's names were Panic, Fear, and Harmony?" Sheffield asked, incredulous.

"Phobus, Deimos, and Harmonia in Greek."

"They had a child named Harmony?" Sheffield cast a look of doubt as if she'd just been told that a horse and a cow could birth an elephant. "How can War and Sex create Harmony?"

Black walked to the table and fished for a photo. Trevor leaned away, staring at the floor.

Black pointed.

"What about Eros and Anteros?"

"By some accounts, Eros is one of the original gods who existed before the Olympian gods. By other accounts, Eros is the offspring of Aphrodite and Ares."

"So Eros is not a cute angel?" Officer Perez smiled warmly, showing his perfect teeth.

"That's the Roman version of Eros—Cupid. The Greeks saw Eros as a young, virile man, not a cherub."

"Anteros." The student flipped open a thick book. "According to this, Anteros represents requited love, and he was the son of Aphrodite and Ares."

"So Fenrir knows his Greek mythology, too." Black sat a cup

of water down in front of Trevor.

As if she were going to share a secret, Sheffield leaned toward Trevor. "Okay, I have to ask. What gives with the jar with the guy's penis in it?"

The informant bit his lip and searched for an answer. "Before I came over here, I was reading some stuff about Ares, and I had forgotten that he was once trapped in a jar by two giants. Eventually, Hermes rescued him."

"So maybe that explains the jar," Perez said. "I'm surprised he didn't stuff the guy's whole body in a big oil drum."

"Be glad he didn't create Ares' throne," he said. "It was supposedly covered in human skin."

"Gross," Sheffield responded. "What about the gavel? The professor didn't know."

"I'm surprised he didn't put it together. Ares was the first one tried for murder. One of Poseidon's sons raped one of Ares' daughters, so he killed him. The gods were convened for a murder trial."

"Wow," Officer Perez gushed. "That's crazy."

"How did Dr. Doom not know that?" Sheffield murmured.

"And these are the gods?" Black pulled out a photo of the painted pewter figurines lined up on the vanity.

"Yep. And Aphrodite slept with most of them. The last one shouldn't be there. It's Hades. He would have been in the Underworld."

"Any children by her husband?" Officer Perez asked.

"No. Hephaestus' only child was conceived when he tried to copulate with Athena, and his sperm fell to earth and impregnated Gaia."

"Doesn't seem like Aphrodite and Hephaestus were a happy couple," Sheffield commented.

"It was an odd match—the most beautiful goddess and the ugly, lame-footed god."

Sheffield and Black were both piqued by his words. The homicide detectives looked knowingly at each other.

"Lame-footed?"

"Yeah. When Hera gave birth to him, he was so hideous that she threw him from Olympus, and his leg was permanently injured. Homer referred to Hephaestus as the 'bandy-legged' god."

"Damn!" Black exclaimed. "We have him on tape!"

Chapter 22

In only seven months, Fenrir the Wolf had taken five victims on three separate occasions. Now, the police were finally looking at his image onscreen. The baggy layers of clothing made it impossible to accurately determine his size, but the detectives guessed he was about 5'10" and somewhere between a scrawny 150 and a beefy 200 pounds. Wiry brown and gray hair protruded from beneath a stained baseball cap, and an unkempt beard hid much of his face. The odd man wore eyeglasses and walked in an unsteady gait as he dragged his right leg. His shirt was partially untucked, his chinos were stained and torn, and his khaki fishing vest was worn through in spots.

Officer Daniels was able to print half a dozen pictures of Fenrir from the surveillance tapes. In some of the photos, he was looking up at the sun and smiling wickedly.

Sheffield was disgusted. "He's not afraid of us. This is a disguise."

"The limp is most definitely faked," Black said. "He's mimicking the lame god."

"The glasses might be real."

"They look like those cheap glasses you buy in the grocery store," Officer Perez commented.

"The hair makes him look like Grizzly Adams," Sheffield said.

"Is that a scar on his forehead?" Black asked, pointing to the picture.

"I can't tell," Sheffield said. "Maybe it's fake, too."

"And how would he know how to make a fake scar?"

"Maybe his Hardy Boys spy kit."

Black's only response was a look of admonishment.

"Makes him more like that disfigured god," Perez said

"Are we going to send the photo out, even though he's heavily disguised?" Sheffield asked.

"I think we have to." Black fished for the clearest image of the Wolf. "Someone may have seen him getting ready or leaving his house like that. Someone may have sold him that ridiculous wig and fake beard."

Perez grabbed the photo and launched into action. "Okay, I'll get it on the wire."

"Who *knows* what he looks like underneath the disguise?" Sheffield pointed her finger emphatically at her partner. "I bet he knows we have his photo, and he's laughing. This asshole thinks he can't be caught."

~~~~~~~

"Three more bodies." Petkov shook her head in dismay. "Too much, I tell you. You must stop him."

"We're doing our best, Doc," Black said.

"Let's go to autopsy room."

They suited up with latex gloves and paper face masks. The detectives weren't sure who was being protected—them or the victims. The CME stood between two tables, on one the body of Felicity Roth, on the other the body of Brad Bender.

"First, I tell you of Ms. Payne. Bruising on knees indicates she fell hard to ground. A large bruise on back of her right calf is consistent with blunt trauma. I think your killer kicked her to knock her down. Death was instantaneous when a strong torque of her neck"—she made the motion with her hands—"separated two cervical vertebrae, ruptured the disks, and tore the cartilage that fastened them together. There were no defensive wounds. She died between 6:00 and 8:00 a.m."

"Isn't that a long time after these two?" Sheffield gestured toward the two bodies.

"Yes. I estimate their deaths around midnight, about seven hours before Ms. Payne's."

Black tried to avoid looking at the cold, lifeless bodies.

"So he either stayed next door with the bodies for seven hours *then* killed Ms. Payne, or he left and came back."

Petkov clicked on the autopsy light over Brad Bender's body.

"These burn marks are caused by stun gun. These abrasions

on his wrists are caused by handcuffs, and these burns on his ankles are caused by rope. There is a stab wound on the bottom of foot, which was inflicted while he was still alive." She walked to the end of the table and touched his foot, and Black looked aghast when she made contact with the body. "It was caused by a standard chef knife. This is very tough part of body."

"Did the killer use the knife we found on the vanity?" Black asked, staying a safe distance away.

Her brunette tendrils peeking out from under her green scrub cap, Petkov moved to the side of the table and pointed to a gash in Brad Bender's side.

"Yes, and this was caused by the same knife. It pierced his right lung, causing it to slowly fill with blood. That is what killed him; he suffocated from lack of oxygen. The victim's penis was removed using same knife, postmortem."

Sheffield said, "The knife was made by the Viking knife company. Bastard must have loved that."

"And these other marks?" Black pointed to numerous abrasions with bruising.

"These are most strange. He was struck hard with a blunt, irregular object. There are 15 such wounds. Given bruising, he was alive when these blows were delivered." She moved a magnifier over one of the livid bruises on his chest and motioned toward the lens. "If you'd like to look. We found traces of dirt and small particles. These wounds are caused by a rock approximately four and a half inches in diameter. According to the lab results, it was sedimentary rock from western desert region—Nevada or Arizona or New Mexico."

"Same place as the scorpions," Black muttered.

"This son of a bitch plans multiple murders at one time," Sheffield declared.

The CME turned to the body on the opposite table. "He didn't use rock on *her*. Ms. Roth's mouth was stuffed with cotton underwear." She pointed back to Brad Bender's body. "So was his. And then taped. She was also restrained with handcuffs and rope. She recently had sex with that man."

"With the killer, too?" Black walked in a wide arc around the autopsy table.

Petkov shook her head. "Not that I can tell. See her left hand?

Pierced like his foot. Blood was transferred from him to her, indicating he was stabbed first." She pointed to the victim's face. "See knuckle marks here."

Once again, Sheffield leaned in to see. "The killer struck her with his fist?"

"Yes."

"Not the rock?" Black asked.

The CME shook her head. "And then there are strange cuts— 15 of them. She went into shock but died from strangulation." Again she turned on the magnifier light and moved it over the stripper's shoulder. Clearly, she wanted them to see what she was referring to. Not really knowing what they were expected to see, both felt obligated to peer through the lens. The skin was brightly illuminated and, under magnification, looked like foreign matter. They might as well have been looking at a satellite photo of the surface of the moon. The blood had been washed from the gash, and now it looked like an uneven fissure on a topographical map. Petkov narrowed her green eyes and shook her head.

"I couldn't figure out what caused such strange cuts. Gashes are unlike any I've seen. Not from knife, but 'what from?' I ask myself. The cuts are jagged, uneven, slightly curved. There is white residue left by the weapon. Since I was having no luck with cut pattern, I focused on the residue and then found the answer." Heightening anticipation, she turned to walk over to the stainless steel counter. She picked up a small, nacreous object and turned to face the detectives. She held up the item as she announced, "This one is from my house."

The two detectives couldn't believe their eyes. Petkov was holding a clamshell.

~~~~~~~

Millicent Deaver had not heard from her boyfriend in several weeks, and she was heartbroken. Not wanting to appear needy, she stopped herself countless times from calling him once again. So far, the lonely zoo employee had left five messages over the space of two weeks. *What if he never calls me back? What if I never see him again? What if he's dead?* Poor Millicent was nearly mad with grief.

An article in the morning newspaper reported a series of murders in southwestern Ohio committed by a man who called himself Fenrir the Wolf. A grainy, indistinct picture of a crazy-looking man with frizzy hair accompanied the piece. The article made her think of her boyfriend, because he had once asked her for wolf hair. It was an easy request to grant because the zoo had a newborn wolf pup named Cheyenne that she fed and groomed. Each day before she left work, Millicent would roll the hair from the brush and place it in a plastic sandwich bag. After a couple of weeks, she had a baggie full of Cheyenne's hair. When she gave it to her lover, he was overjoyed. He gushed about how much he cared for her; then he fucked her like she'd never been fucked, on the table in her dining room. While she was bent over the table with his cock inside her, she could feel him making love to her, but what she couldn't see was the look of menace on his face as he stared at the baggie of wolf hair; what she couldn't see were the images of murder in his head.

Then a detective from Normandy had called to talk about wolf hair. There was no way her boyfriend was responsible, so she lied to the police. Now he would know how much she loved him—if only he'd call her back.

~~~~~~~

A hundred miles away in Chicago, a young woman was going through boxes of old memorabilia. There were old programs and playbills from college plays. She had a VHS tape of her one-and-only commercial, in which she was eagerly selling toothpaste. There were photos and key chains and notes on napkins. Megan Reed even found an old wig she'd kept after a run of *Fiddler on the Roof* one summer in college. Looking like an abandoned rodent nest, it was dusty and flat from the debris pressing down on it for so many years. Before tossing it in the trash pile, she reminisced about her affair with a guy named Cain, the man who played a minor part in the production. When the play closed, she and Cain had absconded with their costumes and wigs and run off to fuck in the backseat of her grandmother's car. As quickly as he had entered her life, he vanished, leaving Megan to wonder how much she really knew about the mysterious man with black eyes.

Spotting a sketch made by an old boyfriend, she tossed the hideous wig aside and confronted the next flood of memories.

~~~~~~~

"Trevor, are you okay?" The voice repeated over the din of the Mexican music and restaurant chatter. Although Marc was a little piece of heaven on earth, Trevor couldn't help but think about the unexpected kiss with Detective Black. "I think I lost you," Marc said.

"I'm sorry, Marc. I guess I'm a little tired."

Marc arched one brow and spoke quietly out of the side of his mouth. "Maybe I can wake you up when we get back to your place."

Trevor offered an obligatory smile. While Marc was the "cool-dude-jock type," Black was the "alpha-male-action type." Both were definitely hot, but *Black* actually kissed Trevor. And what a kiss it had been! He'd barely stopped thinking of it.

"So, can we go back to your place?" Marc leaned a bit closer and whispered. "Maybe have some dessert?"

When they had first arrived at the restaurant, Trevor had slid close, and Marc had recoiled as if Trevor had attacked. Now, when the waitress asked if it would be one check or two, Marc responded facilely, "I'm paying for my bro today." It was painfully obvious that Marc didn't want people to understand the true nature of their relationship.

"Hey, Marc, I need to know something," Trevor said. "Why don't you like to kiss?"

Panicked, Marc's eyes grew wide and his color drained. "Not so loud! Kissing is very…intimate." Marc's voice was barely audible, and his lips didn't move.

"Not when you care about someone," Trevor responded, resolute.

Marc launched into some inane defense, so Trevor's mind drifted to Dylan Black and the serendipitous kiss.

"…just hanging out and having fun." Marc sounded like he was justifying his behavior.

"Marc, I want to kiss you."

"Shh. Can we talk about this later?"

The waitress approached and offered a huge smile. "Can I get you anything else?" she asked.

Marc sat back and puffed out his chest like a gorilla. "I don't think so. Do you want anything else?"

"No, I don't think so," Trevor said. He handed the waitress his debit card. "But tonight, the meal's on me, *bro*." The last word resonated with mimicry.

That night, even though Marc was a closet case who wouldn't kiss, Trevor slept with him again. And while screwing Marc, he pretended he was making love to Black.

~~~~~~~~

"I'll be damned," Black exclaimed. "The bastard used the shell of a Venus clam."

Perez rolled his chair closer as Sheffield walked up behind her partner. The three huddled around Black's desk and gazed at the lab report like it was a lost book of the Bible. Black read aloud from the report.

"The shell fragments were consistent with the *Chione cancellata* species, commonly known as the 'cross-barred Venus clam,' otherwise known as the 'dog clam.'"

"Aye! Dog clam? And he's the wolf!" Perez sat upright and whistled.

Sheffield said, "He used a Venus clam to cut up his Venus. What a sick bastard."

"So where'd he get the clamshells?" Black asked.

"Let me see if I can find out." Perez rolled his chair over to his makeshift workstation, which consisted of a computer, a desk lamp, and an "In/Out" box. While he began clicking furiously, Sheffield and Black continued to read the lab report. The net that Fenrir had thrown over the bodies was a common fishing net made of one-sixteenth-inch hemp rope in three-quarter-inch squares. The lab determined that the net had originated in Mexico before being sanitized and packaged as a craft item. Fenrir's net also showed signs of exposure to salt air.

Perez had his answer: "Anywhere from North Carolina to

Florida. Looks like there are over 400 living species of Venus clams."

"He held the clam by the hinged edge," Sheffield read. "Pulled the skin taut and drew the outer, scalloped edge of the shell across her skin. How painful. Fifteen times. That poor woman."

"Wait—how many names were written on the wall?" Black asked.

"You want me to find out?" Sheffield responded.

"Yeah. You know what I'm getting at?"

Sheffield nodded to Black. "I'm afraid I do. For each name he wrote down, the Wolf sliced her."

"Or pummeled *him*. Like each name was a grievance against them."

While Perez continued to read about clams, Sheffield bent over her desk and searched for the photos of the painted names from the retractable wall in Felicity Roth's bedroom. Black looked out the window and saw snow falling. Suddenly, he had a vision of his nemesis, the Wolf, as a werewolf-like beast standing with a rock in one hand and a clamshell in the other. The detective shuddered.

"Says here that a clam can begin life as a male and become female. Not *quite* a hermaphrodite, but…" Perez's voice trailed off. Trevor had told them that Hermaphroditus was the illicit child of Hermes and Aphrodite. "*Dios mio!* They can live more than 150 years. So it looks like Fenrir could have gone clam digging or bought them in a grocery store."

"But I'm sure he specifically wanted the Venus clams," Black insisted.

"By my count," Sheffield said, "if we add their common enemies and their illegitimate kids, then each had 15 grievances against them."

Black reached for a paperclip. "He wrote a name and then exacted revenge—a beating or a cut."

"And made the other watch." Perez slid his chair closer to the detectives.

Sheffield paced in a large circle around the desks. "Unfortunately, I can see it now. The fear in their eyes every time he walked over to the wall and wrote down a name."

The three sat silently for a minute while they considered the malice. Perez muttered a prayer in Spanish.

"The paint is the same paint found at the previous sites," Black said. "The net was most likely bought at a craft store but was exposed to salty air. The rock was picked up out west, probably from the same expedition as the scorpions. The wig is old. What about the wolf hair?"

"Appears to be a match to that from Adams's place," Sheffield answered.

"And the gavel?"

"No prints," she informed them. "We'll trace it to the manufacturer. Looks like they sell to colleges and schools for mock trials."

"Or for a play," Perez threw out.

"And the figurines?" Sheffield asked.

"Pewter. Painted," Black said cryptically. "Made by a company called 'Treasures from the Past.' They only come in a set of 12 Olympian gods."

"Looks like our guy left the goddesses behind," Sheffield noted.

"Consistent with the myth," Black reminded her.

"So we trace everything and hope for a lead," Sheffield said.

"I'll take the figurines," Perez volunteered. "I don't want the gavel."

Black tossed the paperclip into the holder. "I'll handle the gavel."

Perez and Sheffield headed to their respective desks. Black watched the snow falling heavily outside. The wind suddenly whipped the snow around as if foreboding doom before dying.

~~~~~~~

Six months prior, in a mall in Evansville, Indiana, a group of boys, months away from entering the seventh grade, were loitering in the food court. They were rebellious but generally harmless. On the verge of manhood, they could go either way: end up in college or a detention center, grow up to have a job or a rap sheet. So far, their worst crime had been to light some firecrackers in an old lady's back yard.

When the stranger with the scraggly beard and bushy hair

hobbled over their way, they laughed at him and expected him to pass on by. Instead, he drew out a wad of cash and fixed their gaze with his deep-set, black eyes. After explaining his offer, they responded with a unanimous "Hell, yes!" Once the plan was hatched, they headed directly to the specialty store called the Pirate Shop. When they returned to the stranger in the food court, each received twenty dollars for his artful behavior, and the man with the bum leg hobbled away with six painted-pewter figurines that no one could connect to him.

~~~~~~

The picture of the bearded man with glasses ran on the local TV stations and in the *Normandy Times*. Citizens were asked to come forward if they recognized the killer. The NPD received calls but nothing legitimate or helpful. One caller said the killer was her husband; one man claimed he was the ghost who haunted his turn-of-the-century house; another caller turned in her boss. Four more reports were from mental patients. One man said the photo was his alter ego, and the detectives scrambled to determine if it was indeed Fenrir calling to toy with them. It turned out to be a false alarm from a man who called back to say that he thought he was Dracula. No one seemed to have any genuine leads or to recognize the man in the photo, but everyone was looking for him in crowds, among their neighbors, or in the car next to them at a stoplight. The detectives were intensely disappointed that the picture had led nowhere.

The killer, on the other hand, carefully clipped his photo from the newspaper and taped the local-news broadcast about his hideous deeds. He especially loved the inane, dimwitted responses from the people on the street. The interviews made him laugh hysterically. Their panic was so delectable that it gave him a woody. He wanted to run right out and take another life to further rankle the trembling masses. He loved the paranoia sweeping through Normandy.

It was time now to write another letter to Aggie. He had already written several. What to say *this* time? Without having chosen his next victim—neither the god nor the mortal—it would be impossible to leave a clue. He wanted Aggie to know that he was thinking of her. The urge to kill again hit him like an uncontrollable seizure, and he trembled. There was only one thing to do: Fenrir walked into the bedroom, opened the closet doors wide, and gazed upon his arsenal. Each item gave him a pleasant, almost sexual rush. The scalpels, the bear-paw trap, the bag of wolf hair from the stupid cunt Millicent (he made a mental note to call her), the stun gun, the snake fangs, the hacksaw, the ammonia, the handcuffs. Beneath the shrine were the books his father had made him read: *Greek Myths* by Robert Graves; both of Homer's works; Herodotus's *The Histories*; Hesiod's *Works and Days*; several works by E. A. Wallis Budge; Tacitus's *Germania*; the *Elder Edda* and the *Prose Edda*; *The Epic of Gilgamesh*; Virgil's *Aeneid*; Ovid's *Metamorphoses*; Livy's *History of Rome*; and on and on. Now that father was gone, and mother and the adulterers, he needed to think about whom to take out next. There was an embarrassment of riches, really; so many deserved to die. Then an idea struck Fenrir like a whack from Thor's hammer: to really garner the attention he deserved and capture the imaginations of the masses, the next victim needed to be more prominent. Through his next attack, he would truly raise the public's fear to an unparalleled level and show his immense power.

Chapter 23

It was the conversation Black had hoped to avoid forever, but here he was, once again, on Sycamore Lane. Though it had lasted mere seconds, the kiss had had an irreparable impact, opening doors he'd rather left closed. As an explanation, Black thought of attributing the kiss to a misdirected act of kindness or a stupid mistake. He thought of claiming he had taken some medicine that made him disoriented. He considered a dozen other options, but ultimately, he decided it might be best to say nothing and let Trevor do all the talking. Surely, Trevor would see through any excuse that he made up, anyway.

Still, the kiss had been glorious. He dreamed of it at night and thought of it throughout the day. In bed, he pressed his body into the pillow and imagined Trevor lying next to him—peaceful, innocent, precious. Why did these feelings cause him such duress? Would his parents stop loving him? Would Sheffield request a new partner? Would Jenny hate him? Would the world look at him differently? Maybe none of these things would happen. On the short drive to his destination, he had vacillated from utter denial to complete acceptance and every variation in between, and as he put the car into park, he still had no idea what he would say. But it was time to face the future—wrestle with destiny.

~~~~~~~

In 1989, at a small college in upstate New York, the Pre-Law Society had regular meetings on Tuesday nights. Once a month while school was in session, they staged a mock trial, and faculty advisors served as judges and adjudicators. The leading counsel roles were highly sought positions, and students competed aggressively for them.

Martin Tillman was the president of the Pre-Law Society. He maintained a 3.9 GPA with a major in Political Science and a minor in Philosophy, volunteered for a children's literacy program, and served as a student representative on the university's General Education Review Committee. His faculty advisor, Dr. Straight, said Martin was the best student he had taught in twenty years. While Martin lived the perfect life on the outside, on the inside he harbored a secret that he feared would alienate him from the rest of the world. No one suspected or could even hope to guess the nature of his hidden identity, because Martin was proficient at compartmentalizing his life.

Then one day, a stranger who called himself Cain walked into a meeting and flashed a smile, and something inside Martin stirred irrepressibly. The young Cain stayed after the meeting to help clean up, walked Martin to his dormitory room, and talked to him for hours. That week, the two men spent time together every day. Martin was falling in love, and he thought Cain was none the wiser. What he didn't realize was the almost preternatural ability Cain had to read people, to ferret out their weaknesses, and to exploit them. One day, Cain convinced Martin to meet him in the office. Cain locked the door behind them and moved close to Martin, so close that the Pre-law Society president could smell the spearmint gum in his mouth. Cain grabbed Martin and pulled him close, and Martin swooned despite himself. The two men kissed as if they meant to devour each other. Papers, books, tapes, and more slid from the desk like flotsam washed away by a violent wave. Cain pushed Martin down on the desk and ripped the buttons from his shirt with one energetic tug. Knowing it was wrong, but feeling like a dam had burst, Martin gave himself over to his lust, and he reached for Cain's crotch. Suddenly, the man with the white smile and the black eyes flew into a paroxysm, yelling, "You dirty faggot! I knew it! I'm going to tell everyone your shameful secret, you fucking pervert!" As Cain's voice grew louder and he spat off the kisses, fear unlike any Martin had ever felt overtook him. He apologized profusely and begged the man to stay quiet, but Cain ran from the office threatening to ruin his life.

After the man with the black eyes had fled the room, Martin calmly stacked papers, organized books, and returned everything to its proper place. In his numbness, he failed to even notice the missing gavel, a gift from a retired judge, that was now lost to the Pre-Law Society forever. Martin locked the cabinet, turned off the lights, exited the room, and returned to his dorm room, where he immediately hung himself.

~~~~~~~

The soft knock was uncharacteristic of the confident detective. It was as if he didn't want to be heard, but mere seconds after he rapped on the door, the tenant opened it to find him standing there, raw and exposed. He emphatically motioned the detective inside.

"I just got home," Trevor said. "I smell like fajitas, and I'm covered in grease. You have to wait a few minutes, because I can't have this conversation until I've showered."

The directive left no room for discussion. The younger man retreated quickly down the hallway, discarding his shoes and shirt on the way. Shortly after entering the bedroom, he reappeared in the hallway for a brief flash on his way to the bathroom. The older man stood still in his spot as if bound by some invisible force. Water echoed in the tub, the faucet emitted a metallic click, and then the rain-like sound of the shower drifted toward the living room. Dylan Black finally moved. Nervous, he shuffled over to the couch, yet his eyes peered expectantly down the hall. No amount of emotional defenses could suppress, project, supplant, or divert his mind from his sexual desire for the man in the shower, a man who was seven years his junior.

Black took in details of the room: a stone stele of three dancing women hanging on one wall, and on another, a framed print of Waterhouse's *Circe*. Two imitation Cycladic statues stood next to two bronze Spartan statues on the glass table beside the door. The replica mask of Agamemnon adorned the end table.

After only minutes, the shower stopped, and panic rose in Black's chest. He stared anxiously down the hall like Beowulf waiting for Grendel's mother to emerge from her cave.

Another minute passed with barely a sound. Black stood and then sat; then, he stood again. For no reason at all, he walked to the bar and leaned against it, as if posing for an advertisement. He felt like he'd lost control, and he hated that more than anything else.

Trevor's figure stepped from the bathroom into the hallway.

There was a glimpse of naked torso, and the bathroom light illuminated the college student like an angel. The detective took a deep breath to steel his constitution.

"Much better," the younger man said as he walked into the living room. "Thanks for waiting." Trevor wore flannel lounge pants and a ripped t-shirt, but his toes were invitingly bare. His dirty-blond hair was damp and disheveled. Black-rimmed glasses made him look intellectual. *This conversation would be much easier if Trevor didn't look so adorable*, Black thought.

Trevor blurted out, "Dylan, are you gay?"

Staring into those green eyes, the detective weighed the words without saying anything.

"If you're not, then why'd you kiss me?" Trevor asked.

"Trevor, I'm sorry I kissed you."

"*I'm* not."

"I didn't mean to confuse you."

"Confuse *me* or confuse *you*? Because I'm pretty sure I'm gay, and that kiss meant something to me. It meant there was hope. What did it mean to you?"

"Look, I don't know what to say." Deep in thought, the detective broke eye contact and hung his head.

"Just tell me the truth. It can't be that bad." His voice was soothing and melodious, not confrontational. "Have you ever had feelings for another man?"

"Yes."

"Romantic feelings?"

"Yes."

"Sexual feelings?"

"Yes."

"Have you ever acted on those feelings?"

"A few times."

"So you're gay?"

"Most of my relationships have been with women, but I've had a few encounters with men."

"So you're bi?"

"Maybe."

"Let's forget about labels." Trevor took a deep breath to regroup. "Dylan, if you found the right guy—whatever that means— would you have a relationship with him like you would with a woman?"

"Yes."

"And when we kissed, did it mean something to you?"

Time to face the truth. Black glanced up at the picture of Circe and waited for her to speak to him. After a moment of silence, he looked directly into Trevor's eyes and nodded.

"Thank you for your honesty," Trevor said. "The first time I saw you, I was in shock over finding Lawrence. I kept expecting to wake up from this nightmare. It was the worst night of my life, but then you came into my apartment. I remember you so clearly. You were all business, and I was high on the drugs the paramedic gave me. I never thought I'd see you after that night. Then you called four months later, and I was so excited to hear from you." Having expected an argument, Black felt a surge of relief as Trevor spoke.

The phone rang, interrupting them. Trevor held up a "wait a minute" finger and answered.

"Marc, hi." Pause. "Hey listen, can I call you back? I'm in the middle of something." Pause. "Yeah, okay." He snapped the phone shut and said to Black, "Sorry. So are we okay?"

"Sure."

"Can we be friends?"

Black nodded.

Trevor walked over to the detective and embraced him. Black felt Trevor's skin against his and smelled the citrus scent of his damp hair. There was a hint of vanilla, and Black wanted to lick his neck to see if he could taste it. Unable to stop himself, he slid his hand down Trevor's back. *That's it*, he thought, *I'm going to throw him down on this couch, strip off his clothes and ravish him.*

Then Trevor said, "Maybe I'll get over you if things work out with Marc."

Black froze. "You're dating someone?"

"Yeah."

The two let go their embrace.

"I've got to go," the detective said abruptly. Black patted his shoulder, as a friend might, and then quickly made his exit.

~~~~~~

The frustrated detective walked toward his Lexus without a glance back, but the memories of those precious moments were emblazoned in his mind. The smell of vanilla, the warmth of Trevor's bright eyes, and the feel of the young man's naked skin all haunted Black. But destiny had intervened. Trevor had another love interest, so Black had to let him go. He tried to convince himself that it was all for the better; now, he wouldn't have to carry on a secret affair or come out. But it would have been nice to finally hold someone again, to have sex again, to feel alive again. His only regret was not licking Trevor's vanilla-scented neck while he had the chance.

Chapter 24

Over the next three months, the investigation into the Myth Murders led to several dead ends. The gavel was traced to a retired judge who had died the previous year. His wife believed he had donated the gavel to a school, but she couldn't be certain. The wig was made from artificial fibers, and the manufacturing date was narrowed to sometime between 1979 and 1983, which was no help at all. The net, with residue from the salty Atlantic air, was a mystery as well. Meanwhile, the number on the pewter figurines led directly to a store called the Pirate Shop in a mall in Evansville, Indiana; however, the store could provide no information on sales of the pewter sets to specific customers. Though bombarded with calls, the tip line again proved fruitless. The widely circulated photo of the bandy-legged mystery man who had patronized the Columbus strip club Sexcapade generated lots of false accusations and crazy ramblings, but no viable suspects. New notes had been scrawled, additional interviews had been conducted, the wall of information had blossomed, and still the NPD had nothing solid. Lawrence Adams, Kelly Robison, Felicity Roth, Brad Bender, LuWanda Payne and the gods Odin, Isis, Aphrodite, and Ares were all represented on the murder board. Chief Titus McNally cussed and fussed about the unsolved crimes, though he knew his team was doing its best with limited resources. Other murders took the detectives away, but they kept coming back to the Wolf.

Having reached a détente concerning the kiss, Black and Trevor kept in regular contact, because neither wanted to let go of the other. Their mutual attraction never came up in the conversation. In fact, usually the two talked about nothing of much importance at all. The detective often called under the ruse of providing Trevor with an update on the case when most times there was virtually nothing new to tell. Both men were surprised by how easily their friendship developed. Trevor began to think of the detective as a confidant and friend (albeit a gorgeous, blue-eyed, dreamy one), and

Black considered Trevor a welcome distraction (much like Colin, nearly seven years prior). Late at night, when their words would fall to whispers over the phone, each would secretly hug a pillow as if it were the man on the other end of the line. The only verboten topic seemed to be their feelings for the other.

Sheffield accidentally caught her partner talking with Myth Boy on a couple of occasions when Black thought no one was around. She wanted to express her surprise but didn't want to piss him off, so she let it go. *Why am I making a big deal out of this,* she wondered. *Because of cognitive dissonance,* came her own answer. *This just isn't the behavior I expect from the partner I think I know pretty well. It's an unlikely friendship—one gay and friendly, the other straight and gruff.* On the bright side, it appeared Black wasn't the homophobe she thought.

Aggie Rhodes received two letters from Fenrir between February and May. The reporter searched each correspondence for codes—reading the text backwards, looking for anagrams, searching for any play on words. Meanwhile, just to be safe, she drove her kids to school, carried her Mace as she walked to her car, and set the security alarm as soon as she arrived home.

Fenrir, on the other hand, continued to plot. The next victim was chosen. He stalked very carefully to learn the habits of his prey: the comings and goings at the house, the favorite restaurant, the place of worship, trash night, bedtime, the route to and from work, location of preferred ATM, and more. The killer had an in, a way to enter the house. He knew the god he'd punish. This time, Black and Sheffield would truly be amazed. They were doing all the right things, but he was too talented to get caught. It really was like a game of cat and mouse—or, more accurately, Wolf and mouse.

~~~~~~

The red Mustang turned onto a residential street and raced down the road at twice the legal speed. Unbeknownst to the driver, he was being tailed by a homicide detective.

Marc deftly maneuvered the muscle car into a parking spot and honked. A woman emerged from the house and rushed to the car. Dressed in gray cotton slacks and a pink sweater, her bone-straight, bottle-blonde hair dancing in the breeze, she shuffled through the yard as if running toward her long-lost lover. Her heel caught a tree root, and she almost fell. Black couldn't help but laugh. The moment called for Linkin Park, so he popped the CD in and turned it low.

Black phoned Trevor to ask about the blonde bimbo. "Are you busy?"

"Just getting ready to go to work at the restaurant."

"Have you talked to Marc today?"

"Actually, about an hour ago."

The couple in the Mustang kissed romantically. *The guy is playing both sides of the fence.*

"So are you guys getting along okay?"

"Yeah. He's coming over tonight after I get off work."

"So, he makes you happy?"

"Yeah. Other than the fact that he won't kiss, but I won't go into that."

"You're going to keep seeing him?"

"Um…yeah. I mean I will as long as he still treats me right and makes me happy."

Black realized there was no way he could interfere in Trevor's love life. "I'll talk to you later," he said.

"Okay." Trevor started to hang up and then stopped. "Did you need something?"

"Nope. Just called to say hi."

"It was good to hear from you, Dylan."

And that was the end of that.

~~~~~~~

Time for another note to Aggie. Should I toy with her again? Maybe it would be fun to give her the name of the next victim. The cow is too stupid to figure it out. This is the role I was born to play— judge, executioner, dispenser of fury. Father has been speared, mother was beheaded, the cheating lovers were strangled, and now I will smite the warrior. I can hear his whisper now, smell the urine he releases from his frightened bladder, see his fearful eyes, and taste the copper of his blood.

Yes, I must write to the cow-bitch reporter. It's too good to resist. Now how will I conceal a clue? It can't be an anagram like before. I've got it. The lines will be irregular, but I can make it work. The stupid cunt will never catch on until it's too late. Here is what I'll write:

Dear Ms. Rhodes,

My reign of destruction is about to
continue. Prepare to be shocked and awed.
No one can escape my vigilant eye,
always watching, always judging. At
last, I am ready to be recognized by all as
lord of the world, judge of mortals, and
you are powerless to stop me.

Take heed, and note well, that all humans shall
yield to my dominion. Another victim's blood will run
red soon.

Yours truly,
Fenrir the Wolf

~~~~~~~~

When Vivienne Sheffield returned to her desk, she found Jennifer Black standing there in sassy, black pumps.

"I love those shoes," Sheffield said.

"Oh, thanks." Jennifer bent her leg as if modeling the shoes. She wore a charcoal pinstripe skirt and matching jacket over a melon-colored button-down blouse. Her auburn hair was straightened, and her glasses were designer.

"Not Jimmy Choo, but I still paid more than I should have; I couldn't help myself. And *you* look amazing. I'm loving those pants."

"Got them off the clearance rack. Shh." Sheffield wore tan faux-suede pants and a black crochet sweater.

"Dylan's expecting me," Jennifer told her.

Sheffield leaned back against her desk. "He should be back

any minute. Just went to get a file."

"How're things going with this case?"

"You mean *the* case?"

Jennifer nodded.

"Not good."

"And how's our boy?"

"Okay. Been working hard on it."

"I remember those days."

Sheffield looked a bit uncomfortable, as if Jennifer had shared a secret. She glanced toward the doorway in search of her partner.

"This job can be tough on a relationship," she said.

"Are you seeing someone?"

"Yeah. His name is Viktor," Sheffield replied.

"Good."

Jennifer realized that she and Sheffield were tied together by their love for her ex-husband. She wondered whether she was luckier for having had Dylan's love at one time. Was there a possibility that Sheffield suspected Dylan was gay?

"Viv, is this guy Trevor still friends with Dylan?"

"Yeah, I think so. I know they talk occasionally. You know I call him Myth Boy?"

Jennifer chuckled. "That's an appropriate name, from what I hear." She weighed her next words carefully. "Hey, Viv, have you ever…" Her voice trailed off. She tried again. "Do you think Dylan might…"

"What are you trying to ask, Jennifer?" Sheffield folded her arms.

"Is Dylan happy?"

"I don't know." Sheffield's curiosity was piqued.

"Do you think he gets lonely?"

"He never brings it up." The detective wondered where this conversation was going.

"I think he needs somebody special in his life, someone to take care of him."

Sheffield shifted her weight and cocked her head. "What *aren't* you saying?"

Jennifer's throat felt like it was closing. Could she utter the words aloud, especially to one so close to Dylan? Knowing she should say no more, she just shook her head in resignation.

"Are you saying Dylan and I should date?" Sheffield asked, incredulous.

"What? No!" Jennifer panicked and rubbed her temples. *What had she done?*

With files in hand, Black emerged from the inner sanctum of the NPD and interrupted their conversation.

"Hope you haven't been waiting long." He kissed his ex-wife on the cheek.

"Not long."

"You two been catching up?"

They responded in unison: "Yes."

"It was nice talking with you again, Viv," Jennifer said tenuously. "I'm sorry if there was any confusion."

As she watched them walk away, Sheffield found herself wondering what Jennifer had been intimating. If not a nudge for Sheffield to hook up with Black—an affair Sheffield would eagerly welcome—then *what*?

~~~~~~~~

"This is where you brought me for our first date." Jennifer remembered how sexy Dylan had looked in his leather jacket and silk tie.

"I know." He remembered how sexy *she* had been in her red satin dress.

"And our first meal once I returned from rehab."

"That, too." Black opened a pack of crackers and began snacking. Jennifer tucked her hair behind her right ear and smiled at the memories.

"We've been through some tough times. You working yourself to death; me drinking myself to cirrhosis."

He chuckled. "Yeah, but we survived."

"I'm glad we stayed friends."

"Me, too, Jenny."

The lunch crowd had cleared and the restaurant was quiet. Though it was a seafood place, there was no netting like that used by Fenrir. Instead, the walls were decorated with metal art, and the music was classical. The waitress brought their drinks, and Jennifer stirred sweetener into her iced tea while she contemplated their past.

"How's the hunt for this killer? Viv says no leads yet." Black raised his brow and rolled his eyes in a "yeah that's right" expression. With intense focus, he stirred his soda to expel some of the carbonation. "This case creeps me out." She leaned forward as if Fenrir might overhear. "He's writing to the press. He's killed five people. Dylan, I'm worried about you."

"*Don't* worry." Black touched her hand. To divert her attention, he asked about her publishing job in Columbus. Once that subject was exhausted, they talked about their parents. Before long, their seared mahi salads arrived, along with a shrimp cocktail that they shared.

"So, this new guy is treating you okay?" Black asked.

Finally, the subject she'd been waiting for—the entire purpose for this rendezvous.

"Yeah. He seems like a keeper. We're taking it slowly."

"That's nice."

Jennifer sipped her tea and asked nonchalantly, "What about you? Seeing anyone?" He didn't even look up from his soda; he just shook his head. "Dylan, you need somebody in your life."

"I think I do a pretty good job of taking care of myself. I'm still horrible at laundry, but I get by." The joke was his way of dissembling. "So, what else is going on in your life?"

She wouldn't be dissuaded. "It seems like you're running from something."

"I don't think I'm running from *anything*, Jenny."

"Don't worry about everyone else. You have to be true to yourself."

He bit into another shrimp and then looked at her quizzically, as if she were the Sphinx asking her riddle.

"Your friends and family want you to be happy." Her palms were sweating as she pushed her plate aside. "Look, all I know is that I feel like I need to say this. Don't get mad at me. Face your demons. Dylan, you're stronger than you realize."

"Right now there's one demon I need to slay, and he goes by the name Fenrir."

She folded her arms and gave him a look of frustration. "I'm trying to make a point here, and it's difficult."

"Okay, I'm listening, but I don't know what you're trying to say."

"Don't be one of those people who shuts others out."

As if annoyed by their presence, Black brushed crumbs from the tablecloth as he responded, "I don't."

"Dylan, I know about Colin." There, the words were out!

Her ex-husband forgot about the crumbs and looked her in the eye. Willpower and determination rose within her to continue what she'd started.

"Well, I don't *know* about Colin; I *think* I know. And you've got to move on. You've got to take a chance again. That's the only way you're going to find happiness."

The detective felt betrayed and exposed. *How did Jenny find out about Colin, and how long had she known?* The emotion under the raging panic felt akin to relief.

This time, she placed her hand on his as she continued. "Hate me if you want. Tell me to mind my own business. I just have one more thing to say: go to Trevor."

~~~~~~~~

Early May in Normandy, the spring rain fell, and daily temperatures rose. Trevor and Marc had been together since their first date in February. There were rules when they were together in public: they never gazed into each other's eyes; they sat a respectable distance apart (including never sharing an armrest at the movies); and they never used terms of endearment.

One evening, after finishing a test, Trevor decided to ask Marc out for a bite to eat. Since Marc's cell phone had died, Trevor dialed his apartment number. It was the first time he'd spoken with Marc's roommate.

"Marc's not here, dude," the dismembered voice stated. "He's out with Kim."

"With Kim?" Trevor repeated.

"Yeah." The man sounded like a surfer. "She's been on his ass 'cause he hasn't been spending much time with her. Want to leave a message?"

"That's okay. His cell phone's still not working?"

"Told me the battery won't keep a charge."

Trevor tried to be dispassionate. "Do you know where they went?"

"A movie, I think."

"I met Kim once at a party. She's his girlfriend, right?"

"Yeah. On and off for a couple years."

Now he knew the truth. "That's what I thought."

"And your name?" Marc's roommate asked.

"Apollo. Tell him Apollo called."

Chapter 25

On his drive home from the precinct, Chief McNally called Dolores, his loving wife of 39 years, to ask if she wanted to go out to eat. Dolores was an excellent cook, but her arthritis had been bothering her recently, and she always seemed so tired, so he wanted to do something nice for her. At a florist shop a couple blocks from the station, he picked up an arrangement of birds of paradise and a box of Godiva chocolates, two of her favorites. Dolores didn't answer the phone, but sometimes when she gardened, she forgot to take the phone with her. Titus McNally pulled his Volvo into the garage, lowered the door, and entered the house through the side door.

As soon as he walked into the kitchen, the aromatic scent of roast beef tantalized his senses, but the house seemed unusually still. He set the flowers and chocolates on the island in the kitchen and called to his wife. No answer. He dropped his jacket on the back of a chair and headed to the living room.

As if napping, Dolores rested in an ivory, faux-leather recliner, her head tilted to the side, her eyes shut. He lovingly called to wake her—still no movement. The concerned husband reached to touch his wife's face and found her skin unnaturally cool. Her head slipped gracelessly forward.

Chief McNally had no way of knowing that his doting, faithful wife Dolores had answered a knock on the door from a man claiming to be sent by him.

"Hello, ma'am." The voice had been polite and jovial. "I have a delivery for Mrs. McNally."

"That's me," Dolores had said through the screen door.

The man had looked down at the paper in his hand. "It's from a Mr. Titus McNally."

"That's my husband." She had looked past him and seen a van sitting in her driveway.

"It's a garden statue." The man had worn gray overalls with the name Teddy stitched into them. He had consulted his paper again.

"The Laughing Cherub. Where should I put it?"

"Oh! I can't wait to see it!"

"You're going to *love* it." Dolores had been too excited to see the malice behind the man's smile.

"Come around to the gate, and I'll let you into the backyard," she told him. As she had headed for the backdoor, Dolores had already been contemplating exactly where to put the garden statue— maybe under the great oak tree or maybe in the flower garden or maybe next to the gate close to the rhododendrons. She had wondered how big it was.

What Dolores had not known was that the delivery man in the gray overalls had not returned to the stolen van for the statue; instead, he had slipped into the house behind her, quiet as a hunting wolf. Before she had exited the patio door, one of her own knives had ripped into her back, lacerating her kidney and spleen and killing her instantly. After the assassin had carefully posed her like a sleeping rag doll, he had used the same knife to cut off some roast beef to eat. Hunkered down behind the bar, he had waited patiently for his real prey.

When Chief McNally removed his hand from his dead wife's skin, a jolt of electricity surged through his body, incapacitating him.

~~~~~~~

The Saturn pulled out of one parking spot and into another, closer to its target. Throngs of people ebbed and flowed like human waves in and out of the movie theater. A group of teenage boys drew near a red Mustang, and the spy leaned forward to observe their every move. One of the boys touched the polished hood, and the others whistled. Through the half-open window came a puerile exchange that was all too common in young men trying desperately to prove their masculinity to themselves and others. Suddenly, the spy detected his mark. Like a cheetah in the grass watching a gazelle, he hunkered low and waited calmly. The couple was holding hands. Friends do that. Then the woman put her hand around the man's waist—still not a definitive sign.

Then Marc kissed Kim, and the kiss said it all.

Trevor didn't know whether to feel shame or anger. An acidic enmity rose in him. Not usually one for histrionics, he nonetheless envisioned walking up to the lovey-dovey couple, introducing himself to the woman, and planting a kiss on her boyfriend's lips. *His* boyfriend's lips.

But not today. After all, everyone knows that revenge is a dish best served cold.

Chapter 26

The dead stare of Dolores McNally looked out across the carnage in the once-pristine living room. Like a Pollack painting, the beige carpet was splattered with red. The man on the floor was missing his right hand, which rested on the coffee table three feet away. Next to him was a metallic-gold cord with one end tied into a noose. From the edge of the coffee table hung a lone action figure, dangling like a plastic hanged man. A set of odd, ominous symbols were painted in red and black on the opposite wall next to the fireplace. The worst of the butchery was the man's throat, which looked like it'd been torn out by a lion.

The man responsible for the tragedy wiped his hands and smiled as he admired his work. An intense thrill of satisfaction made him shudder with joy. The time was early—only 9:33 p.m. He savored one last look around, and his entire body vibrated with excitement. He took a mental picture to remember every last detail. Only one thing left to do. The killer reached for the phone, dialed three numbers, and waited for a response.

"911. What's your emergency?"

No answer.

"911. What's your emergency?"

No answer. He almost laughed as he looked at the fallen warrior.

"Is anyone there? This is 911. Do you need assistance?"

Click. He hung up the phone, peeled off the latex gloves, and shoved them into his pocket. Before he exited the house, the phone rang. The killer smiled and continued on his way.

~~~~~~~~

"Dylan, I'm sorry to bother you." Trevor pulled the detective into his apartment and shut out the rest of the world. "Thanks so much for coming over. I know this isn't something you want to hear about, but I have a problem. It's Marc."

The detective knew what was coming. "You sounded upset on the phone."

His green eyes ablaze with anger, Trevor paced. "I found out that he has a girlfriend, and I'm not talking about a Grace to his Will."

"You certain?" It was a question to which he already knew the answer.

"Oh, yeah." The young man ran his hands through his blond hair as if he was going to pull it out.

"How'd you find out?"

"His cell phone's dead. Called his apartment. Roommate told me he was out with some chick named Kim. They've been dating on and off for two years."

Black walked up to Trevor and patted his shoulder. "I'm sorry."

"I'm such a fool." Trevor dived into the detective's arms. Despite himself, Black hugged the young man back. "I should have known."

"How were you supposed to know? Did he ever let on that he was living a double life?"

"No."

"So, don't beat yourself up too much; you trusted him. You're a good guy, Trevor."

"It's not like I loved the bastard, but we had fun together. It was better than being alone."

Black led him over to the couch. "Sit. You want me to get you anything?" Trevor nodded.

"I can't believe he kept this from me for the past three months. He must really be desperate to have his cake and eat it, too." The two men laughed. Trevor flopped back on the couch and looked up at the ceiling. "I'm sorry for dragging you over here." He let out a long sigh. "What am I going to do?"

"You want me to have him arrested?" Black joked, as he sat next to the young man.

"I'd pay to see that."

"He'll be sorry. You know a woman can't please him as much as a man." The detective gave him a wry smile. Trevor laughed and covered his face with his hands. "You going to be okay?" Black asked as he slapped the young man's leg.

"Eventually. Once I go through the phases: shock, anger, revenge then ice cream. Thanks for listening to me."

Without forethought, Trevor leaned over and kissed Black on the cheek. It was an intimate move, but it felt right. He sat back halfway, still hovering close to the detective. In that moment, their eyes did all the talking. Slowly, they leaned forward until their lips softly touched. Black tilted his head and gave three short kisses before deeply kissing Trevor. As the kiss grew more passionate, their hands explored—one reached for a leg, another curled around a neck. Suddenly, Black pulled back.

"Are you okay with this?" he asked.

"Are you kidding?" Trevor grabbed the detective and kissed him again. Then he added, "Just one question: you don't have a girlfriend, do you?"

Black grinned broadly, pushed the younger man back on the couch, and pressed his weight into him. Trevor's hand slid over the curve of Black's hip. Both men were lost in passion. Suddenly, Black's phone rang, and the kissing stopped abruptly, reluctantly. Trevor reached down and pulled the cell phone from the detective's belt and held it up.

"It's Sheff. Might be important," Black said.

"Answer it. Then we can go back to what we were doing."

Holding the phone in his right hand, Black shifted his weight onto his left arm and remained perched over Trevor, who reached up and playfully pinched the detective's nipples through his shirt. Sheffield was speaking loudly and seemed highly agitated, but Trevor couldn't make out her words. Suddenly, the detective's expression dramatically changed, and he bolted upright. Black snapped the phone shut and jumped up.

"It's the chief. There was a 911 call from his house, and no one on the other end of the line. I've got to go."

"Go," Trevor replied.

Chapter 27

The Lincoln skidded to a stop behind the Lexus, which was kissing the police car in front of it. Sheffield jumped out and ran to her partner's side.

"I just got here," Black told her.

They were rushing toward the front door when Officer Ramsey exited the residence.

"What happened?" Black asked, as his partner called out, "Is everything okay?" Officer Ramsey was already calling for help.

"I need an ambulance at 3636 Mayfair Court. We have two dead. It's the chief of police and his wife."

"Oh, no!" Sheffield cried.

The homicide detectives rushed into the house. The first thing they saw was the back of Dolores's head resting unnaturally against the back of the white recliner. Her open eyes stared blankly toward the ceiling, as if mesmerized by the chandelier above. Two legs, lifeless and still, protruded into their line of sight. They wanted to run away, but instead, they inched forward until the mangled body came fully into view. It looked like Chief McNally had been mauled by a bear—or a wolf. Sheffield uttered a whimper. They were too late. Fenrir the Wolf had made an emphatic statement with a bloody exclamation point.

"What did he do?" Sheffield put the back of her hand to her mouth.

"I can't believe this." Black studied the blood pattern surrounding the body and felt his throat close. "How? Dolores was a smart woman. She wouldn't let a stranger in the house."

"Maybe this man *isn't* a stranger. Maybe he's one of us." The two exchanged uncomfortable glances and chose to ignore the possibility for now.

"The Wolf thinks he's invincible and can't be caught," Black averred.

"The chief was the one who gave me my job," Sheffield

lamented.

"He promoted *me*."

"Oh, God." Sheffield felt raw and exposed, like Fenrir had touched her.

Black pointed. On the wall beside the fireplace, they saw some odd writing and a symbol:

Without question, the letters were some archaic form of writing that spelled out the name "Fenrir." The symbol beneath the name appeared to have no special meaning. It simply looked like an arrow pointing to the name above.

"Look at what that psycho did to him." Sheffield choked back tears.

Though there was plenty of commotion outside, for a brief moment inside the McNally residence, only the dark whispers of the dead stirred the air. The quiet was abruptly shattered by the arrival of three officers and two techs. One officer informed the detectives of the presence of reporters clamoring for information; another announced that Petkov was on her way; the third officer let them know that the perimeter was secured.

"It's Tuesday, right?" Black asked, out of the blue. He took out his phone, turned on the speaker, and dialed the man he had left a mere 15 minutes before. After only one ring, the young man answered.

"Trevor, who is Tuesday named after?"

"The god Tyr. He's the Norse god of war and courage."

"Was he one of the gods who died in the final battle—that 'Twilight' thing?"

"At Ragnarok. Yeah. He died from wounds inflicted by the hel-hound Garm." Sheffield and Black looked at each other.

"If I send a cruiser to pick you up, would you come to the crime scene?"

"Oh, god. Fenrir got him?" He needed no answer. "Sure. I'll wait out front."

Sheffield gave Black a questioning look and mouthed "Here?" Black nodded. "I'll send Perez if I can. If not, it'll be Donahue. Ask to see his badge." He pushed the button and ended the call.

Sheffield asked, "Are you sure it's wise to bring him here?"

"No, but we need some answers. The shit's *really* going to hit the fan now."

Sheffield saw Dolores in her peripheral vision and wished she could turn back time to save the gentle woman from the brutal attack. Perez had the night off, so Black gave Officer Donahue Trevor's address and instructions to sneak the informant in through the back of the house.

"His hand is missing," Sheffield muttered.

For the first time, Black walked closer to the body. "What?"

"His hand." She pointed. "It's on the coffee table."

"What the hell is this guy's issue with hands?"

Sheffield leaned over the chief's dead body and inspected the stump. "Looks like he ripped it off."

"Must be part of the myth."

"Maybe it's symbolic. You know, the right hand of the law or something like that."

"Trevor will know."

"Dylan?"

"Yeah."

"We've got to stop this guy. I can't stand much more of this."

Officer Ramsey stepped into the doorway. "There's a reporter named Agatha Rhodes from the *Normandy Times* who called. She says it is important that she talk to one of you immediately. I told her you were busy, but she said it was about Chief McNally." Sheffield already had her cell phone out and was dialing the number.

"Aggie, it's Vivienne Sheffield. We got your message. What's up?" After a short silence, Sheffield continued. "He's already dead."

~~~~~~~

Aggie Rhodes had heard that the police were rushing to Chief McNally's residence because of a mysterious 911 call. She instantly went back to Fenrir's last correspondence. Without reading the entire letter again, since she already knew the rant of superiority within, Aggie began collecting letters—first letter of each word, first letter of each sentence. It had to be there. Fenrir had dropped the postscript, so the code had to be embedded in the body of the letter. Aggie was on a mission. The bastard had to have hidden a message about the chief.

She approached the puzzle in reverse. She wrote out several words: chief, police, titus, mcnally. If he was the next victim, Fenrir had said as much somehow in this last correspondence. One of these words, or something similar, was hidden, and she was like a hunting dog on the trail of a rabbit. Something seemed amiss with the length of the lines. Clearly, Fenrir had used manual returns. Why would he do that instead of letting the word processor wrap the sentences? That couldn't be accidental. Why hadn't she noticed it before?

Finally, it hit her. There in front of her were the words. The cool, calculating killer had told her about his next murder, but not in an anagram like before. This time, it was written down the left-hand column, using the first letter of each line. Aggie was looking at the two words encoded in the message: "mcnally" and "tyr."

~~~~~~~

Petkov arrived at the McNally residence minutes ahead of Trevor. Soon, there were four people standing in the living room: Sheffield, Black, the CME and Trevor. After taking temperature readings, Petkov spoke.

"Death for Mrs. McNally was approximately two to two and half hours ago. For chief, it was approximately forty-five minutes to an hour."

"We found the knife used to kill Dolores." Black held up the baggie containing the weapon. "He left it sitting on the island in the kitchen. One of their own."

"He didn't use that knife on Chief McNally," Petkov contended. "To remove his hand, the killer used large, serrated knife or saw and tugged violently as he cut, as if trying to tear off his hand. And what he did to the throat is a butcher job. Such violence."

Pressed against the wall, Trevor watched the woman with the accent. He studied her precise, delicate movements in order to avoid looking at the carnage.

"I will do autopsy and tell you what I find, but this is savage. So sad." Petkov looked down at the body of the man who had been one of her strongest allies.

Black walked over to Trevor and squeezed his shoulder. He nodded at Trevor and then turned toward the heart of the crime scene. The younger man glanced down at the paper booties on his feet and walked slowly, stopping about four feet from the body of the man he now knew had been the Normandy chief of police. Trying to dissociate from the murder and focus on the mythology, Trevor slowly scanned the room. His stomach did flips, and he thought that he might throw up at any moment, but he tried to put on a brave face. On the coffee table, blood had oozed across the glass and dried in an asymmetrical puddle that looked like a grotesque lava flow. In the center of the pool of blood lay the dismembered hand of the chief. The bone and ligaments were visible, and the appendage looked like a horror movie prop or a morbid Halloween decoration. The G.I. Joe figure dangling off the side of the wrought iron coffee table puzzled him at first. In quick succession, he glanced at the symbol on the wall, the ancient letters, and the gold cord on the floor next to the chief's body. Finally, unable to avoid it any longer, he cast his eyes upon the body on the floor in front of him. The man had been a large and intimidating man in life. Fenrir had removed his shirt, but not his navy blue trousers. In the stark white light, Trevor could see bruising, indigo against the man's dark skin.

"This has to be Tyr, the Norse god of war. Unlike Ares, Tyr

was a god of courage." Black, Sheffield, and Petkov stood in random spots around the room, like chess pieces on a life-sized board. As the informant continued, the three listened intently.

"When the children of Loki and Angrboda were born, Odin was warned that the three children would wreak havoc on earth, so Hel was banished to the Land of the Dead and the serpent Jormungand was cast into the ocean, but the wolf Fenrir was allowed to roam free because he seemed harmless. Tyr took care of him, but then Fenrir grew so big and dangerous that he had to be bound. The wolf was too strong to be restrained by anything known to the gods, so the dwarves made a magical rope." Trevor pointed down at the gold cord tied in a noose. "When the gods wanted to slip the thin rope around his neck, Fenrir grew suspicious. He would only allow them to do it if one of the gods put a hand in his mouth first."

Black motioned to the hand. The young man nodded. "Tyr was the one who put his hand in the wolf's mouth?

"When he couldn't break the fetter, the wolf bit off Tyr's hand. So Tyr hung his shield on his injured arm and learned to use his sword with his other hand."

"That's why he placed the chief's gun in his left hand," Black observed. Petkov stared at Trevor as if he were telling her about the mysterious land of Atlantis. She peeled off her latex gloves and stepped closer to him.

"What about the doll?" Sheffield asked, pointing to the plastic figure dangling from the strip of cord.

"I'm not really sure about that. I'll see what I can find." Trevor paused briefly. "Before the battle of good and evil began, the hel-hound Garm howled, and the earth shook. At the battle, Garm and Tyr killed each other. I've never read specifics about the wounds, so I think he took latitude with tearing out his throat."

Petkov said, "You are a smart man."

"Thank you." He felt self-conscious and looked to Black for guidance.

Black motioned toward the wall. "That has to say Fenrir, but what's with the arrow?"

"It must be the rune symbol of Tyr. I'll check on that, too."

Sheffield looked down at the dismembered hand. "So Fenrir actually bit off this god's hand?"

"Yes."

Black walked over to Trevor but looked at Sheffield as he spoke.

"This psychopath knew from day one that he was going to kill Odin and Tyr. He took the name of the wolf that swallowed one god and bit off the hand of the other. How could he resist?"

"And who better to represent the god of war and justice than the chief of police?" Sheffield added.

"Was Tyr married?" Petkov asked.

"Not that I know of."

"So Dolores was just collateral damage—like LuWanda Payne," Sheffield pointed out.

"That's why her death was instantaneous and her body was placed off to the side, away from the real murder." Black shook his head.

"Her body was probably used to lure the chief to where the Wolf wanted him so he could pounce." Sheffield turned to look at the front door. "She let him in. He used some story that made her open the door. We'll check with the neighbors. Hopefully, they saw something."

Suddenly, someone entered through the side door and called to them. "Detectives, we found this in the garage." In his gloved hand, the officer held aloft a hacksaw with a blood-stained blade.

"That is how he cut chief's wrist and throat," Petkov said.

Chapter 28

Nikolina Petkov arrived home after midnight. The bodies she left behind had been bagged and stored on refrigerated slabs in the morgue. Tomorrow, she would autopsy both bodies to search for clues to catch the killer. Tonight, however, she crept quietly into her daughter's bedroom and gazed upon her angelic, serene face. She hoped little Petia was dreaming of butterflies and birds and puppies; maybe she was a princess in her dreams. Nikolina was glad that her daughter was so far removed from the evil that she witnessed. She pushed her job from her mind, kissed the sleeping child on the cheek, and whispered a prayer in her native tongue.

~~~~~~~~

Aggie Rhodes finished her article minutes before the deadline; it was going to be the next day's headline story:
"Chief of Police Dead: God Killer Strikes Again."
Fenrir would love it. Aggie included text from Fenrir's letter, but she didn't reveal that McNally's name was embedded in the message. She wouldn't let the killer know she found his clue; the next time, she would be ready. Having been an investigative reporter for more than eight years, Aggie had written about some heinous, inhumane acts, but these attacks were more vicious and disturbing than any she'd ever known. Before leaving the office, she sat down at her computer, checked the clock, and gave herself one half hour to wrap up. Skillfully searching the web, Aggie found several helpful sites about codes, cryptography, and hidden messages. To her surprise, many sites were about hidden messages in the Bible, which she skipped over. When she discovered that anagrams were first created by a Greek poet named Lycophon in AD 280, she thought aloud, "Fenrir must love that."
Copies of each of the Wolf's letters lay in chronological

order on her credenza; there were nine in all. Each was addressed the same and signed the same. In hindsight, the odd cadence of the first postscript gave it away as an anagram. The insult, not so subtle, in the second was the same. The uneven lines in the ninth note were a sign that something was amiss. Now, she knew to look for something that wasn't quite right.

Aggie glanced over at the picture of her kids in a silver, scalloped frame that read "World's Greatest Kids." Beside it sat a picture of her and her husband, John, in a matching frame that read "World's Greatest Parents." Then and there, the realization hit her that she *had* to outwit Fenrir.

Once she turned off her computer and packed up her carryall, she headed for the exit. As the reporter peered out into the vast, dimly lit parking lot, her bravado faded. Aggie had a sudden fear that a grotesque half-man, half-wolf would jump out and tear her limb from limb. *I won't let you get to me*, she thought, as she reached for her cell phone and Mace.

"John, it's me," she said into her phone. "No, I'm fine. I'm heading to my car now." Then she boldly threw open the door and strolled out into the night air. "Are the kids asleep?" She looked around and continued to walk briskly. "Uh-huh." A breeze rustled the trees. "Mm-hmm." An owl hooted. "I think I'm going to keep the kids home with me tomorrow." Each click of her heels on the pavement made her cringe. "No. Everything's fine. They could use the day off. Why don't you take off, too? We can make it a family day."

A trucker's horn sounded from the nearby highway. Aggie jumped, almost dropping her phone.

"You will? Good." She was halfway to her car. The urge to glance around and survey her surroundings hit her, and she picked up her pace.

"We can go to the zoo or the arboretum. We haven't been since the kids were small. Or we could drive down to visit your parents." A raccoon raiding the garbage darted for the trees, and the reporter shuffled quickly toward her sedan. "I just need to be with my family right now." She let go of the Mace and fumbled for her keys. "I love you, too." Tears pooled on her bottom lids and her voice cracked. "No. I'm fine—actually, I'm scared. Talk to me, honey, until I get into the car. I hate to be such a scaredy-cat."

Aggie clutched the phone close to her ear and focused on the sound of her husband's voice. He comforted her by telling her a story about the masterpiece their son Jake finger-painted that looked like a whale but was actually, according to Jake, a rocket. As she pushed the keys into the ignition, John continued to calm his wife, and she laughed at herself for letting anxiety get the best of her. Then she saw the cream-colored envelope on her windshield under the wiper blade. Should she jump out and grab the note or should she speed away and turn on the wipers to sweep the note away forever into the moonlit night? Aggie reached for a tissue from her purse. While John rattled on about their oldest son, Ben, helping fix dinner, Aggie jumped out and instantly folded the tissue around the edge of the envelope. She violently yanked it free and dived back into the car and locked the doors. Suddenly, she tossed the letter in the passenger seat as if she were casting aside a hot ingot.

While hearing about Jasmine's latest song, Aggie retrieved a fingernail file from her purse and used it to open the envelope. Careful not to touch the paper, she extracted the page.

Dear Ms. Rhodes,

You think you can stop me, but you never will. Simply put, I'm smarter than you. I think I've proven that. I'm smarter than the police, especially those ignorant detectives, Black and Sheffield, and the psychologists and the chief medical examiner. At least you have your beautiful family. Your husband, John; your boys, Jake and Ben; and your daughter, Jasmine.

If you had been smarter, you might have foiled my plan to kill the chief of police, but you are just as inept as the rest. You dumb bitch. I hope you keep writing those articles about me. I love reading them. Your descriptions are sublime. They make me sound like a real monster. You have no idea! You and the rest of the world can't even conceive of my abilities. I'm so much better than you will ever be.

Don't worry, I don't intend to stop. Who will it be next? When will I kill again? Did I hide another clue in this note? I do hope that you've written another great exposé on my latest crime, the savage murder of Chief McNally.

Remember that I'm watching you, Aggie. I may even be spying on you now as you tremble uncontrollably reading this. I'll be in touch again soon, my dear. Kiss Jake and Ben and Jasmine for me.

Yours truly,
Fenrir the Wolf

The bastard had mentioned her family to frighten her, to get under her skin, and it had worked. *This is war*, Aggie thought. Focusing on her husband's voice, she dropped the note on the passenger seat, put her car into gear, and sped out of the lot.

~~~~~~~~

The two men said nothing on the drive from the McNally house to Trevor's apartment. The radio was turned low. When the newscast about the chief's murder ended, the angelic voice of Annie Lennox assuaged them. Black patted Trevor's leg; the young man responded by rubbing the detective's hand. The May air was cool and refreshing, but a chill ran through Trevor's body. The monster who had first killed his friend and neighbor had now taken someone from Black. The young man needed to forget the horror. The pain he felt over Marc's betrayal paled in comparison and now seemed almost folly. He just wanted to feel safe, protected.

Once inside the apartment, the two men embraced intensely as if they were trying to become one. Trevor could smell Black's cologne, and Black could smell the faint scent of baby powder. Letting out a deep sigh, Black picked Trevor up in a bear hug. With his toes barely touching the carpet, Trevor grabbed the nape of Black's neck and kissed him below his ear. To an outsider, it would appear that Trevor was attempting to drink like a vampire from Black's jugular; instead, he ran his tongue erotically over the tender skin and planted small kisses there. The detective lowered Trevor to the ground and loosened his embrace.

His voice husky, Black touched his forehead to Trevor's and said, "I want to stay here tonight."

"Are you sure? I mean I want you to, but—"

Black placed his thumb over Trevor's lips. Their eyes were locked, and their bodies ached with desire. The kiss that followed made everything else fade away. As the moonlight bathed them in effervescent glow, they made love, exploring each other's body, taking turns conquering and surrendering to each other. Their lovemaking was unhurried and tender. Spent, they collapsed onto the bed and basked in the afterglow. As Selene, goddess of the moon, looked on, the two somehow forgot everything else that had happened and slept peacefully in each other's arms. A few hours later, Selene faded as her sister Eos, goddess of the dawn, greeted the two lovers with her gentle morning light.

Chapter 29

When Sheffield awoke the next morning, she rolled over to look at the clock: 7:43. It had taken a sleeping pill to knock her out, and the effects of the drug lingered in her system. Her cats were next to her, wrapped like yin and yang. As Louis and Lestat began to purr, Sheffield began to sob. The psychopath Fenrir had succeeded in taking someone from her inner circle. Though she had seen unspeakable acts during her six years as a homicide detective, this time it felt as if she were seeing pure evil. For a brief moment, she suspected that Fenrir wasn't human and she doubted her ability to catch him.

The phone rang, startling both her and the cats.

"Are you still in bed?" the smooth, baritone voice inquired.

"I overslept. I don't know how."

"It's because you're exhausted."

She was silent as fresh tears slipped down her cheeks.

"I wish I could be there, hon," the man said. "I hate that I'm out of town when you need me."

"Yeah, I miss you, Vik. How's your trip?" Viktor Edwards was an easygoing and successful businessman whom Sheffield had been dating for nearly two months. Their schedules gave them little time to connect, but they'd managed a handful of dates and the occasional sleepover. Both were hopeful of the burgeoning relationship.

"Boring. I want to lay in that bed with you and wrap my arms around you and tell you that I love you. Babe, you're the bravest, most fearless person I know."

"You're so sweet." She sat up in the bed and wiped her face.

"You were crying, weren't you?"

She said nothing. The cats walked toward her and sniffed the air suspiciously.

"Viktor, I've got to go. I need to get to work."

"I'll be thinking of you."

"We'll talk tonight?"

"Absolutely. Vivienne, if you need me, call."

"I'll be fine. Besides, you'll be in meetings."

"Don't worry about that. I'll keep my phone on vibrate. I can duck out anytime."

"Thank you for calling."

"My momma raised me right."

Sheffield chuckled softly. "Yeah, I guess she did."

~~~~~~~

While Sheffield was drying her tears, Trevor and Black were engaged in other activities. It was as if their bodies were in harmonic symbiosis. Afterwards, the nascent lovers showered and dressed together. Because he hadn't brought a change of clothes, Black wore a pair of Trevor's underwear, which was a bit snug. The detective's head was swirling with a strange mixture of emotions. The previous night had been both the worst and best night of his life. His boss had been murdered by the psychopath terrorizing the city; then, he'd experienced his most intense sexual relationship since Colin. It was hard to know what to feel—dread, hope, fear, excitement—but there was no time to process emotions now. He had to get to work to continue the hunt for that bastard Fenrir.

"I'll fix breakfast," Trevor said. "Eggs, waffles, oatmeal?"

"I've got to get to the station." Black wrapped his holster around his torso. "You got any coffee?"

"Sorry. I could make tea."

Thinking Trevor looked cute in his tan chinos and powder blue shirt, Black responded,"That's okay."

"You sure you can't eat something?"

Black walked over, smiled, and grabbed Trevor by the waist. "No. I've really got to go." Then he kissed him.

"At least take a banana." He tore one free and held it aloft.

"Okay. I'll take the banana." Then Black said earnestly, "Last night with you was nice."

"The next time we're in bed, I'll tell you one of the *good* myths—a love story. I mean, if there *is* a next time. I'm going to shut up before I say the wrong thing." Trevor took a sip of tea.

Black pushed Trevor's hair away from his eyes and looked at him tenderly.

"There'll be a next time." Then he kissed him again.

"You're such a good kisser."

"It takes two." Black grabbed the banana and headed for the door. "I'll call later."

"I've got work and then class," Trevor responded.

Black felt compelled to say, "Lock the door behind me."

~~~~~~~

Sheffield and Black looked distracted and tired when they arrived at the station. A pall permeated the building, though it was a hive of activity. They found Perez at his desk. He had requisitioned the tape of the 911 call made from the McNally residence and typed notes from the interviews with the neighbors. One neighbor had confirmed that the hacksaw belonged to the McNallys. Petkov had already phoned to say she would conduct the autopsies first thing and call as soon as she had more information. Other divisions of the crime lab were analyzing the gold elastic cord, the paint from the wall, and the action figure. Aggie Rhodes had left a message that she would drop by around 10:00 with the latest Fenrir letter.

"So, Amadeo, looks like you got here early," Black declared as he surveyed the paperwork on his desk.

"Jesus, what time *did* you get here?" Sheffield asked.

"Early; let's leave it at that. I can't believe the chief and Dolores are dead. The Wolf had to know that'd make him public enemy number one."

"Oh, he knew," Black grumbled.

"It still hasn't sunk in yet." Sheffield dropped into the chair at her desk.

"We got the tape from the 911 call." Perez spun his chair around to face them. "Aggie will be here in a couple hours. She seems fired up about something—*besides* the fact that our killer left her a nice little message on her vehicle last night."

Sheffield almost dropped her coffee and Black slapped his

hand down hard on his desk.

"Ease up." Perez held up his hands. "She's bringing us the letter, and I've already requested surveillance tapes. Thought I'd work on the tapes while you talk with her."

"Perez, you are a gift from God." Sheffield stood and kissed him on the forehead.

"Tell that to my wife." He gave her a cheesy, crooked smile.

"He *had* to be caught on tape," Black said.

"I bet he was disguised like before." She studied Black's shirt and swore it was the same one he'd been wearing the night before.

"Sheff, we need to find out if there were prints on the hacksaw."

"Got that," Perez offered. "Our killer didn't leave prints. Wiped clean. The knife too."

"Just what we expected."

"Did Trevor cough up any more details?" She poured a second sugar into her coffee.

Black started at the mention of Trevor's name. He felt embarrassed, as if Sheffield and Perez knew about his late night dalliance.

"He found the arrow on the Internet. It's the rune symbol of the god Tyr. Then he looked in some of his books and found something about the Vikings hanging men as a sacrifice to Tyr."

"That explains the hanged G.I. Joe." She studied his shirt again. "Last night probably reminded him of his friend Adams. Was he okay?"

"Yeah, I think so." He started filling out the forms in front of him.

"Hey, when the dust settles, we need to hit up Radford again." Sheffield swirled the coffee in her insulated cup. "Something about that guy bugs me, but I keep thinking he might give us some answers."

"Unless you need me, I'm off to get the tapes from the *Times*," Perez announced.

"No, go ahead." Black waved at him. "And thanks for all your help, buddy."

"We're going to get him this time. I feel it in my Puerto Rican soul."

"From your mouth to God's ear." Sheffield repeated the phrase she'd heard her grandmother use often.

"But which god?" Black said.

~~~~~~

A couple hours later, Aggie and the detectives sat in the conference room staring at the letters, as if they were an ancient find that raised many questions but provided no answers. Though calm when she entered the station, Aggie became flustered as she relived the events of the night before—walking to her car and discovering the threatening letter. Sheffield consoled her with a friendly pat on the shoulder while Black brought her a cup of coffee. As he sat it down, he realized that the caffeine would do nothing to suppress the reporter's anxiety. The day's edition of the *Normandy Times*, with its startling headline, lay at the end of the battered conference table. Lines creased the reporter's forehead, and puffy bags underlined her eyes. Finally, the woman stopped picking her nails and slammed her hands down on the table.

"He will *not* ruin my life! That bastard is not going to win."

"Aggie, Officer Perez is getting the tapes for the Time's parking lot." Sheffield leaned against the conference table. "He isn't invisible. He *has* to be on those tapes."

"What if he's disguised again?"

Black rubbed his temples. "Let's hope he's not, but if he is, we'll deal with it."

"You know he's toying with us." A wave of the hand pointed to the letters as proof.

"It's there. I didn't find it until I knew the answer. When I heard that the police were heading to the chief's house, I searched the letter for his name, and *bingo*, there it was." Her voice boomed as she tried to make her point. "See along the left side? It's the chief's name. And the second paragraph is a Norse god. If only I'd seen it earlier!"

"No one could have predicted what this psycho would do next," Sheffield said, trying to calm her. "You can't blame yourself."

"Yeah, well, the next time I'm going to find his hidden message, and you're going to catch this son of a bitch before he kills again." The woman met both of their gazes with a resolute expression of determination. "He's talking about my family here."

~~~~~~~~

Black, Sheffield, and Perez gathered in the media room, listening to the static and hoping for a miracle.

"911. What's your emergency?" Silence.

"911. What's your emergency?" Silence.

"Is anyone there? This is 911. Do you need assistance?" The call ended.

The three listened to the message a second and a third time. All they heard was a single soft breath at one point—almost like a sigh—and a metallic clink at another point. Neither sound was revealing.

"Sounds like the caller started to laugh," Officer Daniels, the de facto NPD technology "expert," said. His red shirt matched his red hair. "And that slight ping is something striking the edge of the table."

"Like the saw?" Black posited.

"Nothing that heavy or that large."

"Maybe his belt buckle," Sheffield offered.

"Could be."

"Can you at least verify it's a male whose breath we heard?"

"I'm sorry. I've listened to this with a lot of different filters, and there's nothing else there. Whoever it is didn't whisper a word or make any other sound."

"Damn," Sheffield exclaimed.

Black added, "I thought for certain that there'd be a wolf howl in the background."

~~~~~~~~

At the coroner's lab, the bodies of Chief McNally and his wife had been returned to refrigeration. Petkov sat at her desk signing death certificates and budget forms. There were requests for vacation leave from two of her staff, an invitation to a career fair, a flyer about a forensics conference in Las Vegas, and mail she had ignored for two weeks. Reporters had been calling, but RayAnne, true to form, had fended them off like a pro. A soft knock on the door drew her attention.

RayAnne, Petkov's matronly administrative assistant, poked her head in and quietly said, "Detectives Sheffield and Black are here. Do you want me to ask them to wait?"

"No. Send them in." Seconds later, the gray-haired woman returned with the two homicide detectives.

"Doc, we appreciate you seeing us so quickly," Sheffield said.

"I finished both autopsies, but I have to wait for toxicology and lab results. Sit here." She gestured to the furniture surrounding the stone coffee table. She uncapped a cranberry juice and took a sip before beginning.

"Mrs. McNally was killed first, as you know, by single stab wound to her back. The blade pierced her kidney and spleen. She died very quickly. Dolores was maybe lucky." The comment took them by surprise, and the detectives exchanged a questioning glance. Both presumed she meant that Dolores was lucky because she didn't suffer.

"Mrs. McNally had terminal cancer. Based on metastasis into major organs, she would likely have died within the year, probably much sooner."

"The chief never talked about it," Sheffield said.

"Maybe he didn't know."

"Would Dolores have known she had cancer?"

"She would have felt pain and unusual fatigue, even if she had no other symptoms."

"So you think she'd been diagnosed?"

Petkov shook her head and took another drink. "I see no signs of biopsy, chemotherapy, or radiation, but she must have known she was sick. Toxicology will probably show pain-management drugs."

"Poor woman," Sheffield muttered.

"And now for the chief: burn marks on his back were consistent with stun gun. Fibers in his mouth matched dishrag found near his body. Bruising around his left wrist indicates he struggled against handcuffs."

"Probably his *own* cuffs." Black crossed his legs and fixed the cuff of his gray slacks.

"There is bruising on the chief's right upper thoracic and underarm, which confused me at first. As I examined severed right hand, I figured it out. The killer placed his foot at chief's underarm and savagely pulled on his arm as he sawed."

The imagery made Black's stomach turn.

"There are 16 bite marks, like ones on original victim's body but with slightly different dimensions and pattern. They were caused by *dog* mandibles—not wolf's."

"Consistent with the myth," Sheffield noted.

"He was the hel-hound Garm," Black added.

"My guess is that the chief was alive, although certainly in shock, at this point."

"Oh, God," Sheffield uttered.

Black was in disbelief. "Didn't he die from blood loss once his hand was removed?"

The CME shook her head. "No. The killer tied tourniquet to limit blood loss. Effective in keeping him alive longer."

"Oh."

"The trauma to his throat killed chief. One deep saw cut and his windpipe filled with blood. At that point, it was a quick death from suffocation."

"Please tell me you're done with the descriptions," Black begged.

"Almost. The killer sawed through thyroid cartilage and into trachea. Then he pulled at vocal chords but didn't remove them."

"He wanted it to look like his throat had been torn out by a wolf." Sheffield said.

"A hel-hound," Black corrected her.

"In the neck wound, I found wolf hair."

"Any human DNA?" Black asked.

"None. Our killer is neat and clean. He doesn't even seem to leave hair that I can find. Maybe he shaves his head; maybe he shaves his body."

"Bastard can't even leave an eyelash behind!" Sheffield declared.

Petkov walked over to her desk. "Here are the preliminary lab reports on elastic cord, paint, and plastic action figure. I'm afraid there's nothing of significance." The CME paused and sighed before adding, "A child's toy used by a killer. I think of Petia when I see this. She loves dolls."

"She's adorable." Sheffield pointed to the family photo on Petkov's desk.

"Zlatko is good father and good husband—the best." She gesticulated to make her point. "He followed me to the United States from Varna in Bulgaria and never complained once in his life. Now I worry about this madman who calls himself Wolf and ruins this city. He is a monster to rip out man's throat."

Chapter 30

They had him on tape again. Dressed in jeans and a sweatshirt, he appeared to be normal—no oversized clothing, wig, or beard. The man looked around nervously and then walked briskly, without a limp, toward the red sedan belonging to Agatha Rhodes. Once he arrived, he acted quickly, placing the envelope under the wiper. He turned to dart away and then turned back to check the license plate to verify he had the right car. Anxious, the man scanned the parking lot; then, he practically ran to a white pickup truck and jumped in. As he peeled out, he almost sideswiped a cleaning van pulling into the lot.

Just as he'd done from the Sexcapade tapes, Officer Daniels captured the man's image. The photo filled the computer screen: buzz cut, thin build, approximately 5'8" and 140 pounds. The sleeves of his sweatshirt were pushed up, and on his right forearm was a large tattoo of a Celtic cross. He was wearing black cotton gloves to avoid leaving prints.

"That's great clarity," Sheffield said.

"Yeah, I can't believe we got this lucky," Perez added.

"It's the new surveillance system they installed a few months ago," Officer Daniels explained. "Top of the line. Very powerful."

Black said, "Let's run the photo for ID."

"I'll run it now," Perez responded.

~~~~~~~

When Radford read the article about the killings, he couldn't help but smile. His father had loved Norse mythology. So the God Killer had bitten off the hand of the great warrior and torn out his throat. Radford's father had told the story of Ragnarok, the Twilight of the Gods, so often that little Sheldon (though that wasn't his name then) knew it almost as well as any Greek myth. Every day, little

Sheldon sat quietly and listened to his father tell violent, licentious myths about the gods' wrath and retribution. The obsequious son was scared of his father. Growing up, the boy believed the gods and goddesses were indeed real. He even thought that sometimes they reached out with their invisible hands and touched him. Little Sheldon prayed to the ancient gods to deliver him from the parents he hated.

One day, unwilling to wait on the gods any longer, he drove to the community college where his father worked, walked into his office, and stabbed him until he was dead. Calmly, he returned home, strung up a rope and hung his mother. It was like a Greek tragedy, like the death of Agamemnon and Clytemnestra after the Trojan War. The police found a suicide note on the bedside table and presumed his mother had killed her husband before hanging herself.

Sheldon was 18 years old and sole heir of their estate, which he'd verified before executing his plan. He was finally rid of them, and that night, he unyoked himself from the gods of his father and never prayed to them again. In fact, he decided he was better than the gods.

The recent spate of murders in Normandy reminded him of his parents, and he laughed. Then he thought, *I'll probably get a visit from Detectives Tweedledee and Tweedledum.*

~~~~~~~

"Viv, I'm at my layover in Chicago," Viktor said.

"Do you need me to pick you up when you get back?" The detective was sitting at her desk, pouring through photos of felons.

"No, I've got my car at the airport. I'm landing in Columbus late, but I'd like to come over if you'll be up."

"Sure."

"So, how's the hunt going? Any leads?" She could hear airport sounds in the background.

"We think we've got him on surveillance tape, and we're searching for a match. We may actually have him by the time you land."

"That would be amazing."

"It's about time."

"See? I knew you'd get him."

"Well, he's not in custody yet." She leaned over and eyed a photo of someone looking similar to the man on the tape.

"After you catch him, we should plan a vacation. Maybe something Caribbean or Hawaiian."

"Oh, god, yes." Sheffield turned her chair around and cupped her hand around the mouth of the phone. "What did I do to deserve you? I can't wait to see you."

~~~~~~~

Black waited for his partner to walk away before calling Trevor.

"We may have him."

"Yeah?"

"We're trying to match him to surveillance tapes."

"I can't believe you might finally catch this freak."

"It's been a crazy day. I've got a feeling about this. I can't figure out why he got so reckless."

Trevor stopped outside his classroom. "He got cocky. No disguise?"

"Nope."

"Man, I won't be able to concentrate in class. I'll be wondering if you're knocking on his door like Jodi Foster in *Silence of the Lambs*."

"She was FBI."

"And you're cuter than her. Much more manly and rugged, too."

"You think so?" Black looked around nervously to see if anyone could overhear the conversation. The sound of Trevor's voice was making him horny.

"And sexy. Did I forget to mention sexy?"

"Will you stop!" Black shifted in his seat.

"So I'll see you tonight?"

"Do you *want* to see me?"

"Does Jodi Foster know how to act?"

Black laughed out loud and drew a few glances. "*Now* you're drawing attention to me."

Trevor feigned a sexy voice. "Oh, officer, you aren't going to arrest me, are you?"

"I got to get to work." Black spotted his partner heading his way.

"And I've got class."

"It may be late, so I'll call."

"We need code names," Trevor blurted out.

"You mean like 'the eagle has landed' kind of thing?"

"Names we can call each other, and no one will know who we're talking to."

"Like Fred and Ethel?"

"I was thinking something more romantic and classical, like Alexander and Hephaestion or Apollo and Hyacinthus. I'll think on it."

"Okay, I trust you'll pick something I can actually pronounce." Sheffield arrived at her desk as Black said into the phone, "Good-bye, Alexander."

"No, *you* would be Alexander," Trevor insisted. "I would be Hephaestion. Now, go catch a wolf!"

Chapter 31

Bravo Lane resembled a war zone. More than half a dozen patrol cars and a handful of unmarked police vehicles had descended upon a plain, dilapidated house with chipped, faded blue siding, a broken, rusty gate, and a sorely neglected lawn. In the driveway sat a worn white truck, the one from the surveillance tape of the newspaper building's parking lot. The damp May air was cool and made the pavement slick. A dog barked next door. Three teens—each a different ethnicity—watched in silence, without any effort to scatter. They lit another cigarette and huddled in anticipation, as if a parade was about to commence. Three officers headed into the backyard of the dilapidated house, while two covered the sides. The remaining officers remained by their squad cars, ready to open fire or make chase. It was a moment portrayed on TV and in movies all the time, but it had never happened in Normandy—until now.

The dog in the yard next door continued to bark.

One teenager said to the others, "He's fucked."

Another said, "Grammy's going to be pissed."

A figure moved in the window.

Everyone was in place as Sheffield and Black approached with guns drawn. A hard knock on the door.

The woman in the house next door yelled at her dog to shut up.

"Police! Open up!" Black said.

The figure moved across the window again. Another hard knock on the door.

"Police! Open up *now*! The place is surrounded!"

The two detectives saw a figure through the cracked glass in the door. Inside the house, it was too dark to discern a body or a weapon. They ducked to the sides of the door. Tension was high. With guns raised, the detectives were ready for anything, even a confrontation with Fenrir.

The deadbolt turned. Was it being locked or unlocked? Their

nerves on full alert, Sheffield and Black exchanged glances. Suddenly, the rusty handle turned, and the front door swung open. The detectives acted instantaneously, swinging in unison toward the figure in the doorway. The police illuminated the house with bright lights. The dog stopped barking. One of the teenagers on the sidewalk muttered, "Oh, shit!"

In front of the officers stood a petite, elderly woman dressed in a worn, blue housecoat. Cataracts clouded her once-blue eyes, and she didn't even squint at the light.

"Ma'am, we're looking for a Mr. Mickey Riley," Black announced. "Do you know where we can find him?"

She held up a gnarled finger and turned slowly. Sheffield yanked open the screen door. Then, over the old woman's shoulder, a body moved in the dark, descending the stairs.

"Mickey's upstairs," the old woman rasped in a feeble voice. "No, here he comes now."

"Freeze!" the detectives yelled, as they pushed their way into the house.

"Grammy!" the man on the stairs called out. Sheffield pushed the old woman against the door to move her from the line of fire. Black raised his weapon and continued forward, barking orders.

"Stay right there! Raise your hands *now*, and turn around! *Now*!" Sheffield could see the man's lower body in the flood of white light, but she couldn't see his face.

"Now! Raise your hands and turn around!"

"Grammy, are you okay?" the man on the stairs called out. Black charged forward, gun raised, and rushed the man. Sheffield followed behind. Everything seemed to move in slow motion. The man stopped mid-step, raised his hands and turned.

"Don't hurt my grandmother!" he pleaded. "She can't see!"

"Don't move!" Black took two stairs at a time. He grabbed the man's right hand, cuffed it, spun it behind his back and cuffed it to his left. Sheffield hit the light switch beside the door and scanned the house. No one else was there. Officers rushed inside. In the yellow light of the naked bulb, Sheffield and Black saw that the man on the stairs wore only pajama bottoms. On his back was a large tattoo of a menacing wolf, fangs exposed. They exchanged quick glances.

"Are you Mickey Riley?" Black yelled.

"Yes."

"You're under arrest for murder. You have the right to remain silent."

~~~~~~~~

Somehow, amid all the craziness of the past few weeks, Trevor managed to ace his finals. Another semester was behind him, and he wasn't registered for summer classes. The end of the semester, his burgeoning relationship with a hot detective, and now the impending capture of Fenrir all seemed portents of a bright future. Once emptied, the book bag was stored in the closet, where it would wait out the summer. Class notes and syllabuses were filed, and textbooks found a permanent home on the bookshelves, based on their size and topic. College was officially out of sight and out of mind for the next few months. After sorting the mail and starting dinner, Trevor hit the button on the blinking answering machine.

"Hey, Trev, haven't heard from you in a couple of days," the voice on the machine said. "Sorry I've been so busy. Was hoping I could come over for some fun tonight. What do you say? Give me a call on my cell. It's working now. Ring me, bro. Later." It was a familiar voice: Marc Lindberg's.

"I'd like to wring your neck," Trevor seethed.

No sooner had Trevor downed the pasta and a bottle of white tea than the phone rang. Hoping it was Dylan reporting the capture of the Wolf, he jumped to his feet and lunged for the phone, but it was Marc. He couldn't avoid him forever, so he answered.

"Hello." It was cool and brusque.

"Hey, guy. How've you been? I've been thinking about that hot body of yours. I'm horny as hell and was hoping we could play."

"Uh, I've been busy with finals and all."

"So can I come over? I'm leaving work now. Can be there in fifteen minutes."

"Actually, I don't think so." Trevor wondered if he should confront Marc about Kim. Maybe he should break things off with a simple "It's not going to work out."

"What's going on? You don't want me naked and hard in your bed? I'm sporting a woody right now."

Better show it to Kim, he thought, but he responded, "Something happened. I can't tonight."

"Are you okay? I can come over, and we can talk."

And fuck? "No. It's my parents. Everything'll be fine. Have a good night."

"Why does this sound like good-bye?"

Maybe because it is. "Give me a couple of days, and then we'll talk."

"Yeah. I hope your folks are okay."

Trevor hung up the phone and instantly turned his thoughts to Black. Had he caught Fenrir by now? He resisted the impulse to call the detective and instead turned on Food Network to watch Paula Deen make something with butter.

~~~~~~~~

Things were wrong. Things were very wrong.

Mickey Riley had been arrested, fingerprinted, and ushered into an interrogation room. Before anyone had said a word to him, officers were checking his driving record, employment history, criminal record, financial background, family history, and more. One officer was already trying to find out about his wolf tattoo, which seemed to confirm to some that he was indeed the dreaded Fenrir. A female officer remained with the suspect's grandmother, Celia Dandridge, who was usually called CeCe by anyone who didn't call her Grammy. When he was fourteen, Mickey's parents had left for a road trip and never returned. Celia Dandridge had never heard from her daughter and son-in-law again, nor did she even know if they were still alive. The irresponsible couple had, in her words, "likely drunk themselves into oblivion and fell off a cliff." The police were trying to locate the couple now.

The elderly woman had said she'd never once regretted raising her grandson. With only an eighth-grade education and a history of unemployment, Mickey never reached his potential, and Grammy was old and halfway blind when Mickey was 14. He had taken care of her and had never so much as spoken harshly to her. Grammy knew her grandson was imperfect—he'd run with a dangerous crowd, he'd earned money in illegal ways—but he'd never forsaken her like his parents had done to him. Two years prior, the old woman found her way downtown when Mickey was arrested for selling pirated DVDs and CDs, and she paid his bond. Unable to pay his fine, Mickey served a short prison sentence.

Mickey Riley sat hunched over in the aluminum chair with his arms crossed. The detectives had given him a shirt and shoes at the station, but not before they had photographed the tattoos—a Celtic cross on one forearm, a lotus blossom on his abdomen, a serpent on his other forearm, an eagle on his chest, the wolf on his back, and more. In another life, Mickey Riley might have been attractive, but now he looked like a poor, dejected man with nothing to look forward to and no chance for a better life. Sheffield felt pity and not anger when she looked at him. Where was her rage? Every prescient, intuitive bone in her body screamed *This is not Fenrir!*

"He's not our killer." She pointed to the man on the other side of the glass.

"The tats say he might be." Black couldn't muster his full conviction.

She shook her head emphatically. "It doesn't feel right. He's uneducated; he has no means to gather the items we've found at the crime scenes; he probably doesn't know a single pagan god."

"He left the note on Aggie's car."

"Okay. I'll give you that, but killing seven people and posing five of them as ancient gods? I'm not buying it." Insistent, she shook her head again. "Not at all."

The two hovered in the hall outside the interrogation room. As if he meant to storm off, Black took three big steps away from her and then stopped. Sheffield stood in place, chewing her bottom lip and eyeing her partner, who looked like a caged lion ready to growl.

"I don't know, Sheff. Just because he didn't finish high school and hasn't held a job doesn't mean he's not smart. And I can almost guarantee his parents neglected or abused him. That's how Dr. Canter described our killer's childhood."

"Okay, but it's not him." She gesticulated wildly. "He's not the Wolf. That fucker is still out there, and he's using this kid to toy with us. Cat and mouse again, and he's laughing because he's thrown us another red herring."

"He's got some tattoos that look like some of that mythology mumbo jumbo."

"Bull cocky," Sheffield protested, a hand on each hip.

"Let's do this."

They entered the gray interrogation room. Black sat across from Mickey, and Sheffield stood behind him, off to one side. Mickey looked up and eyed Black tentatively before hanging his head. It looked like the boy was praying. Sheffield noticed a tattoo of an ankh on his neck and thought about Kelly Robison and the bloody Knot of Isis.

"So, Mickey," Black began, "we have a few questions for you. We'd like the answers now, but you can wait for counsel if you'd like. The longer we have to wait, though, the less friendly we'll be. You see, I think you're a killer, and we're ready to prove it."

"I ain't no killer." The suspect raised his eyes and met Black's gaze defiantly. Still hunched forward, he seemed like a man partially deflated.

"You ever hear of Agatha Rhodes?" Black asked.

"No."

"Really. Because you left a note on her car last night."

"I was just delivering it for someone, but I don't know her."

"Who were you delivering it for?"

"I don't know."

Black grumbled in doubt. Sheffield watched in silence.

"Some guy," the deflated man insisted.

"I think you're lying. Where were you last night from 4:00 to 8:00?"

"Home. In my room."

"Anyone else with you?" the detective asked.

"No. But Grammy knows I was there."

"Really. She says you may have slipped out, because you do that sometimes." Sheffield stood silent and still, watching the suspect's nonverbals.

"I didn't," Mickey insisted.

"When did you leave to deliver the note?" Black asked coolly.

"Around 9:00."

"Here's what really happened, Mickey: you slipped out and went to the McNally residence; then, after killing the chief and his wife, you drove to the *Times* offices and planted a note on Aggie's car."

"No!" the man objected, sitting upright. "I didn't kill anyone. I dropped off the note for some guy who paid me cash."

"How'd you meet this guy?" Black asked.

"I didn't." He slunk forward again. "I found the letter in my truck with some money. There were instructions to put the letter on that lady's car."

"Where're the instructions?"

"I threw them out," Mickey said, with a burst of energy.

"Where?"

"The kitchen trash."

"And the money? How much was there?"

"Five hundred. The instructions said I'd get another five hundred after I delivered the letter. I can use the money, so I did it."

Black whistled, sat back, and folded his arms. "That's some pretty good money for delivering a letter. When were these instructions left in your truck?"

"Monday. I didn't think it'd be a problem."

Mickey looked like he might cry, and Sheffield shifted her gaze to her partner, who could feel her stare. She folded her arms and walked around the table.

"I don't believe you," Black continued.

Sheffield leaned over the table and looked directly into Mickey's bloodshot eyes. "Do you know who Odin is?"

"A god." He maintained eye contact.

"Mm-hmm. And Tyr?" she followed up.

Mickey shrugged.

"And Fenrir?"

"I don't know."

"He was an evil, homicidal wolf in Norse mythology," Black interjected. "Where'd you get the tattoo?"

"Which one? The wolf?" Mickey sat upright again, as if he'd become interested in something. "About five years ago at this place on King Street."

"Why the wolf?" she asked.

"Because wolves are like dogs. They take care of each other."

"And they're killers." Black continued his bad-cop routine

but was losing his resolve.

"They don't kill each other."

"But they kill defenseless animals," Black said.

"They have to for survival," Mickey stated as if it was a mystical truism.

"Did you ever kill anyone?" Sheffield asked.

"No. Never." Mickey was clearly frazzled. "You gotta believe me."

"Actually, we think you're the God Killer."

"That psycho who's been slicing up people? That ain't me!"

"It *is*," Black said accusingly. "You've got the tat, no alibi, and we've got you on tape."

"It isn't me. Why would I kill those people?"

"Because your folks abandoned you, you got no education, no skills, you can't hold down a job, and you're pissed off that life dealt you a shitty hand. On top of that, you get off on this mythology stuff, because it's full of violence and gore. You get a tattoo of a badass wolf and you start thinking you're some Viking monster come back to punish people."

Mickey grew insistent. "No. It's not that way. I delivered the letter to that reporter 'cause some guy was going to pay me a thousand dollars. He said that she was writing lies about him."

"He told you this in the note?" Black asked, doubtful.

"Yeah."

"I don't suppose this note was signed?" Black shrugged. "Did the guy have a name?"

"Yeah. It was a weird one. I think he might have misspelled it."

"What was it?" Sheffield asked.

"Garm."

Chapter 32

Oh, Mickey, my messenger, you finally fulfilled your purpose.

When I saw you in the tattoo parlor with the ferocious-wolf tattoo, I knew you would one day unwittingly serve me. I struck up a conversation, knowing I needed to brand you as mine. And then it hit me: since you would serve as my messenger one day, you needed the mark of a messenger god. A winged helmet or golden-winged sandals or caduceus. You liked the sound of the caduceus, and you went about drawing it as I described it. Rather than the typical, placid version, you sketched a thick, gnarled staff and entwined it with two serpents with open mouths, fangs proudly on display. Such menace. I couldn't have been more pleased.

I love tattoo joints because they're filled with such interesting people—gangbangers, Goths, frat boys, bikers, freaks, women wanting to do something wild. I've been to dozens of tattoo shops, though I haven't one single tattoo; I have always been fascinated by body scarification, branding, and tribal markings. It's somehow primeval and visceral. Humans are too civilized now for such animalistic displays, and yet they're not as civilized as they think. Instead, they're weak and cruel. They file into their offices and eat their protein bars and drink their lattes and drop their kids off at soccer practice. Most are myrmidons, obsequious and numb. Anymore no one dances around a fire in a lion skin hopped up on peyote or mescaline for spiritual enlightenment. So when they feel wild, they get a tattoo or a piercing. It's the closest they'll come to their true animal selves, the primal being within.

The day I met you, I left the tattoo parlor knowing that upon my command my messenger would execute his duties, and you did so brilliantly.

Chapter 33

Sheffield took three steps in one direction, pivoted on the ball of her foot, and returned to her original spot. She looked down at Mickey Riley and then over at her partner. Disillusionment tugged at her soul. As the interview progressed, her certainty that this man wasn't Fenrir grew.

"So the instructions from the killer are in the trashcan?" Black asked.

"Yes," Mickey said.

"The ones with the name Garm signed to it?"

"Yes. They're there."

"And this message was typed?"

"Yes. It was in one of those big, yellow envelopes." Mickey's eyes were wide.

"And you never got the other five hundred dollars that Garm promised you?" Sheffield asked.

"I got it."

Confusion registered on the detectives' faces. "You got it?" Sheffield asked, shocked. "When? How?"

"After I put the letter on the reporter's car, I stopped for some ice cream, and when I got home, Grammy had an envelope with the rest of the money. She said some guy dropped it off."

"She saw him?" Black demanded. "Your grandmother saw this man, Garm?"

"Well, she doesn't see too well because of her eyes, but she saw what she could. Talked to him, too." His voice had a childlike quality. "Am I going to prison again?"

~~~~~~

In the hallway outside the interrogation room, the two detectives discussed the situation.

"He's not our guy," Sheffield stated.

"No, he's not," Black acquiesced. "Looks like he's going to be no help in finding him, either."

"But the letter and his grandma might. Do we hold him overnight?"

"Why? We can't even get him for complicity. The Wolf used that poor guy to lead us on a bogus chase."

"We take him home now, get the letter and the envelope, and talk to the grandmother."

"Think she saw anything?"

"Maybe something. That's better than nothing."

"It's late. Tomorrow, let's get some guys out interviewing the neighbors."

~~~~~~~~

Aggie Rhodes and her family had spent the day eating Southern cuisine, riding horses, and shopping for antiques. The day with John's parents had been blissful. Aggie had all but forgotten about the letters, the crimes, and her tormentor. Her family—John, Ben, Jasmine, and Jake—were everything to her. Though she loved her job, she would give it up without regret in order to keep her family safe. Though she loved Normandy, she would move without a second thought to protect them. Losing a member of her family would be more than she could bear, especially if one of them was taken by this madman. After heartfelt hugs and kisses, the Rhodes family, loaded down with preserves and canned vegetables foisted upon them by John's mother, headed to their vehicle. The mere sight of the red sedan turned Aggie's veins to ice and her bowels to liquid. At first, she saw a cream-colored envelope under the wiper blade, but it was merely a reflection on the windshield. She took two more steps forward, and then she heard an owl hoot in the distance. Her feet wouldn't move; the world seemed frightening and malicious again. As her kids piled into the sedan, Aggie waited for Fenrir the Wolf to charge out from behind a tree and gobble them up right before her eyes. John turned toward her.

"It's okay, babe," he cooed. "He's not here. He's not going to hurt you." He took the box from her arms and placed it in the trunk.

"What about our *kids*?" she asked. "And *you*?"

"Aggie, the police will catch him. You'll help them get him."

A tear slipped down each cheek, and she immediately reached to wipe them away. Ben was watching her, and she wouldn't let her kids see her fear. She smiled at Ben.

"I had so much fun, I hate to leave."

"Bye, Grandma and Grandpa," the three kids called from the car. After one last wave to her in-laws, Aggie took her keys from her purse, settled into the driver's seat, and asked Jasmine to sing them a song as they started home.

~~~~~~

"Sure, I saw him." CeCe bobbed her head like Kathryn Hepburn. "Took the envelope from him, didn't I?"

"Ma'am, can you tell us what he looked like?" Sheffield asked.

"Well, I didn't see him like *that*," she said, indignant. "Heard him better than I saw him."

"And what did he sound like?"

"Manly voice. Deep, like a singer. He used words sparingly, and they were very crisp. Seemed polite—he called me ma'am and wished me a good night."

"Can you walk us through what happened?" Black asked.

"There was a knock on the door at about 9:30. The man says, 'Ma'am, I was wondering if I could leave something for my friend Mickey.' He put an envelope in my hand. I asked his name. He says, 'It's Garm.' I thought I'd heard wrong so I asked, 'Did you say "Garm"?' He laughed and says, "Yes, ma'am. I know it sounds more like a monster than a man. Guess my parents weren't thinking when they named me.' Then he left." CeCe gave one emphatic nod to signify she'd finished her tale completely and accurately.

Sheffield asked, "Ms. Dandridge, did you see or hear anything else that might help us identify this man?"

"Well, I don't see much. He was about Mickey's height. Not a big guy. Just average. I think he had on a red or orange shirt."

"His hair and eyes?"

She snickered. "I ain't seen no one's eyes for nearly ten

years."

"Did anyone else see him?"

She shrugged. "Don't know. I did *smell* two things. One was a powder scent, like those gloves in the doctor's office. The other was a smell like liver."

"Liver?"

"Yeah. You know, kinda iron-y."

"Like blood?"

"Yeah. Just like blood."

~~~~~~~

Sheffield felt as if the day had heaped layers of soot on her until she was completely weighed down by it. Before a hot shower, she had to feed the cats rubbing against her legs in a figure eight. Before she'd even set down the bowl of Iams, the phone rang, and Viktor said he was bringing Thai food and a bottle of wine. Under the hot stream of water, the detritus of the day gradually washed away, but Sheffield couldn't get the face of Mickey Riley out of her mind. Though he'd done nothing to warrant it, she almost felt sorry for him. Fenrir had chosen him for obvious reasons: he was tractable, dirt poor, and had that wolf tattoo. She'd bet money that Fenrir had "discovered" Mickey long ago. Maybe if she pursued that angle, she'd get closer to finding the elusive Wolf.

When she wrapped herself in the towel, she put away all thought of her job and turned to thoughts of Viktor. She dressed in cotton pajama bottoms and a tank top and allowed her blonde locks to float freely. Feeling clean, refreshed, and excited, she rushed downstairs to light candles and turn on romantic music.

Viktor arrived on time. First order of business: a passionate kiss. Second order of business: compliments and another kiss. Third order of business: groping and more kissing. The cats were left to sniff at the bag of Thai food while the wine warmed in its place on the floor and the couple ravished each other in bed. Sheffield had three orgasms—a record for her—before Viktor stopped. They followed their lovemaking with her second shower of the evening.

~~~~~~~

While Black told Trevor about the false alarm with Mickey Riley, the two fixed a late-night snack of grilled cheese and slice-and-bake walnut-and-chocolate-chip cookies. After warm cookies and ice-cold milk, their hunger was sated, but their libidos were warming up. They started in the kitchen, progressed to the dining room, continued in the living room, and ended on the bed, where they lay panting in bliss, unable to speak for a while.

"That was amazing," Black finally gushed.

"*You're* amazing. Your body's like Hugh Jackman's. And that's a compliment, 'cause he's *fine*."

Black laughed heartily. He rolled to face Trevor and placed a hand on his chest. His lover's heart still beat rapidly.

"You're pretty fine yourself, Mr. Green Eyes."

"I'm glad you like."

"So what's our code names?"

Trevor ran the back of his hand over Black's chest. "I've got some choices."

"Do I need paper to write these down?" Black waved his hand down his body to point out that he had none.

"No paper required." Trevor poked his lover playfully. Black tangled his legs between Trevor's. "Maybe we could be Alexander the Great and Hephaestion. Alexander was wont to call Hephaestion 'Philalexandros,' which means 'beloved of Alexander.' Or there are the Greek heroes Achilles and Patroclus, who fought together in the Trojan War."

"How come I didn't learn these things in history class?"

"If they taught you this in school, it might have made you gay," Trevor joked.

Black scoffed. "Oh, yeah—*that* worked." He reached up and tousled Trevor's blond hair lightly and then ran his thumb along his lover's jaw line.

"There were Apollo and Hyacinthus. The god Zephyr was jealous and blew Apollo's discus so it struck Hyacinthus and killed him. Then Apollo turned him into a flower."

"Too tragic."

"And Apollo had other male lovers. Then there was Heracles and Iolus. Also Heracles and Hyllus."

"Keep going. I know you've got more."

"Poseidon and Pelops. Zeus and the blond prince Ganymede."

"So you would be Ganymede and I would be Zeus." Black curled a lock of Trevor's hair around his finger.

Trevor nodded. "But I was thinking Gilgamesh and Enkidu. Enkidu was made by the gods just for Gilgamesh, to be his perfect companion."

"I like that."

"The text isn't clear on whether they were lovers or not, but they were soul mates."

"I like that."

"Gilgamesh was the King of Uruk. He started as a tyrant but became a kind ruler."

"Are you implying I was a jerk before I met you?'

"Never! We could call each other Gil and Enk."

"This isn't Norse?"

"Uh-uh. Mesopotamian, long before the Vikings—even before the Greeks. I think the *Epic of Gilgamesh* is the oldest book known." Trevor sat up and let his eyes wander down Black's naked body.

"Tell me about Gil and Enk," Black encouraged him.

Trevor pulled Black toward him. The detective lay with his back to the younger man's chest. Trevor rested his chin on Black's shoulder.

"Well, the Sumerian king Gilgamesh was two-thirds god and one-third mortal, so he was super strong…"

His voice was smooth and melodic, and Black was mesmerized by his words and the imagery they evoked. For a spell, he was transported to another place and another time when gods walked the earth. Soon, Black was more relaxed than he ever remembered being. With the soft thump of Trevor's heart beating against his back and soft words in his ear, Black drifted to sleep.

Chapter 34

The elastic cord matched the one braided into Kelly Robison's hair and was virtually untraceable. The plastic figure—whether doll or action figure depended on who was talking—was manufactured around 1978 and was sold nationwide. The figure showed typical wear from play, like marks where it might have been stepped on or dashed against a rough surface. Recently, the plastic figure had been washed in soap and water, followed by an alcohol bath. Fingerprints would have formed nicely on the plastic surface, and yet there were none. The toy's missing clothes were nowhere to be found. A curious pattern of indentations on the torso was identified as the teeth marks of a child. Even if the killer was caught and these marks were left by his teeth, his adult bite wouldn't bear resemblance to his childhood bite. Early dental records would be necessary to match the bite pattern—if such records were even available. The choice of G.I. Joe was an obvious attempt by Fenrir to show his superiority over an iconic warrior.

One of the technicians at the lab made a curious discovery about the hair found in Titus McNally's gaping throat: the hair was similar, but not identical, to the wolf hair found at the previous murder scenes. Upon closer inspection, it was found to be canine, but not wolf hair. Rather, it came from *Canis lupus familiaris*—a dog, a Siberian husky to be exact. The trace experts determined the animal had been treated with the largest-selling brand of flea and tick medicine. This was an animal that was cared for by its owner. They wondered if it belonged to Fenrir but knew that serial killers didn't tend to make effective caretakers, even for pets. While one officer checked on the cord and another on the action figure, a third retrieved a list of Siberian huskies licensed to owners in Normandy and the surrounding municipalities.

The news stations were still rampant with reports of the "local serial killer." Retired FBI agents, who had never tracked a serial killer in their lives, were interviewed. Psychologists who knew very little about sociopaths and antisocial personality disorders gave their perspectives on the "disturbed killer." Angry citizens once again blamed the police for failing to do their jobs. Meanwhile, Aggie Rhodes remained oddly silent after her last exposé on the murders of the McNallys. She was, in fact, lying in wait for the megalomaniac Fenrir to write her again with a message she could decode.

~~~~~~~

The 13-year-old boy standing in front of the police desk had a Hispanic accent. "Will I get in trouble for leaving my bike on the grass?"

Young and petite, Officer Anita Flowers leaned on the desk to respond. "No, son. Can I help you with something?"

"I found a dead guy," the boy said calmly

"Dead?" Officer Flowers asked in disbelief. "Where?"

"In his house."

"You actually saw this dead body?"

"Yes."

"Where exactly?"

"In his bed."

"You were in his room?"

"When he didn't answer the door, I let myself in. Am I going to get in trouble for that?" The young boy bowed his head in contrition.

Officer Flowers leaned over so far that her body was touching the counter. "I think we can overlook it this time, son. Tell me what you saw."

"I found him in his bed. There's blood."

"Where does he live?"

"On Bravo Lane. His name is Mickey. It's his grandma's house. And I think she's dead, too."

Officer Flowers gave Hector Ramirez a soda, told him to have a seat, and rushed to get detectives Black and Sheffield.

~~~~~~~

When Trevor arrived home, he found a familiar red Mustang parked out front. *Damn*, he thought, *I don't want to have this conversation now—or ever!* As Trevor considered pulling away, Marc glanced his way and stepped from the muscle car. Trevor put his Saturn in park and looked down as if organizing something. His nerves twitched, and his stomach flipped, because he hated confrontation. Had it really been less than a week since he'd shared his bed with this duplicitous lover? After a deep breath, he stepped from his car.

"Hey, I was hoping to see you," Marc said with a seductive smile. "Are your folks okay?"

"Uh, yeah."

"I missed you."

"Yeah." Avoiding eye contact, Trevor walked ahead.

"I was worried about you."

Trevor almost lambasted Marc about his double life, but he stopped when a jogger breezed by.

"I'm fine, but we need to talk."

Once inside, Marc kicked off his shoes as if he were about to make himself comfortable. Trevor dropped his bag on the counter and grabbed a soda from the refrigerator.

"Something seems different in here," Marc said. Trevor poured his soda over ice and grabbed a bottle of water for Marc. With a sigh of resignation, he picked up the drinks and headed into the living room. Marc stood in the middle of the room, naked, with his hands outstretched as if to say, "Here I am!" Trevor found himself thinking, *He shaved his privates,* and chastised himself for the inane thought.

"Don't you want a piece of this?" the buff man asked.

"Marc, put your clothes back on." Trevor set the drinks on the counter and plopped down on a stool.

Marc studied him suspiciously as he dressed. "What's going on?"

"There's something I found out."

"What?"

"Kim."

"Who's Kim?" He tried to feign ignorance.

He's a cold liar, Trevor thought. *He isn't even nervous.* "Kim is your girlfriend."

"She and I are through."

"Your roommate doesn't think so."

"I told you that I'm not out to him."

"Does Kim know she's not your girlfriend?"

Marc was no longer excited. "Yeah. She's my friend."

"Does she know you fuck guys? Does she know that guys fuck you?"

"We don't talk about it."

"She doesn't know you're gay?"

"I don't talk to anyone about guys."

Trevor tried to maintain his equanimity. "Kim looked like your girlfriend at the movies."

"You were spying on me?" Marc yelled in disbelief.

"Oh, don't try to act offended." Trevor coolly took a sip of his soda. "Your roommate told me you were out with your girlfriend, and I had to see for myself if she was a friend or a girlfriend."

Marc pulled on his jeans. "And what did you see?"

"You still fuck her?"

A cold stare was the only response. Marc fastened his belt and pulled on his t-shirt.

"Look, Marc, we need to call it quits."

His demeanor changed. "There's another guy?"

"Marc, I wasn't cheating on you. Anyway, you can't get mad at me for liking another guy when you were hiding a girlfriend."

Marc twisted his face into a grimace. "You're going to miss me and my hot body." It was a ridiculous gesture, but Marc grabbed his crotch in his hand and squeezed.

Trevor tried to mollify him. "Yeah, I'll miss you."

"You'll want me back."

What an ego. Glad I found out now. "You might be right."

"You're sleeping with another guy, aren't you?" Marc blurted out as if he'd solve the Da Vinci Code.

Trevor said nothing.

"Fuck you, asshole!" Marc slammed the door behind him as he stormed out. A minute later, the tires of the Mustang squealed like a dragster at the racetracks.

For a closet case, he sure can make an exit like a drama queen.

~~~~~~~

    The indignant man stormed from the apartment, a trail of
fumes behind him. He kicked an aluminum can resting on the grass,
and it started a trajectory toward a jogger stretching by a tree. The
two men made eye contact for a brief moment, and the jogger
halfway expected the angry man to rush at him. Instead, the hothead
jumped into his red Mustang and peeled out.
    After the sound of the revving engine faded and the smell of
rubber dissipated, the jogger smiled. He knew about the guy who
lived in the apartment, the guy who had infuriated the Mustang
owner. The occupant of the apartment had had a different guest the
night before—a homicide detective working the local serial-killer
case. The jogger looked around one last time before heading down
the sidewalk in a steady jaunt. His endorphins were flowing—not
because of the exercise, but because he'd now selected his next
victim.

Chapter 35

The old woman on the couch looked peaceful, as if she'd merely fallen asleep in front of the TV. At 68 years of age, she was a wisp of a woman. With her eyelids closed, no one could see the clouds on her eyes. CeCe Dandridge had been killed and laid on the couch like a geriatric Sleeping Beauty. There were no signs of violence, no evidence of foul play, no indications of the manner of death. By all accounts, it appeared as if she had just slipped away from this world.

The scene in an upstairs bedroom was vastly different. The naked body of a 25-year-old man rested on bloody sheets, a knife protruding from his abdomen. His arms were splayed out beside him, turning his body into a large cross. A menagerie of tattoos adorned his body, most notably the eagle spread across his chest. Less than twenty-four hours earlier, the authorities had been certain that this man was the dreaded Wolf. Now he was dead, almost certainly at the hands of the real Fenrir.

The detectives waved in the forensic photographer and crime-scene technicians. Petkov estimated the time of death as midnight, barely an hour after the last officer had left the house. Fenrir, if this was his work, had not left any of his usual markers: no names in ancient letters, no wolf hair, no props; but then, this wasn't a ritual murder. This was an elimination—a silencing.

"Make sure to get photos of all of his tattoos," Sheffield instructed.

The two detectives walked around, taking in the story the room had to tell, including the mismatched sheets, the posters of lions and wolves, and sketches signed with the initials "MAR." In the drawers, under faded, holey underwear, were three adult magazines of hermaphrodites. The room was bleak, barren, and dilapidated. The dark paneling was dated and stark; the single window was yellowed, and one pane was cracked; the wood around the window was half rotted, and most of the white paint had flaked away. On the sill were old footprints from Mickey's tennis shoes.

The trellis he used to climb down was visible over the eave. The single closet had no door, and the ceiling was stained in one corner from water damage.

"Nothing extraordinary here," Sheffield commented. "A little porn. Pretty vanilla."

"The killer disposed of him—but *why*?"

Suddenly, Petkov interrupted them. "Uh, detectives, you might want to see this."

The two turned to see a gruesome sight. They had rolled Mickey Riley's body on its side and uncovered the work of Fenrir. The skin had been flayed from his back; the tattoo of the snarling wolf had been effectively removed. All that remained were raw muscles and bloody pulp. The sight made Black turn away, and Sheffield instinctively grimaced.

"How did he do that?" Sheffield asked in bewilderment.

"This took some precision," Petkov responded. "Most likely he used a scalpel.

"We didn't think about him taking out his messenger," Black said. "He removed the tattoo to make a statement: Riley is not the Wolf."

"Probably killed the grandmother then came up here and stabbed Mickey." Sheffield walked closer to the victim's mutilated body. "The bastard let us interview him before ending his life."

Black noted a torn poster of an eagle in flight hanging beside the dresser. "Because he's taunting us."

"But he mixed up the mythology. Garm wasn't killed by Fenrir; he was killed by the god Tyr. He's not sticking to the myths."

"This isn't about the myths; this is about the Wolf showing off. This is about showing us that he's the ultimate killer. This is him silencing his underlings."

"So five posed victims and four collateral damage. He certainly loves to kill." Sheffield sighed.

"God, I'm beginning to hate my job."

~~~~~~~

Sheffield had thought all day about Viktor's proposal of cohabitation. She hadn't expected him to recommend they move in together. It seemed early, but it also felt right. He was even receptive to living in her house instead of his. It was smaller but still roomy, close to his office and the NPD station, in a nice neighborhood, and, most importantly, the cats considered it home. Viktor was so eloquent that he essentially won her over with words. Not one for tears, she nonetheless got misty eyed. Finally, she answered, saying she needed to think about it, and the next day she thought of almost nothing else. Not the impulsive type, she surprised herself by deciding to give it a go.

~~~~~~

"Honey, I'm home," Black deadpanned as he entered the apartment, his arms extended wide.

"And how was your day?" Trevor approached the detective.

"I've had better." He kissed him then held up a folder. "I need your expertise with some mythology."

"Oh, no," Trevor groaned.

"Yeah, our guy struck again. Killed his delivery boy and the grandmother."

"Did he pose the bodies?"

Black shook his head. "Nothing. Killed them quickly, cut the large wolf tattoo from the guy's back, and left."

"No calling card?" Trevor took Black's jacket.

"Nope. In and out, and no one seems to have seen him." Trevor was wearing khaki shorts and an old sweatshirt, and he looked like a typical college student. In that moment, Black found himself thinking, *I could come home to this every night.*

"So where do the symbols come from?" Trevor headed into the kitchen.

"Tattoos on the body. I recognized the ankh thing and thought you might have some insight on the others." The detective moved closer to the bar and opened the folder. Trevor set the tea down and stared at Black's gun in the shoulder holster. He wondered what it was like to hold a gun, pull the trigger, and take a life. He imagined the steel would feel cold, the kick would be violent, and emotion would be akin to power. Black picked up a bottle of tea and took a swig.

"Wow, he has some interesting tattoos." Trevor moved around the counter and stood next to Black. Though he was engrossed in the pictures, the smell of Black's cologne distracted him.

"These are the ones I was curious about."

Trevor picked up the photos one by one. "You're right: that's the ankh. This one's Mesoamerican." He pointed.

"Yeah, it looks like some of the art on the wall at a Chipotle restaurant."

"I've only read a little of Aztec and Mayan mythologies. There's a little bit too much blood and sacrifice for my liking." Black leaned toward Trevor and their bodies touched. "This is a step pyramid."

"He had a poster on his wall"—Black fished through the photos—"with something about the Mayan world." He located the photo and pulled it out. "Here it is."

Trevor looked at it. "This right here is the plumed serpent representing the god Quetzalcoatl."

"He's the one the Aztecs thought was Cortez?" Trevor nodded, although he knew Black meant it the other way around: the Aztecs thought Cortez was Quetzalcoatl returning to earth.

"So our poor accomplice had some knowledge of mythology."

"Or he took images he liked from pictures." Trevor cocked his head. "He had a huge wolf tattoo on his back, but it was removed by Fenrir, and I'll spare you the graphic description. This kid Hector Ramirez was friends with Mickey—I'm not sure what I make of that, but I won't digress—and he claims that Mickey drew all his own tattoos."

"He wasn't a half-bad artist." Trevor put his hand on Black's shoulder.

Black swigged half the bottle of tea. "Fenrir effectively removed the symbol from the vessel. Mickey couldn't have a wolf tattoo, because it was the mark of the Great One himself."

"And the other tattoos didn't threaten Fenrir?"

"You got it."

"Look at the massive eagle on his chest." Trevor was amazed. "He drew this?"

Black shrugged. "Is this from mythology?"

"Could be, but maybe he liked the bird because it's an American symbol or because it's a raptor. In mythology, Zeus swooped down as an eagle to carry off the young Trojan prince Ganymede."

"So this could represent Zeus."

The younger man hesitated. "Or not. It's an eagle, Dylan. It's not specifically mythological."

Black shrugged in resignation. "What about this one on his thigh?" He slid another photo over and tapped his finger on it.

"Wow." Trevor held it closer. "Looks like an angrier version of the caduceus. It's also called the 'Wand of Hermes.' The symbol for medicine." Black nodded and sat down on the stool. "Anyway, the story says that the god Hermes laid his herald's staff between two snakes that were either fighting or mating and they attached themselves permanently to the staff."

The detective unfastened his holster and removed his gun.

"Hold on." Trevor walked over to the bookshelf and selected a book. He flipped to the index, flipped to a page, and then scanned quickly. Not finding answers, he tossed it aside and selected another. Black cracked some nuts that were in a bowl next to him. As he munched on Brazil nuts, he admired Trevor and his tenacity to find answers. In the third book, the mythology buff finally found his answer: "Looks like the staff was originally wrapped in ribbons. It says Hermes was a god of incantations—which I never knew—so he was associated with alchemy. That carried over to medicine. Oh, and he was associated by the Germans with the god Woden, which is the Norse god Odin."

"What!" Black dropped a nut. "So he was killing Odin all over again?"

"Eh, I don't know. This is getting complicated. Only the psycho committing these murders knows what he's thinking."

"This one isn't about the myths. Otherwise, he would have posed the bodies and done all of that other stuff."

Trevor walked back toward Black. "Hermes was the messenger god of Zeus. He carried messages, helped travelers, and took souls to the River Styx. Basically, he was a delivery boy."

"So this guy was Fenrir's messenger. He delivered Fenrir's message like a good boy, and then he was eliminated because he wasn't needed anymore."

"Do you think he knew Fenrir or at least met him?" Trevor asked.

"I don't know. It looks to me like he was branded by Fenrir. I don't believe this tattoo is a coincidence."

"You know," Trevor said, "Hermes was the father of Pan, and Pan was a trickster god like Loki. So, in one sense, Fenrir killed his grandfather by taking out Hermes."

Black growled. "Wait till I try to explain this to Sheff. Her head'll explode."

Chapter 36

"So you're going to move in together?" Black mused.

"I don't know yet, but I'm thinking yeah." Sheffield wasn't ready to admit her final decision out loud.

"And you're okay with that?"

"I wouldn't say yes if I wasn't, dumbass."

"And the cats are okay with it?"

"*Now* you're going too far." She slipped off her sunglasses.

With the help of copious notes, Black was able to tell Sheffield what he'd found out about the tattoos on Mickey Riley's body. After listening intently, her only comment was "Fenrir is a nutcase." Not the response he was expecting, but accurate enough. Black navigated the Lexus toward the campus of Normandy University.

"So where were you last night?" she asked her partner. "I called and left a message. You always answer my calls. What's up? You avoiding me?"

He shifted his weight. "You caught me."

"What time did you leave Myth Boy's place? You two have become fast friends."

He scoffed in response. "I went over when I left the station and asked him to look at the photos. He told me what he knew, and I left."

"Seriously, why didn't you call me back?" She checked her reflection in the visor mirror.

"I was tired and thought it could wait."

"So after you left Trevor's, you went home and went to bed?"

"Yeah. I just crashed. Slept like a rock."

She closed the visor and poked him in the side. "So why don't you look more rested today? You look like hell—got dark circles under your eyes."

"You're crazy."

"What's with the mischievous smile? What's up? You got secrets you're keeping from me, partner? You *know* I'll find out."

"I was tired, Sheff." He was getting flustered.

She shot him a sideways glance. "I got my eye on you, mister."

"You know I got nothing to hide."

"Yeah, yeah. Just get us to the university so we can grill Professor Stick-Up-His-Ass."

Sheffield looked out the window and watched the street signs pass by. She thought about her evening. After going home to check on the cats, she had gone over the case in her head and decided they should check tattoo parlors. Needing an escape, she had driven over to Black's house, but he wasn't home. She had waited a half hour before giving up and going home. His mysterious whereabouts the night before intrigued her, especially now that he was lying to her.

~~~~~~~

Aggie Rhodes eagerly searched her office mail every day in hopes there'd be another letter from the Wolf. Since the last note, the one on her car, nothing had surfaced. To counteract her feelings of inadequacy, she wrote about the philanthropic life of Dolores McNally. The article was unlike anything she'd written before. While some dismissed it as a puff piece, she took pride in detailing Dolores's numerous humanitarian works. While researching the story, Aggie's loathing for Fenrir grew. He was the antithesis of what Dolores McNally represented, and yet he had eliminated her as if she were vermin.

It was now week after the murders, and there was still no message from Fenrir. Aggie knew it would only be a matter of time before the killer wrote her again. *This* time, she would be indefatigable in her quest for the hidden clues.

~~~~~~~

The lab was quiet following the birthday celebration for two of the techs. They were twins—one worked in Trace, the other in DNA/Genetics—and were identical. It was difficult to tell them apart, but Petkov thought she was beginning to recognize subtle differences. Reese tended to squint and hold his shoulders tighter, and Reed moved his lips when he read and habitually brushed his hair from his eyes. After cake and punch, the worker bees scattered to their labs.

Petkov finalized her report on the autopsy of Titus McNally. Though she couldn't be certain, the CME was hopeful that the human hair she had found on the body actually belonged to the killer. It was small; it appeared to have come from an eyebrow. She had already theorized that Fenrir clipped or shaved the hair on his body to minimize shedding at the crime scene. He might, in fact, even keep his head shaved—which was more and more common those days, so he wouldn't necessarily stand out. She found herself thinking of the actor Vin Diesel and wondering if Fenrir resembled him in any way. There was no way he'd shave his eyebrows, though, because *that* would have the opposite effect: he'd actually stand out. She took great care in saving the hair for DNA matching later. This single hair, which could place the killer at the scene beyond any reasonable doubt, might be the only thing that ensured Fenrir's conviction at trial. While she saw this as a breakthrough, the detectives were less than ecstatic. They realized that it would be important in the long run but would do nothing to help them in the short run.

The autopsy of Celia Dandridge had been quick; she had died from suffocation. Particles in her mouth and esophagus matched the pillow found under her head. Petkov returned to Mickey Riley's body. He had been stabbed in the abdomen, probably while sleeping. The knife had caused a mortal wound, but it hadn't cause instantaneous death. The attacker had withdrawn the knife and plunged it in again. Marks on the side of his body were consistent with someone straddling him. Unfortunately, Mickey may have been clinging to life when he was rolled over and had the tattoo unceremoniously removed with a scalpel. The killer had outlined the tattoo, lifted the skin, and flayed it from his back. Red cotton fibers from a sweatshirt had been found among the raw carnage of Mickey's back.

So, two elements were left by the killer: human hair on McNally's body and red cotton fibers on Mickey's. Petkov wondered if the killer was growing careless or cocksure. Either way, she had the evidence and would relish the day she could present it in court.

Chapter 37

With the spring semester over and summer classes yet to begin, the campus of the University of Normandy was empty and quiet. The detectives parked in a faculty spot close to Bainbridge Hall. Sheffield had gotten eerily quiet during the drive. Black couldn't help but notice that she'd begun to fiddle nervously with a button on her jacket, and he wondered what was up.

They found Radford eating a peanut butter and jelly sandwich and drinking an orange Shasta while staring at his computer screen. Making no effort to stop what he was doing, he waved them into his cluttered office.

"Thank you for seeing us again, professor," Sheffield said.

Without looking up, Radford held up a hand to silence her. Sheffield was infuriated. The professor continued to ignore the detectives. Black opened the file in his hand. Sheffield cleared her throat. Radford bit off a large chunk of the sandwich and continued to study his computer monitor. It appeared he was playing a game.

Livid, Sheffield opted for shock value. "Professor, can you tell us where you were Tuesday between 4:00 and 9:00 p.m.?"

It had the desired effect. He snapped his head up sharply, bumping the desk violently with a leg. His face grew flushed and indignant. Though she wanted to smile, Sheffield returned his gaze with one of complacency.

"Are you implying I'm a suspect in these crimes?" He dropped his sandwich onto a plastic baggie.

"We have to consider all possibilities," Sheffield responded matter-of-factly. "I'm sure you understand."

He certainly *didn't* understand. How could they even hint at accusations that were so fallacious! "I can promise you that I'm not your killer. You can see that my degrees are in Greco-Roman history."

Black nodded toward the diplomas.

"And you never studied Norse or Egyptian myths?"

"Are you serious about this?"

"It's a simple question," Black responded without a hint of emotion.

"Maybe some of them at my father's insistence."

"So your father knows Norse mythology?" Sheffield walked toward the wall of diplomas.

"Knew. My father is dead."

"I'm sorry. And your mother?"

"Dead, too. They died in an automobile accident when I was at Brown."

"How tragic." She couldn't help but sound disingenuous. This was verbal sparring. "And your siblings?"

"I'm an only child."

"And Tuesday night?" Sheffield asked.

He was unable to disguise the vitriol in his tone. "I had dinner at my place with a faculty member. Her name is Marlena Goodrich. I fixed antipasto. We watched a movie."

Black opened his notepad. "We'll need her number for verification. I'm sure you're telling the truth."

Of course I'm not, but Marlena will lie for me, Radford thought. What he actually said, though, was "Of course."

"We were wondering if you could tell us what you know about the Norse god Tyr."

"God of war, much like the Roman Mars. Shield and spear. Wasn't Tuesday named after him?" Neither detective responded. The epiphany hit Radford.

"Ingenious! What a macabre intellect your killer has. I can tell by his letters that he's quite full of himself." Then he muttered under his breath, "Like my father."

"Excuse me?" Black said.

"Did I say that aloud?" He stood up from his desk. "My father was very impressed with his knowledge. He didn't even have his doctorate, but he thought he was *so* erudite…" He trailed off for a minute.

Sheffield's distaste for the professor was growing by the minute.

"What can you tell us about the caduceus?"

"The herald's staff. Now you're entering my territory. Carried by the god Hermes. You know of the god Hermes, I take it.

The winged hat and winged sandals?"

"Yes, we know," Black responded. "Messenger god; helped travelers; patron of athletes; did the bidding of Zeus."

"Impressive for an officer," he deigned, purposely demoting the detective. "Sometimes called the Wand of Hermes. Akin to the wizard's wand. Wrapped by two serpents." Black nodded. "What does the caduceus have to do with the god Tyr? Is your man mixing up his mythologies?"

"No." Sheffield answered too quickly.

"So there's been another murder?"

Black closed his notepad and slipped it into his pocket. "We're trying to gather information that may help us figure out our killer's motives."

The professor actually laughed out loud. "A bit presumptuous, don't you think? You'll never figure him out. Besides, you wouldn't want to know his troubled, twisted mind. Be glad you don't understand him, detective. Just accept that he's smarter than you."

~~~~~~~

"That man really perturbs me," Sheffield seethed.

"Yeah, I think that showed," Black responded.

The click of her heels on the sidewalk punctuated her words. Her rapid, forceful steps reverberated across the abandoned quad, broadcasting her anger. One of the things Black liked the most about his partner was her passion.

"Dr. Marlena Goodrich. I'm going to give her a call. You know that cocky bastard gets on my nerves."

Black couldn't help but smile. "Put Perez on it."

"Nah. I'm calling her myself. I want to know what kind of self-respecting woman would go out with a prick like Radford."

"Maybe it's his witty conversation."

"Yeah—and maybe monkeys fly."

They arrived at Black's Lexus. A click of the button, and then both climbed inside. Sheffield slammed her door a little too forcefully.

"Sorry," she apologized.

"He really gets you worked up."

"There's something about him, Dylan, that bugs me."

"He's not our killer."

"I know, but I still want to check his background."

"So do it."

"I'm calling Perez now."

"Before you do, let's decide on lunch."

"Something spicy," she stated.

"To match your mood?"

~~~~~~~

The food hadn't arrived, but Sheffield attacked the chips as if she had a grudge. She'd already gone through a whole basket and a bowl of salsa. Black found himself watching her with a mixture of shock and adoration. Between bites, Sheffield laid out her plan: review all of the murders side-by-side, and search for unseen common threads. There must be a pattern that would help them predict the next murder—something almost imperceptible.

Black's cell phone vibrated and forced Sheffield to stop mid-sentence. She reached for his bowl of salsa and continued to eat.

"Hi, Gil." Trevor tried the new code name.

"Hi, Enk." Black hoped he'd remembered the name correctly. Sheffield's brow furrowed with inquisitiveness.

"Just wanted to say I'm thinking of you," Trevor said.

"Where are you calling from?"

"The museum. I'm on a break. How's your day?"

"It's getting better."

"Because of me?"

"Mm-hmm."

"Ah. You sure know how to make a boy blush. I'll let you get back to work."

"Okay."

"So I'll see you at my place later?"

Black avoided eye contact with his partner. "How about mine?" he asked.

"You mean I get to see the Bat Cave? I can't wait."

Black laughed, and Sheffield studied him closely, her

curiosity piqued.

"Tonight I get to sex you in your own bed," Trevor continued. "I'm growing quite fond of you, Gil."

"Same here, Enk." He gazed at his partner as he disconnected the call.

Vivienne Sheffield had polished off the last chip and sat staring at her partner. "Oh, good; here comes our food. So who the hell is Enk? He sounds like Superman's arch-nemesis."

"Someone I met recently. The enchiladas look delicious."

"Yeah. The only thing that would make this better is a margarita."

~~~~~~~

When Trevor returned to the museum store after his break, he was ebullient. A bald man flipping through greeting cards looked up and smiled, and Trevor smiled back. A middle-aged woman stepped to the register with a basket of goodies. While Trevor rang up her order—a postcard book of Impressionistic paintings, a Kandinsky-inspired stained glass, and a Van Gogh screensaver—the bald man eyed him surreptitiously. The bald man's expression grew cold. The woman at the register made idle chatter about the warming weather and the new outdoor exhibit. It made the onlooker nauseated; bile rose in his mouth. Happy, stupid, weak people always made him sick. They should have enough decency to fear the violent, turbulent world around them—to fear people like him. The woman left with her purchases, and Trevor arranged some Russian stacking dolls. Finally, the bald man found something of interest, a card sealed in cellophane. On the front was a statue of a beautiful youth, a child born of incest who was loved by two goddesses and killed by a jealous god. Drunk with delirium, he carried the card to the register and laid it down.

"Did you need anything else?" Trevor asked cheerily.

"No," the stranger said in a cool, baritone voice.

"Ah, Adonis. I've seen this statue in real life in Philadelphia. It's amazing."

"I bet." The man handed Trevor a five-dollar bill.

As soon as he was out of sight, Trevor forgot about the

strange customer with the black eyes and the bald head.

Chapter 38

"Okay, I spoke with the ice princess, Dr. Marlena Goodrich, and she vows that Sheldon cooked for her last night, antipasto, and then they watched a movie, *Cold Mountain*. Love that movie; now they've ruined it for me."

"So you're buying her alibi?" Black asked. Like a pouting child, Sheffield shrugged and plopped down in her chair.

"I take it she's like the crazy doctor." Black tossed a Cheez-It into his mouth.

"Cold, arrogant, and indignant," Sheffield answered. "They both have something lodged where the sun doesn't shine." Black offered her a cracker. "Meanwhile, Fenrir is planning his next attack."

"And we have no clues."

Officer Perez rushed toward their desks, took a deep breath, and waved a piece of paper as if brandishing an oracle from Delphi.

Black set down his snack and said, "You look flustered, Amadeo."

"No one named Sheldon Radford ever attended Brown University, let alone graduated from there."

"What?" Black was stunned.

Sheffield jumped to her feet. "I *knew* the bastard was a liar!"

"That confounded me, so I did some digging. It seems that Sheldon Radford is the legal name of one Timothy Finnegan."

Sheffield scrunched up her face. "Someone actually *chose* the name Sheldon Radford?"

Perez took a deep breath. "He changed it before going to grad school."

"So he did graduate from Brown?"

"Yes. And Columbia and Johns Hopkins."

"Why would he change his name?" Sheffield mused.

Black took the paper from Perez. "Why does *anybody* change their name?"

Perez dropped his pièce de résistance: "Maybe it was because his parents died before he left for college."

"Car accident?" Black asked.

"Not exactly. Dad was knifed to death in his office at the local community college by mom; then mom returned home and hung herself. Looks like the whole family was *muy loco*."

"He told us they died in a car accident." Sheffield paced by her desk.

"Any evidence to support the murder-suicide theory?" Black asked.

"Her fingerprints on the knife, no defense wounds, and a suicide note on the nightstand."

Sheffield stopped pacing and reached for Black's Cheez-Its. "Why'd he lie?"

"With you accusing him of being the Wolf, maybe he didn't want to talk about the Sophoclean tragedy of his childhood," Black said. Her look screamed "Ooh, big word." Black ignored it. "And little Timmy was the only heir?"

"The entire inheritance went to him. I'm still checking on background. Dad taught Mythology at the two-year school in their hometown."

"See?" Sheffield exclaimed. "I knew there was something odd about that man."

"Sheffield, just because he lied about his deranged parents doesn't make him our psycho."

"I'm not saying he's our killer. I'm just saying there's something disturbing about him. And I don't like him."

~~~~~~~~

The Lexus pulled onto Sycamore Lane shortly after 7:00 p.m. Black was excited to take his lover to his home for the first time. In anticipation, he'd stopped at CVS to buy a pack of condoms and lube.

The homicide detective was surprised to find another attractive man in Trevor's apartment.

"Dylan," Trevor said, "do you know Marc?" The two men shook hands tightly and all but puffed out their chests like rival gorillas vying for dominance.

"Are you here on police business?" Marc asked inquisitively. "If not, this is kind of a bad time."

"Actually, I'm here on personal business."

"Oh." Marc wasn't certain what that meant. "Trevor and I have something we need to work out, dude."

Trevor responded, "I don't think we have anything else to say."

"Does Kim know you mess around with guys?" Black asked boldly. Marc's head snapped in Black's direction, and his eyes narrowed to cold slits. His chest heaved as he breathed deeply. Unflinching, Black returned his stare.

"You two got a thing?" Marc asked Trevor. "You dumped me for *him?*"

"Maybe you should go back to your girlfriend now—*dude.*" Black placed his hand on Trevor's shoulder.

Emboldened by his anger yet wisely afraid, Marc glowered at the detective. Silence. A jut of his jaw. The shift of his weight. A sharp exhalation of breath accompanying a shake of his head.

"You'll regret this, Trevor," Marc admonished.

Black stepped toward him. "Is that a threat, Marc?"

"Marc, don't be like this." Trevor tried to assuage his anger.

The detective continued, "Because it sounded like a threat, and I know you're not foolish enough to threaten my boyfriend in front of me. I'd hate to have to shoot you and make it look like an accident." He didn't crack a smile.

Realizing the enormity of his mistake, Marc fumbled for an explanation. "I'm not going to hurt him…any more than he's going to hurt from losing me."

"You made your point. Now take off." Black nodded toward the door.

"I hope you two lovebirds are happy." Venom dripped from every word. Marc turned toward the door, turned back as if to add something, and then exited the apartment in a huff.

"What a jackass," Trevor muttered. Black only laughed. Next, he greeted Trevor properly with a long, slow kiss followed by a warm embrace.

"What if he tries to out you at work?" Trevor asked, concerned.

"I'm a big boy. I can take care of myself. Now, get your stuff, and let's go to my place."

"I got my gym bag all set."

"Then move that ass, Enk!"

On the way out, Black watched Trevor closely to be certain that he locked the deadbolt. As they walked to the car, he told Trevor that their code names had made Sheffield suspicious, to which Trevor laughed maniacally.

~~~~~~~

Jennifer Black had dreamed of her ex-husband the previous night. It was the type of nightmare that left a lasting chill throughout the day. In the nightmare, he chased a dark, shapeless, ghostlike killer. After being cornered in a park, the supernatural evil turned and mauled the detective under the blue light of the moon, and she was helpless to save him. It was her heaving sobs that finally wrested her from the disturbing dream. For the entire day, the nightmare nagged at her, distracting her from her work.

Shortly before 6:00 p.m., Jennifer left her office, pulled her car out of the parking garage, and, without any forethought, veered onto SR 70 and headed west toward Normandy.

~~~~~~~

Trevor was stunned when he stepped into the house. He was prepared for plain white walls, posters for art, an empty refrigerator, a paucity of knickknacks, a dearth of color, the box springs and mattress on the floor, clothes strewn about, and an institutional plastic shower curtain with hard-water stains. Instead, Black's house was decorated in a minimalist style, with neutral earth tones throughout. Stainless-steel appliances, dark wood, glass-and-chrome lighting, granite countertops, and geometric shapes gave it a masculine and modern feel. On the queen-sized bed, Egyptian cotton in sage and black covered an expensive mattress. While Trevor's apartment was soft and warm, Black's house was crisp and sleek.

Once the tour was over, the two men prepared dinner: chopping vegetables, steaming rice, searing chicken, and cleaning strawberries. In the background, Josh Groban sang a love song in Italian. Suddenly, there was a knock on the door.

"That better not be a Jehovah's Witness," the detective grumbled, heading for the door.

"Maybe it's a neighbor wanting to borrow a cup of sugar."

"Nah. They're all intimidated by me, 'cause I see dead bodies for a living."

"Well, I certainly hope it's not an ex-boyfriend." Black laughed before opening the door.

"Hi, Dylan," a female voice gushed. "Hope you don't mind me dropping by."

"No, Jenny, come in." He kissed her cheek.

With the grace of a dancer, Jennifer Black stepped into the house. Trevor watched the attractive woman float into the room. Her auburn hair was tucked behind her diamond-studded ears and flowed over her shoulders like silk. She wore a celery-colored blouse with a pinstriped, charcoal skirt and a beaded necklace in emerald and blue. The woman was tall and slender with perfect feminine curves. Their eyes met, and she stopped abruptly.

"Oh. Hi." She smiled widely.

"Hi."

"I'm Jennifer. Are you Trevor?"

"That's me."

"We were fixing something to eat," Black stated. "You're welcome to join us."

"I won't intrude. I just wanted to make sure you're okay."

Black put his hands on her shoulders and looked directly into her eyes. "Did you have another dream?"

"Guilty."

"Everything's fine." He turned toward the kitchen. "Trevor, Jennifer is my ex-wife."

Trevor tried to hide his surprise. "Oh. It's nice to meet you."

"We stayed friends after the divorce." Her expression said, "Imagine that."

"How long were you married?" Once the question escaped his lips, he apologized. "I'm sorry. That's personal."

"Honey, it's okay. We have nothing to hide, and you have every right to ask."

"We were married for two years," Black answered.

"You're beautiful," Trevor said.

"I love this man," she told Black, laughing. "You two should enjoy your meal, and I should head back to Columbus."

"Jenny, you can't head back right now. You drove an hour to get here. Knowing Columbus traffic, probably longer."

"Please stay." Trevor approached. "We fixed more than enough for the three of us. It's stir-fry. We have strawberries for dessert."

"You two should be alone." With that simple sentence, Jennifer Black made clear her understanding of their relationship.

"Jenny, you can't leave," Black insisted.

"The food is done," Trevor announced. "I'll get you a plate." She shrugged in resignation and sat down at the oak dining-room table.

"What do you want to drink?" her ex-husband asked.

"Tea is fine. Do you need help with anything?"

Trevor brought a bowl of stir-fry to the table. "Everything's done."

"Jennifer actually taught me how to cook," Black said. "If we'd stayed married, I'd weigh 300 pounds by now."

"Tell the truth, Dylan. I'm a decent cook *when* I cook. I found any excuse not to prepare a real meal. Whenever I could, it was microwave dinners."

"Her tiramisu is to die for."

"I haven't made that in months. I'll have to make some for Randy."

"I love tiramisu," Trevor said.

Black set the drinks down. "Randy? New boyfriend?"

"That word sounds so high school—'boyfriend.' I just refer to him as my friend. It's good."

"I'm glad."

"And I'm happy for you two," she returned.

Neither responded to her words.

Chapter 39

Sheffield couldn't help herself; she simply *had* to dig into the past of Dr. Radford, formerly Timothy Finnegan. She found newspaper articles and death certificates for Mr. and Mrs. Reginald Finnegan. From the material, it appeared to be just what it said: a homicide-suicide by a jealous and disturbed wife. Yet, no one believed Cathy Finnegan was capable of such violence—not her neighbors, not her mailman, not her high-school teachers. Then again, given the Finnegan family's insular existence, no one really *knew* her at all.

The house was immediately abandoned and then sold the following year at a ridiculously low price to a fan of the occult. In an interview, he claimed that Cathy Finnegan's ghost walked the halls, cried in the night, and caused the lights to flicker. Soon after, the Finnegan family of Edinburgh, Connecticut, disappeared from the news all together. One of the articles talked about "the children," who were homeschooled and had few friends. Maybe little Timmy had multiple personalities. Maybe the neighbors were confused about the hermetic Finnegan family. After a few transfers and a number of minutes on hold, Sheffield eventually had the fortune to talk with the associate registrar at Brown University. She explained the nature of her call and faxed her credentials to the office.

"His name was Timothy Finnegan, and he was from Edinburgh, Connecticut. He studied Classical Humanities. He would have matriculated in the fall of 1986," Sheffield said.

"And you say you're a homicide detective?"

"Yes." Sheffield bit into a Mounds bar.

"So did Mr. Finnegan kill someone?"

"We don't believe so, but his name came up during our investigation."

"I'm pulling up the information. We have an excellent Classics program. If he attended here, I'm sure he's doing well."

He certainly thinks so, Sheffield thought. "He's now a professor here in Normandy."

"The Alumni Office would love to know that."

"Yes," Sheffield commented blankly.

"Hmm. That's interesting."

"What?" Nerves always made Sheffield eat, and she took another bite of Mounds.

"I did a search under the name T Finnegan from Connecticut."

"What did you find?"

"There were *two* T Finnegans—with the *same address* in Edinburgh."

"Excuse me?" Sheffield launched to her feet.

"Both studied Classics. One is Timothy, and one is Tobias. They appear to be brothers. Must be twins because they share a birthday. Ooh, the other brother didn't do well. He dropped out before the end of his first year."

"You're sure there were two of them?"

"Absolutely."

"And you couldn't be mistaken?"

"Of course not," she responded, indignant. "We keep very accurate records."

"I'm sorry. Can you fax me a copy of anything you have about these two?"

"There's little else to give you. I have their old address. I have their student ID numbers and their names. The brother you asked about was named Timothy Frey Finnegan. The other was named Tobias Fenrir Finnegan."

Vivienne Sheffield was speechless. She dropped the rest of her candy bar.

Chapter 40

With some effort, Jennifer Black was finally able to convince her ex-husband to sing a couple stanzas of "American Pie" and do his best Robert De Niro imitation. The three laughed until their sides hurt. She also regaled them with stories of the publishing world. When she talked about her new boyfriend, Randy, she peppered it with comments like "you know how it is" and "you know the feeling." After the meal, she thanked them both for letting her crash their evening.

Black winked at her. "It's nice having you here."

When the CD ended, Jennifer walked over and changed the disk to Etta James. "I think you two make a cute couple," she said. Neither of them responded as they put the last dishes away. "Oh, get over it, you guys! I'm just trying to tell you I'm happy for you."

"Thanks, Jenny," Black said. "You always were good to me."

"Well, not *always*," she replied. He smiled at her. "I'm just glad you have somebody." She held up her hand, pretending to block Black from hearing. "Make sure he doesn't work too hard and that he takes care of himself."

Trevor copied her gesture, pretending to block Black's view. "I will."

Before she left for Columbus, Jennifer told her ex-husband about her dark and disturbing dream. Then she kissed each man on the cheek and slipped away, leaving them to their solitude.

~~~~~~

The Lincoln pulled up to the curb, and Sheffield reached for the file on the passenger seat. From the stereo came the melodic voice of Celine Dion. Though she hated to cut her off in mid-chorus, Sheffield was eager to tell her partner what she had discovered about the weird Classics professor's secret twin. But before her hand reached the stereo button, a light from Black's house caught her eyes. A woman emerged through his front door. Sheffield was unfazed to see Jennifer Black leaving her ex-husband's home. However, Sheffield was surprised to see the third party visible in the doorway. Trevor kissed Jennifer on the cheek; Black did the same. Then, the slightly taller man draped an arm on Trevor's shoulder. Stunned and confused, Sheffield turned off the stereo, as if she would be able to hear their conversation. Jennifer gracefully strode toward her vehicle and immediately pulled away. The front door closed, and Sheffield realized that she had remained undetected.

Unwilling to face the truth, she ignored the meaning of what she'd seen. It stirred in her head like an elusive thought. Then, like a repressed memory emerging from the subconscious, Sheffield heard Jennifer's voice in her head. At the station when she had talked about Black being happy, Jennifer must have been referring to Black's sexuality. Jennifer hadn't been trying to get *Sheffield* to date Black; she had been implying that *Trevor* should date him.

Sheffield decided to confront Radford on her own. Overcoming her shock, she hit the button to resume playing the CD and then pulled onto the road.

~~~~~~~

Oh, what tangled webs we weave, Fenrir thought. First, Jennifer exited the home, and then Sheffield pulled away without making her presence known. Now his ex-wife and his partner knew about his illicit affair. This wasn't the Golden Age of Greece; there were bound to be complicated ramifications to Black's homosexual affair. Fenrir had never understood puritanical views of sexuality; men with women, men with men, women with women, it made no difference to him. He saw homophobia as a sign of fear born from weakness, and he loathed weakness. He was willing to use anyone he could to get what he wanted. He would have even slept with Martin Tillman, president of the Pre-Law Society at that college in New York, if he'd had to in order to get the gavel. He had needed it for his collection, and Martin had been weak.

Now Fenrir watched in silence as the lights inside the home dimmed. Achilles, the adored Achaean hero, and his lover Patroclus, leader of the Myrmidons, were going to bed. Now that Sheffield knew her partner's secret, their relationship would be strained, like that of Achilles and Agamemnon during the Trojan War. Once Achilles and his lover were dead, he would pursue his damnable brother. And then Vivienne Sheffield as the goddess Ishtar, and then Aggie Rhodes as Cassandra, and then…

Chapter 41

After Jennifer Black said her good-byes and they were alone once again, the men began caressing and kissing, playfully teasing each other. Black's and Trevor's passion quickly drew them to the bedroom, where their lovemaking was both tender and carnal. Exhausted but happy, they soaked in a tub of warm, bubbly water. Candles and soft music added ambience. Dancing shadows, like little Kokopellis, reflected on the tiles.

"I'm glad you came to my place tonight," Black whispered in Trevor's ear.

"So am I. It really is a beautiful home."

"When I bought it, I did nothing for the first few months. Once I settled into my new job, I decided to tackle one room at a time. My dad and mom helped." Black ran his fingers through Trevor's wet hair.

"I really like Jennifer," Trevor told him softly.

"Yeah, she's amazing. We went through some tough times when I started realizing I was gay, and she started drinking. I was gone a lot, and then I met Colin. I didn't know how to tell her that I'd fallen in love with a man."

Trevor sponged some warm water on their bodies. "I like her laugh."

"Me, too."

"Did you know you were gay when you married her?"

"Not really. I was confused and in deep, deep denial."

"When did you figure it out?"

"Early on. Within the first year or so. When I met Colin, I realized that I loved Jennifer in a completely different way than I loved him."

"Did she figure it out?"

"Actually, I didn't know that she had until a few months ago, when she told me that she knew about Colin."

Trevor made small circles in the water with his hand.

"Wow."

"Yeah. She's a better friend than I realized."

"Does Viv know? About you, I mean."

"I don't think so. I've never told anybody at the station."

"Hmm."

"I should tell her someday."

"So your parents don't know?"

"I think both of my folks probably suspect. If I'd stayed with Colin, I would have definitely taken him to meet them, and they would have loved him."

"I wish I'd known Colin."

"Sometimes I think if I hadn't met him in that café and ended up in his bed, then I would still be lost and miserable. With Colin, I stopped being afraid of what I felt for another man."

"That's deep."

"But then, I still didn't feel like part of a movement or a subculture. Does that make me sound too much like Marc?"

"No!" Trevor scoffed. Black rubbed his hand over Trevor's chest.

"You know I followed him and saw him with Kim." Trevor turned to face Black but said nothing. "Yeah. I kinda had a crush on you, and I was afraid he was bad news."

"Why didn't you tell me?"

"It wasn't my place. I also did a background check on him."

The young man rubbed Black's chin playfully. "Did you do a background check on me?"

"Sheffield did, when we started the investigation."

"Did you find anything?"

"Clean as a whistle."

"Speaking of, let's get out of this water."

The two men stepped into the shower to rinse the bubbles from their bodies. Then they dried off, dressed in pajama bottoms, blew out the candles, and crawled into bed.

"So we were visited by your ex and my ex in the same night," Black said. "That must be the craziest cosmic coincidence ever."

Trevor chuckled.

Black folded his hands behind his head and said, "Tell me a story."

"What do you want to hear?"

"I don't care. Surprise me."

"Let me think. I want to come up with a romantic one."

The detective said, "I have a question for you: who was Andromeda?"

Trevor rose up on his elbow. "She was a princess who was rescued by Perseus after he killed Medusa. The Greeks believed that from their son Perses came the Persian race."

"How did I know you'd know that?" Black turned on his side and plumped a pillow under his head.

"You thought she was just the name of a ship on a show?" Trevor joked.

Black chuckled. "You get a serious look on your face when you talk about these myths." Self-conscious, Trevor put a hand over his face. "No, no. It's cute." Black caressed the side of Trevor's cheek with his thumb. "And was Adonis a god?"

"He was mortal and later became a demigod. His mother, Smyrna, was cursed by Aphrodite—cursed to sleep with her own father." Trevor made an "ick" face. "When her father tried to kill her, she was turned into a myrrh tree. When the trunk was split open, out tumbled a beautiful baby. Aphrodite locked him in a chest and asked the goddess Persephone to keep him safe in Hades. When he grew up, both goddesses fell in love and fought to have him. Finally, Zeus decided Adonis would spend part of the year with one goddess and part with the other."

"Interesting."

"Yeah, especially since both goddesses were married to other gods."

"Mmm."

"One day, Ares disguised himself as a boar and killed Adonis, because he was jealous."

Black brushed the hair from Trevor's brow. "Our adulterers."

"Yep."

"Everyone knows that Adonis was a beautiful man, but I don't think many of them know the incest stuff," Black said.

"There are some great sculptures of Adonis. In fact, today some guy bought a card with Adonis on it at the store."

Black rolled on top of Trevor.

"All this talk of beautiful men is making me horny, Enkidu."

Chapter 42

Aggie was still unaccustomed to her notoriety as the reporter chosen by Fenrir to be his pen pal. TV stations requested interviews with her, other newspapers asked her to author articles about the madman, and one publishing company had already contacted her about writing a book. She eschewed most of the attention. Refusing to let Fenrir control her life, she shopped at the grocery store, attended her son's recital, spoke at the opening of the new children's oncology wing of the hospital, and continued to report to her job at the *Times*. But Aggie always expected the Wolf to pop out at any moment.

Then it arrived—a new letter from Fenrir. With the slightest quiver, she unfolded the parchment.

> Dear Ms. Rhodes,
>
> Opportunity can still present routes: schools, clubs, outdoors, estates. Attack or death—ever more present.
>
> And you fell for the ruse. You believed it would be you. Stupid cunt. Why would I destroy you when you write such flattering articles about me and my work? You are my pawn. You serve a purpose: to shock and awe the public.
>
> Oh, don't get me wrong. You will die one day at my hands. As will those beautiful children and that loving husband. Get over yourself, you fat cow bitch.
>
> Yours truly,
> Fenrir the Wolf

The detectives had been notified, but before they arrived, she had work to do. With deliberate care and precision, she laid the letter in the copy machine and pressed the green button. The light blinked, the machine hummed, and the copy rolled into the tray. After carefully retrieving the original from the glass top, she transported it as if it were explosives and returned it to the envelope to await the police.

Chapter 43

*My damnable brother was always the good one. I was the elder by
all of ten minutes, and father and mother saw me as the evil Cain
and him as the lovable Abel. Truth be told, Timothy never hurt me,
but I hated him nonetheless. My parents liked to tell me that mother
carried one evil and one good child in the same womb. Then they
gave us both Norse middle names, he a lord and me a monster. As if
they had foresight like Prometheus, they labeled me at birth. They
said I was born with a caul and Timothy was born with a black eye.*

*When we were children, he would break a vase and blame it
on me, and I would be punished. I can't fault him, really. I would
have done the same if the tables were turned, but I still hated him for
it. He had the better toys. One Christmas, he was given a G.I. Joe,
which I had begged for; I was given a copy of the* Iliad. *One day, I
couldn't take his taunts any longer, so I bit into his G.I. Joe and left
my teeth marks. My metamorphosis into the Wolf had begun; I would
become the monster they'd accused me of being.*

*In truth, though, Timothy hated them more than me. It was
relief I felt when he finally killed them. How surprised they must
have been when he showed up on that mission of death. Oh, the
irony! When I heard of their deaths, I knew beyond any doubt that
Timothy had orchestrated them. It was greed that drove him to it. He
had them cremated and buried with no funerals and no good-byes.
When I finally confronted him, he coolly laughed off my accusations,
and then I knew my brother was every bit the monster I was.*

*After the cremation, I found out that Timmy had inherited
everything, and I nothing.*

*To keep me quiet, he agreed to pay for my first year of
college and took me to Brown with him. There, I learned how easily
manipulated mortals are. It was during this time that I started my
collection, my shrine, which was funded by my brother's blood
money. Each day, I stood before my shrine talking to the gods as if I
were their peer, for I was better than other mortals, I was better than*

the demigods and heroes of yore. Soon, I realized that I was better than the ancient, antiquated deities themselves.

Toward the end of the second semester, I demanded more money from Timmy. He lambasted me for my indignation. Then he tried to kill me but failed miserably. My power prevailed. Now I knew how he had felt when he had ended life. It was a rush to think of actually doing it, but I didn't kill my brother that day. Thereafter, I would play the scene in my head and imagine slaying him, like Cain slaying Abel. Yet, I restrained myself and merely left him battered, bloody, and much poorer that day.

It was then that I struck upon the idea of killing my mortal foes—father, mother, lover, brother—as a god. Then I imagined Timmy dead as the Egyptian god Osiris, diced into 13 pieces and filled with lead. I would be his murderous brother, Seth. It was a delicious image.

After years of wandering from city to city, place to place, I lucked upon an article written by my brother, who was now going by the name Sheldon Radford. He still looked like me, except he had hair. I thought of making him my first victim, but what was the fun in that? I wanted him to know I'd become the monster that he and our parents had predicted. I wanted him to know fear again.

Yes, dear Timmy, there's a powerful enemy in your midst, and it's almost time to die. However, I must first kill the hero and his lover, because this cop is fucking pissing me off! I've prepared the devices, readied my plan, and rehearsed the execution. Oh, to rain devastation upon the great hero Achilles by killing his obsequious lover. After he grieves and rages and beats his manly chest, I will then reduce him to bones and flesh and send his cursed soul to the dark house of Hades.

Once Patroclus and Achilles are dead, then I will murder my last remaining relative—my damnable brother.

Chapter 44

Under a new moon and cloudless sky, Sheffield arrived at the
residence of Professor Radford, formerly Timothy Finnegan. In the
abyss of night, the two dimly lit windows resembled golden eyes,
and the red siding appeared black. No movement was evident inside,
but Radford's Saab was parked in the driveway. *Why didn't he park
it inside the garage?* she wondered. Was he going somewhere
tonight? Was his garage full of Greco-Roman artifacts or jars of
fetuses or bodies posed like ancient gods? Was his brother the Wolf,
and was the Wolf living inside the garage like the crazy wife in the
attic in *Jane Eyre*? *Now* she knew she was losing her mind.

There was only one way to uncover the answers. Before
stepping from the Lincoln, she checked her Beretta and left her
jacket open for easy access to her weapon—just in case.

Approaching the front porch, she wished her partner was at
her side. Only her boyfriend, Viktor, knew where she was, and he
had wanted to come along, but she had adamantly refused. Bold and
determined, Sheffield stepped up to the door and pressed the
doorbell. Radford answered almost immediately.

"Detective Sheffield! To what do I owe this pleasure?"

"I'm sorry to disturb you so late unannounced, but I have
some questions for you."

Wearing only a white t-shirt and plaid boxers, he grinned at
her. "Come in. I'm afraid I've had a little too much vino, so forgive
my loose tongue."

Sheffield stepped inside, careful not to move too close to the
professor.

"Would you like some wine?" He proceeded to the kitchen.

"No, thanks. I'm on duty." She found herself studying his
physique as he walked away. She never would have expected him to
have such defined muscles. If he weren't such an arrogant prick, she
might even find him attractive. Sheffield realized that he was a
powerful man, capable of committing the crimes of the Wolf. She

quickly scanned her surroundings. The living room was dark except
for the image on the TV screen. No signs of anyone, including
Marlena Goodrich. Light from the kitchen spilled into the dining
room, and Sheffield could smell wine and cumin, a nauseating
combination.

"This will be quick. Can we sit here to talk?" She pointed to
the dining-room table. Up went his glass, and down went the
chardonnay. He was on the other side of the counter, and, though she
couldn't be certain, she thought he was rubbing his crotch.

"Certainly," he replied, smiling wolfishly.

She selected the seat closest to the exit. As she reached for
her notepad and pen, he rounded the counter, and she could see he
was semi-aroused.

"I'd put on something else, but it's warm in here. Or maybe
it's just the wine."

Showing no fear, the detective met his gaze steadily. She
shifted her arm and felt her gun against her elbow. At that instant,
she realized she might have to kill this man before the night was
through.

"It's about your family," she announced.

"They're dead."

"What's your middle name?"

"Morgan."

"I mean your *previous* middle name."

He looked down and traced some invisible pattern on the
table with his poorly manicured finger. He licked his lips and opened
his mouth, but nothing came out.

"Isn't your birth name Timothy Frey Finnegan?"

"Yes."

"Why'd you change it?"

"It stank." He winked at her.

"And your middle name, Frey, is the name of a Norse god."

"Yes, it means 'lord.' And 'Timothy' means 'he who honors
God.'"

"And your parents didn't die in an automobile accident."
Sheffield watched the man's expression change. The professor
pursed his lips and continued to draw something invisible on the
wooden table. "Why did you lie about your parents' deaths?" she
asked pointedly.

Again, he gave no reply. He made no eye contact. Sheffield expected him to explode and lunge at her.

"Am I under investigation for something?"

"Where's your brother? I don't find a death certificate for him."

"He killed them," Radford muttered.

She waited for him to continue, but he didn't, so she asked, "Your brother killed who? Your parents?"

"Yes."

"Did you tell the police this?"

"I was afraid of him, so I never told the authorities. They thought my mother killed my father then herself, but *he* killed them. Toby hated them. Oh, god, I loved them." He pretended to sob and laid his head down on his arms.

"His name is Tobias Fenrir. Has he changed it?"

"Not that I know of," he mumbled, without looking up. "'Tobias' means 'God is good.'"

"I'm confused. Why would your parents give him a first name that means 'God is good' and a middle name that comes from some monster in Norse mythology?"

"Why would they do *anything* they did? I loved them"—he raised his head—"but they were disturbed. They believed in duality: good and evil, dark and light, and all that. Tobias was named after Christian good and pagan evil, but he was never good."

"But you were only named after Christian good and pagan good?"

"Maybe they knew Toby would grow up to be violent and mean."

"How could they? He was an infant when they named him. They had no way of knowing what he'd be."

Radford slammed his fist on the table. "No! Toby was born evil. I was born with a black eye. His evil started before he was born. My mother felt it in her womb."

She looked at him with a mixture of shock and confusion. How fucking loony could he be? It would be so satisfying to pull her gun and shoot the crazy bastard. The whole family must have been batty.

"I'm sorry," he continued. "The wine makes me demonstrative. My brother was a bad kid. He pulled the legs off bugs and burned them under a magnifying glass. He chased cats into trees and then climbed up and shook the branches 'till they fell to the ground. Don't misunderstand, Detective Sheffield, Toby was deeply disturbed."

Sheffield shrugged.

"*I* had to be good." Radford poked himself hard in the chest. "Toby was more than my parents could bear. They disciplined him, but it had no effect."

"So Toby killed your parents?"

"Right before I went off to college. At first, I didn't know it was him. My parents left me everything, but I agreed to help him get a college degree and turn his life around. One day, he threatened to kill me. I agreed to give him half the money if he disappeared and left me alone forever. That was 15 years ago, and I haven't seen him since."

Sheffield studied her hand just to avoid looking at him.

He cast a plaintive glance and placed both hands on her arms. "*Now* I'm afraid he's followed me here. He wants to kill me—I *know* he does. Please protect me."

His touch was more than she could bear. She pulled her arm away and leaned back in her chair. Weighing her words carefully, she formulated a response.

"Professor, why do you think your brother is out to kill you?"

"Because he's here in Normandy committing these murders!" Spittle flew from his mouth. "He's the serial killer you're looking for. He came here to torment me. I'm his prime target."

"So you think your brother is capable of these killings?"

"Absolutely. My father and mother beat ancient religions into us."

"And you never thought to mention this to us before?"

"I didn't think it could be Toby."

Sheffield eyed him suspiciously.

"Maybe I should have figured it out," Radford defended himself. "You have to understand, I didn't think Toby was *this* crazy!"

Doubting his every word, Sheffield remained stoic.

"Okay, I did start to think it might be Toby after Chief McNally was killed."

"And again, you didn't tell us *why*?" Her disgust was

showing.

"I didn't want you to kill him. He is my brother, my only living relative. But he's coming for *me* now."

Now I know *he's lying. The bastard hates his brother and hopes we'll kill him. Maybe it's about the money.*

"Dr. Radford, we'll need a picture of your brother—the most recent one you have. I'll have a patrol car cruise your neighborhood, but we're stretched thin, and I can't guarantee you protection."

He ran his hand through his unruly hair. "There are no pictures of my brother. I kept nothing after he threatened to kill me."

"Is he your identical twin? Does he look like you?"

"No. Toby and I are fraternal. He is—*was*—a little heavier than me with darker eyes and darker hair. I have no idea what he looks like now."

"Are there any old photos of him from school or social events that we could dig up?"

"We were homeschooled. I don't know of any pictures."

"I'll need you to describe him to a sketch artist tomorrow." She stood. "I'll let you sleep off your wine."

Radford jumped to his feet. "Officer Sheffield, would you stay here tonight?"

She was taken aback. It took the utmost restraint to hide her indignation and revulsion.

"I don't think that will be necessary, Professor. Lock your door, and call the station if you hear from your brother."

She fled the house before Radford could say another word.

~~~~~~~

Again, Aggie studied the correspondence from the serial killer. The margins weren't altered, and there were no hard returns. Still, she read the letters down the left-hand margin, followed by the right-hand margin. She read it in backwards. Then she tried to make words by rearranging the first letters of each line.

There was no postscript, so he hadn't resorted to his original method. No surprise there. The Wolf was too smart to use the same trick again. The first paragraph disturbed her. It was poorly written, almost nonsensical. That had to be where the message was hidden.

Aggie carefully collected the first letter of each word from both sentences:

o c s p r s c o e
a o d e m p

There were three vowels and seven consonants in the first sentence. She formed words:
"cops score"
"press coco"
"cross cope"
The second sentence yielded nonsense as well:
"mad poe"
"pa dome"
"ad poem"
She tried using all 15 first letters, which led to gobbledygook:
"access mud pro bop"
"poem scoop crease"
"doom press cape oc"
"dream scope coos"
"scare doom copes"
"process amo cope"
Still nothing arose from the morass.

It had to be in the first paragraph. The message had to exist somewhere in those 15 words, those 94 letters. But how many possibilities were there? Online descramblers proved useless.

After two hours, she put the letter aside and took a break. Opening a can of diet soda, she said, "You will not win, you bastard."

Chapter 45

Catching up on paperwork, Petkov rubbed her eyes, which she
wasn't in the habit of doing; rubbing tired eyes at the wrong time in
a lab could mean big problems. Since she'd performed no autopsies
this day, she briefly allowed herself the abandon. At that moment,
she wondered what the notorious serial killer who called himself
Fenrir was doing. His crimes had kept her and her staff involved in
some of their most challenging work; yet, for all their efforts, he was
still free to continue acting out his violent urges. The talented doctor
questioned her own part in the investigation. She was supposed to
provide answers, clues that would lead to the killer. So far, she had
provided them little to narrow down their search, but what could she
do? When provided options, she could eliminate or incriminate: the
killer was left-handed; the murderer was female; the DNA from the
crime scene matched the suspect's DNA. She couldn't cull the
perpetrator's address or identity from nothing.

　　　Still, Petkov wondered if she had somehow missed
something—*anything*—that might help bring in Fenrir. She
imagined him: medium build, lean but strong, close-cropped hair,
beady eyes, moderately attractive, deceptively taciturn demeanor,
eerie grin with perfect teeth. She made herself picture him in a
rage—gouging Lawrence Adams in the side, sawing off Kelly
Robison's head after piercing her with a harpoon and handling her
internal organs, slicing Felicity Roth dozens of times with a serrated
clamshell and pummeling Brad Bender with a rock, and slicing off
Chief McNally's hand and then ripping into his throat.

　　　RayAnne, her administrative specialist, knocked and entered.
　　　"Dr. Petkov, you look tired. Why don't you go home early?
There's nothing going on here that can't wait."
　　　"Are those for me, RayAnne?"
　　　"No." Knowing her boss was over-exerting herself, the
protective secretary clutched the folders in her hand and lied, "They
are for the labs." Petkov raised her brow in suspicion. "Petia is

getting so big, and she adores you. Go home to your family."

The CME rose and walked toward the skeleton by her bookcases. "I think I should review these serial killer cases."

"No," RayAnne declared, maternally. "Nothing will be solved here today. I will call Mr. Petkov."

Normally, Nikolina Petkov would have taken offense to her secretary's brazenness—she didn't deal well with having others tell her what to do—but today, she was simply too tired to argue.

"Petia will be surprised to see me home early," she said. "I may even have time for a bubble bath before she arrives."

"Give her a hug for me."

Petkov clicked off her computer and her desk light. It felt decadent to leave work so early. On the drive home, she found herself singing an old Bulgarian song and thinking about where she had put the bath salts.

~~~~~~

"You went to his place without me!" Black yelled. "Why would you *do* that? His brother is probably our killer."

"Relax, will you?" Sheffield flipped her ponytail behind her. "And stop yelling. You're acting like a parent, and if you don't stop yelling, I'll hit you."

Officer Perez couldn't help but smile, though the interrogation room where the three had gathered was feeling cramped. Black muttered threateningly under his breath.

"Besides," she continued, "weren't you otherwise occupied last night?"

Casting a sideways glance at her, Black remained mute. She could see that she'd rankled him.

"So what'd he say?" Perez asked impatiently.

"First off, he creeped me out. He was half lit and half dressed. He cried tears and put on a good show, but he clearly hated his parents." She gesticulated as she spoke.

"Then he tells me how Tobias—he called him Toby—was a bad seed who tortured animals for sport and constantly misbehaved. Said he was born with a black eye where Toby socked him in the womb. Like I'd believe that shit. He claimed his brother scared him into giving up a wad of money."

"Their poor parents," Perez said.

"He says his brother killed them."

Perez exclaimed, "*Dios mio!*"

"Radford says he hasn't seen his brother since they were undergrads in college. He thinks his brother is coming after him. Why he didn't think this before, I have no idea. He actually asked me to stay at his place."

"He *what?*" they yelled in unison.

She mouthed the words "*Oh*, yeah." Then she added, "He's even more of a freak than I thought. I'm not buying the whole 'I was the good son and Toby was the devil's spawn' routine. And I *swear* he was touching himself while we talked. Freak with a capital F."

"Damn, I'm getting goose bumps." Perez held out his arm and shivered.

"So, no pictures of his brother, no address—nothing?" Black asked.

"Nope. But I wouldn't be surprised if he's protecting him."

"Why would he do that? Maybe they're working in consorts."

"A killing team, like Bianchi and Buono, the Hillside Stranglers," Perez offered.

"I don't think so," she responded, "because he seems to really hate his brother. One thing I know is that he's a fucking liar besides a creepy perv. I was ready to shoot the son of a bitch if he touched me again."

"Again?" Black and Perez said in unison.

"Relax, dads. He merely touched my arm. It made my skin crawl."

"So we put out an APB on this Tobias Finnegan?" Perez asked.

"Radford is coming in to help us get a sketch. They're apparently fraternal twins, so *not* an identical match. I wonder how much they look alike. Anyway, after he comes in for the sketch, I think we play it cool and don't spook Fenrir."

Black said, "Perez, can you check neighbors, relatives, and friends in Connecticut? Sheff, I'll start checking addresses, name changes, and driving records."

"And I'll check financial records, accounts, and taxes."

"He's within our reach. We're going to get him this time."

Before they exited the interrogation room, Sheffield remembered the letter.

"Oh, yeah, we need to talk with Aggie about the letter she received yesterday."

"It can wait," Black said. "We've got to find Tobias Finnegan now."

Chapter 46

Sitting at the kitchen table, Jasmine Rhodes giggled as she looked up from her *Dora the Explorer* book. Her mother had cut out dozens of letters, and they danced around the table as her mother pushed them this way and that. Little Jasmine, who would start kindergarten in the fall, knew she couldn't read the words her mother was making and suspected that her mom had no idea what she was doing. Aggie mumbled something unintelligible, and Jasmine giggled again. Her mom could be so funny.

Aggie had spent hours deciphering. Certain the first paragraph was the key, she ignored the rest of the note, which was classic Fenrir "I'm better than everyone else" rant.

Jasmine turned a page, and then mother and daughter looked up from their respective texts and made eye contact. Both smiled and winked. Jasmine giggled, closed her book, and rose up on her feet. Standing in the chair, she leaned over the table and studied her mother's work, as if she were going to assist her.

Aggie started sliding letters again. She put the sentences back to their original form: "Opportunity can still present routes: schools, clubs, outdoors, estates. Attacks or death, ever more present." Then she started with the first letter of each word:

o c s p r s c o e
a o d e m p

Knowing this had led nowhere before, she started collecting the second letter of each word and placing them in front of the others. She planned to continue until she was out of letters. Jasmine was so engrossed in her mother's antics that she forgot the rules and sat down on the edge of the table. The girl watched her mother slide more letters. After fixing the messy rows, her mother continued shifting the scraps of paper. Soon, she had a string of nonsense:

o c s p r s c b u   p a t r o c l u s   p n i e e u h u s e
a o d e m p   t r e v o r   t - a e r e

Over half the letters were resituated, and two of the words

were completely used up. Before continuing, Aggie stopped and glanced at her work. There it was! She had it! She had him!

Aggie jumped up, and Jasmine stood upright in the chair and giggled. Surely her mom was trying to make her laugh. She was turning in circles with her fists clutched in the air and saying "I got you, you son of a bitch!" Jasmine couldn't help but clap at her mother's fantastic performance, and yet she had no idea that her mother had just outfoxed a wolf.

~~~~~~~~

There was no house, no apartment, no condo, and no hotel room in Normandy in the name of Tobias Fenrir Finnegan. His last driver's license was issued in Connecticut but had expired in 1989. His last bank account had been closed after he had cashed a check for $250,000 and withdrawn the last $52.19 from his savings. His last known residence was a dormitory at Brown University. There were no credit cards, loans, or other financial accounts in his name. For all intents and purposes, Tobias Finnegan had simply ceased to exist.

"How can he just disappear?" Black asked, exasperated. Sheffield pushed her chair away from her desk.

"He must be living off the money he extorted from his brother Timothy."

"And he hasn't bought a car? He doesn't have a checking account?"

"Obviously, he's figured out some living arrangement without signing Tobias Finnegan—or Fenrir the Wolf—on a piece of paper."

"Maybe he's squatting on unused property." Perez clicked away on the computer.

"Like staying in someone's house for the winter?" Black wasn't buying it.

Sheffield put her hands on her hips and stared out the window. "I've been thinking; he's been traveling all over, collecting wolf hair and scorpions and pewter figurines, so maybe he doesn't live in Normandy at all. Maybe he just drifts into town to commit murder and freak out his brother and then leaves."

Perez chimed in. "Maybe he still lives in Connecticut. Or Arizona, where he got the scorpions and the rock."

"I don't know." Black disfigured a paperclip. "My gut tells me he's here watching and stalking. The letters to Aggie, which are all postmarked in the Normandy area, and the randomness of the murders."

"So where do we look next?" Sheffield asked.

Perez slid his chair over to their desks. "We got someone watching his brother. Maybe he'll go after him next."

"Could the Wolf know we're on to him?" Sheffield asked.

"That we've figured out he's Tobias? If so, he won't attack Radford and risk getting caught."

Black placed the mangled paperclip on his desk like a piece of modern art. "See, I think that's exactly what he'd do. Nothing would prove his power more than taking someone right in front of us."

"We pulled the prof's phone records," Perez added. "No suspicious activity."

"So you think we watch Radford and wait for Fenrir to show up?" Sheffield asked.

"I think we'll drive him to a killing spree if we run the photo," Black responded.

"But if we don't, and he kills again, the media could eat us alive."

"It's a risk either way."

Sheffield put a hand on Perez's shoulder. "Will you continue looking for any place where Fenrir may be hiding? Someone has to have seen him come and go." She looked at Black. "I think we should canvass some neighborhoods and flash his picture to see what comes up."

Black's cell phone rang. "I'm going to answer this."

It was Trevor. "Hey, sexy. How's my favorite homicide detective?"

"Anxious," Black replied. "We think we know who Fenrir is." Sheffield eyed Black inquisitively while Perez slid over to the computer.

"Holy shit!" Trevor responded. "Who? Can you tell me?"

"Hold on to your hat. It's Radford's twin brother."

"The Classics professor? He has a killer brother?"

"Looks that way. Apparently, his brother Tobias was a bad seed, and dad crammed the 'wrath of the gods' crap down their throats. Radford changed his name after the brother killed their folks."

"Oh, my god! This is like *All My Children* stuff."

Sheffield pretended not to listen while she opened a package of cashews and bit into one.

"Listen, do you have any ideas where the Wolf may be hiding? Is there some place that would make sense symbolically?"

"No. I mean, the mythical Fenrir wandered around Asgard, which was literally 'God Land' or heaven, until he was fettered by Tyr. When he broke free, he fought at Ragnarok on the Vigard Plains and died there."

"So, he didn't live in a cave or underground or something like that?"

"No. Do you think he'll go after his brother?"

"That's what we expect." Black looked up at Sheffield, who mouthed "Trevor" just to let him know that she knew.

"Can you think of what day of the week he may have in mind?" Black asked.

"Well, he's already killed on Wednesday, Tuesday, Friday, and Sunday. That leaves Monday, Thursday, and Saturday—Moon's Day, Thor's Day and Saturn's Day. A wolf ate the moon in Norse mythology, but it was a woman, so not Monday. Thor killed Fenrir's brother Jormungand, so there's a brotherly reference there. Maybe Thursday."

"And it's Wednesday, so we may not have much time. We're keeping a close eye on Dr. Freaky undercover, so Fenrir won't know. Let's hope we get him."

"Be careful."

"So, who *finally* killed Fenrir?"

"Odin's son Vidar; he didn't speak, so he was called 'the Silent God.' At Ragnarok, after Fenrir swallowed Odin, Vidar stepped on Fenrir's lower jaw and pulled on his upper jaw until he ripped Fenrir in two."

"Nice. So Vidar the Silent One it is."

~~~~~~

Millicent Deaver sat crying at her small dining-room table. Her dull hair was a rat's nest, her teeth weren't brushed, her eyes were red, and her face was blotchy. She was a mess. The table was littered with sugar she had spilled trying to sweeten her coffee. The terrycloth robe was stained and ripped, making her look like a vagabond. With her legs folded in front of her, she wiped her nose on the knees of the flannel pajamas. Because her lover had not called in months, her heart had broken in twain. She'd gained weight and stopped cleaning her apartment. She had even lost interest in working at the zoo because it reminded her of him. Something or someone must be keeping her lover from her.

The poor, grieving woman ran a finger over the bold, black newsprint: "Normandy Serial Killer 'the Wolf' Still at Large." Her feelings vacillated from longing to anger, from love to vengeance. She could barely keep herself from calling the Normandy police. Never did she believe that her lover was the killer, but she thought the wolf hair at the crime scenes was most likely the same wolf hair that she'd lovingly and obediently gathered from the pup Cheyenne. The killer must have taken it from her boyfriend, maybe even hurt her lover.

Millicent picked at her toenails while she debated what to do. Should she call the Normandy police? Would her lover be mad at her? What if he was in trouble? Her head was spinning. She wished he'd call her and end her suffering. She wanted him back even if he'd made mistakes. Where was he?

Finally, she put her feet on the floor and sat upright. She wiped her eyes and blew her nose. The headline in the newspaper spoke to her. Millicent felt better for having made a decision. She had finally figured out what to do.

Chapter 47

Because of his late-night trysts with Black, Trevor was yawning all the way through his Wednesday shift at the museum store. It had been a slow day for the most part. After talking with Black on the phone, his adrenaline had surged, but soon, the endorphins faded from his system and left him even more enervated than before. At 6:00 p.m., his shift was finally over. Maybe he could get home and nap before Black arrived. When he grabbed his keys, he remembered the gift he'd bought for his lover—a Celtic pocket cross. He clutched it in his hand and headed to his car.

The June sky was bright blue and the air was warm, but the forecast was calling for rain and thunderstorms. He found himself thinking about Jennifer Black. In the fall semester, he'd be taking a course on addiction, and Jennifer seemed open to talking about her dependence on alcohol and her road to recovery. Maybe she'd be willing to let him interview her for class. More importantly, maybe she'd share some juicy secrets about Black: what he was like when they first met, what was the best gift he ever gave her, what were his pet peeves, what made him happy, where his spot was. He put the key in the door of his Saturn.

Before he lost consciousness, he was blissfully lost in thoughts of Black and the future.

~~~~~~~

The phone on her belt vibrated, and Sheffield looked down to see the incoming number.

"Oh, damn!" she exclaimed. "We didn't pick up the letter sent to Aggie. I'll let it go to voicemail."

"We better send somebody for it," Black said.

Perez jumped up. "I'm on it."

Sheffield paced. "We got to figure out where Fenrir might be.

We're so close."

There was still no record of Tobias Finnegan since he had left during his second semester at Brown. Under suspicion that he was using an assumed identity, they tried to trace a path from Rhode Island back to Connecticut and then to Ohio. They had obtained the photo of Tobias from his last driver's license and decided it was best to release it to the press before Thursday, since they expected him to go for his brother then. Hopefully, someone who knew his whereabouts would come forth. Maybe he'd glommed onto some poor, unsuspecting, lonely woman who was unintentionally harboring the killer. They were so close to finding him and were prepared for anything.

Or so they thought.

Chapter 48

Perez was about to leave when Officer Flowers stopped him to take an urgent call from a reporter at the *Normandy Times*. The timing seemed serendipitous, since he was leaving to go to her house. Unable to reach either homicide detective directly, the reporter had called the station with a desperate plea to speak to anyone associated with the God Killer case. After talking to her, Perez dropped the phone and rushed to catch Black and Sheffield.

"I just talked to Aggie," he exclaimed. "She's got something."

"The last letter?" Sheffield asked.

"No, *more*." The two detectives looked at him. "She's found a message. Aggie knows who he's going for next."

Perez reached for Black's desk phone, hit 'speaker,' and punched the numbers in quick succession. Aggie answered before the first ring.

"Detectives?" the reporter yelled.

"We're here," Black said. "You're on speaker phone. What've you got?"

"Two names. I searched every way I could for some hidden name. I tried anagrams, first letters, last letters, but I wasn't finding anything." She was so anxious that she was hyperventilating. After a couple of deep breaths, she continued. "Then I focused on the first two sentences because they were so awkward. Then I found them, the two names." She took another deep breath.

"Did he give the name Timothy or Sheldon?"

"No," she gasped.

"Frey?" Sheffield asked.

"No."

"Aggie, calm down," Sheffield said. "Tell us the two names."

"The first I didn't recognize, so I didn't realize I'd even *found* a name, but the second was unmistakable. When I looked the first one up on the Internet, I found out he was a character from the

Iliad."

The three waited with anticipation, unable to move. All they could hear was deep breathing. Then a little girl asked, "Mommy, are you okay?"

"Yes, sweetie," Aggie told her daughter. "Now go play in the living room while mommy talks on the phone. I'll be there in a minute." Having sent Jasmine away, she returned to the phone. "Detectives, the first name is 'Patroclus.'"

"Got it." Black wrote it down. "And the second?"

"Trevor."

"Oh, my god," Sheffield blurted out, as Perez said the same in Spanish. Black was frozen for a split second, and then at lightning speed he flipped open his phone and dialed.

One ring.

Two rings.

Please answer, he thought.

Three rings.

Four rings.

Someone answered the phone. Black waited to hear Trevor's voice, but there was only silence. Eyes wide in anticipation, Sheffield and Perez hovered close.

Then Black asked, "Trevor, are you there?"

"He's here, Detective," a cold, unfamiliar voice said. "At the sharp end of my spear. And there's nothing you can do to stop me from murdering your precious, fawning lover. I suppose we need no introductions. I'm Fenrir the Wolf."

Then Black heard the scariest thing of his life: silence.

Suddenly, the phone went dead.

Chapter 49

"Damn it! He's got Trevor."

"What?" Sheffield exclaimed.

Black frantically redialed the number. "The bastard answered his phone."

"What did he say?"

"That he's got him at the end of his spear, that I can't stop him. Then the son of a bitch called himself Fenrir the Wolf."

Sheffield launched into action. She had to maintain composure while her partner tried to keep from exploding as he redialed Trevor's cell phone to no avail. Sheffield took the photo of Tobias from the old Connecticut driver's license and the sketch made from Radford's description and instructed Perez to release them to the media with the story that the killer had abducted a young man. Next, she held up a piece of paper and made Black write down Trevor's phone number. While her partner continued to hit redial, Sheffield initiated a trace on all calls made from and to Trevor's phone.

Black paced feverishly, and Sheffield had no doubt he'd kill Fenrir with his bare hands if he could. Her biggest concern was keeping her partner from self-destructing until they caught the madman—hopefully while Trevor was still alive. Calmly, she led him to the conference room. Officer Davis rushed toward them, but she stopped him with a raised hand. She mouthed the words "one moment," and the man stood in place by some filing cabinets. Once inside the conference room, Sheffield shut the door.

"Dylan, we need to find Fenrir before he hurts Trevor. You need to hold it together."

He looked at her and said nothing. Behind his eyes, his mind was racing a million miles a second. He was desperately trying to formulate a plan. "I've got to stop him," Black said.

"We're running Fenrir's picture on the news. I need a photo of Trevor, so we can run that, too. It'll help in case someone has seen them."

"We'll get one from his apartment."

"We also need to trace Trevor's steps. Do you know where he would have been last?"

"He should have been at the museum until 6:00."

Sheffield looked at her watch and then at the wall. "Dylan, it's only 6:35. He can't have had him more than half an hour. I'll have someone follow up with the museum, and we'll look for his car. If it's gone, we'll put out an APB on it."

"It's a Saturn," Black muttered blankly.

"Okay. We'll run the plates."

"I talked to him less than an hour ago, Sheff. Fenrir must have followed me."

"Or him. Regardless, he knows about your relationship with Trevor." Black gave her a questioning glance. "So he's your boyfriend or lover or whatever. You can have your coming-out crisis later, but Fenrir's got him now. Look, I can do this *alone* if you can't keep it together."

Black shook his head. "No, I have to be involved."

"Then you've got to be a cop—not a boyfriend—right now, if we're going to save Trevor."

"He took him because of me." Black looked crestfallen.

Sheffield grabbed her partner's face in her hands. "Dylan, you got to get a fucking grip. He may have taken Trevor just because he's helping us with the case. He's going to kill him if we don't stop him. I can do this with or without you. What'll it be?"

Something inside Black snapped. "I'll get the photo of Trevor, and you call the museum director."

Sheffield shook her head. "It'll be better if we stay together."

As they exited the conference room, Sheffield spotted Officer Davis still standing by the filing cabinets and waved him over.

"The reporter who gets the letters from the killer faxed these to you." Davis handed her some papers. "She said they might help."

They were printouts about the Greek heroes Patroclus and Achilles and the Trojan War. Sheffield tucked them in her pocket and sped off with her partner.

~~~~~~~

Trevor felt like he was emerging from a coma. His body was weak and unresponsive; his mind was disconnected. *Have I been in a car accident?* But the chandelier above him wasn't standard hospital lighting, and the hard surface beneath him wasn't a bed. Trevor realized that something was covering his mouth, so he wiggled his lips. *Why is there tape on my mouth?* A groan escaped as he tried to roll. That's when he realized that his arms and legs were bound. With great effort, he turned his head to the left and saw a living room. The curtains were closed, and the room appeared almost sepia. He was lying on a dining room table.

As he rolled his head to the right, the hard surface jostled his brain. Wearing a plain white t-shirt and jeans, a bald man with piercing black eyes stood beside him.

"Hello, Trevor."

The man, whose eyes were menacing and emotionless, leaned closer and wiped the hair from Trevor's brow. Because of his baldness, his age was difficult to determine, but Trevor guessed he wasn't even forty. The similarities to Radford were evident: same brow, cheeks, and chin. This had to be Tobias Finnegan, the one who called himself Fenrir the Wolf.

"Don't cower." As he hovered over Trevor, their noses almost touched. His breath had a citrus aroma. "Is that any way for an Achaean hero to act when faced with his enemy? Don't spoil this for me." He grinned. "Of course, I will kill you. But first, I want to taunt your Achilles into a rampage. I bet he's fuming like a bull of Poseidon right now." The killer stood upright and smiled. "Ah, I see you know who I am. You're sleeping with my enemy."

~~~~~~~

The entrance lane of the Normandy Art Museum circled a large sculpture of Cupid and Psyche. To the left of the museum was a small lot for staff parking, while the larger public was situated in front. The parking areas were completely vacant except for one stray car that proved to belong to a woman who had ridden with friends to a nearby restaurant.

The museum director pulled up behind Sheffield's vehicle

while the detectives scanned the lots. A glint on the pavement caught Black's eye. He stooped and picked up a metallic object.

"Director, I'm Detective Sheffield. We spoke on the phone. And that's Detective Black." She pointed to her partner, who was engrossed in the shiny object.

The middle-aged director was extremely skinny. "Yes. On the way over, I did what you asked and called the manager. Trevor worked until 6:00 and left the building alone."

Sheffield turned to her partner. "Find something?"

"This." He held out his hand, and the trio peered down at the object.

"A Celtic cross," the director informed them.

"It's Trevor's," Black said.

"How do you know?" his partner asked.

"I *know*. He's all about this ancient stuff, and he was just reading me a story about how some Celtic queen almost defeated the Romans. Trevor had this when he came to his car."

"Boudicca," the director said. "Queen of the Iceni people in Great Britain."

Sheffield was doubtful of Black's conclusion. "Do you think he was taken from here?"

Black nodded his head. "Fenrir's getting bolder. He thinks he can't get caught."

"Then where's *Trevor's* car?"

"Maybe nearby."

"I'll call in help to canvass the area." She pulled out her cell phone.

"Maybe Fenrir was in Trevor's car and hijacked him."

"So then the killer's car could be nearby. I'll have them look for suspicious vehicles in the surrounding blocks. And check taxis and buses."

While Sheffield dialed the NPD, Black approached the director.

"You got video of every visitor coming into the museum?"

"Yes."

"We'll need it. Maybe he was stalking Trevor."

Repulsed, the director sneered. "I'll get the tapes for you immediately."

"Have them delivered downtown to an Officer Perez."

"Now?"

Black nodded emphatically.

"Okay," Sheffield said, "they'll start canvassing the area. You got the surveillance tapes?"

"Our friend there will get them to Perez."

"Then you and I need to get the photo of Trevor on the news and make sure everyone in Ohio is looking for Fenrir and Trevor."

~~~~~~~~

The TV broadcast his photo, and he was shocked by his image, although he barely resembled it any more since he'd matured and filled out since the photo was taken. So they knew who he was and that he had Trevor, but they still didn't have a fucking clue where he was or what he had planned. Maybe the police thought this gave them a chance, even an advantage, but he knew he was still smarter than them. After killing Patroclus, Achilles, and his brother, he had special plans for Vivienne Sheffield. She may be a bumbling detective, but she was hot, and he couldn't let all that beauty go to waste. After that, he'd move to another city to continue his spree.

He'd do the same thing in the new city that he'd done here: find a lonely, elderly person in an out-of-the-way house, kill the coot, bury the body, and carry on their finances with their ATM card and checks. It was amazing how long you could make people believe that someone was still alive when no one cared. This is what he'd done to Nelly Parker, the former occupant of the house he now resided in. The poor soul now rested in a shallow grave in her backyard by a row of pansies.

Though the news anchor was pleading for anyone with information to come forward, he was confident no one would. He turned from the TV and returned to the kitchen to torment his prey.

"Your damn boyfriend keeps calling. I think I'll answer the next time and tell him that I've removed a finger." He held up a kitchen knife and studied his reflection in the blade. An evil smile crossed his lips; then he gazed at Trevor. "You want to lose a finger now?" After he'd made his introductions, Fenrir had slid Trevor from the table and bound him with handcuffs and rope to a chair. Unable to hold it any longer, Trevor had peed.

"I really want to talk to you," the killer said. "None of my other prey were worthy, but you, Patroclus, know the ancient tales. You know of me, the wolf who devoured Odin and bit off the hand of Tyr. Yes, I want to talk to you, but first I need to know that you'll behave."

The killer walked over to Trevor and placed the flat of the knife against his cheek. Then he slowly drew the cold knife across the young man's skin. They eyed each other coldly, Fenrir showing no compassion and Trevor showing no fear. Next, the killer placed the tip of the blade to his prey's throat. As he pressed the blade, the metal slowly dug into his skin, and the hostage pulled back. Without warning, Fenrir threw the knife in the air, caught it in his grasp, raised it high, and plunged it into Trevor's thigh. The young man's back arched, his eyes grew wide, and a muffled scream escaped through the gag. Until that moment, Trevor had remained defiant. Now he realized that he was going to die at the hands of this killer.

"So are you ready to talk without screaming for help? I don't want to listen to you yelling. It'll ruin my buzz."

With one quick jerk, the Wolf pulled the knife from Trevor's leg and laid the weapon on the table. Warm blood oozed from the wound, and Trevor felt his head begin to swim. Fenrir yanked the tape from his captive's mouth. Instinctively, the hostage stretched his mouth to loosen the muscles.

"So, Patroclus, how are you?" The killer gave a mock expression of concern.

"I've been better." His voice sounded scratchy and foreign to him. So *this* was hell.

"Tell me, are you a fan of my work?"

"Not exactly."

"I'm crushed." He pulled out a chair, sat across from Trevor, and glanced down at the spreading blood. "You aren't going to die on me tonight, I hope. You can't die until tomorrow."

"Thor's Day."

"*Sehr gut*," he said with a flourish.

"So you figured out the significance of the days. I do it because I can. After the way the gods have treated me, it was time for them to die."

"You're so full of yourself," Trevor spat. "You aren't better than the gods. You aren't better than the humans you prey upon.

You're lower than a dog."

"I'm the Wolf; don't fuck with me," Fenrir seethed between clinched teeth. "Guess what I'm going to do to you, you little piss ant?"

"Since you've been calling me Patroclus, I guess you're going to play Hector and kill me."

"What else?" The monster sat back, folded his arms, and placed a foot between Trevor's legs, as if he might kick his chair backwards. "You know my M.O. Describe your murder scene."

"Ants, since Patroclus was a Myrmidon, and the Myrmidons were made from ants."

"Good, good. See I like this. What else?"

"The armor of Achilles."

Fenrir wiggled his socked foot against Trevor's injured leg, and the white cotton started turning red from the blood.

"Nice."

"A lock of Dylan's hair, if you could get it."

"Why?" Awaiting a response, he cocked his head.

"Because Achilles cut off a lock of his hair in mourning." Trevor moved his leg and winced in pain.

"Don't forget that he sacrificed dogs and horses for his lover. Tell me more. You're giving me a hard-on." Fenrir licentiously rubbed his groin.

"Something to represent the funeral games. Maybe a discus."

"Keep going, or I may have to stab the other leg." The beast folded his leg onto his thigh and touched the bloody sock.

Trevor felt pain radiating up his leg. "The ashes of bones."

"Why?"

"Patroclus and Achilles were cremated, and their ashes mixed and buried, so they could be together forever."

"I don't have bone ash, but I should have thought of that." Tobias/Fenrir rubbed his chin in exaggerated contemplation. "Maybe I'll take one of *your* bones to make powder for your lover's murder scene."

"You know who killed Fenrir the Wolf?" With little to lose, Trevor decided to challenge the beast. "Odin's son Vidar. Dylan Black is your Vidar, and he's going to rip you in two."

The Wolf's expression grew hard and he froze for a moment before reaching over and digging his fingers into the wound on

Trevor's leg. The poor, injured hostage felt the most intense pain of his life before he lost consciousness for the second time.

~~~~~~~

After slipping off her heels and dress, Jennifer Black stood in her bra and panties and debated jeans or sweats. The flat-screen TV mounted to the wall broadcast the local news. Ultimately, she opted for a pair of lavender sweats. Once she'd pulled on the pants, while still finagling with the top, she glanced at the TV screen and felt her chest tighten. It was Trevor, the man she'd met days before, the man sleeping with her ex-husband. Frantically looking for the remote, she spotted it on the bedside table and lunged for it. Though she caught only a small portion of the broadcast, it was exactly what she had thought: Trevor was missing, and Fenrir had him. She said a quick prayer before changing into jeans, packing a small suitcase, and setting the house alarm. Once behind the wheel of her car, Jennifer dialed her ex-husband's cell phone. As expected, his voicemail picked up.

"Dylan, I saw the news. I know you're upset, and you have to be busy trying to find him. Listen, I saw the guy who calls himself the Wolf outside your house."

~~~~~~~

Radford was unpleasantly surprised to see the homicide detectives at his door. They appeared highly agitated and entirely unamused by his salutation: "Are the Fates smiling on me today?"

"We need to talk now," Black insisted.

"Have you caught my brother?" Radford asked.

"No, and we believe he has another victim."

Radford was crushed. "It's not me? He went after someone else?"

"Very astute," Black stated dryly.

"We need answers." Sheffield pushed her way inside.

When Radford tried to offer them a drink, the detectives spoke over him. He loathed being ignored more than anything else. How dare they treat him like he was nothing! They were getting on his bad side.

Sheffield tried to keep her partner from talking. "Professor, do you know of any aliases your brother may be using? Could someone be sheltering him?"

"If I knew anything, I would have told you, wouldn't I? After all, my life is in danger here. Toby is crazy, and he hates me."

"Yeah, about that." Black's voice was set to stun. "Now that he has another victim, he clearly isn't coming for you, so we can remove the officer watching you."

"What? But you don't know that he won't come for me after he's butchered this poor schmuck he's torturing now."

Black grabbed the professor by his shirt and slammed him against the wall. The force dislodged something on the other side of the wall, and it crashed to the floor.

"Look, Radford, nothing would make me happier than to hand you over to your psycho brother, you arrogant prick. The way I see it, you withheld information from us over the past *year* while these murders were happening." He leaned close and spoke through clenched teeth. "You knew these killings were the work of your brother, and you didn't say a thing."

Radford didn't respond. He'd suspected from the beginning that his brother was the psychopath committing these murders, but he wanted to get back the money Toby had extorted from him. Radford believed that this time, he could kill his brother. That's why he'd hidden weapons all around his home and even in his office. When Toby showed up, he'd get to the nearest weapon and overpower his loathsome brother. Once he'd extracted information about where the money was, then he'd kill him and be rid of his last fucking family member.

"Have you seen the news?" Sheffield asked the professor. Black let go of the man and walked away. "Your brother's face is out there. Now, we could spread the word that you fingered him. That would probably piss him off. And of course the media would come after you, too. That could make your life interesting—twin brother of a serial killer."

"I don't know what you want, but these lame threats aren't going to help. I've told you everything I know."

Black flipped open his phone. He dialed a number and waited. "Yeah, this is Black. Call off the plainclothes watching the

Radford place." Black looked at Sheffield for a brief moment and then headed out the door.

"You're as disturbed as your brother." Sheffield stopped on the threshold. "Better lock your doors and check your windows. Not that it's stopped your brother up to this point. If he wants you, he'll get you."

As he watched the detectives pull away, Radford's eyes grew narrow and inflamed. An effluvium of anger roiled forth, and he pounded the wall until his knuckles bled. He hadn't felt such hatred since killing his harpy mother and controlling father. Somehow, he would exact retribution on the detectives for treating him like a nobody.

~~~~~~~

As Sheffield reached the car, Black's phone rang. His face was still red, and he was breathing heavily.

"Hello."

"Your boyfriend is no fun," Fenrir said. "He's already passed out again."

"You filthy fucker! You'd better not hurt him."

"Too late."

"Where are you? Why don't you come and face me like a real man?"

"Oh, Detective Black, you really are a buffoon. Did you think you could challenge me to a duel, and I'd show up at high noon?"

"Listen, you want *me*, not Trevor. Take me. We'll set up an exchange."

"That wouldn't be right. Your lover must die first."

"No! He's not Patroclus."

The killer paused. "So, Agatha Rhodes found my hidden message? That cunt! I didn't think she had the brains to figure it out. Well, it doesn't change anything. Patroclus must die."

"And that makes me Achilles? So you're coming for me next."

"What do you think?"

"I think you have some sick fantasy and want to piss me off

by killing Trevor."

"You should see your lover—fallen, bloody, battered."

"So you start with your parents and think you can go on killing?"

"My parents? Timmy told you that *I* killed our parents?" Fenrir laughed out loud. "Oh, that is wonderful. Why don't you ask Timmy how he drove the knife into father's gut and then how he strangled our mother and hung her from the rafters? My dear Achilles, my brother has lied to you. He killed our folks, even though they trusted him. Actually, I admired him for doing it— though he's a fucking toad."

"Why would he do that?"

Fenrir screamed into the phone, *"BECAUSE HE HATED THEM!"* Then he regained some semblance of composure. "Tell Timmy that I'm coming for him after I kill you."

Black was going to try to negotiate a trade, but the line went dead before he got the chance to say another word.

Chapter 50

Jennifer hadn't found her ex-husband at home—but then, she hadn't expected to. On her way to the police station, thoughts of Trevor suffering at the hands of this madman made tears well up in her eyes. Maybe she could have stopped his abduction. First Colin, and now Trevor. This would devastate Black beyond all reckoning. She whipped into the parking lot, ran into the station, and was informed that Black and Sheffield were out. She waited patiently in an interview room with a cup of hot tea in hand. A sketch artist arrived to update the drawing of Fenrir. With a bald head and a fuller face, he became much more recognizable. She called her boyfriend, Randy, but he couldn't talk. She tried reading an old copy of *People*, but even an interview with Jake Gyllenhaal couldn't distract her, so she gave up and sat quietly sipping tea.

Finally, Black walked into the room. "Jenny, what are you doing here? It's not a good time."

"They didn't tell you?"

"Tell me what?"

"I saw the Wolf."

"What!"

"When I left your house, I saw this man standing on the sidewalk lighting a cigarette about two houses down from yours. When he saw me coming, he started walking away, but I saw his face."

"Holy shit! So he was watching me."

"Dylan, I'm sorry. I didn't realize it was him. He might not have Trevor now if I'd said something." Jennifer wept into her hands, and Black embraced her. Standing by the door, Sheffield silently watched the exchange.

"Jenny, you can't blame yourself. You had no way of knowing it was him."

She fished in her purse and pulled out a tissue. "I could have prevented this."

Sheffield finally spoke. "Jennifer, I saw you leaving Dylan's house that night, and I didn't see anyone standing around on the sidewalk."

So that's how Sheff knew about Trevor and me, Black thought.

"He was by a big tree across the street," Jennifer explained.

Sheffield exchanged a glance with her partner; then she walked over to Jennifer and put a hand on her shoulder.

"You may have just saved Trevor's life by providing that sketch, so don't kick yourself over this. The Wolf has fooled all of us."

~~~~~~~

"Does your leg hurt?"

The voice was distant. His arms were stiff, and his wrists ached from the handcuffs. When he realized that he'd drooled and his mouth was crusty, he instinctively felt embarrassment, which was ridiculous given his predicament. The embarrassment was quickly eclipsed by an intense pain when he tried to move his leg. The wound lit up like it was on fire and started to throb. Trevor rubbed his mouth against his shoulder. His khaki pants were bloody and stained, the buttons had been cut off his dress shirt, and his socks and shoes had been removed.

"Ooh, it *does* hurt," his captor said ecstatically. "I can tell. So, Patroclus, would you like a drink? Can't have you dying before the fun is over."

Trevor said nothing. He simply met his captor's eyes with a steely gaze. Even with the curtains closed, daylight seeped into the rooms. The man facing Trevor looked human, not like some half-beast. Trevor even suspected he could take him in hand-to-hand combat, if only he had the chance.

"Such a brave one. You are my Patroclus."

Like an alarm going off, Trevor suddenly yelled as loud as he had ever yelled before: "Helllllp!"

Fenrir stiffened as if an electric charge ran through his body. He rushed at his captive and toppled him backwards. Eyes wide with rage, the crazed man pressed a hand tightly over Trevor's mouth and drove his head into the linoleum. Trevor's hands were pinned underneath the two men's bodies, and it felt as if the right one might be ripped from his arm. Trevor shifted his weight to keep his wrist from breaking, but then the wound in his leg flared with pain.

"Don't! Do! That! Again!" Fenrir looked like an animal. "Today is Thor's Day, so you can die any time. I'll stuff your bloody sock in your mouth and tape your trap shut if I have to."

Trevor took satisfaction in knowing he had riled his captor.

Empowered by his rage, Fenrir deftly lifted Trevor and the chair.

After a moment of intense stares, Trevor finally said, "I'd like something to drink."

"That's more like it." He reached in the fridge for a carton of orange juice. "So tell me how I should torture you."

"Fire ants," Trevor said. The killer laughed.

"Wouldn't that be fantastic! Unfortunately, I haven't made it to Africa to get any."

Fenrir held a glass of orange juice to Trevor's lips and watched him drink. The liquid stung his throat, and Trevor wondered how much longer he could live. Every part of his body ached, and he felt like he could sleep for a year.

"Tell me about your life, Patroclus." The madman poured the acidic juice on Trevor's wounded leg. The gash had reopened when Fenrir had toppled him, and the juice now burned like alcohol. His mind on autopilot, Trevor closed his eyes.

"Grew up with Achilles in Thessaly. Achilles and I were tutored by the centaur Chiron."

The victim had done exactly what the killer had wanted: he'd said "I." He'd taken on the mantle of Patroclus and played his role. Fenrir rubbed his crotch and licked his lips as a sexual charge ran through his body. If only it could be like this every time. Alas, no murder could ever equal this one.

"And you and Achilles were lovers." It was a simple acknowledgment.

"Homer doesn't say so."

"Homer didn't have to. It's well-known. Don't trifle with me." He reached up and lovingly fondled Trevor's nipple; the action seemed incongruent. "And who did you kill?"

"A friend during an argument."

"Clysonymus." The Wolf was smiling. "Who else?"

"Hector's charioteer in the war."

"Cebriones was his name—Hector's charioteer. And don't forget Zeus' son Sarpedon. That was a noble kill." Fenrir leaned so close that Trevor thought he meant to kiss him. "How do you die, Patroclus?" he whispered.

Trevor's skin crawled. The beady eyes studied him.

"A spear thrust by Hector."

The killer sat back.

"You're injured first by Euphorbus, don't forget. *Then* Hector finishes you off."

"Euphorbus." Trevor repeated the name, because he'd never heard it before.

Fenrir sat on the edge of the chair. "Why are you killed, Patroclus?"

"I'm an Achaean and Hector's a Trojan, and we're enemies."

"Don't fuck with me!" He became instantly enraged. "You know why you die."

Trevor looked down at his injured leg. Fresh blood mixed with the piss and orange juice on his pants. If he didn't come up with the right answer, Fenrir might inflict another wound, maybe his other thigh. *Think, think, think!* Was it prophesied? After all, Apollo was on the side of the Trojans, and he was the god of prophecy. Achilles had been fated to die in Ilium (as Homer called Troy), and his mother, Thetis, the sea nymph, understood this. Trevor knew of no such prophecy about Patroclus. He played the events in his head: Achilles and the Myrmidons had withdrawn from the war; the Greeks were losing, and morale was low; Patroclus borrowed Achilles' armor and went out to intimidate the Trojans; he disobeyed Achilles' orders and confronted Hector in hopes of turning the tides of war. That's it!

"My arrogance, thinking I could take on Hector."

Fenrir clapped his hands together.

"Bravo. You are such a worthy adversary. It was your hubris, Patroclus, thinking you could defeat the Prince of Troy."

"My bad," Trevor muttered.

"So, how should I kill you, Prince of the Myrmidons? Tell me." The Wolf stood, swung his chair away, and looked down, as if ready to hear his pleas.

"Spear thrust."

"But it must be a slow death. Nothing excites me like the suffering of the gods."

"But I'm not a god."

"Psssh. *You're* not, but your lover's one." Fenrir paused. "Your lover, Achilles, flies into a rage over your death." Fenrir waved his arms maniacally as if he was fending off bees. "Then he's killed by an arrow in the heel, his only vulnerable spot. That will be quite painful, I imagine. I can't wait. Your bodies were burned, and the ashes were buried together. Ah, romance! That means I have to burn *you*, and I have to burn *him*. You don't mind a little fire, do you?" The monster smiled eerily and lit a match.

Trevor saw the inhumanity in Fenrir's eyes and remained silent. What could he say to the beast?

~~~~~~

Viktor had fallen asleep on the couch with Lestat on his belly and Louis on his legs, but he awoke when Sheffield arrived home.

"Hey, babe."

"I was going to stay with Dylan tonight…" She leaned against the counter as if she needed its support. The cats stretched, and Lestat accidentally rolled off Viktor.

"You're exhausted. You need to rest." He stood and held her in an embrace. "You want something to eat?"

"No."

"You want to sleep?"

Sheffield grabbed his face and kissed him passionately, and his penis responded immediately.

"Viv?"

"Shh. Just make me forget." She needed to make love to him. She needed him inside of her, on top of her, stimulating her, gratifying her. For a brief period, the world would be beautiful again; she could forget the madness. And she could forget her attraction to Black.

~~~~~~

Still at the NPD station, Black had not slept all night. He had read and reread the Wikipedia articles about Patroclus and Achilles and the Trojan War. He called Trevor's phone a dozen times, but Fenrir didn't picked up. Unable to grieve publicly, Black withdrew. Closing his eyes, he remembered Trevor lying next to him, telling stories about ancient gods and heroes. He thought about Gilgamesh and Enkidu. He thought about Alexander and his beloved Hephaestion. He mostly thought of Achilles and Patroclus.

Jennifer had spent the night in a hotel and gotten up early. She brought Black a change of clothes and breakfast. Sheffield found her partner with his ex-wife, sitting quietly at his desk.

"Dylan, they have the cigarette butt from the sidewalk outside of your house. Doc says she can get his saliva off it for a match. They also have a plaster cast of the shoe imprint in the grass where he stood."

"Sheff, I want out of here," Black pleaded. "I'm going crazy."

Sheffield exchanged glances with Jennifer. "Sure."

"I should get out of here, too," Jennifer said.

"Fenrir knows about Trevor and me." Black's voice was husky, almost *rusty*, as if he hadn't spoken in a hundred years. He looked at both women.

"That means he plans on coming for you next," Sheffield said. Jennifer clutched her arms tightly around herself, as if warding off the evil.

"Looks that way. You've read the articles. After Patroclus is killed, Achilles goes into a rage. Then he dies."

Sheffield broke off a piece of bagel. "But if Fenrir is taking on the role of Hector, then that means you kill him. Achilles wasn't killed by Hector."

"Paris," Jennifer said. "Achilles was shot by Hector's brother, Paris."

"Yeah, so if he's Hector, then you're his killer."

Black had ruminated over the psychology of their killer. "Fenrir thinks he's a super killer, like a modern-day Jack the Ripper. He's reenacting these stories, but he's not psychotic."

"So what?" Sheffield asked.

"He doesn't see himself as Hector or Paris—or even Fenrir. It's just a name he takes, like Son of Sam. He's twisted, and he's pissed because his crazy parents crammed this mythology crap down his throat, so he's getting even. The mythology just gives him a context for his rampages. Now, he'd better start believing in God, because I'm sending him to his Judgment Day."

~~~~~~

Millicent Deaver didn't have an Internet connection at her house to look up the phone number she needed. She hated the charge for an information call, but she finally decided to break down and pay it. After giving her the number of the Normandy Police Department, the system offered to connect her for a fee, but she declined. She had decided, before calling the NPD, to go to the sandwich shop down the street to eat something. She made herself presentable—brushed her teeth, combed her hair into a bushy ponytail, and dressed in wrinkled clothing. If there was still no word from her lover by the time she got back, then she'd definitely call the Normandy police and report what she knew about the wolf hair and her lover.

Chapter 51

The shrine was a place of comfort and joy for him. There were weapons, histories, guides, and symbols of power. Before burning down the house with Patroclus' body, he would need to pack up the shrine. It was all he'd brought to Normandy, besides the cash. The item he was looking for was propped against the wall. He pulled it out and held it up like a Greek warrior. This would be perfect. Of course, he wasn't ready for Patroclus to die yet, but this would deal the final deathblow. It was relatively light; the tip was made of a metal alloy. Oh, what pain this weapon would cause! Before that, however, he needed to inflict a non-mortal wound to represent the injury inflicted by Euphorbus. When he had meted out all the torment the poor boy could take, he would deliver the coup de grace with the weapon in his hand and burn down the house. He'd have to remember to take one of Patroclus' bones—a big one, maybe the femur—so he could burn it with Achilles' body.

When Trevor saw the spear in Fenrir's hand, his heart raced, and his eyes grew wide. Was it time to die? Already, he felt weak from blood loss and lack of food. It was only midday, and he had expected Fenrir to toy with him more. He had been drifting in and out of consciousness, though, so maybe Fenrir wanted to drive the spear home before Trevor could cheat him of his murder. He was, in fact, ready to die. The smile on Fenrir's face was disturbing. He rushed at Trevor and thrust the spear. Trevor winced and turned his head. Then he heard Fenrir laugh.

"You didn't think I'd do it so soon, did you? Here's the dice." He laid two dice on the table. "You killed Clysonymus, your friend, over a game of dice, so I'm going to stuff these down your throat before I light your body on fire. I still have to find the right accelerant." He shrugged and rounded the table. "Oh, well. I'll figure it out."

Trevor moaned in spite of himself.

"Your beloved Achilles will find only charred remains of

you, Patroclus. That'll unleash his wrath."

The serial killer stopped pontificating and laid down the spear. The metal was shaped like an arrowhead; the wooden shank was ash. The killer stooped to untie the rope around Trevor's ankles. Next, he stepped behind him and un-cuffed his right hand. Once free, Trevor's arm flopped forward and dangled at his side. Fenrir grabbed the young man's shoulder as if to hold him in place.

Trevor debated his next move. He probably couldn't run on his injured leg; maybe he could whirl around and overpower the madman. Fenrir couldn't have more than 10 pounds on him. Trevor breathed deeply, trying to muster strength and courage. The killer's hand still clutched his left shoulder. In one moment of Technicolor clarity, Trevor saw the face of his lover. Then he heard Black's husky voice and felt the warmth of his hard body. He could taste his kiss and smell his cologne. The hallucination was so real it made him smile. Trevor knew that he'd do anything in his power to get back to Black—or at least to save him from the Wolf.

While Trevor was imagining his lover, Fenrir reached for the scimitar that was lodged in the back of his belt.

"Tell me, Patroclus, which god you would pray to for help."

Trevor was silent for a moment. Was this another trick? Was the psychopath looking for a certain answer?

"What?"

"If you were to pray right now for mercy, for release from this pain, who would you pray to? The Christian God?"

"Maybe."

"Maybe? *Maybe?* Who would it be?" Fenrir shook him violently like a large rattle.

"I'd pray to them all: Odin, Zeus, Osiris, God, Allah. Maybe they're all one-and-the-same anyway."

He placed his lips against Trevor's ear and whispered, "Oh, you are a worthy foe, Patroclus. I almost hate to do this." Tightly gripping Trevor's left shoulder, Fenrir pressed him forward and then plunged the scimitar into his back. Trevor let out a gasp and heard Fenrir's voice—"The wound of Euphorbus"—before losing consciousness yet again.

~~~~~~~

The phone call made little sense to the dispatcher who answered, and she knew that detectives Black and Sheffield were overwhelmed trying to find the serial killer who'd been terrorizing the city. It was probably a prank, but the caller swore she'd gathered wolf hair, like that used in the God Killer cases, and given it to her boyfriend. There was something about working at the Toledo Zoo and something about a boyfriend whom she hadn't heard from in months. Though the woman seemed a little crazy, Officer Anita Flowers couldn't take any chances. With a curt interjection, she silenced the rambling caller so she could get help. By the time Officer Perez arrived, the woman had hung up.

"Damn it, she's not there anymore," Perez blurted. "Did she leave her name?"

"No, she wouldn't give me her name." He muttered something in Spanish, which made Officer Flowers smile.

"But this may help." She held out a piece of paper. Perez looked at the ten digits written there. "She was acting skittish, so I copied the number off the phone before I put her on hold."

"*Dios mio.*"

~~~~~~~~

"Wakey, wakey," came a distant voice.

"Patroclus, my boy, come back to me."

"It's not time to pay Charon yet."

"Don't disappoint me, my valiant Myrmidon."

A cool cloth on his forehead revived him from his comatose sleep. When he opened his eyes, it was the face of evil he saw.

"You have to wait for the spear," Fenrir said matter-of-factly.

Trevor felt as if a building had fallen on him and he'd been left for dead. He was once again lying on top of the wood dining-room table. There were layers of newspaper underneath his body. His shirt was missing, and he felt like his blood had stopped flowing.

"I must say: you've looked *better*, my brave warrior! Take a drink." The predator dribbled water from a straw into the mouth of his prey. "You'll be so dehydrated, you'll burn like kindling." The killer smiled at him and patted him on the cheek. "Of course, I almost wish I could burn you alive, Patroclus, but don't worry, I'll be faithful to the story. You'll die by the spear. After all, that's what I stole it for—just such an occasion.

"Drink some more." He dripped more water into Trevor's mouth and watched him swallow with great effort. "Can you talk? Say something profound."

"Fuck you." The young man's voice was raspy.

"I understand why you're bitter. Achilles is going to let you die."

Trevor still felt as though his body was no longer connected to his brain. There was no doubt that Death would claim him soon.

"I know your shoulder must hurt. I couldn't help but twist the knife a little." He winked.

"Dylan," Trevor whispered.

"What?" The killer leaned over him.

"Dylan. Please don't hurt him." Every word was labored, and emotions threatened to overtake him.

"Oh, you foolish twit. What do you think my killing you will do to him? It'll devastate him. He is Achilles." He snarled.

"You'll never hurt him." A tear belied his bravado.

"Achilles had a son. Do you know his name?"

"Neoptolemus." Though his body was devastated, his brain was oddly alert, drifting from image to image, myth to myth. Trevor felt ancient, and he sensed the gods standing around him, beckoning him.

"Sometimes known as Pyrrhus because of his fiery hair," the Wolf stated.

"He killed Hector's son, Astyanax, by throwing him from the walls of Troy, and he took Hector's wife, Andromache, as a slave."

Fenrir walked around the table. "Oh, you keep enticing me with your knowledge. You and I are similar in so many ways."

"I'm a hero, and you're a monster." Trevor's breathing was irregular.

"Yes, yes. Patroclus and Achilles. The greatest male love story of all time."

"No, it wasn't."

Fenrir leaned further over the table and cast an inquisitive glance at his immobile captive.

"Lestat and Louis."

Fenrir bellowed with laughter.

"Maybe you're right. Let's see what you know, Patroclus." He placed the blade against his captive's abdomen. "Who was Achilles' mother?"

"Thetis."

"And why did she marry a mortal?" He watched the knife intently.

Was this some sick game? *Trojan War for $500, Alex.*

"Because Prometheus knew that she would bear a child greater than the father," Trevor answered.

"And which god did she save?"

What is this madman up to? Trevor wondered.

"*Save?* She retrieved Hephaestus after Hera threw him from Olympus."

Fenrir was so focused on the knife that he appeared to be in a trance.

"Good. And why does Thetis abandon her beautiful boy, Achilles?"

The knife felt cold on Trevor's skin. With each breath, he felt the weight of it pressing into his side. Was Fenrir trying to trick him? Thetis loved Achilles to the point that she disguised him as a woman to prevent him from going to war.

"She didn't."

"Wrong!" Fenrir yelled, as he drew the knife delicately over his skin, leaving a gash. Trevor couldn't help but groan aloud. The warm blood collected on the surface of his abdomen before starting a ticklish trail down the side of the table.

"She left because her meddling husband stopped her from making him immortal." As if a switch had been flipped, his eyes went from enflamed to steely. Then he placed the blade against the young man's arm. "Now, let's try another question."

Knowing what lay ahead, Trevor closed his eyes and mined his brain for every detail—every person, every event in the life of Achilles.

~~~~~~~

Officer Perez ran the Toledo phone number to find out the

identity of the caller. The number was registered to a Millicent
Deaver. Perez hit 'dial' and prayed Millicent picked up.

"Ms. Deaver, please don't hang up. This is Officer Perez of
the Normandy Police Department. I want you to know that you're
not in trouble. I have a few questions I need to ask you. Your
answers might save a life."

"I don't want to get him into trouble," the woman cried. "I
just wanted you to tell him that I love him, and I miss him."

"Who?"

"Cain?"

"Is Cain your boyfriend?"

"He's going to hate me for turning him in. I'm a terrible
girlfriend for doing so, but I miss him. Someone must have stolen
the wolf hair I gave him. It couldn't be Cain committing these
crimes." The woman was talking so fast.

"Millicent, I need to know who Cain is. Where does he live?
We need to make sure he's okay. We want to ask him a few
questions. We'll tell him how much you care for him."

Sheffield and Black approached. He waved them over and
pointed to the name and number on the paper. Sheffield immediately
called the Toledo Police Department. Meanwhile, Black worked on
getting the phone records for calls made to and from her cell phone.

"Ms. Deaver, everything will be okay."

"No, it won't. I might as well be dead. He's going to hate me,
and I don't want to live without him."

"No, we can make things better."

The phone went dead.

~~~~~~~

"You've made this my best kill ever," the assassin beamed.
"You make me want to keep you alive." Trevor's body was
decorated with red gashes.

Fenrir walked over to the counter and picked up the spear. It
was light, and he lifted it aloft as if he were going to throw it. Then
he stepped up on a chair and onto the dining room table. With one
foot on each side of Trevor's body, the killer stood over him. The
chandelier danced near his face. Silently, Trevor asked the gods to

look over Black. Fenrir raised the spear and plunged it toward Trevor's chest. He felt the tip actually dig into the wood of the dining room table.

Chapter 52

Before the Toledo police arrived, Millicent Deaver had jumped from the roof and ended her young life. The officers searched her sparsely furnished apartment, which told the tale of a sad, lonely woman. They found a diary in which she had written profusely about her boyfriend. Before jumping, she had scribbled out his number in her empty address book and cleared the numbers from her cell phone. Millicent Deaver had changed her mind and tried to erase all evidence of Cain before taking to the roof for her final act. The Toledo PD called the Normandy PD to let them know what they'd found.

~~~~~~

Black had already gotten the call records for Millicent's phone. The list was brief—a testament to her friendless life—and one number stood out. It was a southwestern Ohio area code and Normandy extension, and she had called it several times over the past months. They traced the number to a Nelly Parker. When the address came back, the homicide detectives couldn't believe their eyes.

"This is a few houses down from Radford," Sheffield noted anxiously.

"Fenrir is living in a house close to his brother?" Black grabbed his keys.

"Maybe."

"How else would you explain Millicent having that phone number? He must have hunted down his brother and rented a room from this woman."

Perez turned to them. "Guys, looks like Nelly Parker is a widow who lives alone."

"We've got to get there now!" Black was already running.

"Should I call the number?" Perez called out.

Sheffield responded, before running out, "No. And no sirens."

As they raced to Nelly Parker's house, Black thought of his Patroclus.

~~~~~~~

Fenrir cursed. The gods had answered Trevor's prayer and given him enough strength to roll his body before the spear pierced his flesh. The weapon had grazed his arm and embedded into the wood. The angry killer pulled it vigorously to free it from the dining-room table.

Trevor ached from head to toe. He was bleeding from a half a dozen places on his body. Though he was cold, he didn't even have the energy to shiver. Life was draining from him.

The Wolf leaned over and pressed the young man flat against the table. He entertained thoughts of stomping him to death, but resolved to use the spear.

"That was valiant. From where did you muster that burst of energy? Look at me, Patroclus. Look at me!"

Trevor looked up and saw Fenrir's black eyes.

"Go ahead and piss yourself if you want. Tremble in fear. Cry if you must. I'm going to take your life now. Then I'm going to take your lover's life, and then I'm going to keep killing—because I'm untouchable." He was yelling like he was testifying from the pulpit "I'm above the law. I'm better than the gods." He raised the spear with both hands and gripped tightly.

"No one is above the gods," Trevor whispered hoarsely. "Dylan will stop you."

The tip was poised high in the air.

"Oh, yeah? Look what I've accomplished already. I'm unstoppable. More will fall at my feet and perish by my will."

"You're full of shit!" Trevor said.

In a violent motion, Fenrir arched his back to plunge the spear. Trevor closed his eyes to avoid seeing his end.

Next, he heard a pop and glass breaking. He opened his eyes to see blood gushing from the Wolf's side. Another bullet tore into the killer's arm, and he toppled like a crumbling statue onto the floor. Trevor heard more glass break and then a familiar voice.

"Trevor! We're here!"

The helpless captive turned his head toward the door and saw the homicide detectives charge in with guns fully drawn.

"Where's Fenrir?" Sheffield yelled.

"He fell on the other side of the table," Black answered.

"You got him." Trevor felt like he was talking in slow motion.

"I don't see him," Sheffield yelled.

Trevor repeated, "You got him."

Suddenly, flames danced across the floor and licked at the underside of the table. Fenrir had poured out the accelerant and started a fire. Sheffield ran toward the kitchen island as Black ran toward Trevor. The newspaper covering the table ignited, and Trevor felt the heat against his skin. He was so cold that the fire actually felt good. He was unable to do more than raise his head a few inches; doing so caused extreme pain, and he felt the tacky blood pull at the paper underneath him. The flames jumped higher. There was no way he would be able to get himself off the table before he burned alive.

"Where is he?" Sheffield yelled as she pointed her gun toward the floor.

Black reached over the flames and picked up his lover. The entire wooden table was burning. Trevor cried out in pain as the two men fell to the dining-room floor. Black patted the burning newspaper stuck to Trevor's body. Seeing the extent of his lover's injuries, he thought, *Maybe I'm too late.*

Sheffield dove around the wall of fire. The scimitar flew in her direction and struck her arm, causing her to drop her gun. Luckily, the sharpened side didn't hit her, so she had no gash. The flames were blocking her view of the killer. More glass shattered. Officers battered the front door as others stormed in through the backdoor. Sheffield rounded the flaming table, and the killer swept the spear across the floor and knocked her off her feet. She spotted her gun within her reach and lunged for it.

The Wolf leapt into the air, his face twisted in rage. He drew back the spear to charge at the fallen detective. Another shot tore into his neck. Blood flew in an arc as his body tottered. Another shot ripped into his abdomen. Black and Sheffield both pumped bullets into him. The Wolf fell, and flames licked his white shirt, scorching it.

Black made his way back to Trevor and lifted him to his chest. He was lifeless and limp.

"Trevor, don't die," he begged. Sheffield was the only one to hear what he whispered in Trevor's ear: "Stay with me. I don't want to lose you, my Enkidu."

Chapter 53

The chief medical examiner looked down at the battered body. She remembered this young man from the McNally residence; he was the one who had explained the Norse mythology, the one whom Sheffield had fondly called Myth Boy. Petkov remembered admiring him that day. What a smart, adorable young man! Now, looking at his angelic face, she realized that he was even more attractive than she had remembered. The CME did something she never did with her charges: she touched his cheek with the back of her hand.

"I never wanted to see you in my lab, you beautiful boy." She muttered something else in her native tongue. The door opened and Black and Sheffield filed into the room.

"So?" Sheffield asked.

"I talked to the doctors." Petkov put a hand on Trevor's arm and turned to face the detectives. "They say he lost a lot of blood, and it was touch-and-go in surgery, but they expect him to recover."

Sheffield breathed a heavy sigh and clapped her partner on the back.

"Any permanent damage?" Black asked.

"His leg should heal, but it will be tough at first. They drained blood from lung and fixed shoulder. He should have no long-term effects. You gave blood?"

"I gave blood," Sheffield answered.

"Uh," Black stuttered.

"Now I go. Petia has first dance lesson today. Ah, my little rose." Black smiled, knowing that Bulgaria is known as "the Land of Roses."

"Officer Perez and my ex-wife are in the lobby. Will you tell them how he's doing?"

"Of course," she responded before exiting the room.

The detectives approached the bed and looked down at the unconscious man. Black took Trevor's hand in his.

"Like a sleeping prince," Sheffield whispered.

"Like Endymion asleep on the mountain," Black said.

"Well, listen to *you*, Mr. Smarty Pants!"

"What can I say? I'm getting into this mythology stuff."

Sheffield put her arm around Black's shoulder.

"We did good."

Black nodded.

"What about the brother?" she asked. They both knew she was talking about Sheldon Radford, aka Timothy Finnegan, who had cleared out his bank account, packed up his Saab, and slipped out of town.

"I don't care about him."

"But what if he really is the one who killed their parents?"

"We'll put the Connecticut police on it."

"I'd sure love to send him to prison." She walked over to a beeping monitor.

Black felt a squeeze of his hand. "He's waking up."

Trevor opened his eyes and looked around to orient himself. When he saw Black's face, he smiled.

"Did you get him?" he asked.

"Don't you remember?" Sheffield said. "That's all you kept saying: 'You got him.'"

"He's dead." Black squeezed Trevor's hand.

"I *told* him you were going to kill him. The great Achilles."

"The doctors say you're going to be fine." Sheffield patted his arm tenderly. "We're all pulling for you, Myth Boy."

"Jenny's here." Black said.

"And Perez," Sheffield added. "I've got to make some calls, so I'll leave you two alone." Sheffield grabbed her purse and slipped quietly from the room.

Trevor closed his eyes for a minute. When he opened them, he asked, "Does she know?"

Black shrugged his shoulders and caressed Trevor's hand. "I don't care who knows." Trevor found the energy to smile.

"When you get better, I say we take a trip to Greece, so you can show me where all of these myths took place. What do you say?"

Epilogue

Timothy Finnegan slowed to the speed limit as he headed south on SR 75. He didn't know what his brother might have told the police, and he couldn't risk going to prison, so he had taken off with no plan. Now, he needed to get off the highway and slip into some small town for a while. He thought about his twisted family. He had to admit that he admired his brother for being so malicious, but he was glad that Toby was dead. It would only have been a matter of time before Toby came after him, and, though he'd like to think he could have won, Toby probably would have killed him. Now, *no one* could stop him.

He pulled over at a piece-of-shit diner. The food was horrendous, and the people were all losers. Finnegan sat and remembered killing his parents when he was 18. He also remembered trying to kill Toby a year later. As he looked around, he saw a young man in his early twenties standing in the parking lot. Timothy laid his money down on the table and exited the restaurant.

That's when he thought it: *Yeah, I could kill him. It would feel good to do it. It'd be like killing my brother.*

Biography

Charles Alan Long works full-time at a university and likes writing novels, short stories, and poems. His first novel, *The God Killer*, combines his interests in both detective stories and mythology.

He has traveled to more than 25 countries, loves dark chocolate, and is a romantic at heart.